Book Two of the Jack S

PURSUED BY LIGHT

DAVID G. KIRBY

Pursued by Light
Trilogy Christian Publishers A Wholly Owned Subsidiary of Trinity Broadcasting Network
2442 Michelle Drive Tustin, CA 92780

Cover design by: __
For information about special discounts for bulk purchases, please contact Trilogy Christian Publishing.
Manufactured in the United States of America
10 9 8 7 6 5 4 3 2 1
Library of Congress Cataloging-in-Publication Data is available.
ISBN: 979-8-88738-153-4
E-ISBN: 979-8-88738-154-1

To

My children, their spouses, the precious grandchildren, and all the sons and daughters of God who turned toward the irresistible Light when it pursued them into the darkest of all Stygian Forests...

It all began when you were fearfully and wonderfully made by the Designer of all things.

Then you fell.

You were born in darkness, and so you loved the darkness. You walked a path that took you far from your Maker. You suppressed the truth and were strangers to God and aliens to heaven. You were hopelessly lost.

But then—the Father sent His Son.

Jesus pursued you with rich mercy and great love. He paid your ransom with His own life. He called out to you by name!

You stopped running from the Light. You turned and saw the glorious face of The Only One who could quench your deepest thirst and satisfy your fiercest hunger.

One look, and you ran into His arms—finally found, finally free, finally home.

Acknowledgments

Who I am and everything I write flows from the people who have congregated in my soul since birth—family, friends, and others who entered my life along the way. I am especially grateful to those who introduced me to Christ, taught me about the life of faith, and mentored me throughout the years. I have met some of these people. Many I have not. They have influenced me through words from a distance.

I am eternally thankful to those who pointed me to Jesus, especially Billy Graham, David Hunt, and Gene Block.

I am indebted to those who fueled my infant faith, men like Roy Paulson, George Bonnema, Mr. Den Herder, Pastor Caley, Dr. Grady Spires, Don Mostrom, and Bernie Grunstra from Camp Peniel in upstate New York. Many of these men have graduated from this world and now behold Jesus face to face. I look forward to seeing them again and thanking them properly.

Then there are those who challenged me to move on from the milk of faith to the meat. Once again, some of them I have never met. I list only a few here, namely, Chuck Colson, Francis Schaeffer, A. W. Tozer, John Eldredge, Tim Keller, Chuck Swindoll, Bill Bright, Paul Lindberg, Stanley Oawster, Chaplain Glen Bloomstrom, Gary Setterberg, Norman Plasch, Arlan Rolfsen, and Steve Unruh. I leave unmentioned the names of mentors who influenced me through the words they wrote and the lives they lived centuries ago.

I would not be writing at all if it was not for the influence of authors in my youth, such as Edgar Rice Burroughs, Jules Verne, Louis L'Amour, and John Bunyan. As I grew older, other writers influenced me like J. R. R. Tolkien, G. K. Chesterton, Charles Dickens, Chaim Potok, C. S. Lewis, Randy Alcorn, Frank Peretti, John Lennox, Sigmund Freud, Frederick Nietzsche, James Michener, Fyodor Dostoevsky, Tom Clancy, Lee Strobel, Nabeel Qureshi, John Piper, and Scott Peck. All these authors opened doors to rooms I had never entered before. Although I do not embrace the beliefs or philosophies of all these writers, they now sit at a table in my heart, some as acquaintances and some as dear friends. Jesus stands at the head of the table.

Also, God has brought beautiful biological children and spiritual sons and daughters into my life over the years to teach me how to love, serve, lead, and mentor. They are catalysts for much of what I write. I love these young people deeply.

I am so thankful to Nancy, my faithful wife and the humblest servant I know, who has encouraged my writing and tolerated the many hours I lived in another world. She is God's gift to me. I am also grateful to Travis Dye, a friend who early on read my manuscripts and inspired me to keep writing. Other encouragers along the way were Nick Terlizzi, Debbi Terlizzi, Boni Caine, and my son, Jon Kirby.

Above all, of course, I write because of Him. Jesus Christ has been my best friend since he tracked me down at seventeen. Everything has changed for me—inside and out—since the day he delivered me from the kingdom of darkness and transferred me into the kingdom of his Son. To Him be the glory and the honor and the praise. He alone is worthy. I live to speak

His name to men and women so that they, too, might know His love and experience inexpressible joy.

There are many who stumble in the noon-day, not for want of light, but for want of eyes.

—John Newton

Grace comes into the soul, as the morning sun into the world; first a dawning; then a light; and at last the sun in his full and excellent brightness.

—Thomas Adams

The issue is now clear. It is between light and darkness and everyone must choose his side.

—G. K. Chesterton

And this is the judgment: the light has come into the world, and people loved the darkness rather than the light because their works were evil. For everyone who does wicked things hates the light and does not come to the light, lest his works should be exposed. But whoever does what is true comes to the light, so that it may be clearly seen that his works have been carried out in God.

John 3:19–21

For it is you who light my lamp; the LORD my God lightens my darkness. For by you I can run against a troop, and by my God I can leap over a wall. This God—His way is perfect; the word of the LORD proves true; He is a shield for all those who take refuge in Him.

Psalm 18:28–30

Table of Contents

PURSUED BY LIGHT

CHAPTER 1

Jack and Armando in the Southland

The most harrowing adventure of Jack's life begins when his flight to LAX lands at 12:52 p.m., ten minutes ahead of the predicted ETA. He retrieves his computer bag from under the seat and his carry-on backpack from the overhead storage compartment and disembarks the Boeing 737 that flew through a Colorado snowstorm late that morning.

Half an hour after arriving at the airport in LA, Jack is outside waiting for his ground transportation on a sunny but cool SoCal day. He does not have long to wait.

His ride pulls up to the curb in the form of a late-model silver Mercedes sedan. Armando, his roommate from the Academy, jumps out of the luxury vehicle, a broad grin brightening his goateed face. He is wearing shorts, sandals, and a loose-fitting, pastel-blue polo shirt. He gives Jack a quick slap on the shoulder and then grabs the two pieces of luggage out of his hands and throws them into the backseat.

"Let's go, ese!" he shouts as he climbs back into the driver's seat. "Time and tide and LA traffic wait for no one, not even a gringo from Colorado!"

Jack lingers on the sidewalk, trying to do the math of the Iridium silver metallic Mercedes and the ex-gangster known as Syko Loco, whose teardrop tattoo beneath his right eye whispers of a darker past. The two values of the equation simply do not add up in Jack's mental calculator.

Shaking his head, Jack slides into the black leather passenger seat and asks, "Where in the world did you get these wheels, bro? Isn't the S-class sedan the flagship model of Mercedes-Benz?"

"I already told you, Juan," Armando replies as he glances in his side mirror and accelerates smoothly into the flow of traffic. "I told you that my mother comes from a wealthy family. And she married well enough after her forgettable one-night stand with my father."

The young man with the close-cropped black hair laughs and adds, "Which reminds me, Juan—what do you get when you cross an Orange County girl with a gangster from the hood? You get a very special hybrid dude named Armando Vasquez!" he exclaims, taking both hands off the steering wheel and spreading out his arms dramatically.

Jack pushes Armando's right hand back onto the steering wheel. "Yeah, you're a special dude—no doubt about that. But if you don't keep your special hands on the wheel, soon you'll be a special dead, dude, and I'll be like you—not special, but dead."

Both men laugh, and then Jack asks, "What do you mean that your mom married well enough? Are you talking *dinero* or character?"

"She married a legit guy," Armando replies as he slows to match the flow of traffic in front of him. "He doesn't love Jesus yet, but he's close. Trust me, I'm working on his soul."

"I'll bet you are," Jack says with a smile as he continues to check out the interior of the S-Class sedan with its natural grain ash wood trim. He locates the seat air conditioner and adjusts the cooling level until it is set where Jack wants it.

"What I don't remember—" Jack begins to say as he glances out the heavily tinted window at bright red bougainvillea flowers and a cluster of palm trees towering up into the copper-tinted sky.

"What are those?" Jack asks, interrupting himself. He points out the driver-side window at a row of fifty-foot-tall trees with vivid flowers. "I've never seen such amazingly blue flowers before, especially on a tree!" he exclaims.

Armando momentarily glances away from the traffic and says, "Jacarandas." He smirks and then adds, "They're named after you, Jack. See, you are special after all. And like you, people love those trees, or they hate them."

"Ha-ha," Jack replies, shaking his head.

"Seriously, those trees are a blessing and a curse," Armando observes. "As you can see, they grow beautiful flowers—like the cherry blossoms in Japan except for the color, of course—but their beauty comes at a price."

"What price is that?" Jack asks curiously, still looking at the trees.

"The Jacarandas produce those blue, trumpet-shaped flowers twice a year here in LA," his friend explains. "As long as those flowers remain on the tree, they are our friends. But as soon as they fall to the ground, they become our enemies. People walk on the blue carpet of the fallen flowers and grind them under their feet. When they do that, it's like treading grapes in a vat. A sticky juice is crushed out of them, either from the flower itself or the aphids living inside of them—I don't remember which."

Armando glances over at his friend and says, "The crushed flowers make the sidewalk very sticky—sometimes even slippery. I know some old lady down in Dana Point who slipped on Jacaranda juice and broke her hip. Three weeks later, she died of pneumonia. The tree killed her. The saying around southern California is that Jacarandas are best observed in your neighbor's yard."

Jack turns his head slowly as his eyes follow the flowered trees until they are out of sight. "I think there's a life metaphor in the Jacaranda tree," he says, chuckling. "Something like, 'Beware the beast behind the beauty.'"

"Good one, Juan," the driver says, nodding his head. Then he adds, "The Jacaranda bears fruit just like the fateful tree in the Garden of Eden that led to the fall of humankind. Who would have thought it: trees are the root of all evil."

Jack finally turns his attention back to the road ahead and says, "Before those homicidal Jacarandas interrupted our conversation, I was going to ask if your mom had any other kids besides you."

Armando's brown eyes glance in the rearview mirror. Then he looks over his shoulder and accelerates. He switches lanes smoothly despite a brief warning from the car's blind spot monitoring system.

"Two children with Alberto," he replies. "But I'm blessed," he adds as he shoots a look in Jack's general direction. "I didn't experience what Rachel did with her parents—you know, how they favored her sister over her. My mother made sure my stepdad didn't treat me any differently than their two kids."

"Even when you identified with your gangland father and dressed like a gangster, tats and all?" Jack asks with disbelief in his voice.

"Even then—most of the time," Armando says.

"She wasn't worried about you being a bad influence on your younger sibs?"

"Not really," replies the young man with the olive skin face interrupted only by his black goatee and the fine white scar running the length of his left cheek.

Armando pauses for a moment and then corrects himself, "I lied. There was a period of two years when she wouldn't let me in the house if I was using drugs or alcohol and acting like an all-around bad dude. She really had only three rules: no smoking, no drinking, and no weapons. Okay, and no low rider pants, baseball caps, or any other gang attire."

"Did you obey her?" Jack inquires as he looks at the right profile of his friend's face.

Armando nods his head as he switches lanes again. "My mother is strong—a 'no nonsense *esposa y madre*,' as my stepdad likes to say. She learned a lot the hard way during her teenage years. She had wise, loving parents—Eusebio and Gabby—but they were strict Catholics who never missed mass. Maybe they were a bit too harsh and controlling with my mom, especially when she was younger. That's probably part of the reason she pushed back so hard as a teen. But they learned to be more reasonable with her brothers and sisters. Mom was the oldest. She was their guinea pig."

Jack nods his head and looks out the passenger window again. "Seriously," he comments a moment later.

"What is it, Juan?"

"Eight lanes of concrete, and we're only going twenty miles an hour?"

Armando laughs. "Welcome to the 405 freeway and most every other freeway in LA. You're not in Denver anymore, mi amigo."

Jack looks over at his friend and says, "But LA traffic is not as dangerous as Colorado traffic."

"Are you serious?" the driver disagrees with a disbelieving snort. "How could Colorado traffic be more dangerous than this war zone?"

"Mainly in one part of Colorado," Jack clarifies, "between Craig and Rifle." "Rifle," Armando repeats, shaking his head. "There's really a town named Rifle?"

Jack nods his head. "And the town of Dinosaur is close by," he says. "Loveland isn't all that far away, either."

Armando breaks out in loud laughter and exclaims, "Rifle and Dinosaur and Loveland! Are you kidding me? Who named the towns in your state—a Tyrannosaurus-loving third grader who had a crush on his teacher and whose father was president of the NRA?"

"Yeah, yeah, yeah," Jack replies, glancing in his side mirror. "Loveland does sound a bit lame. But getting back to my point, I drove the ninety miles from Craig to Rifle in the middle of a blizzard on a March night sometime after midnight. The road was covered with ice, and the surrounding grasslands were swarming with pronghorn antelope. I mean, there were thousands of them!

"Those crazy critters kept darting across the road like they wanted to get hit! I felt like I was in an arcade video game. Between the ice and the antelope and the darkness, it took me three hours to get to Rifle, and I still had to drive on to Montrose that night. I think I got there about six in the morning."

"There must've been an antelope convention that night," Armando replies with a crooked smile. "Or maybe they were a bunch of young lovers running away from home so they could ante-elope."

While Jack groans and shakes his head, his friend moves on to another subject. He asks, "By the way, how are your mom and your little *hermanas*?"

Armando switches lanes, and the tires of the Mercedes thump over a dozen raised white reflectors attached to the roadway that serve as lane dividers.

"Good," Jack says as he glances at the driver. "Mom was a bit hurt that I wasn't going to be home longer, but she and the girls are flying down to Arizona on Saturday to stay with her parents for Christmas. So, in the end, I only cheated her out of two days. Besides, I'll see them in Colorado again before I head back for spring semester."

Armando glances at Jack and frowns. "My bad, *ese*," he says with a sigh. "For the record, I feel guilty taking you away from your *familia* over Christmas."

"Yeah, you owe me big time," Jack says with a laugh as he runs his hand through his straw-colored hair.

The driver of the Mercedes changes lanes yet again, and Jack feels the throbbing of the omnipresent reflectors beneath the tires.

"By the way, how's your skull, man?" Armando asks.

"You mean my concussive symptoms?" Jack says. "All cleared up. No more headaches or nausea, or transient dizziness. Recovery was much faster than after the two I sustained playing football."

"Dr. Windsor would be happy," Armando comments randomly.

"That I recovered so fast?" Jack asks, turning to look at his roommate.

"No, that you got a haircut, Juan," the driver replies with a sidelong glance.

"Oh, yeah, I forgot," Jack says. "I did, and he would be."

"Not that it's short enough for the army, but it's an improvement."

"It sounds like Windsor isn't the only one who likes my hair shorter," Jack observes.

"That would be true," his friend admits, applying the brake and coming to a sudden stop as they approach the exit ramp to the southbound 55 Freeway. "I never liked long hair. Neither did any of my homies back in the day, partly because of the hotter LA weather but mostly due to the preferences of our set."

Jack runs his fingers through his shorter hair again. While he is not too concerned about the new look, he is still uncomfortable with the new feel.

Half an hour later, the Mercedes enters the city limits of Newport Beach. Fifteen minutes after that, Armando maneuvers onto the Pacific Coast Highway toward Laguna Beach. Jack begins to catch glimpses of the Pacific Ocean between the trees as they continue to drive southward.

Somewhere between Newport Beach and Laguna, Armando takes a right turn off the PCH 1 and heads west toward the ocean. Shortly after that, they enter a gated community with large stucco houses painted in desert sand tones. In the neighborhood driveways, Jack spots Porsches, Bimmers, more Mercedes, and even a Lamborghini.

Jack shakes his head and remarks, "How can these people afford such high-end vehicles when their houses probably all cost over half a million?"

Armando laughs at his friend's naivety about southern California real estate and says, "Like I said before, Juan, you're not in Colorado anymore. Try 3.5 mil."

Jack jerks his head around and stares at Armando, wide-eyed. "For real?" he asks incredulously. "Why so crazy expensive?"

"To begin with, you're in LA," his roommate explains. "On top of that, you're in Orange County. Then, finally, you're not far from the ocean here in this development. Land is gold down here, my mountain friend."

Armando steers the silver Mercedes onto a wide concrete driveway and parks on the left apron to avoid blocking the three garage doors. "Here we are, Juan," he announces as he depresses the ignition button, killing the engine.

"Where is everybody?" Jack inquires, noting the empty driveway.

"Alberto's at work in Irvine, and Mom and the kids are in San Diego for the day visiting Tio Jorge and Tia Consuela. We're on our own until late tonight."

"So, what's the plan?" Jack asks as he unbuckles his seat belt and looks past Armando at the gleaming Bentley parked in the driveway next door.

Beyond the luxury automobile that is more expensive than his house back in Colorado, Jack sees a small army of landscapers busily mowing the lawn, edging the driveway, and trimming the bushes and other flora that he is not accustomed to seeing back in the foothills of the Rockies. A white Toyota pickup truck with tandem wheels and a small trailer in tow is parked in front of the house. Of greatest interest to Jack is the young man who has climbed a towering palm tree on the boulevard and is busily hacking down dead fronds from beneath the crown of the tree with a machete.

"We'll get you settled into your room and then hit the beach for a few hours," Armando says. "We'll come back here later to shower and then get food at my favorite restaurant in Dana Point."

"Sounds good to me," Jack responds. "Then tomorrow we head to La

Puente?"

"Tomorrow afternoon," Armando says as he chews his lower lip. "And La Puente is not our final stop. We're going to Valinda, the barrio next to La Puente."

There is a short pause as Jack continues to watch the young man up in the palm tree severing one dead frond after another, sending them floating down onto the waiting tarp at the bottom of the tree.

"Amazing, yes?" Armando says as he glances over at the other yard. "He climbed that 65-foot tree with only a lanyard fixed around his waist and spikes on his shoes. People die every year doing exactly what he's doing, and not always from falls. Some people get injured up in the tree when a large frond hits them."

Jack nods his head slowly and says, "Dangerous work. But I was thinking more about tomorrow. I'm waiting to see what amazing things our God will do in the heart of Sniper."

And in my heart as well, Jack thinks, *since my gut gets tied into knots just thinking about going into gangland.*

"Amen to that," his host agrees as he opens his door and steps out into the air that is still cooled by the stubbornly lingering early afternoon marine layer.

The two young men grab Jack's luggage and head into the house. After Armando gives his roommate a quick tour of the property, they change clothes, then drive back north.

They spend the next three hours on the beach just north of the Newport Pier. The water is colder than Jack had anticipated because, according to Armando, La Nina is creating cooler than normal Sea Surface temperatures.

A persistent northwest wind has also impacted the water temp along the coast.

Neither man complains about the cool water simply because they do not stay in the ocean very long. They spend most of their time playing Frisbee on the beach, catching crabs along the stone breakwaters, and lying on the warm sand, talking about what has happened in their respective lives during the first week of their winter break. Since it is the off-season, the two friends have plenty of space to romp around without worrying about kicking sand in the faces of fellow beachgoers. Only five people share the sand with them on this December day, and they are half a football field away.

Instead of returning to Armando's house in Corona Del Mar to get out of their swimsuits and shower, the two roommates decide to change into their clothes in the public restroom on the beach. A little salt and sand on their skin are tolerable for both men. This way, they avoid showering at home and then driving farther down the coast to Dana Point for supper.

Back in their shorts and T-shirts, the two young men amble out onto the Newport pier to have supper at the newly reopened restaurant located at the end of the "giant dock," as the young Coloradan refers to it. Jack is impressed by all the people fishing on the thousand-foot-long pier that rises more than seventy feet above the ocean. He is especially interested in several sand sharks lying on the wooden deck that were caught in the same waters he and Armando were swimming in only an hour earlier.

Armando treats his roommate to a supper of two-pound Dungeness crabs and fries—compliments of his parents. The two men consume their food while sitting on the outdoor plexiglass-protected patio that overlooks the vast Pacific Ocean. They feast and talk and laugh until the sun sets, leaving behind a rich wake of orange-red pastels unsubdued by the smog that has been driven inland by the persistent evening breeze. Far out on the ocean, the distant lights of rocking boats wink on the darkening water.

After supper, the two young men retreat to the lonely beach where they sit and listen to the ocean waves crashing and gliding higher and higher up the sand toward them.

"It's such a different world out here," Jack observes as he digs his bare feet into the cooling sand and stares out over the waters of the Pacific that are now shrouded by night. "It's not only the climate and the ocean, but also the traffic, the racial diversity, the smog, the palm trees, the personalized license plates, and all the luxury cars." He stops and laughs.

"And you haven't even lived through an earthquake yet," Armando says with a smile, his white teeth flashing in the growing darkness.

"I won't feel too deprived if I miss one of those," Jack remarks.

"Then you probably won't mind missing the floods and the fires and the droughts and the mudslides and the riots and the financial insolvency," Armando lists off. "LA may be an interesting place to visit, but it's not as magical as Disneyland might suggest. Since the early nineties, I think more people have actually left California than moved in. The luster is long gone."

"Like anywhere else, I suppose there are pros and cons," Jack remarks as he listens to the shrieking of a nocturnal tern overhead. There is a short silence before he adds, "Can we walk, roomie? I think better when I'm moving."

"Sure," his friend says with a shrug.

The two men get to their feet and walk barefoot down to where the tide is scouring the glistening sand with wave after wave of saline cleanser.

"So much happened at the Academy this fall," Jack says as he wades ankle-deep into the cold water. "I keep thinking about the Windsors, Emily,

Rachel, Stewart, Aly and Mahmoud, Embee, Greenlay—even Miriam and Mr. Fagani."

"And that's not even including the whole mystery in the cemetery," Armando comments.

The heavy salt breeze sweeping in off the dark ocean dampens Jack's shirt and oils his exposed skin. The air has become cool enough for a sweatshirt, but neither man brought one down to the beach.

"How exactly are we going to arrange a meeting with Sniper tomorrow?" Jack asks, abruptly changing topics.

His friend stares ahead as they walk over sand wet from a receding wave. "As you may remember, my father is dead now," Armando eventually replies, "so I obviously can't get any information from him. My stepmom is probably living on the streets somewhere—if she's still alive. I've made some contacts through old friends in La Puente. The word from them is that Sniper is still in Valinda running drugs and working for the Mexican Mafia."

"Does he know we're coming?" Jack asks slowly.

"Not yet," Armando replies as he continues to stare straight ahead into the darkening night.

"I suppose there's really no answer to the question, but will we be safe?" Jack inquires as he reaches down and picks up a fractured shell from the rippling waters of another retreating wave.

"You don't have to come, Juan," Armando replies, a sudden edge in his voice.

"Whoa," Jack responds calmly. "I wouldn't be here if I wasn't committed to this whole deal, bro. God made it very clear to me through Violet's dream and the Holy Spirit speaking in my heart that I'm supposed to be here with you. End of discussion.

"Besides," Jack adds as he kicks the shallow sheet of water covering his feet so that it sprays out ahead of them, "I'm committed to living like Jim Elliot did."

"Who?" Armando inquires as he looks at Jack's face that is dimly illuminated by the boardwalk lights a hundred feet away.

"Jim Elliot," Jack replies. "He was a missionary to the Auca people in Ecuador—or at least he was aspiring to be. He and four other missionaries were speared to death by the natives when they attempted to make face-to-face contact with the dangerous people group. Jim was only twenty-eight years old when he was killed. He's the guy who wrote, 'He is no fool who gives what he cannot keep to gain what he cannot lose.'"

"Sounds like a brave man, Juan," his friend says. "What exactly did he mean by the gaining and losing comment?"

Jack pauses and then responds, "I think he meant that even if living for Jesus resulted in his death—which it did—he wouldn't be a fool because we're all going to die anyway. He knew that he was going to live forever with Jesus in the end, so to give up his earthly life was not a huge loss, especially if he died doing what God had called him to do. In fact, it was a gain because dying meant that he was going to see Jesus face to face."

Armando stops walking and looks down at the water swirling around his bare feet. "I wish I had that kind of faith, Juan." After a short pause, he adds, "But in my heart of hearts, I'm a coward."

"What?" Jack asks incredulously as he turns to look at his friend. "You, a coward? Armando, you're the last person I'd think of as a coward."

"That's kind of you, *ese*," his friend says, looking at him in the darkness. "But you forget that I ran away from Raul when he was being slaughtered."

"You've already told me what happened in that alley," Jack says firmly. "Your brother was already dead when you ran. And if you hadn't run, you would've been dead, too! Then you never would've met Jesus. And I never would've met you. And Sniper would've never had the chance to soon hear the good news about Jesus' love from the man he almost killed! Don't you see the fingerprints of God all over your life story?"

"I do see his fingerprints on my life," Armando agrees, nodding his head. "It's just that my father beat it into me that I was a coward. Literally."

Jack looks directly into his friend's eyes that are darkened by the night and his father's accusations and states, "You probably never considered that even bravery can be an idol."

"What's that supposed to mean?" his friend asks, frowning.

"I don't really know," Jack replies with a laugh, "I've never thought about it until just now."

After Armando punches him in the arm, Jack explains, "What I'm thinking is that some men are so obsessed with being macho and alpha male to the point of stupidity that they make it a pride thing, more important than loving God or loving others. So, you see, even courage can be an idol if we exalt it as the most important thing in our lives. Remember all the passages in the Field Manual that tell us how Jesus doesn't want us to be self-sufficient—He wants us to know that our strength comes from Him."

Armando rubs his goatee thoughtfully and stares at Jack. "Hmm. You make an interesting point, amigo," he says as the two men begin walking again. "I'll have to think on that for a while."

"Why do you think Jim Elliot was willing to give up his life so freely?" Jack asks. "Because he believed that he was a strong man or because he trusted in a strong God?"

"It sounds like it was all about God's strength for him," Armando replies.

Jack nods his head as he steps over a clump of dark weeds lying on the sand. "That's right," he says. "What Jim Elliot and you and I have in common is not that we are inherently courageous men, but that we're all brothers who have the same amazingly strong Father who goes with us wherever we go."

There is a short pause as the two men wade through the rising tide that is feeling colder on their feet and ankles by the minute.

"I think I answered my own question about if it will be safe going to find Sniper," Jack eventually reflects aloud. "The bottom line for me, for you, for Jim Elliot, is not about if it's going to be safe but if we're obeying God. If He wants us to go and share the good news about His love, we need to obey and go, even if it's in the primitive jungles of South America. Life is too short to make safety our primary objective."

"In this case, we won't be going to the primitive jungles of South America," Armando replies with a chuckle. "We'll be going to the primitive jungles of the barrio."

The two men continue their slow walk through the alternating rhythm of wave and sand until Jack says, "Let's find a place to pray. I'm sensing that we need to be super prepared for tomorrow."

Soon Jack and Armando are sitting on the dry sand halfway between the waves and the boardwalk that runs in front of the beach houses.

They begin by praying for the ongoing comfort of Dr. Windsor as he experiences his first Christmas without Violet. Then they thank God for the amazing new faith in Mahmoud's heart and ask that he and Aly might grow close since they are now brother and sister twice over—physically and spiritually. They pray also that the Holy Spirit might make himself known to Drew in such a personal way that he will not doubt the soundness of his decision to follow Jesus. They ask the Father to be with Stewart and Rachel as they go home to potentially difficult encounters with family members.

They also petition God on Emily's behalf—totally unaware that she also is sitting on a beach in Florida at that same exact moment, just under very different circumstance—praying that God might awaken her enigmatic heart to know the presence of His love. They lift their mothers and siblings, as well as Armando's stepdad, up to Jesus, asking their Savior to draw all their loved ones into a relationship with him.

Lastly, they pray about tomorrow's "tip of the spear" adventure into Valinda, asking for wisdom and safety.

As they walk back to the car in the fifty-eight-degree air that is much fresher than the California air Jack first encountered outside the airport, he confides to his Academy roommate, "I know nothing about gangs, Armando. I'll totally be relying on your lead tomorrow. I'll just do my best to have your back."

Armando does not reply immediately because he is lost in thought. Eventually, he says, "I don't want to admit that I'm scared about tomorrow. I don't want to admit it because that makes my father right about me being a coward. Besides, I don't want to increase your fear, Juan. But after you talked about having the same attitude as Jim Elliot, I know you're going to be okay. And I think I'll be okay, too, because just as Jesus saved me through Juan Ortega, so I believe Jesus will save Sniper through me."

Neither man says another word as they walk through the parking lot.

A few minutes later, they climb into the car and navigate back to the PCH. They do not talk to each other as they drive south toward Armando's house because they are too busy talking to Jesus about tomorrow's adventure in the hood.

Both men are also thinking that even though Jim Elliot walked in obedience to God, his blood still spilled over the rocks of the Curaray River in Ecuador.

CHAPTER 2

Rachel and Drew in Connecticut

The talkative, energetic, auburn-haired Rachel Biandi flies into the Providence, Rhode Island, airport in the late afternoon of December 21st. Since her father, as usual, is working late at the hospital and her mother is writing up a non-contingent, no inspection sales contract for a real estate client, Rachel schedules an Uber to bring her home.

She spends the next hour traveling to Mystic with a talkative forty-year-old driver whose day job is collecting rare coins. It does not cross Rachel's mind to ask the numismatic lover for information about the 1870-S Seated Lady Liberty Silver Dollar until hours later.

As they drive toward the Biandi family home, Rachel stares out the window at the islands of snow scattered in the ditches like white archipelagos and, closer to home, at the ribbons that curl like scarves around the base of old stone walls and trunks of trees bereft of leaves. Her eyes see nothing because she is deep in thought.

On the one hand, she is elated about seeing her parents. *Hope springs eternal,* she thinks to herself knowingly. On the other hand, she is aware that if things go the way they have in the past, whenever she visits her Mystic home, her hope and anticipation soon will be shredded by the serrated blade of something Rachel experiences as emotional abandonment.

The driver deposits her at the end of the long driveway that meanders through fir trees and around several large stone outcroppings before it ends at a contemporary-style home eighty feet from the street.

Rachel stands in the twilight for a long time, staring at the house of memories. Eventually, she picks up her luggage and trudges toward the Biandi home, whose roofline, with all its unusual angles, resembles a Picasso painting. Hope flickers in her heart as she enters the dark house.

Susan Biandi arrives home an hour after her adopted daughter and enters the kitchen from the garage. Rachel is at the stove preparing her father's favorite stir-fry razor clams and turns to greet her mother. The younger woman opens her mouth to speak but then notices that her mother is leaning into her phone. The older woman, dressed in a gray suit and a white blouse, waves two fingers at her daughter while the rest of her hand grips her cell phone. Her other hand is busy with the strap of her purse and the valise that is hanging from her shoulder. She smiles at Rachel brightly, then walks into the adjoining room.

Rachel watches her mother disappear into the living room and remembers why the woman reminds her of a fragrance. She sweeps into a room with her radiant face and brilliant smile but never remains long. Her presence is a sweet bouquet that fills a room with an enticing aroma, promising wonder and substance. But in the end, it proves ephemeral. She disappears, literally and figuratively, leaving a transient fragrance that lingers for a while before it dissipates into nothingness. Initially, so promising—in the end, so disappointing.

It is almost worse that she appeared at all.

Rachel experiences a familiar sinking feeling in her stomach, and she instinctively searches the kitchen cupboards for her comfort food of choice. Before long, she finds a stash of chocolate bars and consumes not just one piece but two whole bars. She is feverishly swallowing the last bite when the inviting fragrance returns to the kitchen with its alluring promise of delight.

Rachel's mother has changed into a fashionable navy and white jogging suit that highlights her svelte body and her glossy black hair that is cut in a bob. The elegant woman says, "Rachel," in a way that a grandmother might greet her five-year-old granddaughter or a kitten lover might respond to the sight of an adorable little feline. Rachel almost expects her mother to pet her on the head. Susan does not hug her daughter; she sweeps up to her and takes her face in her hands. Then she gives Rachel air kisses in the general direction of both cheeks.

Her younger sister always gets kisses on the skin of her cheeks.

"Hi, Mom," Rachel responds. Her face is a pleasant veneer that masks the throbbing ache lurking in her heart—a forever shadow. Too late, she realizes that she opened her mouth far too close to her mother's legendary nose that is known to detect the smell of food and alcohol fifty yards away.

Her mother steps back, and her face stiffens into a look of judgment. "Eating chocolate again?" she says in a cool voice that stands in sharp contrast to her beautiful fragrance.

The fifty-something woman turns and walks over to the sink. With her back to Rachel, she adds, "Have you so quickly forgotten that a healthy body means a healthy life?"

Rachel feels something warm rise in her cheeks as she stares at her mother's impenetrable back. She entertains a strong urge to rise up against her mother's subtle shame, as she occasionally did when she was a teenager. In the end, she restrains herself. Instead, she takes a deep breath and manipulates her countenance into the Biandi pseudo-smile that will never be censored.

"When is Dad getting home?" she asks agreeably.

"Your guess is as good as mine," her mother replies as she walks over to the Thermador refrigerator and opens the door. "I'm quite certain Celeste will arrive home before he does."

"Celeste is coming home tonight?" Rachel inquires as the sinking feeling in her stomach intensifies into a free fall.

"Yes, that's what I just said," the mother comments as she pours herself a glass of cranberry juice. "She's riding home from the University with Jason Tibbets from Stonington. Surely, you must remember his parents, John and Stacy. We play bridge with them every Thursday night."

As Susan Biandi busies herself with various tasks around the kitchen, she chats about the Tibbets, the Browns from Ledyard, the Williams from Norwich, and the Smiths who recently moved to New London. She bemoans the invasion of the gypsy moth caterpillars last summer that stripped the trees bare and wonders aloud if some of the trees in their yard will die after three consecutive years of infestation. She talks to the lettuce salad she is making about the country music concert that is coming to the Mohican Sun Casino in early January and informs the dishwasher about the seafood restaurant on the coast where she and her aunt Mattie recently consumed "the most delicious scallops ever—not too 'chewy' and with surprising flavor for such a bland shellfish."

Susan begins to inform Rachel about the new exhibit at the Mystic Aquarium when the front door opens.

"Mom, I'm home!" a female voice that Rachel loves and hates cries out from the living room. Her tone is so dramatic one might think the new arrival had been lost in the wilderness for five weeks and given up for dead but now is miraculously stumbling into the home of her deliriously worried parents.

Rachel instinctively turns away from the stove and watches her mother.

The Biandi matron wipes her hands on the dishtowel and announces excitedly to the kitchen, "Celeste is home!"

She drops the towel on the counter and glances at Rachel. "Chop, chop!" she says in a staccato voice that is as gentle as a meat cleaver on a butcher's block. "What are you waiting for? Let's give baby girl Biandi a huge welcome!"

Rachel follows the suddenly animated woman into the living room with its twenty-foot ceiling that only accentuates the emptiness in her heart and watches the dreaded drama unfold. When Susan lays eyes on her special daughter, she raises her hands into the air and releases a high-pitched squeal. "Celeste!" she cries as she scurries over to her daughter and throws elated arms around "baby girl" as if she had not seen her just three weeks ago at Thanksgiving.

As the mother and daughter embrace, Rachel watches the reunion. She does not view the display of affection as excessive or inappropriate. Rather, her heart longs for what she sees on display before her eyes—her mother's total affection—and her heart aches even more. The ache is so strong she can barely contain it. She feels like weeping. She feels like doubling over in pain.

Instead, she walks back into the kitchen to check on supper. While the two biological Biandi women chat away furiously in the living room, Rachel sneaks another chocolate bar, and then another and another.

She hates herself.

Feeling forgotten by the universe, Rachel slips into the bathroom and purges. She hates herself even more.

She escapes outside to the deck, whose creaks and groans from the cold echo the pain in her heart. She weeps bitterly.

Between sobs, she chokes out words heavy with bitterness and sarcasm: "Jesus, have you also forgotten me? Please...remember me—your poor, pathetic, unwanted, unlovable Hagar."

The next morning, Rachel and Celeste, along with Mom and Dad Biandi, are perched on stools around the kitchen island, properly eating vegetarian omelets prepared by Rachel. Like two schoolgirls, Celeste and her mother are planning the itinerary of their trip to the mall in New London to do Christmas shopping while Rachel's father is scheduled to work yet another shift at the hospital that will be inhabited by his ghost when he dies.

Rachel watches the two women talk excitedly across the island from her. Mother and daughter both have short black hair, ivory skin without blemish, and slim, athletic physiques. As always, Rachel cannot resist comparing her own red hair, freckled skin, and slightly larger body to that of her adoptive mother and sister. She feels different, less than them—even alien.

Rachel is playing with her food on the elegant white stoneware that reminds her of her mother's flawless skin when the older woman asks, "Rachel, do you want to join Celeste and I at the mall?"

Rachel lifts her eyes from the perfect plate. She glances at her mother and then at her sister. Their faces are as readable as flashing neon lights on a dark night. She immediately discerns that her mother's inquiry is voiced out of obligation instead of desire.

Rachel shakes her head and looks back down at her plate. "No thanks," she says, uttering the correct response. "It's been a busy semester. I just need some downtime."

"Fine, then," her mother replies so quickly that Rachel knows beyond any doubt that she has responded appropriately. "Have it your way."

"The gym is open every day except Christmas," her bespectacled father with salt and pepper hair interjects as he looks up from his phone and glances briefly at his adopted daughter. "Please don't waste your time lounging about and reading, Rach."

The father turns to Celeste, and his face brightens. He says, "I apologize again for missing the championship game last week, Cellie. I had no idea you were going to start. The coach obviously made the right decision to insert you in the lineup after that Jenny girl went down with an ACL."

His voice is alive with a proud energy reserved only for athletic achievements. "I did watch the game on the school livestream site, though," he adds. "Your header goal off that corner kick was truly amazing! You timed your run perfectly! It reminds me of the goal I scored against Rutgers back in '87. Did I ever tell you about my left-footed, game-winning, set play strike from midfield?"

Celeste smiles sweetly and sets her pristine hand on her father's arm. "Only a thousand times, Daddy," she says with a laugh. Then she gives her paternal admirer a peck on the cheek and announces, "Mom and I really should run. The mall is going to be crazy today!"

Dr. Samuel Biandi rises from his stool and says, "I have to run, too. Have a super time, Super Girl."

Turning to his other daughter, he says, "See you later, Rach. Great pancakes! Next time, though, add more apples. You know how much I love fruit."

The last sentence is not spoken with a smile but with the sober countenance, he displays so often with Rachel, one that she always interprets as communicating disappointment. She is not surprised by his criticism. She learned a long time ago that her father rarely says goodbye to her without throwing a parting hand grenade. Why he feels compelled to do so, she has never been able to fathom. What she does know is that it always leaves her feeling like she is never good enough.

Soon the house is empty. Not even Gizmo, Rachel's chocolate Siamese cat, is around for company. *Probably sleeping on Celeste's bed.* The stillness is total. The aloneness is suffocating.

Rachel wanders aimlessly around the house that looks magical with its Christmas adornments: the fifteen-foot-tall spruce tree decorated with sparkling silver bows and glittering red balls; the garland with its small pinecones wrapped precisely around the railings and windows; and the twenty-five houses, banks, stores, schools, and churches of the Charles Dickens' village arranged methodically and symmetrically on a bed of snow-white cotton as only a perfectionist like Susan Biandi can do.

Rachel sighs and wonders if any woman living in the era of Dickens' novel, *A Tale of Two Cities*, ever obsessed about chocolate in the cupboard. The drawing power of the candy is nearly impossible for her to resist when she is emotionally starved. A veritable trance descends on her, and she has no power to resist the summons of the gratifying morsels.

She gazes somberly through the sliding glass doors at the large cedar wood deck and then out into the thick forest of firs and hardwood trees. A fresh blanket of white covers the mid-December world compliments of the whispering snow that fell during the night.

Pure snow. Beautiful sparkling snow. Her mother's skin. Celeste's skin.

Rachel sighs again and then begins to quietly sing a song she wrote shortly after she became a believer in Jesus. It has long been a comfort to her, especially when her heart is heavy with sadness. One of the lines is, "When I am unseen by those who once promised to love me, I thank you, Jesus, that in your embrace I will always be."

As she continues to sing, the powerful grip of the ancient trance with its irresistible summoning begins to weaken. The throbbing ache that resides inside her chest and abdomen slowly downgrades from a category five hurricane to a tropical depression.

But then two things happen that thrust her back into the eye of the emotional maelstrom that has often been her closest acquaintance—not a friend, of course, but an abiding companion.

First, she walks into her father's home office and notices several new pictures on his desk. All but one of them are action shots of Celeste playing her father's favorite sport. In one framed photo, her athletic sister is fiercely shielding the ball from a defender; in another, she is leaping high into the air to head the ball; and in the last one, she is running at top speed down the pitch, an opposing player on either side of her, dribbling the ball toward the net. Her face is a study in determination. Her eyes are on fire, her ponytail is flying behind her like the tail of a comet, and her lips are twisted into a snarl, revealing barred teeth. Her whole face cries out, "You can't stop me."

The last picture on the desk is one of her workaholic father—who never returns from the distant provinces of his ever-consuming job in the medical world—standing next to Rachel's sister after a soccer game. He is smiling for a posed picture—how rare. His hand is resting on Celeste's shoulder—how unusual.

The fact that he is available at all for a family event instead of living at the hospital anesthetizing patients is unprecedented. *Gently putting strangers to sleep for two decades while his daughter is at home, hungry for the comforting presence of her father's voice and touch,* Rachel ponders with bitterness. How many nights had she longed for her daddy to be in her room, putting her to sleep with a bedtime story?

Rachel lifts her chin and begins singing a little louder to fend off a resurgence of the storm in her chest. She pivots quickly and walks out of Dr. Biandi's 'home away from the hospital,' a high and sacred place that Celeste has finally been invited into, but not his other daughter.

Rachel drifts down the glistening hardwood floors of the wide hallway and pauses outside her mother's sewing and craft room. She looks in, and her eyes travel slowly over the orderly desk, the neat shelves, and the meticulously organized sewing thread and fabric. Eventually, she begins to walk down the hallway again but then stops abruptly. Her brain registers that one of the drawers in her mother's desk is slightly open—ever so slightly.

Rachel senses she should not open the drawer, not just because she would be snooping, but for an even more critical reason that she cannot know in the moment. However, the pull of curiosity fueled by a voice beyond physical hearing is so compelling that she relents after only a brief hesitation. In doing so, Rachel puts herself in harm's way for the second time in the last few minutes.

Still singing her song to Jesus, she walks over to the desk and reaches down with a tentative hand. She slides the drawer open and sees a stack of envelopes. In an instant, she recognizes them as past Christmas letters, the missives in which her mother regales extended family members and friends about Biandi family events and news from the previous twelve months.

Rachel has always had mixed emotions about these annual letters. On the one hand, they have stirred tremendous gratitude in her heart—especially since she came to know Jesus—toward her parents for adopting her. She is aware that Samuel and Susan Biandi invested considerable time, effort, and finances pursuing her and securing her as their daughter. For all of that, she is genuinely thankful even though once, when Rachel was eight years old, irritated Susan Biandi let it slip out that her husband had hoped to adopt a boy.

On the other hand, the letters have often touched something painful inside of Rachel. The fact that she was chosen by the Biandis means that she was rejected by somebody else—her birth parents. So, being chosen by the second set of parents has always been tempered with the rejection by her first parents, leaving Rachel with an underlying sense of abandonment that has nagged her ever since she learned she was adopted.

Another reason the Christmas letters are distasteful for Rachel is that they usually mention her parents' travels, Samuel's work at the hospital, Susan's office-leading real estate sales, and a short blurb about Rachel's happenings during the year. The lion's share of the letter, however, is devoted to Celeste and her amazing life.

Rachel has never mentioned the blatant Celeste bias to Susan, but she cannot help but believe that her mother must have some awareness of how she worships her younger daughter—the biological one. Rachel has never been able to decide if her mother loves her sister too much or if she loves her—Rachel—too little. Whatever the case may be, Rachel has never brought the issue to her mother's attention because of her gratitude for being chosen by the Biandi family. She also fears that any comments on her part will be perceived as pettiness or a lack of appreciation.

Rachel removes the top envelope from the drawer and opens it. She slides out the customary folded holiday letter along with the enclosed family picture. She is curious which photo her mother has chosen this year to proudly display the Biandi family to her family and friends. It is not difficult for her to conjure up a mental image of the Christmas picture that was probably taken last summer at the cottage...

Celeste will be standing or sitting between Samuel and Susan, the three of them obviously biologically related with their matching dark hair, light skin tone, and lithe body type. She, Rachel, will be positioned somewhere behind Celeste, looking like she was pulled off the street and inserted into the picture to serve as an inferior contrast to the amazing others: gaudy red versus elegant black, larger versus smaller, artsy versus athletic, emotionally hypersensitive versus resilient and unflappable.

When Rachel removes the family picture from the folded letter, she abruptly stops singing, and her mouth falls open. Her disbelieving eyes behold the usual arrangement of Celeste, the precious jewel, nestled in the setting of her mother and father on either side. Unusually, there is no juxtaposition of the normal with the atypical. No, the outsider is absent altogether. She is excluded from the family picture. The faces smiling back at her are the mother, the father, and the biological daughter.

Rachel's eyes blur with tears as she stares at the *family* photo. Her mind races as she mumbles, "How can this be? I've been the second-class citizen in the past, but this time I'm the excluded one. What have I done wrong?"

She wipes away tears with the tips of her fingers as a darker thought slinks into her mind: *It's not what you've* ***done*** *wrong, Rachel. It's that you* ***are*** *wrong. Don't you get it—there's something inherently undesirable about you.*

Rachel grinds her teeth and fights off a strong urge to rip the picture into a million pieces.

The stunned woman stares at the picture for a long time until disbelief gives way to numbness, and shock is mitigated by despairing acceptance. She has never really been loved by her mother. She has never actually been a part of the inner Biandi circle.

In the beginning, they chose her—at least her mother did—and brought her home. Then they realized that she was not what they wanted after all. But it was too late to get rid of her. They did not have the option, as with an unsavory fish caught in the ocean, to throw her back. They could, however, marginalize her to the periphery of their love and attention—consciously or subconsciously—probably the latter.

Celeste, on the other hand, is the keeper, the "celestial star," as Rachel has thought of her. She is the one the parents truly desire, not out of obligation but because they genuinely cherish her. Yes, Celeste is the precious treasure, and she, Rachel, is the tolerated disappointment.

A wave of nausea washes over Rachel as she places the letter and picture back into the envelope and returns it to the drawer. She walks stiffly out of her mother's room—no, Susan's room—and wanders toward the kitchen. The power of the trance reaches out and clutches her like the tentacles of a monstrous kraken. She feels so empty inside. Food, the magical elixir, will fill her. Lots of food—enough to distend her stomach until she feels like she has a baby bump.

Once again, the cruel battle is lost without so much as a pathetic whimper.

CHAPTER 3

Stewart at the Bottom of the World

Stewart Olson parks the old Dodge pickup, whose fenders are colonized by rust and road salt, at the trailhead twenty miles north of Grand Marais. Although he is more practiced at summer camping, he knows enough about winter camping to survive—especially when it involves a log cabin.

He is alone. He wants to be alone—or at least he thinks he does. When is he not alone, even when he is surrounded by people?

The Intellect climbs out of the cab into the subzero air and lowers the gate of the pickup truck. It shrieks against the cold. He straps on his snowshoes, then grabs his backpack and manipulates it into an upright position so he can slide his arms into the straps and hoist it onto his back.

After he adjusts the pack to a comfortable position on his shoulders, he turns back to the truck and slams the gate. Again, the shriek, followed by a loud bang—cold metal against cold metal. Eerily, it reminds Stewart of...a gunshot.

For a long time, he stands frozen, like the ground beneath his feet. He is transfixed by warring sensations in his heart.

On the one hand, he exults in the peace and safety of being outside in nature—his favorite place, second only to books—where he has sought refuge since he was a boy to escape the anguish of human relationships.

On the other hand, he dreads the heavy ache that throbs in his chest like a sledgehammer striking an empty fifty-five-gallon steel drum.

He is too detached from his own heart to identify the emotion behind the ache. All he knows is that it engulfs him.

Stewart slowly inhales the frigid morning air into his lungs. When he blows it out through his mouth, the warmer exhaled air appears briefly as a white cloud in front of his face before it dissipates into nothingness, swallowed by the fifteen degrees below zero Minnesota air.

Nothingness, Stewart thinks to himself, the world is so full of nothingness. Is that an oxymoron? he asks in his brain that so often ponders irrelevant details. *Full of nothingness.*

He readjusts the backpack on his shoulders one more time. Then he heads across the stone-hard trailhead parking lot that resembles Rocky Road ice cream with its ingredients of gravel, snow, and dirt.

He enters the forest of snow-frosted Norway pines and naked birch trees whose fragile bark peels and shrivels against the cold. He follows the trail as it winds over glacial rock outcroppings and frozen streams that ceased gurgling six weeks ago, reduced to silence by the onslaught of the relentless winter that kills everything in its frigid embrace.

As he trudges forward, he hears the raucous cackling of voices in his head. They clamor under his furry trapper hat, whose flaps resemble the long, floppy ears of a hound dog. He hears his parents, his peers from high school, his middle-school gym teacher, his cell biology professor in college—all of them accusing him.

He attempts to invite the affirming voices of Jack and Rachel into the same head space as his accusers, but the voracious piranhas in his mind that took up residence there even before he was five years old direct their razor-sharp teeth against the encouraging words. Within seconds, the voices are annihilated, shredded into nothingness. Nothingness once again.

Always the nothingness.

The undefinable ache continues to throb beneath his ribs. Like some terrifying alien creature, it attempts to force its way out of his chest. His throat constricts, and he swallows hard. He shakes his head and, only by an act of sheer will, forces his snowshoes forward over the fresh snow.

After half an hour, he encounters a winding river of ice about fifty feet wide. He turns onto the seasonal road and follows it, alone.

In some places, where the wind has blown the snow off the river, he sees water running beneath the fourteen-inches-thick transparent encasement of ice. Fleetingly, he envisions his heart buried beneath the impenetrable layer of frozenness. Then he sees his face, white and dead, rushing past beneath the ice. He shudders.

Fifteen minutes later, he encounters two solitary snowshoers trudging downriver toward him. Neither traveler bothers to lift their face to glance at him as they walk by. He is nobody to them. Nothing.

A short while later, he encounters a party of twenty hikers accompanied by a park guide. The fifty-five-gallon drum in his chest thunders loudly when he hears the hikers laughing and chatting animatedly about the frozen waterfall they have just seen.

Stewart remembers the people—the word "friends" does not enter his mind—at the Academy and wishes they were with him on this journey into—nothingness.

Wanting people with him is new for Stewart. Missing his dog, Moose, or longing for the woods of northern Minnesota, or desiring to retreat to his private study in the basement of his parents' house—these are all familiar longings for him. But wanting people? This yearning is unprecedented.

Why do people hurt you so much when you're with them? he wonders to himself. *If they weren't so highly associated with pain, maybe I'd want to be around others.*

Stewart hikes steadily upriver for two hours, stopping only to shed an outer layer of clothing as his body heats up from the rigors of snowshoeing.

Eventually, he arrives at the towering white pine that signals his departure point from the frozen road. He veers off the icy trail, carefully climbs the steep bank, and then sets out on a snowy path that has been compacted by earlier hikers. It is now nearing 11:30 in the morning.

He glances up into the hazy, iron-gray sky and notices white snow dogs heeling obediently on either side of the sun. He is mildly surprised to see the parhelia so bright and visible this early in the day. His intellectual self knows that sunlight refracted by hexagonal ice crystals suspended in the clouds is creating the appearance of the two "dogs."

He knows so much about *things*.

An hour later, where the compacted trail veers off to the west, Stewart continues in a northerly direction. Now he is trudging through three feet deep snow that has not been compacted by other hikers. His beavertail snowshoes are extremely helpful at this point of his journey. They keep him largely on top of the snow, preventing him from exhaustingly high stepping through the deep drifts.

When he comes to a small stream that is frozen solid, Stewart turns and follows it as it winds among trees and bushes toward the northwest. In the warmer months, this part of the forest would be almost impenetrable with berry bushes that provide a desirable habitat for black bears.

Over the ensuing four hours, he encounters bear scat and the hoof and footprints of deer, wolves, and even one moose. He pauses several times on the frozen stream to rest, snack on trail mix, and drink water sharp with ice slivers. His frigid fingers struggle to open the insulated water bottle and maneuver the raisins and nuts into his mouth. Whenever he comes to a stop, his glasses frustratingly fog up like he is in a hot tub.

As the giant celestial ember drops behind the treetops and the winter air becomes noticeably colder, Stewart espies his destination—a lonely log cabin nestled among the pine trees on the hillside. If he had not been looking for it, he would not have seen it, so well is the structure set back from the flat, open plain that has steadily broadened around the stream over the last half hour.

Stewart has long considered the cabin a metaphor for himself—hidden and alone. It is no larger than a single-stall garage. A stone chimney climbs up its back, and a single window in the front stares menacingly at him like an irritable cyclop's eye. Stewart leaves the frozen stream and snowshoes up to the old cabin.

Mechanically, he removes his snowshoes with their sharp crampons and leans them against the exterior logs of the cabin. The door latch opens with pressure from his mittened hand, and he steps over the threshold into the gloomy interior that smells of wood and the passing of many years. He slips out of his forty-pound backpack, and his body sighs in relief.

As he massages his shoulders, he scans the small room. Everything is how he left it last summer—the ceiling-high stack of split wood next to the fireplace, the small table with its rough-hewn pinewood surface and solitary chair, and the crude wooden bed frame with its box spring made of leather straps.

Next to the bed is a wooden nightstand with knobby birch legs that appear tired and fragile. Resting on top of it are two books as familiar to Stewart as the back of his hand.

Stewart peels off a layer of clothes—his mittens, scarf, puffer jacket, and the winter hat with its hound dog ears. He extracts several items from his backpack, including a small battery-operated lantern, a miniature cook stove, and a pan. He sets these items on the small table along with a packet of freeze-dried beef stroganoff. Then he busies himself with peeling bark off a log.

He uses a cigarette lighter to ignite the bark along with small pieces of kindling wood. Within minutes, flames are crackling in the fireplace that is black from the smoke of six decades of previous fires. The small cabin slowly transitions from an uninviting freezer to a refrigerator—just in time to war with the creeping darkness that invades the room through the cyclop's eye. After stepping outside to collect snow in his pan, he stirs in the freeze-dried meal and heats it up on the small stove.

It is not wasted on Stewart that everything in the miniature cabin is made to accommodate one person—the eight-inch pan, the single serving MRE, the solitary chair, the narrow bed, the small table.

His mother told him a thousand times that he "came by it honestly." What she means is that he inherited a natural bent toward isolation from his father, his uncles, and his grandfather. It was his grandfather, Arnie, who built the cabin back in the early 1950s to shelter him during his observation of moose and timber wolves for the DNR. Grandpa Arnie always referred to the isolated cabin as The Den.

Unlike his mother, Stewart is not persuaded that nature is primarily responsible for the schizoid bent so common in Olson men. After familiarizing himself in recent years with family history and Olson personalities, he is now convinced that nurture, not nurture, provides the best explanatory power for his strong inclination toward aloneness and hiding. For two hundred years, Stewart's predecessors ingrained in their children the value of self-sufficiency and silence.

Common axioms heard in the Olson clan were admonitions like, "you're too big for your britches," "don't get a big head," "children are meant to be seen, not heard," "if you keep crying, I'll give you something to cry about," and "don't speak until you are spoken to."

So much for encouraging the emergence of a child's personality. An acorn under a boulder had a better opportunity to grow tall and strong than an Olson boy or girl.

After supper, Stewart feeds the fire more split wood from the stack in the corner of the cabin and then unrolls his sleeping bag on the latticed bed frame. Exhausted but wanting to warm his core before he falls asleep, he positions the solitary chair in front of the fire and sits down.

As his fatigued body drifts into unconsciousness, something summons his mind into the labyrinthine passages of the first twenty-four years of his life. Initially, he is sitting in Dr. Windsor's warfare class at the Academy. Then, he is planting trees with his fifth-grade science class behind the elementary school in Two Harbors. Finally, he is in his backyard with his sister, Maggie...

Six-year-old Stewart has a baseball bat in his hands. He and four-year-old Maggie are taking turns swinging at the huge dragonflies that buzz lazily through the air like winged dirigibles. The brother and sister have yet to strike one of the insects, but their lack of success does not deter them from further attempts. They are laughing and squealing with childish delight, and their eyes are bright with excitement on this summer afternoon.

Stewart pulls the wooden bat back as he prepares to take another strike at the elusive insects with the bulging eyes and double set of wings. During his backswing, his bat hits something behind him that is much firmer than air. Almost immediately, Maggie cries out in pain. Stewart turns around quickly and watches in horror as blood begins flowing from his sister's nose and upper lip.

Shocked at the sight of the blood, everything fades to a blur in Stewart's brain. Maggie continues to scream lustily, as much from fear as pain since the bat had not hit her hard enough to break any bones or dislodge any teeth. No stitches would even be needed—only a wet washcloth and some ice.

Before Stewart can even think to cry for help, his mother explodes from the back door of the house at a dead run. He remembers thinking that her face resembled a crazed mother bear whose cub had just been shot by a foolish hunter.

He also has enough time to imagine that something akin to the solar plasma arcs he read about in an astronomy book is radiating from his mother's body. It is not the first time he has felt them descending on him. They are almost tangible. He stiffens. A dark curtain falls over his eyes.

The insane she-bear does not choose to do the rational thing, namely, run to assist her screaming daughter, whose face is dripping blood. No, she does something irrational. After all, she is in her emotional mind and so reacts out of emotion. She hurdles herself toward her son with such energy that her body is leaning forward. She stumbles before she reaches her son but recovers herself just in time to tackle him with her shoulder and face.

Once Stewart is on the ground, his mother slaps him hard across the face. Then she slaps him again and again. He sees stars behind his eyes. At first, her punishment is delivered in eerie silence like a mute demon from hell itself. Then she finds her voice. The unhinged woman masquerading as his mother begins to scream curses and character-assassinating names, including one that is new to his boyish ears: "Wicked bastard."

The beating climaxes with him lying on the grass in a fetal position as his mother kicks him repeatedly.

Stewart's body jerks in the wooden chair in front of the fireplace, but he does not awaken. He sighs raggedly, and his brain resets.

Now he is sixteen. He is standing next to a huge pile of wood with only an ax, a wedge, and a thermos of water. His hands are blistered and bloody. He has been splitting wood since the first light of day, and now it is close to suppertime. It is, in fact, the fourth consecutive day he has been splitting wood. His father is angry. Again.

Stewart does not even remember his offense on this occasion; there have been so many. The truck overheated the day after he drove it, he got an A- in industrial arts, he forgot to do a chore, he is constitutionally lazy, he looked disrespectfully at his mother, he said "shut up" to Maggie, and on and on. All he knows is that his father demanded that he split wood for five days as a severe punishment masked behind the euphemism of "integrity formation."

And, oh yes, his father is not speaking to him. The dreaded silent treatment. Stewart knows from repeated experience that this shaming behavior will continue for days, if not weeks, depending on the severity of his offense. His father will not even look at him during this shunning season. He ceases to exist as a person during these periods of punishment. He is a specter.

Yes, both parents are capable of monstrous anger. His mother's version is explosive and unpredictable, often shocking. It is overwhelming to its object but, like a tsunami, is soon over, leaving devastation in its wake. Father's anger, on the other hand, is cold, unforgiving, and has remarkable staying power. Like the Genesis flood, it sometimes covers Stewart's entire world for forty days and forty nights. Its hallmark is annihilation and abandonment.

Both his father's anger and his mother's anger are dangerous. Both have killed his spirit over the years. Both make visibility of self a high-risk venture. Only a truly foolish child would fly above the radar in such an environment. He has wisely chosen to hide. Far away.

Over the years, he has learned that safety lies in not being seen or known. *Don't feel, don't express opinions, don't ask questions, don't disagree, don't have expressions on your face (even positive ones because they will undoubtedly be interpreted as defiant disrespect or ungodly pride), don't exist in any manner as a separate self that might trigger the devastating tsunami or the relentless flood.*

In the Olson family, it is better to be dead than alive.

Yes, he has learned to be dead. Not just playing dead like a person might do when an angry grizzly bear attacks. No—actually *being* dead. And once you have learned to be dead for a long time, only a miraculous resurrection will bring you back to life. These resurrections are very rare in a family system.

Dead is dead.

Stewart awakens to a dark room. The fire has died. He gets up from the lonely chair and grabs an armful of the split logs—mute reminders of his past evils as a teenager. He arouses the dead fire and then steps outside into the dark night.

He is in another world. The gibbous moon, a titan in the sky, illuminates the winter landscape, painting it silver. But the effect is not magical. Rather, the earthly world around him appears eerie, ghastly. The crooked black shadows of skeletal trees and barren bushes race across the snow toward him with sinister intent. They are his mother—enraged and coming for him.

With great effort, Stewart rips his attention away from his onrushing attackers and directs his eyes toward the expanse above him.

The night sky is a mammoth jewelry box full of brilliant diamonds that has been overturned. Thousands of twinkling gems have been scattered across the dark vault above his head.

A shiver only partially caused by the subzero temperature travels down Stewart's spine. He takes several steps away from the cabin and turns to gaze above the roofline and the surrounding trees. In the northern quadrant, he beholds the quivering emerald hues of the aurora borealis snaking across the sky like a living creature.

He stands mesmerized by the undulating sight above him that never fails to fill him with awe. Minutes pass. He folds his arms across his chest to ward off the besieging cold.

As he attempts to internalize the glorious sight shimmering above him like a mirage in the desert ("attempts" because he has never been able to become one with the resplendent beauty of the night sky no matter how hard he has tried), his mind drifts to the two books on his wobbly nightstand and the two opposite personalities who reside between their covers.

One of the books is entitled *Alone*. It is the autobiographical account of Admiral Byrd, the intrepid explorer who spent five months alone in the Antarctic clinging to life in a shack buried in the snow and ice to protect against the minus seventy-five-degree temperature and the frostbiting, flesh-eating wind. Incredibly, the Admiral survived the deadly cold, the devastating aloneness of being buried in an icy crypt by himself, and the near-lethal effects of carbon monoxide poisoning that drove him into bouts of insanity.

Admiral Richard Byrd has been Stewart's hero since the third grade. Hero? Maybe not as much a hero as a man he identified with closely. After all, he and the Admiral are both men who experienced utter aloneness and afterward longed for more of it.

In past years, when Stewart had made trips to the cabin in the north woods alone, he had felt a strange camaraderie with the Admiral. In fact, Stewart felt like a kindred spirit with Byrd. But that term, "kindred spirit," was one that probably neither he nor Richard would ever allow to escape their lips. It is too laden with connotations of intimacy for two men so bent toward voluntary isolation to ever speak aloud.

Whatever their quiet connection might be called, Stewart echoed this man's life and often wished he could have spoken with him. He has always wanted to hear more about the Admiral's adventures in the icy wilderness of the Antarctic and understand how the explorer had survived his five-month-long unending winter of isolation. Unfortunately, Richard Byrd had died forty years before Stewart was even born.

Stewart had often viewed his cabin in the deep woods—especially when he was there in the dead of winter—as a solitary bunker akin to Byrd's buried shack. Never had it entered Stewart's awareness of how tragic it was for him to identify most closely with a dead man who probably never learned to be genuinely intimate with another human being—possibly not even his wife and children.

Unexpectedly, a shock wave rolled through Stewart's life three years ago that breached his lonely existence. It had to do with the second book that rests on the nightstand in the cabin with Admiral Byrd—the Bible.

While at the university, an unexpected encounter altered the trajectory of his life. Stewart was making the familiar, lonely trek from his dorm to the science building when he was approached by two young men who identified themselves as members of a campus ministry. They shared the good news of Jesus' love with the isolated young man. In his hunger for something to feed the deepest desire of his heart, Stewart prayed on the spot to receive Christ into his heart. The two young men subsequently invited him to weekly meetings on campus, where he met other believers and grew in his knowledge of Jesus.

But even with his belief in Jesus and his new friends, Stewart sensed that something was still 'off' inside of him while he was at school. If his heart was a house with many rooms, most of them remained strangely inaccessible to God and to those around him with skin on. He still found himself in a house primarily inhabited only by himself.

So, what was the problem? Was his faith too small, or was God punishing him as his father had—with silence and abandonment? Worse yet, was God merely a myth he believed to feed his existential aloneness?

Stewart awakens from his mental wanderings beneath the night sky because his body is shaking violently from the cold. He takes one last look at the living creature gyrating across the northern sky and at the silvered landscape looming before him with both threat and beauty. Then he retreats into the cabin that is a bunker and a tomb.

He resumes his spot on the lonely wooden chair and touches his burning ears and cheeks. He knows that if he had remained outside much longer, his exposed skin would have been tattooed with frostbite. As it is, his glasses are covered with ice.

Stewart rubs numb fingers together and slides his chair close to the warmth radiating from the fireplace. He glances over at the two books on the nightstand. Both are written in the same language. Both contain perceptions about the universe. Both include reflections on God and His character. But they are so unalike. One is all about Stewart's life story: aloneness. The other is chock full of intimacy and love.

In recent years, Stewart has felt a growing pity for his "friend," Admiral Byrd, who believed that God was an unknowable, impersonal universal intelligence. Stewart harbors no judgment toward the Admiral since he himself had embraced a similar belief about God for most of his life. In fact, he still entertains lingering questions about the personal relationship between the Divine and His human creation. However, over the past three years, Stewart's experience with God has led him to view the Creator of the universe less as a distant, impersonal force and more as a supernatural personality who makes occasional appearances in his life.

Although the inconsistency of the divine presence remains an ongoing issue—an inconsistency due either to God's elusive nature or to Stewart's tendency to hide—the truth of the divine existence is largely indisputable for Stewart. He has tasted God's presence even if it has been sporadic and more on the level of the intellect than the heart.

After his extremities and face are thoroughly warmed, Stewart gets up and takes the two steps over to his backpack. He extracts his personal journal and then retrieves his Bible. With some regret, he drags the chair back to the small table, leaving Admiral Byrd on the nightstand, alone again.

His retreat to the log cabin—which in years past he referred to as

"Byrd's Base Camp" but more recently as "God's Hiding Place"—is motivated on this occasion by deep intention. He is here for five days to fight the battle inside himself between competing sensations: accusation and affirmation, aloneness and intimacy, going through life as the walking dead or the fully alive.

Sitting down at the table, he switches on his lantern and opens Windsor's Field Manual to Joshua 1:5, 6, where he reads: "No man shall be able to stand before you all the days of your life. Just as I was with Moses, so I will be with you. I will not leave you or forsake you. Be strong and courageous..."

After meditating on the inspiring words, he turns to another verse, and then another and another.

Hours pass. At 5:30 in the morning, Stewart gets up from his study of the Word of God and feeds more logs to the dying fire. Then, he retreats to his narrow bed, that is more of a punishment than a respite from fatigue.

As he settles into his insulated sleeping bag, he remembers Admiral Byrd's account of seeking refuge in his bed from the frigid Antarctic air during the eternal night of June when the sun never rose above the horizon. How miserable it must have been for the intrepid explorer when he climbed out of his warmish sleeping bag on minus seventy-five below zero mornings when no heat was being generated in the subterranean shack.

Stewart slips in and out of sleep as he conjures up mental pictures of the Antarctic shack.

In the lonely cabin twenty miles removed from the nearest living person, a battle is being fought in the spiritual world well beyond human awareness. A dark, hateful presence attempts to brand fiery words of shame and accusation onto Stewart's mind while a bright Being defends the son of Adam with truth.

The ancient prosecutor attacks the dozing man with familiar lies: "You're a mistake," and, "If anyone sees your real self, they will be *appalled*," and, predictably enough, "Nobody will ever love you."

The bright Being fights off the accuser by speaking a single phrase into Stewart's besieged heart: "If God is for you, who can be against you?" (Pity the man or woman who has no divine defender to protect them from the accusations of darkness.)

When Stewart eventually falls into a deep sleep, snowflakes the size of silver dollars begin to drift down lazily from a dark firmament that is now starless and moonless. By daybreak, blizzard winds will be gusting over fifty miles an hour. By noon, two feet of fresh snow will cover the ground, and the wind-generated drift in front of the cabin door will reach the roof.

CHAPTER 4

Brother and Sister Twice

A week after they leave the Academy for the six-week winter break, Aly and Mahmoud find themselves at another school just outside of Atlanta, Georgia, called the Institute for Apologetics and God Studies. The Ahmed siblings are sitting in a repurposed, pedestrian classroom, very unlike the exotic ones back at the Teleios Academy.

The current room has a water-stained, drop-down ceiling with flickering fluorescent lights and an ancient olive-green linoleum floor. It is located in a single-story building that, in another lifetime, housed a small printing company. Along with twenty-five other students of varying ages, they are listening to Professor Kameel Majdali wax on about the topic of Jesus, among other world religions.

The class content captivates the Ahmed siblings since they both are relatively young in their new faith—especially Mahmoud, of course, who has known Jesus for only three weeks now. The class is also enthralling because of Professor Majdali, the thirty-year-old professor who hails originally from the city of Alexandria in Egypt. Aly has already decided that the young instructor is the most intelligent man she has ever met.

According to Kameel's testimony, he was "found by Jesus" when he was living with his Coptic Christian parents in the Sinai desert town of Sharm

El Sheikh. His family had moved to Sharm eleven years after the final subdivision of the Sinai wilderness had been quietly and officially transferred to Egypt after being under Israeli rule since the 1967 war.

Kameel's father was hired by the Egyptian Ministry of Tourism as a medical professional at the Hyperbolic Medical Center, a facility specializing in the study of the effects of deep-sea diving on the human body. Kameel became a believer in Jesus in a very unusual manner...

In July of 1995, when Kameel was only ten years old, he and his friends found themselves very bored and hot in the wilderness city of Sharm. So, the young boys did what they always did when they were bored and hot—they rode their bikes to the beach to go snorkeling.

Their familiar routine was to walk out in the shallow water on top of the reef that extended a hundred feet out into the Gulf of Aqaba. Then, when they arrived at the edge of the reef, they would swim out into the open water where they could look down at the breathtaking 500-foot drop-off that was teeming with hundreds of specimens of sea life, including barracuda, grey sharks, stingrays, giant tuna, jellyfish, clown fish, and myriads of other marine species as colorful as Noah's rainbow.

On this particular day, Kameel was thirty feet out on the reef when his right foot slipped into a crevice and was punctured by something sharp. The pain was immediate and excruciating. In the past, his father had often spoken to his children about the dangers of the highly camouflaged and poisonous scorpionfish and stonefish that inhabited the shallow waters of the reef. Equipped with this knowledge, Kameel was immediately terrified when he felt the intense pain in his foot.

As he limped back toward the shoreline, he began screaming for help. Soon, he began to weep loudly. By the time he reached the beach and collapsed onto the sand, his head was exploding with pain, and he began vomiting. To his horror, his foot had already ballooned to twice its normal size.

Slipping in and out of unconsciousness, his heart began to beat irregularly, and his vision was increasingly impeded by a thick, gray curtain. He knew he was going to die. Delirious, he cried out for his grandfather, Nabeel, who had been killed years ago in the fourth Arab-Israeli war.

As if in response to his cry for help, a shadow suddenly fell on him, snatched him up from the beach, and carried him over the sand. By now, half out of his mind, Kameel imagined himself flying through the air on the magic carpet of Solomon. But when he forced open his eyelids that were as heavy as the boulders at Solomon's mines, he saw, as if in a dream, a man whose appearance was angelic. His light skin convinced Kameel that his rescuer was not an Egyptian or a member of the peace-keeping force from Columbia or Fiji. He was convinced that he had been rescued by a supernatural being.

Then everything went black.

When he finally opened his eyes again, albeit briefly, he found himself in a hospital bed surrounded by people who resembled his parents and his three sisters. He could not see their faces well at all without his glasses since his vision, uncorrected, was atrocious.

Being in the hospital was not highly irregular for Kameel. He had received medical treatment frequently in the past due to injuries attributed to his unusually poor eyesight as well as to his overall lack of physical coordination. His pigeon-toed feet, especially, had been a thorn in his flesh since the day he had begun to walk.

What was unusual this time was the fear he saw in the eyes of the woman who resembled his mother when she leaned over his bed to examine him more closely. From her expression, he knew without a doubt that he must be dying or was already dead. Maybe it was not an angel that had come to rescue him after all unless it was the angel of death.

When Kameel lapsed into a coma that persisted for days, his parents were informed that he indeed had stepped on a stonefish, the most poisonous of venomous fish in the Gulf of Aqaba. A stinger from the fish had penetrated the bottom of his right foot and delivered a potentially lethal amount of toxin into his body.

Kameel's condition was exacerbated by anaphylaxis, an allergic reaction that further compromised his grave medical situation. It is certain he would have died had it not been for the immediate intervention of the angel. As it was, his prognosis was grave, according to the attending physician.

The rescuer who had appeared that fateful day on the beach was Joshua Bloomstrom, a captain with the U.S. Army who was stationed in Sharm El Sheikh in Zone C, South Camp. He was a member of the MFO—Multinational Force and Observers—a unit present in the Sinai to oversee the terms of the 1979 peace treaty between Israel and Egypt. Captain Bloomstrom was a twenty-nine-year-old chaplain deployed to the Sinai with the 82nd Airborne Division from Fort Bragg, North Carolina. He had driven to the beach that sweltering July day to do some snorkeling of his own.

Hearing the boy's agonizing screams, Joshua had rushed over to assist Kameel. When he saw the boy's foot, he immediately diagnosed the problem. Grabbing two seashells that were lying on the sand to protect himself from the poisonous barb, he carefully removed the stinger of the stonefish and then snatched up the young boy and ran to his MFO armored vehicle.

By the time Joshua's vehicle screeched to a halt in front of the hospital entrance, Kameel was already experiencing multiple organ failure. A minute later, his heart stopped. It took a crash team seven minutes, employing multiple medications, CPR, and a defibrillator to resuscitate him.

It was later divulged that the resuscitation efforts only went on as long as they did because the attending medical personnel at the hospital recognized Kameel as the son of Anwar Majdali, the revered researcher at the Hyperbaric Medical Center in Sharm. Any other boy would have been declared dead after four or five minutes of unsuccessful resuscitation efforts.

When Kameel opened his eyes three days later, his parents feared extensive brain damage. It was no wonder, then, that they looked far more worried than the time he had crashed through a sliding glass door with his unicycle; or the day he had tripped on a curb and driven his head into a signpost on the street, sustaining a concussion and a laceration that required twenty-one stitches to close his scalp.

His family was relieved beyond words, and the medical personnel were amazed beyond explanation when Kameel's eyes remained open. A few minutes later, the miracle patient asked for his glasses so he could see the faces of those standing around his bed in the hospital room.

Chaplain Joshua Bloomstrom had visited the gravely ill boy in the hospital every day since Kameel's fateful encounter with the stonefish. During these visits, he introduced himself to the whole Majdali family. By the time Kameel left the hospital ten days later, the young captain from the 82nd Airborne had been embraced by Kameel's family as a hero and, indeed, an angel sent from God.

Several weeks later, when Kameel finally felt strong enough to leave his house, his parents welcomed their son's desire to visit "Captain Joshua" every day. On his part, Chaplain Bloomstrom arranged to spend many of his meals with the Egyptian boy, telling him stories about his childhood in Texas and even driving him around Zone C when he was on patrol with the soldiers of the 82nd.

The most amazing thing that the chaplain did—incredibly, even more important than helping to save Kameel's physical life—was to tell the boy about Jesus. The ten-year-old Egyptian had already heard about Jesus, of course, having grown up in a Coptic Christian family that valued the importance of good works and religious rituals aimed at pleasing God. But Kameel and his family did not know God in a personal way. They just knew about him. So, it was totally alien to Kameel's ears when Joshua informed him that he could have a personal friendship with the Maker of the universe instead of relating to him as a largely unknowable sovereign Being as unapproachable as the Allah of Islam.

Six months after that frightful day on the beach, Kameel asked Joshua to pray with him to "receive Jesus into his heart and to believe on him in his head." Within a year, his parents and sisters followed in Kameel's footsteps and committed their lives to Jesus as well. No longer did anyone in the family position their faith in God on the wobbly stilts of good works designed to win God's favor, but on the amazing grace of a loving God who pursued them even when they were not pursuing him.

It was only after they experienced the love of Jesus that Kameel's parents understood why so many of their ancestors over the last millennium had surrendered to Islam with such little resistance. The Coptic emphasis on salvation based on merit was not far removed from the heavily good-works-based Islamic religion, whose adherents were known to hold their breath (literally and figuratively) on the day of their death, hoping against hope that their accumulated good works would be enough to earn them entry into paradise.

Yes, Anwar and his wife, Sarah, now understood what true salvation was. It had nothing to do with their good works or their efforts to reach God. It had everything to do with God's grace reaching down to them through the person of Jesus Christ, offering true life to all who believed in the crucified and risen Savior of the world.

Eventually, Chaplain Bloomstrom's extended period of duty with the MFO came to an end, and his unit returned to Fort Bragg in the United States. Kameel was heartbroken. He felt like he had lost his best friend. But the young captain and the now eleven-year-old boy communicated regularly via letter and occasional phone call. Then, when Kameel was seventeen years old, he and the rest of the Majdali family emigrated from Egypt to Miami.

At this point, the army chaplain—now promoted to the rank of major in the army—and the Egyptian young man traveled back and forth to see each other at least twice a year, even when Joshua moved to Fort Leavenworth in Kansas to attend the United States Army Command and General Staff College (CGSC). As they spent time together, the young major guided his young protégé into a closer walk with God until Jesus became Kameel's best friend, not Joshua.

Kameel went on to acquire his four-year undergraduate degree and then began applying to medical school to follow in his father's footsteps. But as God would have it, a retired army chaplain by the name of Eugene Swenson—who was a mentor to Joshua Bloomstrom—heard about Kameel and his strong faith from his mentee. The retired chaplain, who had joined the Institute of Apologetics and God Studies several years after he had left the military, contacted Kameel and invited him to fill a position at the Institute that focused on reaching Muslims for Christ. Even though Kameel had not come to Christ out of the Muslim faith, his Egyptian ethnicity was viewed as giving him credibility with adherents of Islam.

Kameel accepted the position at the IAGS in Georgia and now, eight years later, was the anchor of their Muslim outreach.

The Ahmed siblings ended up at the Institute under the tutelage of Kameel Majdali because retired Colonel Isaiah Windsor and retired Colonel Eugene Swenson had been contemporaries in the army as well as friends. Familiar with the Institute through his good friend, Dr. Windsor inquired if Aliyah and Mahmoud, the two young Muslim background believers in Jesus, could come and continue to grow in their new faith at the Institute during their six-week winter break at the Academy.

The Ahmeds were welcomed with open arms, and arrangements were quickly made for the two siblings to lodge with Kameel in his small home in Stone Mountain, Georgia, just outside of Atlanta.

Even before Aly and Mahmoud arrived at the Institute on Stone Mountain, Kameel contacted them and inquired if they wished to accompany him on a trip to Israel and Egypt in the middle of January. He informed them that he was participating in an apologetics conference in Jerusalem and then possibly traveling down to Sharm El Sheikh to visit some friends. He also told Aly and Mahmoud that if they wanted to join him, they would need to let him know immediately so he could fast-track the acquisition of their visas through an acquaintance he had in the Israeli embassy.

The Ahmed siblings discussed the invitation and quickly agreed to accompany Kameel to the Middle East. Mahmoud found it incomprehensible that he might soon be walking on despised Israeli soil, a country he had never recognized as legitimate.

So here they sit, only weeks after Mahmoud's incredible encounter with Jesus, at the Institute for Apologetics and God Studies, along with twenty-five other students from the United States and several foreign countries. Today is the last day of classes for Aly and Mahmoud before leaving with Kameel to travel to Fayetteville, North Carolina. Chaplain Joshua Bloomstrom, who eighteen months earlier had been re-stationed at Fort Bragg, has invited them all to join him and his family for the Christmas week. After the first of the year, they will return to the Institute for a week and then fly to Tel Aviv via Rome for the apologetics conference in Jerusalem.

Aly is listening to Kameel Majdali as he juxtaposes the beliefs of Islam, Judaism, Buddhism, Hinduism, and Christianity, highlighting the common theme of monotheism in Islam, Judaism, and Christianity. She smiles to herself as she listens to the young professor who only has a master's degree but sounds to Aly as erudite as a PhD-level educator.

The Egyptian man is wearing a light-colored suit jacket and matching pants—almost white—with a striped-red tie. His curly black hair is tousled all over his head and looks like the waves of a restless sea. His black glasses are larger, and the lenses thicker even than Stewart's. He has a small black mustache and a broader nose.

As the Egyptian lectures, he massages the lobe of his right ear between two fingers and slowly shifts his weight back and forth on his pigeon-toed feet as if he is on the deck of a ship rolling in the ocean. He is not a tall man; in fact, he is only two inches taller than Aly, and that is when he is wearing his thick-soled shoes. Aly admits to herself that even if Professor Kameel Majdali qualifies as a nerd, at least he is a cute nerd.

When the class period is over, Aly and Mahmoud retreat to the library to study. Mahmoud is envious of the knowledge his sister possesses about the wide fractures that travel down to the deepest foundations of Islam. More importantly, he admires the impressive grasp of Christianity she has acquired during her three-year journey of faith in Jesus.

Aly, on the other hand, is jealous of the miraculous personal encounter her brother had with the Messiah.

Most importantly, the siblings have quickly developed a habit of challenging each other to deeper faith as they study the Bible and the Quran as well as Jesus and Muhammed side by side.

There are still moments when Mahmoud's default position is to defend the Prophet. Occasionally, he even feels anger rising fast and hot within him when Aly or the professors at the Institute challenge his old beliefs. However, his faith in Jesus is growing so rapidly that his love for his new best friend increasingly overshadows any impulse to defend Muhammed. He has exchanged belief in a man who claimed to be a prophet for belief in a prophet who claims to be the Creator of the universe.

Mahmoud looks up from reading the Bible and announces matter-of-factly, "I've been thinking about changing my name."

"Changing your name?" Aly repeats with a confused look on her heart-face. "Whatever for, brother?"

"I've been reading about Saul in the book of the Acts of the Disciples," the young man informs his sister.

"When have you had time to do that?" she asks, raising an eyebrow.

"At night, after my studies are done," Mahmoud says as a smile brightens the countenance that just weeks ago was twisted into a malicious frown.

"At night? Do you mean like at midnight?"

"Not exactly," Mahmoud replies, hedging. "More like three in the morning."

Aly shakes her head, and her gleaming, jet-black hair strays over cheeks as delicate as almond blossoms. She comments, "Ever since you gave your life to Jesus, you've hardly slept at all."

"I don't need to sleep," Mahmoud states with twinkling eyes. "The Holy Spirit keeps me awake at night. He knows my heart requires much work to be changed from a desert to a garden."

Aly's brother pauses and then says, "I have read in the Acts of the Disciples how Jesus appeared to Saul and spoke to him from heaven. Do you remember, sister, how some of the professors at the Academy spoke to me about Saul the day I came to faith in Jesus?"

Aly nods her head and replies, "Of course, brother. So, you want to change your name like Saul changed his after his encounter with Jesus?"

"Yes," Mahmoud affirms. "I'm not certain if Saul always had two names or if he adopted a new name after his conversion to Jesus. I just think it would be wise for me to have a new name that will forever remind me of how Jesus raised me from the dead."

Mahmoud gently closes the Bible that is sitting on the table in front of him and observes, "Saul, who becomes Paul, has already been a profound inspiration to me, sister. I see him as a mentor, someone I can identify with in my new faith. Just like Saul was on the way to Damascus to imprison and possibly kill believers in Jesus, so I was on my way to kill you, my own sister. In both cases—Saul and Mahmoud—Jesus appeared and intervened in such a powerful way that we could not doubt what we saw and heard."

Mahmoud looks into his sister's clear eyes and says, "Jesus told Ananias—you remember, the man who Jesus sent to pray with Saul—that Saul would carry the good news to the Gentiles and suffer greatly for doing so. Like him, I sense the Holy Spirit telling me that I will carry the name of Jesus to my Muslim brothers and that I, too, will suffer greatly for doing that.

I need to be ready even to die for the God Most High."

Aly's large almond eyes grow even larger as she places a hand on her brother's arm. "Paul lived for many years before he died the death of a martyr. I want you to live many years before anything happens to you, too, brother. You need not become a new believer and then die immediately for Jesus. You must have time to grow in your faith."

Aly pauses and then adds with a smile, "And you also need time to know your sister better."

Mahmoud nods his head slowly as he stares at the bookshelf behind his sister.

Aly knows her brother's restless brain has already moved on to something else. "What are you thinking now?" she asks with feigned impatience.

"I was just contemplating how both Paul and I were involved in the death of others," Mahmoud replies with a deep sigh. "When I look back on it now, I struggle to believe that I did those evil things. But then I remember that I was gripped by a religion whose prophet taught that warfare and violence against unbelievers were honoring to Allah."

Mahmoud gazes at the bookshelf a while longer, then turns his eyes toward Aly. They are moist with emotion. He reaches out and gently touches her face with the fingers of his right hand. "I am eternally thankful to the Messiah that he prevented me from doing violence to my own sister."

"You and me both," Aly says with a mirthless laugh. "I was so certain I was going to die, and I was so in love with Jesus that I was ready to die."

"Your faith is remarkable," Mahmoud comments. "The Messiah used it to draw me to Him."

Aly nods her head. "And my faith has grown much stronger even in the few days since Jesus interrupted your life with his love. Of all people—Mahmoud Ahmed coming to faith in Yahweh! I always knew my God was big, but when He saved you, I realized just how great He is. He is huge! Mammoth! Sovereign over all things! King of kings and Lord of lords!"

"Praise be to the God of heaven, yes, He is!" Mahmoud agrees, nodding his head. "If He can change my heart from one that kills to one that loves, He indeed is very great!"

Aly grabs her brother's hand in her own and smiles. "So, what will your new name be?"

Mahmoud considers his sister's question for a while before he says, "I've prayed about this decision often over the last fortnight." There is a short silence before he adds, "Just last night, I arrived at a new name. I believe God desires me to be 'Moussa.' The name is that of Moses in the Old Testament, a man who led his people out of slavery. He spoke to his people about listening to God and following Him.

"Like Moses—but a much lesser servant—I have been called to be Jesus' instrument to go to my people and speak of the Name and declare His glory and love. I owe my life to my amazing Father in heaven, who sent His only son to die for me. How can I not be willing now to lay my life down for him?"

The new believer's eyes smolder but not with the hate that had previously burned within him like the fires of Hades. Now he is filled with a deep sense of God's loving presence.

"Sister, I am willing to suffer and even die for him," Moussa says with total confidence, "not by doing violence to others but by speaking to them of Jesus' love."

Little does Mahmoud know how prophetic his words will prove to be, words not for the distant future, as his sister had hoped, but for a time very soon. And words that apply not only to him.

CHAPTER 5

Emily in Fort Myers Beach

It is evening in Fort Myers Beach. Emily is sitting in white shorts and a pink tank top beside the illuminated swimming pool behind her parents' three-bedroom rambler. The house is situated on a canal just a few blocks off Estero Boulevard and a quarter mile from the gulf. She is attempting to read an e-book recommended by Embee, but her attention keeps drifting off past the screened pool enclosure and out over the dark water of the bay that lies beyond the canal. The evening air is warm and moist against her face. Her long blond hair is collected on top of her head instead of resting on her clammy neck and back. She is tempted. She is torn.

In the end, her heart fights off the agonizing dissonance, and her hand reaches for her phone.

"Em, it's about time!" a voice speaks excitedly into the phone after several rings. "Why didn't you respond to my texts? I thought you would have reached out yesterday when you flew in."

Emily hesitates and then says, "Yeah, I was going to call you last night, but I misplaced my phone while unpacking." She grimaces and rolls her eyes, certain that the voice on the other end will see through her lame lie.

"Well, whatever," the voice says dismissively, "we're talking now." There is a brief silence before the voice asks, "So, when are you coming down, babe?"

Emily hesitates again. "I'm not sure—"

"I thought you were coming today," the voice says with a hint of coolness. "It's still not too late to drive down here tonight. It's only an hour to Marco, as you know very well."

"It's getting a bit late to drive down tonight," Emily says as she nibbles on one of her fingernails.

"Em, it's only seven-thirty," the voice on the other end of the phone says now with some exasperation. "Don't you want to see me?"

"Of course, I do," Emily replies slowly.

"Then drive on down, babe!" the voice says convincingly.

"Okay," Emily says, relenting. "I'll pack up and be down there by 9 a.m."

"I like the sound of that!" her friend comments into the phone.

After they say their good-byes, Emily drifts into the house through the three-panel sliding glass door and throws some things into her backpack. Her parents are gone at a Bible study and will not be home until long after she leaves. She scribbles a note to them on the whiteboard in the kitchen, informing them that she is going to visit a friend for the next few days and not to worry. Then she grabs a bottle of water from the fridge and heads out to the driveway, where she jumps into her Volkswagen Super Beetle.

As she turns on the headlights and slips the car into reverse, she glances into the rearview mirror and sees her darkly shadowed face. She has a strange fleeting feeling that the eyes looking back at her are not her own. They look different, somehow. But such thoughts are not to be entertained, so she rips her eyes away from the mirror and backs into the street.

Seventy-five minutes later, on the same evening that Stewart is holed up in his lonely cabin and Armando and Jack are sitting on the sands of Newport Beach, Emily crosses the bridge from the Florida mainland to Marco Island. Soon, she pulls into the parking lot of a condominium development. The jangling, rattling noise of the iconic Super beetle engine triggers two car alarms as she drives between rows of car ports.

After she parks the car, she gets out and heads toward the tall building. As she walks, a cool breeze teases her hair, and the soft sound of distant waves caressing the shoreline reaches her ears. A seagull overhead shrieks in the dark, and she looks up. In that moment, she is only half aware of the weightiness of what she is about to do.

She is going to cross *the* line yet again (if the line even exists anymore), this time with only a whisper of hesitation opposing her more powerful urge to surrender to desire. In her more analytical moments, which are very few these days, she thinks of the strong urge as a trance. It is almost impossible to resist.

The road she has chosen to travel is acquiring deep ruts.

Emily knocks on the eighth-floor door and waits. Her heart is beating with a passion that might be love or forbidden desire or something else she does not want to acknowledge. All she knows for sure is that the feeling inside impacts her physiologically. It feels good, alluring. *How can something that feels this good ever be wrong?*

A moment later, the door opens, and a voice exclaims excitedly, "You made it! You don't know how good it is to see you, Em!"

Emily is aware of a growing smile on her face as she replies, "It's good to see you too, Natalie."

The two women embrace affectionately, and then the door closes behind them. It shuts out everything else.

CHAPTER 6

Jack and Armando in the Hood

Less than an hour after they leave the beach, they arrive back at the house in Corona Del Mar.

Jack meets Armando's mother, Maria, her husband, Peter, and their two kids, Sam and Bridget. Maria is a smaller woman with a large personality—talkative and energetic. Peter, an architect who works in Irvine, is taciturn but has a friendly face and an even temperament. They consume a late supper of tamales smoked in cornhusks that Maria has prepared as a long-standing Christmastime family tradition.

While they devour the tamales that Jack finds delightful, they talk about a wide range of topics: the snow in Colorado, Maria's grandparents who live in Tijuana, Peter's current project in Las Vegas, and the first semester at the Teleios Academy. Jack notes that his roommate does not speak about tomorrow's rendezvous with the murderer of Armando's half-brother.

During the evening conversation, it becomes evident to Jack that Maria and Peter are not followers of Jesus but do not seem hostile to Armando's faith. In fact, Armando's mother seems grateful to Jesus for turning her son away from gangster life, albeit at the cost of three bullet holes in his body.

The six of them talk animatedly until 2:00 a.m. Having grown up without a father for much of his life, Jack always enjoys observing the interaction between a husband and wife. Tonight is no exception.

The next morning, they eat breakfast together in the backyard gazebo adjacent to a kidney-shaped pool replete with a small waterfall. Jack cannot help but notice the four homicidal Jacaranda trees growing in the far corner of the yard, well away from the pool. Many of their flowers, resembling a bright blue carpet, are thick on the ground beneath the trees.

After breakfast, everyone goes their separate ways for the day. Peter flies to Las Vegas from the Orange County Airport (Maria refers to as the John Wayne Airport) to consult with a contractor at a building site; Maria drives to Carlsbad to meet several friends who are brainstorming with her about launching a new online wedding app; Sam leaves to attend an all-day soccer camp for goalkeepers; Bridget heads to a nearby amusement park with some friends; and the two Academy students go to church and then drive toward their anticipated rendezvous with someone far more dangerous than the Jacarandas.

Armando takes Jack up the 57 freeway to a friend's house in Fullerton, where he exchanges vehicles with Julio for the day. Armando explains to Jack that he would rather not cruise around in gang territory in the Mercedes. Julio's 2003 Nissan Maxima is a much lower-profile vehicle than the late model S-Class sedan.

Armando's friend does not appear disappointed in the least about the swap. Jack looks at Julio's beaming face and is convinced that the young man has plans to drive the Mercedes all day, stopping only to pick up his girlfriend and refuel as needed.

Jack and Armando grab four by four burgers and two orders of fries Animal Style at the IN-N-Out in Placentia, then drive to a nearby city park. As they eat their lunch next to a small pond, Jack watches a handful of people navigate their whining, remote-control speedboats across the water at break-neck speeds, all the while hoping to avoid a collision with other boats. He also notices that the marine layer has rolled all the way inland to where they are sitting. The late morning sky is a confluence of the light gray clouds of the marine layer and the copper dome that is the smog.

"Is it cloudy like this most days?" Jack asks as he bites into his huge burger, thick with four patties. "This isn't exactly the sunny California I imagined."

"I hear you, Juan," Armando replies as he reaches for some fries. "We call this the 'May Grey' or the 'June Gloom' because it messes with the sunlight. It's not as common in December, and it often doesn't come inland this far in the winter, but we never know out here. It'll burn off soon, though."

When they finish consuming their IN-N-Out lunch, Armando drives them to the nearby city of Brea to kill some time before they head to La Puente and then to Valinda.

They stop at the Carbon Canyon Regional Park to hike the 2.5-mile trail that leads through a forest of several hundred redwood trees. Jack finds their size disappointing since they are about a third the size of the redwoods he has seen along the coast of northern California. Nonetheless, he is still surprised to see them thriving in the desert-like conditions of the LA basin.

After they leave the forest and follow a trail lined with walnut trees, Armando says, "Twelve years ago, a man was mountain biking through the Santa Ana hills not far from here when a mountain lion attacked and killed him. Shortly after that, it attacked two other bikers. It almost ripped one lady's face off."

Jack glances at his tour guide and says, "You couldn't have waited to tell me that until we were back at the car?"

"Sorry, ese," Armando replies with a darker laugh than usual. "The good news is that it's a rare tragedy. The bad news is that we never know when unforeseen events will cut us down like grass before the reaper's scythe. I'm sure that man didn't climb on his bike that morning thinking he would never come home again. Fortunately, nothing surprises God."

As the two men hike over a dry creek bed, Jack says, "We have plenty of mountain lions out in Colorado—we usually refer to them as cougars—but they're rarely seen. I did hear about an attack last year where the targeted victim was a five-year-old boy. Fortunately, his mother scared off the big cat, and her son survived."

"One of those brave moms," Armando replies, shaking his head slowly. "I could see my mom doing something like that, small as she is."

Jack nods. "Yeah, your mother seems like that kind of woman."

There is a long pause and then Jack comments, "Speaking of mountain lions and cougars, Satan is referred to as a lion seeking someone to devour."

"How weird is that," Armando says, giving his friend a shove. "I was just thinking the same thing."

The men walk further down the trail that meanders between the walnut trees. They meet only three other people as they hike forward. Eventually, Jack says, "Maybe we're both thinking the same thing because we're going into Satan's territory tonight."

"Yeah, like in about four hours," Armando says in a subdued voice, licking his lips.

"You know what else is weird?" Jack says.

"What's that?" Armando asks.

"Remember Violet's dream? She saw us walking through a forest of angry trees that were trying to harm us."

"And we just got done hiking through the mini-Redwood Forest," Armando responds as he glances at his friend.

"For what it's worth," Jack observes, "Violet's dream about Aly also had a lion in it."

"So here we are today talking about mountain lions and walking through a forest," Armando says. "Coincidence or a message from God?"

"I'm not the kind of guy who sees every bald eagle or dragonfly as a supernatural sign," Jack muses aloud, "but I am convinced that God is telling us to be ready for an encounter with evil tonight."

When they come to the end of the trail, Armando says, "Yeah, I think the lion in Violet's dreams is Satan, and the trees are those who serve him, for sure, Sniper and his homies."

When they reach Julio's car, Jack looks over the roof at his roommate and comments, "I think we have a lot of praying to do."

"Do you know what I'm thinking?" Armando asks as the two men climb into the car.

Jack laughs and shakes his head. "Sorry, I've known you for four months now, but I still can't read your mind, bro."

The man with the close-cropped black hair and matching goatee smiles and says, "Believe it or not, Juan, I'm thinking about what Samwise Gamgee says to Frodo after they survive the attack by the evil Nazgul in the city of Osgiliath in the territory of Gondor."

"Wow, you clearly know your *Lord of the Rings* trivia—at least the *Two Towers* section," Jack observes.

"Sí, Juan, I've read the book twice and watched the movies a dozen times," Armando replies. "I was a boy when *The Fellowship of the Ring* came out in theaters. I was more interested in watching it than a bullfight in Tijuana or an episode of Cops on TV. Even to this day, when I watch *LOTR*, I experience this overwhelming sensation that light and darkness are at war in the world. I get chills up my spine. I definitely feel like there's more going on in the universe than meets the eye."

"I hear you," Jack says.

"Anyway," Armando says, getting back to his original point, "after that attack by the Nazgul who was riding on a Fell-beast, Frodo doesn't feel like he can go on fighting anymore. He wants to give up. He's exhausted and scared. He feels like he's in way over his head."

"Kind of like us," Jack interjects.

Armando pauses to nod his head and then continues. "Sam, who's along on the journey to help Frodo, makes some comment about how they shouldn't even be there. Two peace-loving hobbits like them should be back in the Shire where they belong instead of in the middle of a fierce battle against darkness. He wonders how the world can go back to being good when so much evil is happening. But then Sam adds something that has forever been burned onto the frontal lobes of my mind, as my ninth-grade history teacher used to say."

"Remind me what Sam said," Jack says.

"Sam tells Frodo that even darkness is a fleeting thing," Armando replies, "and that a new day will come when the sun will shine bright—even in southern California with the marine layer," he adds with a laugh. "Samwise tells his weary friend that what they're going through is like one of the great stories of battles against shadow where the heroes could have turned back instead of facing the encounter with darkness. But they keep fighting because they're holding onto something."

Jack smiles knowingly at his roommate from the passenger seat of the Maxima and asks, "What are we holding onto, Samwise?"

Armando glances at his friend with his piercing brown eyes and is silent for a moment. Then he answers, "That there's some good in this world, Mr. Frodo—and it's worth fighting for."

The two friends high-five each other and let out a simultaneous whoop that sounds like they're charging out of Helm's Deep to counterattack the sea of evil Uruk-hai.

After Armando fires up the Maxima and pulls out of the Carbon Canyon parking lot, both men are quiet for a long time.

Eventually, as he gazes out the window at the brown, treeless hills around them, Jack comments, "Both Windsor and McNeely talk a lot about the battle in this world—the unseen battle. I think that's what Tolkien was getting at when he wrote *the Lord of the Rings*. It's all one big metaphor for the world we are living in right now."

Armando nods affirmatively as he merges onto the 57 Freeway. "Yeah, there certainly is a theme of the conflict between good and evil in Tolkien's book."

"Do you know what I'm thinking?" Jack asks, turning the tables on his friend.

"Are you serious or just playing with me?" Armando asks wryly.

"Serious, scout's honor," Jack says, raising his hand and giving his friend the three-finger salute.

"Okay, then," Armando replies. "No, I don't. Do you think I can read your mind?"

"What goes around, comes around," Jack replies with a laugh. "Except I don't believe in karma. I just believe that payback from a roommate is deserved on occasion." He pauses and then says, "Sticking with *the Lord of the Rings* theme, I'm thinking about the Prancing Pony."

"The Inn of the Prancing Pony in Bree?" Armando inquires without hesitation.

"Wow, I'm impressed!" Jack exclaims. "You've proven again that you know your LOTR trivia."

"Almost as well as the Bible, but not quite," his friend replies with a smile. "But what were you going to say about the Inn of the Prancing Pony?"

Jack continues to gaze out the passenger window. "I'm thinking of the old gatekeeper at the village," he muses thoughtfully, "how he had no idea what terrible darkness was descending on him and his little village in the terrible persons of the ring wraiths. One minute he gets up from his cozy fire to peer through his peephole for the ten thousandth time, and the next, he's crushed under the gate by the evil riders and their devilish horses."

There is a long pause that Armando does not interrupt because he senses that his friend from Colorado is building toward something.

Jack eventually turns to look at the man in the driver's seat and says, "And then I think about the people in the inn who are eating and drinking and laughing seemingly without a care in the world. Just like the gatekeeper, they have no clue about the darkness that's invading their village that night. They're totally oblivious."

"Good point, ese," the driver comments as he glances in his rearview mirror.

Jack continues to philosophize aloud. "I think the men and women in this world we're living in are like the gatekeeper and the people inside the Inn of the Prancing Pony—they're totally oblivious to the evil in the world. They're unaware of the spiritual war raging all around us, far more dangerous than politics or cancer or acts of terrorism—as terrible as those things can be."

"But we have been given eyes to see that evil and that war," Armando says in reply.

"Exactly," Jack agrees. "So, as we head to La Puente tonight—sorry, Valinda—we're engaging in a battle far more significant than simple gang warfare, as ugly as that is. We're going up against spiritual powers of darkness."

"Like Samwise and Frodo," Armando says, "we're fighting because we see that there's some good in this world."

"Even better than that," Jack says as a shiver travels down his spine, "we're fighting because we see that there's *Someone* good in this universe and that *Someone* gave his life for us, so how can we not be willing to do the same for him?"

The two young men drive up the 57 toward Diamond Bar and then slow down when they reach the interchange to go west on the 60. It does not help their progress that minor construction work is underway in the area. Traffic is heavy on the Pomona Freeway, but they keep moving, albeit slowly, since they are driving against the flow of rush hour traffic.

As Armando focuses on the road, Jack observes the multitude of personalized license plates, how black and oily the middle of the freeway lanes are, and how strange it is in LA that some of the freeways are built above the houses enabling people in their cars to look down on rooftops and back yards while other freeways are level with the surrounding neighborhoods.

Twenty minutes later, Armando exits the five-lane freeway and turns onto a surface street. As they drive north, he asks Jack, "Do you see the San Gabriel mountains over there?"

Jack leans forward in the passenger seat and scans the horizon in front of them. All he can see are palm trees and hazy skies. "Can't say that I do. Is this a trick question?"

Armando laughs and says, "No, Juan, not a trick question. If it were raining today, the sky would be clear, and you'd see a whole mountain range emerge in front of your eyes, stretching from east to west. But since it isn't raining, the smog is so thick today that you'd never guess there are any mountains there at all. It's not usually quite this bad in December."

"Crazy!" Jack exclaims. "I would've never guessed there's anything out there except the desert."

"If you stay long enough in LA, you'd get used to the frequent smog alerts that warn everybody to stay inside their homes except for people wearing gas masks," Armando exaggerates. "Someone once told me that breathing the air in the LA basin is like smoking two packs of cigarettes every day."

Jack turns to his roommate and exclaims, "No way! So why does anybody still live out here?"

Armando shrugs his shoulders. "The weather? The ocean? The mountains? To be near Hollyweird or Mexico? Because they don't believe anything exists in the U.S. between LA and New York City, and they don't like the thought of the winters on the east coast or the humidity in Florida?"

Jack laughs and runs his fingers through his shorter hair. "Yeah, I've heard some people comment that there's LA and the Big Apple and that the rest of the United States is 'flyover' country."

"It's true," Armando says. "The east coast and the left coast are all there is."

"I think I'll stay in Colorado," Jack remarks, "even though bougainvillea flowers, palm trees, and sixty-five degrees in December are tempting. I think I'd rather avoid the two packs of cigarettes every day."

The next few hours are a blast from the past for Armando as he gives his friend a tour of La Puente and its environs. He drives Jack past Nelson Elementary, Sparks Junior High, and La Puente High, all schools Armando attended for periods of time while he was living with his father. Jack notices that all the schools have outdoor, porticoed walkways, so foreign to him after growing up with all his school hallways inside the building to protect the students against the ravages of the winter months.

After the school tours, Armando takes Jack to his father's old house, where he spent many weekends, several whole summers, and even parts of some school years when he was younger.

The L-shaped stucco house is painted a drab tan color, not much different in hue than the smog-filled sky. Its latticed windows and decorative white fascia remind Jack of a gingerbread house. The grass around the rambler is patchy, intermixed with areas that are barren—just exposed dirt. An island of a half dozen mini-palm trees grows up helter-skelter next to the front door of the house. Jack thinks they look like giant carrots jutting halfway out of the ground with huge green sprouts on top. There is no garage, only an ancient carport that can accommodate one vehicle.

Two large palm trees growing close to the street climb into the hazy oblivion that is the sky. Both trees boast huge green fronds high up on top, and a brown skirt of dead fronds collapsed around their narrow waists. The frond skirts remind Jack of Hulu dancers—so different from the neatly trimmed trees in Corona del Mar.

Armando climbs out from behind the wheel and rests his arms across the roof of the car. He stares at the house for a long time. He is far away in another world.

While his roommate is lost in distant memories, most of them undoubtedly dark, Jack gazes out the side window of the car at the house and the sky and the surrounding neighborhood that, like a dead body, appear to be in a state of decomposition.

He feels strangely depressed, heavy. His wandering eyes observe the iron bars on the windows of the houses and the flamboyant gang graffiti painted on the cinder block wall across the street.

He observes the sky that feels simultaneously large and small. Large, because only a few insubstantial palm trees interrupt the expanse of the sky, unlike the trees he is accustomed to seeing in Colorado that crowd the immediate horizon with lush growth. Small because the smoggy sky feels like the lid of a burial vault encasing the city. Jack feels mild claustrophobia as he surveys Armando's old stomping grounds.

An intangible gloom also crushes down on the neighborhood like a concrete blanket. Jack senses that the world around him is not just a barrio, personal turf that a gang has staked out to defend with blood and honor. It feels more like a kingdom that darkness rules.

Someone more sinister than a gang has claimed this territory for his own.

CHAPTER 7

Rachel's Surprise

Rachel is trudging like a captured slave toward the kitchen when the dark, powerful summoning of her addiction collides with an immovable object. Words from her devotional reading that morning rise like a towering wall against the typically irresistible temptation that commands her to fill herself with created things instead of the Creator.

She hears the words from Isaiah 55, and the turbulent waters of her mind begin to calm a bit: "Come, everyone who thirsts, come to the waters; and he who has no money, come, buy and eat! Come, buy wine and milk without money and without price. Why do you spend your money for that which is not bread and your labor for that which does not satisfy? Listen diligently to me, and eat what is good, and delight yourselves in rich food."

Immediately, Rachel's runaway train of addiction is derailed from its incorrigible steel track. She halts a step away from the pantry where the siren call of counterfeit comfort has invited her—no, demanded her—to partake of its fleeting pleasure that, at its core, is idolatry. Instead, the ears of her heart hear more words from Isaiah 55: "For you shall go out in joy and be led forth in peace; the mountains and the hills before you shall break forth into singing, and all the trees of the field shall clap their hands.

The joyful promises flow gently into Rachel's shame-filled heart. She lingers only a moment, then turns and strides out of the kitchen. When she hears the word "run," cry out in her mind, she grabs her purse and coat and literally jogs out of the house to her old car sitting in the driveway—Celeste's car is parked in the third stall of the garage. She brushes off the fluffy snow that had accumulated on the vehicle during the night with her bare hands and jumps behind the wheel. Without hesitation, she backs up onto the turn-around apron, then accelerates up the long driveway and out into the street.

As she drives, the choppy waters of her mind begin to calm even more. Soon, she remembers another favorite Isaiah passage in God's love letter: "Can a woman forget her nursing child, that she should have no compassion on the son of her womb? Even these may forget, yet I will not forget you. Behold, I have engraved you on the palms of my hands (Isaiah 49:15)."

Rachel breathes more deeply as the visceral ache in her stomach, and the tightness in her chest melts away. Her grip on the steering wheel relaxes, and she prays aloud as she begins to weep softly, "Abba, Daddy, you are my loving Father. You never forget me. Where would I be without your love? Where would I be?"

Then, remembering the promises in Romans 8 that Embee encouraged her to store away for just such times of darkness, she says aloud, "You work all things together for good in my life, Daddy, no matter how painful they might be. Who can be against me if you are for me, Abba? And nothing, not even my own self-hatred, is able to separate me from your love, Father."

Rachel continues to recite other promises from the Field Manual, as Dr. Windsor refers to it until she arrives at the small seashore village. She parks her car and then walks around the corner to her favorite coffee shop.

She enters, orders her coffee, and retreats to a small couch next to the gas fireplace that exhales cozy warmth on this cold day. As she settles into the soft couch, she sighs and says, "Thank you, Jesus, for providing a way to escape the addiction that has driven me into such deep despair for so many years. I praise you, and I love you."

Rachel pins her hair behind her ears, then takes a sip of coffee as she pulls her phone out of her back pocket to text her friends. She considers sending a group text but decides against it. She wants to personalize her message to each person. Currently, texting is her only medium since she decided to take an extended leave of absence from binging on social media. Last summer, she felt convicted by the Holy Spirit to unplug from the world of likes and friends and other false measures of self-worth that fed her natural penchant for the praise of people instead of the love of God.

Taking her time, she composes and sends lengthy texts to Aly, Emily, and Stewart. She also texts Embee and Amanda, one of her roommates. She is beginning to type a message to Jack when she receives a text. She does not recognize the number, so she almost ignores it. Fortunately, her eyes read the first line, and she is immediately prompted to open the text.

"I need someone to talk to," the message reads. "Things aren't going so well. Oh yeah, I'm Drew, the guy you and Jack talked to on campus at the U a while back. Did Jack tell you I gave my life to Jesus last week? Did he let you know I might be contacting you?"

Jack—a typical guy, Rachel thinks to herself as she smiles and shakes her head. *No, Jack didn't tell me that you gave your life to Jesus, and no, he didn't tell me that you might be contacting me.*

Rachel pauses to consider her response to the student as she sips her mint chocolate java. Soon, she sends him her message: "Drew, I'm so excited to hear about your faith in Jesus Christ! You made the most amazing decision of your lifetime that will change absolutely everything! Feel free to text me as needed."

After her message has been delivered, Rachel shakes her head in disgust and whispers to herself, "'Text me as *needed*.' I sound like a pharmacist prescribing the frequency of medication dosages. You've got to do better than that, Rach."

Rachel sighs and turns her attention back to composing her text to Jack. Just after she sends it, her phone pings with another message from Drew.

That was fast, she says to herself. *Maybe I should always communicate like a pharmacist—people seem to take me more seriously.* The text message from Drew simply says, "Can I call you?"

Rachel sets her phone on the table in front of her and stares into the dancing flame of the gas fireplace.

She tries not to feel it, but she is excited. She is excited because she remembers being attracted to the young man when she met him in the student commons at the university. She did not allow herself to like him too much, however, since he was not a believer. Besides, as a university student, he was probably four years younger than her. But there is no denying that she was attracted to something about him. Was it his unmistakable sensitivity? His thoughtful questions regarding faith? His obvious potential as a leader? Oh, yeah, he also was easy to look at, she admits to herself with an embarrassed smile.

Eventually, Rachel picks up her phone and texts Drew that she is at a coffee shop and probably has a two-hour window to talk if he is available. Thirty seconds later, her phone begins playing the opening notes of the organ piece, Toccata and Fugue in D minor. She lets the music play for six measures before she answers.

"Hey, this is Rachel," she says, trying to sound calm even though her heart is beating so hard she fears her caller will somehow hear it through the phone.

Over the beating of her heart, she hears a deep voice say, "Rachel, this is Drew—Drew Johnson."

Instantly, Rachel recalls another reason she noticed the university student—his rich bass voice. It triggers the memory of a song Johnny Cash recorded called "Hurt." Rachel stumbled across the cover song when she was fifteen years old. At the time, it resonated perfectly with what was going on in her life: cutting herself to distract from her overwhelming emotional pain; feeling rejected by the people who were supposed to love her; and believing that she was worthless and would, sooner or later, be a disappointment to everyone.

"Rachel, are you there?" the deep voice inquires gently.

"Yeah, sorry," she stammers, "I'm still here. Just a bit distracted." She feels the familiar warmth rise into her cheeks, no doubt turning them as red as her hair.

"Is this a good time for you?" the voice asks.

"Yes!" she exclaims with more energy than she intends. "Yes," she says a second time in a more controlled, matter-of-fact voice, "this is an acceptable time. This is actually a very good time," she says, correcting herself as she shakes her head and rolls her eyes at herself.

There is a short pause. Rachel wonders if her uneasiness has been off-putting to the young man, but he does not seem to notice it. "I'm really struggling," he admits. "Like I told you in my text, I need someone to talk to. I spoke with Jack several times in the last week and a half, but I haven't bothered him since he left for Los Angeles to visit his friend." Drew pauses and then adds, "I don't want to come across as too needy."

Rachel knows exactly what the young man is referring to, and so she responds quickly, almost reflexively. "I think we all fear being too needy, if we're honest."

"Really?" Drew says, sounding relieved. "I thought I was the only one."

"Not a chance," Rachel replies with a conviction based on extensive experience with the fear of being too transparent. "The lie of the universe is that I am the only one who is too needy. The truth of the universe is that every single one of us is afraid of being too needy or too vulnerable, or too unacceptable. So, we hide."

"That's helpful to hear," the deep voice resonates, "especially since I'm not used to needing anything from anybody."

"Well," Rachel comments wryly, "you must remember that you've got three strikes against you: You're male, you're a football player, and with a last name like Johnson, you're probably Scandinavian. You don't stand a chance to need anyone—ever."

Drew laughs quietly on the other end of the phone. "So, you're saying there's no hope for me," he says facetiously.

"None," Rachel says with feigned seriousness. "Not one in a billion unless, of course, you happen to know Jesus."

"Ah, so there is a ray of hope, at least since a week ago Tuesday," the man replies.

"Absolutely," Rachel replies. "There's all the hope in the universe for you now, Drew. Jesus told us that apart from Him, we can do nothing, but with Him, all things are possible." She pauses and adds, "So, for you, three strikes don't add up to an out. When you know Jesus, there are no such things as strikes, only home runs."

Drew laughs again and says, "A woman who talks in sports metaphors—how impressive is that?"

Rachel feels the need to clarify her comments. "Before you think too highly of me, I confess that I've never played a sport unless you call gymnastics at age five a sport. I learned about sports because that's one of my father's interests. He didn't know how to enter into my world, so I learned how to enter into his world."

"No matter how you got there, it's still impressive to me," Drew says again. "And the reverse is true for me—I've always enjoyed sports, but not my father, so, I also had to find a way to enter my father's world of interests."

"How did that work for you?" Rachel asks.

"Not so good," Drew admits. "And in some ways, that relates to why I need to talk to someone who knows things."

"Oh yeah, how so?" Rachel asks.

"Well, as you know," he begins, "I gave my life to Jesus like ten days ago now, and then immediately after that came home for the holiday break."

"Okay."

"I told my parents what happened back at the university, not just about Jesus, but also about...my roommate. I don't know if Jack told you what happened to Pete," the young man says, his voice trailing off at the end.

"No," Rachel says as an uninvited cold wave crashes over her heart. "Do you mean the Pete who was with you the day we talked to you in the Commons?"

"Yes, that, Pete," Drew replies quietly, or at least as quietly as his deep voice can speak.

"What—what happened to Pete?" Rachel asks, bracing herself for what she is about to hear. She can tell by Drew's serious tone that it is not going to be good news. Ever since she was a little girl, she wished that the world could stop at these moments before the painful reality is spoken and it becomes known. Before it is spoken, it remains not real; it has not yet happened. But once it is spoken, the cruel reality is chiseled forever into the stone of truth. Then it can never be taken back. At that point, she is left with the equally unsavory choice of accepting the harsh truth or spending the rest of her life trying to deny it or run from it.

Drew shares with Rachel the news of Pete's tragic death and the circumstances surrounding it. He relates, pausing often, how devastated his roommate's parents were and how "insanely painful" the funeral was. He confides with Rachel how Pete's death opened the door to his faith in God. He speaks excitedly about his meeting with Jack at the university and his long overdue surrender to the love of Jesus. Finally, he tells Rachel about returning to his parents' house in upstate New York, where he encountered major resistance to his new faith from his atheistic mother and his agnostic father.

Rachel leans forward on the couch and sets her coffee cup down on the table. She swallows hard and fights back the tears that well up in her eyes. "Oh, Drew," she says, shaking her head slowly as if the young man is sitting across from her, "life can be so unbearably unfair and cruel. I'm so sorry for everything that's happened to you!"

"Yeah, it's been a rough stretch," Drew admits. "I never saw any of this coming two weeks ago, and then, boom—everything changes." He pauses briefly and says, "Oh, and by the way, my parents are getting divorced."

"How awful!" Rachel empathizes. She wipes away a tear with her napkin and asks, "Is there anything I can do to help?"

She hears Drew sigh into his phone. "I'm not sure where to go from here," he confesses. "Jack told me to read the Bible and hang out with other believers, but my family doesn't have a single Bible in the whole house, and I don't really know where to go to meet other believers."

He hesitates just a moment and then qualifies, "I know that stuff is on me. I'm not helpless. I need to go out and buy a Bible and find some believers. It's just that I think—I think I'm kind of lost right now. I'm certainly off to a great start as a Christian, right?"

Rachel feels a strong desire to defend this young man. She slaps the table in front of her—unusually oblivious to the glances of the people around her—and announces, "It's a huge change in the infrastructure of your life to believe in Jesus, Drew, but it's not like everything suddenly and magically changes.

Yes, God gave you a new heart, and you've become a new creation, and now you have ears to hear and understand spiritual things," she says, "but it's not like 'welcome to easy street.' You've chosen the amazing step to follow the Maker of the universe, but now comes the challenging journey of growth. And growth is uphill and against the current. It's always the road less traveled. Dr. Windsor says that this journey is opposed fiercely by the enemy."

"Wow," she hears Drew say, "'the journey' you're describing sounds very similar to what Jack mentioned. I obviously need to make an intentional effort to set out on this journey you're referring to." There is a short pause, and he asks, "But where do I start?"

"Well," Rachel says, closing her eyes and massaging her forehead, "as Jack said, you need other believers in your life to help you grow—to teach you, pray with you, answer your questions, let you know that you are not alone on the journey, and so on. What I was told as a young believer is that one log in the fireplace doesn't burn very well. You need at least two logs and ideally three or more to have a good fire. It's the same for a believer: you don't grow well alone."

Drew laughs quietly into the phone and says, "I really like that metaphor. And yeah, I feel like I'm just smoldering right now; lots of smoke but no fire. I'm certainly alone in the fireplace—a log flying solo."

Rachel nods her head again. "This is a critical time in your journey—just after the seed has been sown and it begins to grow. Jesus told a parable about the farmer who sowed seeds and how only some soils received the seeds and only some seeds went on to produce an actual crop."

There is a silence after Rachel is done talking. "Drew?" she finally inquires. "Drew, are you there?"

"Yeah, I'm here," the bass voice intones. "I was just distracted by a crazy idea."

"Oh, what's that?" Rachel says, taking the bait.

"How insane would it be for me to drive down to where you're at and spend a day with you?" he says. "You could be the second log in the fireplace with me for a few hours."

Rachel does not know what to say. Drew must sense her hesitation because he hurries on to say," I know it's crazy because you don't even know me, but we could just hang out at that coffee shop you're at or some other public place. I can promise you I have no ulterior motives. Not that you're an unattractive woman or anything," he qualifies, "but I just see you and Jack as lifelines for me right now, like a brother and a sister."

Rachel finds safe ground and asks, "Where do you live anyway?

Probably not Fargo."

"No, not Fargo," he replies with a chuckle. "I live in Lake Luzerne, upstate, not far from Lake George, if you know where that is. If you're in Connecticut, you're probably only four or five hours away from me."

"I'm in Mystic," Rachel says, "not far from New London—out by the coast."

"So, what do you think?" Drew asks. "I could drive down and be there by 9:00 a.m. any morning, spend the day with you, then head home after supper. Eight to ten hours with you should get me pointed in the right direction. Then you never have to see me again."

Rachel's head hesitates, but her heart answers for her. "I think that's a good idea."

"What's a good idea?" he asks. "To come down or to never see me again?"

"Someone's being a wise guy," Rachel replies as she smiles into the phone. "I meant it would be a good idea to meet you and help draw up a map for your journey."

"Oh, okay," the young man says with a laugh.

"When do you think you could make it down here?" Rachel asks.

"I could come tomorrow, if that works for you," he replies. "Or if that's too close to Christmas, I can do any day besides Christmas Day. Shoot, I could even do Christmas Day since my parents don't celebrate it anyway."

"Tomorrow is fine," Rachel says. "I'm not working over winter break, so that means my schedule is very flexible. I'll text you the address of the coffee shop. We might as well meet here. Does ten o'clock tomorrow morning work for you?"

"Awesome!" Drew exclaims, and Rachel thinks she can hear the young smiling into the phone. "I really appreciate you doing this, Rachel. As a way of showing some gratitude, I'll pay for all the coffee and food we consume tomorrow!"

The auburn-haired woman laughs in such a melodious way that beautiful chimes could not have produced a more pleasant resonance in the young man's ears.

"Sounds like a plan to me, Drew," she says.

"Rachel," the deep voice says, "before you hang up, I want you to know I never forgot one thing you told us back at the Commons. Do you remember what you said about walking to Australia? I thought of it before I called Jack ten days ago. Those words reminded me that there was no way I could make myself good enough for Jesus and that I didn't have to. I could come to Him just as I am. Thanks for those words."

"You're welcome, Drew," Rachel replies. "How good that you were listening so well." There is a pause before she says awkwardly, "See you tomorrow, then."

She touches the red button with her thumb and lays her phone on her lap. Then she laughs quietly and says inside her head, *Well, Jesus, I never saw that coming!*

A second later, her smile fades. She sighs as her mood plummets in consonance with her thoughts. *Please, Lord, don't let me get my expectations twisted in the wrong direction. I don't think I can weather another disappointment this week.*

Ten minutes later, Drew enters the greenhouse that is connected to the family pole-barn behind the Johnson house just outside Lake Luzerne. He is met by a warm wave of humid air scented with the fragrance of growing things. Both his mother and father are working in the passive solar-heated structure equipped with roof panels positioned at a 60-degree angle to most efficiently capture the energy of the mid-winter sunlight.

As is their custom, his parents are working with their backs to each other.

Drew stands in the doorway of the giant incubator and observes the cabbage, radishes, lettuce, turnips, beets, kale, and tomatoes. The produce is not meant only for his family's consumption but also for two dozen other families in the area that purchase the winter vegetables and fruits from the Johnsons.

Drew swallows hard, dreading the imminent encounter.

Just then, his mother glances up and spots her son standing at the far end of the greenhouse. "Andrew," she says in her familiar no-nonsense tone as she looks back down at the task before her, "did you feed the livestock?"

Drew moves forward slowly as if walking into a stiff headwind toward where his mother is planting a second winter crop of lettuce and his father is harvesting kale. "I did," he replies, "and I checked on the dogs, too," referring to the post-surgical residents in his mother's small-animal veterinarian clinic adjacent to the barn and greenhouse.

Having served a four-year stint in the army before college, Drew is accustomed to interacting with authority figures of all ranks. Nonetheless, the mystical foreboding that has always been generated by the tandem of his pragmatic mother and his reticent father has always proved intimidating to Drew, especially as an only child. He has never had siblings to confer with concerning how to best approach the parental team that is soon to be dissolved anyway.

Before he can open his mouth to announce that he is going to Connecticut tomorrow, his mother glances at him briefly with her penetrating eagle eyes and asks, "So, are you still a Christian, or did you sleep it off?"

Drew hesitates, taking a quick mental inventory to decide if it is productive to engage his mother. When he decides that it is not a wise idea, he ignores the bait and announces, "I'm going to be gone tomorrow—just for the day."

"Oh," his mother replies in her inimitable manner of delivering disappointment with one syllable.

One word, one look, and I feel ashamed, Drew thinks to himself. *The power I give them is way out of proportion. Not even a four-star general wields that kind of power over me.*

"Yeah," he says, sounding relaxed and casual on the outside, "I'm going to meet a friend."

"What gender?" his mother inquires without looking up.

"A girl," Drew responds. "Someone I met at school." He braces for the interrogation.

"Oh?" his mother says again, this time looking up. One eyebrow is raised. She looks like a principal eyeing a student accused of classroom misconduct. "Local?"

"No, she's down in Connecticut," Drew says.

This time even his father turns to glance at him briefly. Then both parents return to their plants.

"I'll take Franklin because I'll get the best gas mileage with him," Drew informs them, referencing the family's old Volvo wagon that is a fuel hog but still gets better mileage than the Ford Econoline van.

There is a profound silence in the greenhouse that, as always, is unsettling for Drew. Yes, he knows that his parents see and hear him, that he is special to them in some mysterious way. But he also knows that they have no clue how to communicate affection to him. He wishes they could offer more, but years of experience have taught him to be thankful for whatever they can give.

"I'm going to go pack and then hit the rack," he says, pivoting toward the door, "unless you need me to help with something else."

"I expect you'll be departing early," his mother observes coolly as she looks up at her broad-shouldered son again and raises her chin slightly. "Check on the clinic animals before you leave."

"Will do," Drew says over his shoulder as he walks toward the door.

Just when his hand reaches to unlatch the insulated door and escape to safety, his mother intones, "Andrew."

"What, Mom?" he says as he stops and looks up at the ceiling.

"Give it up, son," she says flatly. "Myths are for fools. I don't want you to waste your life on supernatural legends and fairy dust."

Drew hesitates for a moment, debating. In the end, he says nothing. He steps out of the tropical climate of the greenhouse and into the cold breezeway that leads to the pole barn.

As the door closes behind him, he gazes through the triple-panel glass sliding door on his right that offers a view into his father's art studio. The large table in the center of the room and the countertops lining all four walls are populated with ceramic creations and framed photographs. A dozen easels are scattered around the room, cradling paintings in various stages of completion.

On one of the tripods, he sees a painting of a male turkey, its plume of feathers fully spread as it stands majestically erect in a golden cornfield. Resting on another easel is a 3' x 4' canvas depicting a scene from Lake George. Glistening water and towering fir trees appear in the distance. In the foreground, two white Adirondack chairs sit peacefully on the grass beside the lake, mutely waiting for someone to discover them.

It is not insignificant that the chairs are empty. To Drew's knowledge, his father has never painted a picture with a person in it. Sadly, the dearth of humans in his father's art is representative of both his and his wife's affections. The Johnsons love animals, plants, trees, birds, and water. But they have no awareness that they lack the desire or the tools—or both—to love or even like humans. Despite the splendor of his father's artwork, the room is heavy with emptiness.

Drew turns his back on the lifeless studio and walks out into the cold.

CHAPTER 8

Mahmoud's Interrogation

Eight days after they return to the institute from their glorious Christmas celebration at Joshua Bloomstrom's home, Kameel Majdali and the Ahmed siblings board the Boeing 777-300 and complete the nonstop flight to Rome.

After the ten-hour flight, they have a five-hour layover in Rome. The downtime turns out to be a godsend since Aly, the most ostensibly innocent of the three travelers, is unexpectedly detained for several hours by a random security check. When she is finally released, Mahmoud-become-Moussa and even the more restrained Kameel tease Aly that she was selected by security because she simply looks guilty.

Eventually, the three travelers board the El Al airplane and jet from the Eternal City to Tel Aviv-Yafo, arriving there in three and a half hours. It is close to 5:00 p.m. when they deplane and set out to retrieve their luggage.

Impacted by her experience in Rome, Aly begins to whisper but then fears that such behavior may not be wise in the Ben Gurion airport, so she says in a louder voice, "I was worried they wouldn't let me leave Rome. As I told you earlier, they became very suspicious when they learned that my father was born in Saudi Arabia. I'm afraid of what will happen if we're detained here, in Israel."

"Welcome to the world of hyper-security," Kameel remarks in a hushed voice. "At this moment, of course, you're walking through the most secure airport in the world. Israelis perceive themselves as an island surrounded by enemies who detest that they even entered Palestine back in 1948 and ever since have literally wanted to push them into the ocean. Living with such a heightened sense of external threat, you develop a bit of paranoia, some of it well founded."

Moussa directs a sidelong glance at the Egyptian professor next to him and grips the straps of his backpack more tightly. "Customs and immigration will be challenging here," he says, half as a statement, half as a question.

"Yes," Kameel agrees, "you'll be asked many questions by airport security. You'll be asked many questions repeatedly. Just be honest and relaxed, and all will be fine. Easily said, harder done, I know. But I think it's safe to say that our entry into Israel should be less unpleasant than it would be under normal circumstances.

"Several weeks ago, I asked my friend, David, to contact the department of immigration and inform them of our arrival and our purpose for entering the country. His position in the government affords him credibility and access far beyond that of the average citizen. He will pave the way for us," Kameel says confidently.

The professor crinkles his nose for the twentieth time since he deplaned, possibly to remove an itch without the use of his fingers that are engaged with two briefcases or simply out of chronic habit. The Ahmed siblings have known Kameel long enough to know it is for the latter reason.

"David is an Israeli?" Aly asks.

"Born and raised," Kameel says, nodding his head. "A true sabra, although that status is not esteemed as highly as it was thirty years ago. His grandfather was a member of the Israeli secret service who tracked down

WW II war criminals all the way to Argentina. His father is also connected to the government and serves as an adjunct professor at the Hebrew University."

"In what manner did two such diverse individuals come to meet—you and David, I mean?" Moussa asks. Even as he is asking the question, he eyes several Uzi-carrying soldiers walking past them in terminal number three.

"I'll tell you later," the young Egyptian replies. "We're approaching customs. Get in the queue on the right. The other one is for Israeli citizens. Aly, you should be fine here. I'm still not sure why they singled you out in Rome. If anyone has trouble, it will be me since this is my fifth trip to Israel. Repeat visits invite more scrutiny."

Turning to Mahmoud, Kameel says, "Your passport, last name, and country of your father's birth will be questioned. It's never a positive thing to have stamps in your passport from Iran and Saudi Arabia when you enter Israel. However, the information David passed on to immigration should make this process much smoother."

Moussa licks his lips and takes a deep breath. "I don't have a good feeling about this, professor. I always hated Zionists in the past. I fear that my face alone will give me away. I may be a new creation in Jesus, but I come with a lot of bad history that still oozes out of me on occasion."

Even while the young man with citizenship in three countries is still speaking, a middle-aged man built like a tank with a pocked face and a head as bald as an ostrich egg approaches them. He appears ominous. A wall cloud would look more inviting.

"Mahmoud Ahmed," the man announces in a grave, thickly accented voice that immediately awakens a ball of anxiety in Aly's stomach.

"I am he," Moussa replies in English without hesitation.

"Come with me," the man commands. His passionless eyes travel over Kameel's face, displaying what might be a spark of recognition.

Moussa glances quickly at Kameel and Aly, then nods once at the Israeli official. He follows the man across the modern, airy terminal building to a nondescript door that looks like the entrance to a maintenance closet. Aly's anxiety spikes even more when she sees a soldier dressed in an olive-green uniform standing beside the door, cradling what looks to her like a machine gun.

She turns alarmed eyes on Kameel and grabs the young man's arm. "What's going to happen to him?"

"Pray to God," the Egyptian man says with a shake of his head. "I believe he'll be fine, but this will be a serious test for him. That man who detained him is not your typical security officer. He's one of the highest-ranking members of Shin Beth."

Moussa enters an 8x8 room that feels much smaller than that. He is instructed with a grunt and a tilt of the ostrich egg to take a seat on a flimsy plastic chair in front of a desk. The small desk is bare except for a laptop computer and a black file folder.

The grave man sits down across from Moussa and rolls up the sleeves of his khaki shirt, exposing beefy, hairy forearms. His thick fingers open the laptop slowly, methodically, indicating to Moussa that he is a man of precision; he is a man who pays attention to every detail. The young believer in Jesus swallows hard and shifts in his robin-egg blue chair, which seems so incongruous with the dark fear that is mounting in his chest.

Moussa is uncertain if his fear is due to the presence of the intimidating man or of his past sins, which might soon be laid bare.

The interrogator extracts reading glasses from his shirt pocket and positions them precisely on his ears and large nose. While he taps some keys on the keyboard and leans toward the screen to examine its content, his brows furrow menacingly, and his fish lips twist into a scowl. Moussa thinks the man's incredibly pocked face resembles the cratered surface of the moon.

Several minutes pass. Moussa crosses his legs and grabs his right foot to stop it from bouncing around wildly. He attempts to take deep breaths and makes several futile attempts to relax his tight neck and shoulder muscles.

Somewhere in the back of his brain, an empathy unexpectedly awakens for all the people he has placed in a similar position in the not-so-distant past. The empathy is soon washed away by a red wave of ancient anger toward the infidel sitting in front of him.

Moussa closes his eyes and prays in his head, *Help me, Father, or I will soon go mad.*

After what seems like an eternity, the airport official peers over the top of his glasses at Moussa with a face as expressionless as a snake and announces, "I am Moshe Abramovich, a colonel in Shabak, otherwise known as the Israeli Security Agency."

The powerfully built man pauses to pull a cigarette out of his pants pocket. He does not light it but inserts it carefully into the left corner of his mouth between his thick lips.

"It is not my custom to bother myself with hands-on airport security," the ISA agent says, "but you, Mr. Ahmed—how shall I say it—you are worthy of an exception." As the man talks, the unlit cigarette bounces around in front of his face like a windsock in a typhoon.

The intimidating colonel looks down at his laptop again, and his thick forefinger appears to follow words on the screen. "I could arrest you on the spot," he announces in a thick accent rendered almost unintelligible by the presence of the wagging cigarette. "You have a reputation that precedes you from Thailand all the way to this airport. All hyperbole set aside, you are a terrorist and a murderer."

He pauses, and his face lifts from the screen. His gaze finds Moussa's eyes and melts them with revulsion. He says in a voice rendered more chilling by its subdued nature, "You are meshugana to show up in my country. Do you understand Yiddish, Mr. Ahmed? I'm telling you that you're raving crazy to even think about setting foot on my soil."

Moussa shifts his body in the robin-egg chair for the twentieth time and licks lips that have become as dry as bones in a midsummer wadi. His tongue is just as dry—a stick in his mouth. He begins to pray to Yahweh.

The Shabak officer stares through his subject for a long time until Moussa stops breathing. The young man becomes light-headed and fears that he will pass out.

Finally, Colonel Abramovich turns his attention back to his laptop. As he studies the screen, the index finger of his right-hand massages a large mole on his cheek that, like a lunar mountain, rises impressively above the meteor craters scattered over the rest of his face.

The man stares over his glasses at Moussa once again and comments matter-of-factly, "I merely type your name into my computer, and much condemning information appears," he says, loudly tapping the screen with a thick finger.

The brawny inquisitor pauses and fingers the floppy cigarette for a few moments before he transfers the slim cylinder to the opposite corner of his mouth. His gaze remains fixed on the object of his inquisition. The man's eyes now appear relaxed, even nonchalant, but Moussa knows they are closely observing the frequency of his breathing and registering every twitch of his facial muscles. He swallows hard and distracts himself by examining the exceptional lunar mountain on his interrogator's cheek.

"People like you don't show up on my doorstep every day," Colonel Abramovich observes as he spreads out his hands in a casual gesture. "They certainly do not come and knock on my front door and violate my mezuzah with the gaze of their filthy eyes as you have done today, Mr. Ahmed. Typically, they enter my country impersonally via a Scud missile or very personally by watercraft intent on setting foot on my soil and gunning down innocent civilians or blowing themselves up in the marketplace."

Moussa glances at the man's small, bullet eyes and senses competing emotions in his chest—hatred and love. Less than a month ago, he was on social media with his "colleagues," excoriating Israel and the United States, both Christians and Jews alike. No, worse than that, he was condemning them to death. So, yes, by all rights, he is insane to walk into this country. It is not dissimilar to threatening to assassinate the president of the United States and then walking into the White House.

At that moment, Moussa's brain agrees that he is *meshugana* to be in Israel. But in his heart, a still, small voice speaks to him that he is exactly where he is meant to be.

"Yes, I have done my research," the colonel announces as the mole is further massaged and the cigarette bounces wildly between the robust lips. "You are a terrorist, Mr. Ahmed, which makes you an assassin. You hate Israel and all western nations. You have traveled to Iran and Saudi Arabia within the last six months. Your shameless posts on the Internet betray your Jihadist loyalties," the security officer states as he ominously taps the laptop screen with his thick finger. "It is but a superfluous detail that your father was born in Saudi Arabia and that you lived there yourself for several years.

You already stand guilty before one even considers your country of origin."

The cigarette stops bobbing as the security officer stares silently at his subject. "So, Mr. Ahmed," he finally says, "what do you have to say for yourself?"

Moussa feels like the proverbial goldfish in a bowl. He has been laid bare as never before and in a place he cannot escape. Worst of all, he cannot disavow the evidence that has been presented against him. He could point out that he never actually built or placed the bombs in the motorbikes that claimed lives in Songkhla. He could argue that he never personally wielded the sword that decapitated the Hindus south of Yala. Both defenses would be true. But his new heart admits that he is complicit in these acts of violence in Thailand since he not only encouraged them but also assisted in their planning.

The young man who was born in America, raised Muslim, lived in Saudi Arabia and then in Thailand, and who recently converted to faith in Jesus, feels the need to place his hands on the desk, palms up, as a gesture of peace.

"I am guilty of all you say," Moussa confesses as his piercing brown eyes ensconced beneath thick, black brows focus on the colonel, who is only four feet away.

Moshe Abramovich removes the mangled cigarette from his mouth and turns it over and over in his stout fingers. He eyes it dispassionately like a man might examine a damaged toy to see if it is worth salvaging. His polished head, like a mirror, reflects the harsh light from the ceiling fixture above the desk.

Still examining the cigarette, the intimidating man begins talking to the room. "I was fifteen years old when the terrorists landed their rigid-hulled inflatable boat on the beach forty miles north of where we are now sitting. That was 1978, over forty years ago, now," he remarks, his voice trailing off into a maze of memories.

"Strange, isn't it?" he comments to the cigarette that is beginning to disintegrate in his hands. "Forty miles and forty years. Forty—a significant number in the Old Testament. Did it not rain forty days and forty nights when Noah was in the ark when God destroyed all the wicked men and women from the face of the earth?"

The colonel's large hand abruptly crushes the cigarette. The interrogator then rolls it between his palms, reducing it to a jumbled mess of tobacco and paper. He deposits the disintegrated cigarette on the desktop that serves as a flimsy buffer between him and the subject of his interrogation and rubs his thick hands together to rid them of any remaining particles. At this moment, the young believer in Jesus wishes the desk was a wall of steel.

The Bet Shin officer eventually lifts his small eyes to stare at Moussa. They have become stones—cold and hard.

"March 11, 1978, to be exact," he intones, picking up where he left off. His voice betrays no emotion, but his nostrils flare out like wind-filled sails. "On that day, the terrorists infiltrated my country with their Kalashnikov rifles and RPGs and powerful explosives. Coincidentally—or not so coincidentally—that was the same day I swore my allegiance to the Israeli Security Agency.

"I chose ISA over Mossad, where my father worked," the bulky man reflects aloud. "I shunned overseas intelligence because I wanted to get out of bed every morning knowing I was going to protect my backyard from cowardly terrorists. I swore to myself on that day that I would never countenance the presence of evil jihadists who presume they can arrogantly saunter into my homeland and slaughter whomever they wish."

The colonel pauses, and his finger touches the mole on his cheek as if to ensure that it is still attached to his face. "On that day, twenty-five men and women and thirteen children were massacred like so many sheep," he mutters through clenched teeth. He looks down at the remains of the demolished cigarette on his desk and then begins to absently push the remains around with his index finger that is apparently done attending to the mole.

"One child was only two years old," Moshe Abramovich announces. His voice trails off as he tilts his head sideways and stares at Moussa in a manner that seems borderline insane to the young man.

Mahmoud's anxiety level skyrockets, and his heart races in his chest. He begins to pray even more fervently. He is so distressed that he automatically begins reciting in his mind a sura from the Quran. Distraught, he quickly switches to the Psalm he had read earlier on the plane: *I waited patiently for the LORD; He inclined to me and heard my cry. He drew me up from the pit of destruction, out of the miry bog, and set my feet upon a rock, making my steps secure.*

"So, you see, Mr. Mahmoud Ahmed," the officer states too slowly, too calmly as he sweeps the remains of the mangled cigarette onto the floor with the back of his hand, "it's all quite simple. I despise you as much as you despise me."

The interrogator places his hands palm to palm in front of his mouth and gazes at the young man seated across from him. The flat eyes have returned.

Moussa shifts uneasily in his chair, wishing that it would swallow him up. He is afraid to say anything for fear that it will only incite the wrath of this zealous guardian of his country. However, when the formidable

Colonel Abramovich continues to stare at him, Moussa feels compelled to break the torturous silence. He throws all caution to the wind and professes, "I am everything you said I was, as I stated earlier, but I am no longer that man. I no longer hate everyone who isn't me." Moussa pauses and dares to glance in the direction of the bullet eyes. He is surprised that his voice is steady and strong.

After a long silence, he goes on, "If you allow it, Colonel Abramovich, I wish it to be a matter of record that I have recently been pursued and arrested by the most dangerous of anti-terrorist agents—Jesus Christ—fully against my old will. He apprehended me so that he might set me free from the prison of my own hatred and selfishness and conscript me into his service.

"As I sit here before you, I serve no man or religion or cause, only the God of the Old and the New Testaments. And yes, I sit here guilty and worthy of death." Moussa pauses and then says softly, "My only defense is the righteousness of Jesus the Christ."

The Beth Shin veteran continues to examine Moussa's face as only an experienced interrogator can. His eyes crawl like a scorpion over the young man's eyes, mouth, and forehead. Finally, he says, "So you now claim to be a Christian." He pronounces the last word in a tone that communicates deep doubt with a hint of distaste.

Moussa nods his head. "Except that I do not call myself by that name. It is offensive to many of my brothers and sisters. I hope to reach with the love of God. I prefer to call myself a follower of Jesus."

As an afterthought, he says, "And I no longer answer to the name Mahmoud. I now have a new name. In Arabic, it is Moussa. Of course, strangely, you have the same name—Moshe—in Hebrew. I feel called to lead my people out of Egypt, as it were, as Moses did in the great Exodus. Although, I certainly make no claim to be his peer. None whatsoever."

The interrogator snorts and smacks his lips. "It's tragic, really," he bemoans, shaking his head. "It's tragic that you no longer are Mahmoud because if you were, everything would be so easy. I would cast you into the deepest, darkest dungeon in Israel and throw away the key. But now," the colonel says with a sigh, "you have muddled things badly—Moussa. So badly."

The bald man with the cratered face stares at his subject a while longer, then sighs again, this time with resignation. Shaking his head, he pulls a phone out of his pocket. He punches in a speed dial number, waits a few seconds, then says, "Send them in."

Moussa feels a wave of fear crash through his brain. He looks at Moshe Abramovich's face and discerns immediately that the man has detected his worry. *Be my strength, Jesus the Christ, and bless me with the peace of your presence,* the young man prays as he attempts to calm his anxiety.

"Fear not, Moussa, I do not summon the executioner," the man across the desk from him mutters as the fluorescent light glares off the tight skin of his skull. "At least, not yet."

A moment later, the door swings open, and a small procession files into the room. Moussa turns and watches as four people squeeze into the confined space.

The first person through the door is an airport security officer dressed in an army uniform and holding an Uzi. His finger looks to be poised on the trigger. Behind him is the familiar face of Aly, who is followed by the pigeon-toed, curly-haired Kameel. The last person to enter the room is a man dressed in a suit and tie with sunglasses perched on the top of his thick black hair. He appears to be the antitype of Colonel Abramovich.

Moussa and Moshe stand up in unison as the door closes behind the four new people whose presence mercifully represents the conclusion of the interrogation session. The room suddenly feels much larger to Moussa and less forbidding. The young man takes a deep breath and lets it out slowly. Then he closes his eyes and gives silent thanks to his new savior.

Kameel extends his hand to Colonel Abramovich and says, "Shalom! What a pleasure to see you again, sir. This woman," he says, turning to touch Aly's arm, "is Mahmoud's sister, Aliyah Ahmed."

The Beth Shin officer hesitates briefly, then reaches out his beefy hand to Aly. A grimace cracks the lunar surface of his cratered face as he says, "Welcome to Israel, Ms. Ahmed. I hope your stay with us is—uneventful."

By this time, Mahmoud, a.k.a. Moussa, is at a total loss. His confusion does not abate much when Kameel turns to him and says, "Mahmoud—sorry, I mean, Moussa—I would like you to meet my friend, David, who I spoke to you about earlier."

The Israeli man in the suit, who looks to be a tad south of thirty, reaches out and shakes Mahmoud's hand with energy. "Marhaba," he says in good Arabic. Switching to English, he adds, "My name is David Abramovich, son of the esteemed Colonel Moshe Abramovich, with whom you've already had the pleasure to engage in some—intimate conversation, I see."

Moussa's eyes widen as he looks from David to Colonel Abramovich to Kameel and finally to Aly.

"Oh," David adds, "this other gentleman with us is Daniel," he says, nodding toward the officer who entered the room first. "He's a mutual friend of both Kameel and I. He's here to ensure your safety while you visit our fine country."

Daniel does not smile as he lifts his chin slightly and examines Moussa. "David informs us that you and your sister are here in Israel to attend the conference in Jerusalem," he comments in a voice thick with a Hebrew accent.

Mahmoud, recently become Moussa, sizes up the young man dressed in military fatigues who is wielding the hated Uzi. The Israeli's face is not unfriendly, but neither is it welcoming.

Kameel reaches out and touches the shoulders of Aly and Moussa. "Are you curious how an Egyptian like me is friends with two Israelis?" he asks. "Well, I'll explain that to you. You already may know a little about David from our previous conversations."

The Egyptian man adjusts his glasses with their thick lenses and begins another one of his stories from the Sinai.

"When I was growing up in Sharm el Sheikh, David and his family were living in Zone D, a narrow strip of land between Israel and the much larger Zone C where my family lived in the South Camp. His father was a member of Beth Shin but had been stationed in the Sinai along with the Israeli infantry battalions. He and his family traveled down to visit the reefs in the Bay of Aqaba whenever possible—at least once a month, if I recall correctly. That's where I met him one day—on the beach near Sharm. He and I became fast friends even though he was an Israeli and I was an Egyptian."

Kameel gestures toward Moshe Abramovich and adds, "David's father was open-minded enough to allow the two of us to become friends when he discovered that my family was Coptic Christian, not Muslim. The colonel has a strong aversion to Muslims; you may have discovered. Muslims who are terrorists, that is," Kameel adds elliptically.

"The dynamics between our families were initially quite tenuous," Kameel explains, "especially between our fathers, but before long, the Abramovichs and the Majdalis hung out together at least one Sunday a month in Sharm or Ras Muhammed or even occasionally up at Eilat.

"It's amazing how children can tear down barriers between the parents. It also helped my father to remember that if the prime minister of Israel, Menahem Begin, and the president of Egypt, Anwar Sadat, were able to set aside their differences and sign the peace treaty of 1979, he could do the same with David's father."

Moussa steals a glance at Colonel Abramovich. The man's face reveals nothing. It is forged of steel.

"What about Daniel—when does he come into the picture?" Aly inquires as she gazes at the soldier whose long sideburns flow generously over his cheeks like lamb's wool. A black yarmulke rests on top of his head. Aly is wondering if the young Israeli soldier is a believer in Jesus but is still wearing his yarmulke like she had continued to wear her hijab even after her encounter with Jesus.

The soldier considers Aly with the same expressionless face as the Colonel. Unlike the Beth Shin officer, however, his eyes appear to be smiling.

"I was living in Sharm as well," he says. "My father owned a dive shop in the city and rented scuba gear to people from all over the world. They came to dive in the reefs and explore the Thistlegorm, a ship that was sunk by a German bomber plane during World War II.

"Kameel and I met because our fathers' professions were both connected to deep sea diving. Since both fathers shared the same interest, they often sat around exchanging obscure facts and swapping stories. It was through Kameel that I later met David. He and I got along just fine, of course, since we were both Israelis."

Daniel hesitates and then adds, "Oh, we had our moments, though, right, David?"

David nods his head and winks at Daniel. Moussa looks at Daniel and David and finally at Kameel. He does not permit himself to even glance at David's father anymore. Instead, he asks, "Are they...are they all—"

When Kameel glances at the colonel and says nothing, David interjects, "If you're wondering if all of us love Yeshua, the answer, unfortunately, is no. Daniel and I are brothers under the lordship of the Messiah, but my father, well, I will let him speak for himself."

The five young people squeezed into the claustrophobic room—one Egyptian, two Israelis, and two American-Saudi-Thai siblings—turn to look at Moshe Abramovich, who is still standing behind the small desk. The broad-shouldered, bald man with the round lunar face reaches into his pocket and fishes out another cigarette that he will never smoke.

After he inserts the slender cylinder into the corner of his mouth, he announces to his audience, "I do not serve the God of the Old Testament or the New. I am a nonbeliever—an atheist. My father taught me that God must have died sometime before the Holocaust because if He did exist, he was either too weak to protect his children from evil or too unloving to even care what happened to them—and my father could not believe in such a deity."

Aly probes her hijab-less hair with both hands and turns to David. "So how—"

Before she can finish her thought, David interrupts her and completes her sentence, "How did two good Jewish boys—both raised by non-religious fathers—fall in love with the Messiah?"

At this point, Kameel touches his frail mustache and comments, "David, I already told Aly and Mahmoud—Moussa, rather—the story about my encounter with Chaplain Joshua Bloomstrom in Sharm."

"Ah," David replies as a broad smile spreads over his gregarious face, "so they know about how God sent a fish to bring you to faith in Jesus! God does indeed work in mysterious ways."

The other young Israeli, Daniel, elbows Kameel in the ribs. His face finally betrays the hint of a smile as he quips, "Jonah had his giant fish, and Balaam his talking donkey, but you got stuck with a stonefish—literally stuck! Of all the accursed luck!"

"But truly, the story does not end there," David interjects enthusiastically. "That dreadful little fish caused Joshua Bloomstrom's life to collide with Kameel's, which, in turn, led Kameel to encounter Jesus, which then led Kameel and later, Joshua, to eventually share their faith with Daniel and me. We didn't become believers immediately, but in that moment, God amazingly planted the seed of faith in our young hearts only to sprout and grow later."

"You may already know we were there that day," Daniel explains to Moussa and Aly. "We were there at the beach with Kameel when he stepped on that providential stonefish. Our families were in the city, but the three of us were at the bay to snorkel. One minute, David and I knew Kameel was going to die, and the next, the man who was sent by Jesus appeared out of nowhere to save our friend."

Daniel adjusts the Uzi strap on his shoulder and continues. "As David already said, when Chaplain Bloomstrom later shared his faith with us, our hearts were unusually open to his message because of everything that had already happened to Kameel. Even though I didn't surrender to Jesus as a boy, Joshua planted the words of the Good News in my heart. When I was twenty-two, I came to faith."

David laughs and says, "Just as God used the huge fish to take Jonah where he wanted the Old Testament prophet to go, so God used a much smaller fish to bring all three of us to where he wanted us to go—into his family as brothers."

The younger Abramovich pauses and smiles respectfully at his father. "It's actually quite amazing, don't you think, that everyone in this room except for one are brothers and sisters, especially when you consider where we all came from."

Moussa notices that David's eyes are intense with joy beneath the fluorescent light—*how different the father is from the son*. Amazingly, Moussa's heart feels connected to this young man—an Israeli.

The senior Abramovich rests the tips of his thick fingers on the top of the desk and looks at his son. His previously hard face and stony eyes soften a degree as he says, "I do not share my son's faith in Jesus, as you already know. My heart remains unconvinced."

Moshe Abramovich glances from his son to Moussa. "Yet, I must confess that I am deeply impacted by the transformation I've witnessed in my son's life. Previously, he was a young man given to selfish pleasures and angry rebellion against his father, a man who was often absent from his life—even when I was in the same room with him. Sadly, I was often harsh, often demanding."

The colonel pauses and leans forward on his fingertips. His eyes return to his son. "But since he embraced the alleged Messiah, he has slowly become a new man. He serves others and does not think of himself. In fact, I've never met a more unselfish man."

The Beth Shin officer hesitates before he adds, "He even respects his difficult father now. So how can I be a strong critic of his faith? Personally, I do not believe in Jesus, but how can I be against Him?"

Moshe Abramovich turns to look at Moussa again, and everyone in the room rivets their eyes on the colonel's cratered face.

"I despise terrorists with all my being," the colonel says unequivocally, his voice threatening and tight with emotion. "I want them all dead or locked away behind thick walls of concrete and steel. If you were still Mahmoud," he announces to Moussa as his eyes drill through the young man like jackhammers, "such would be my sentiment toward you. You would represent all the butchers and murderers who killed my people over the last seventy years and beyond, and I would kill you with my bare hands."

There is a long pause. The room is thick with tension as everyone falls silent. Moussa feels like he cannot breathe. The interrogation room once again shrinks to the size of a broom closet. The Muslim-become-Christ-follower senses the rage of decades vibrating off the colonel's body with an intensity that is almost tangible.

"However." The fierce protector of his country speaks the word as if it is a stand-alone comment. He repeats the word a few seconds later. "However."

Another silence follows. A few people in the room are breathing again. Not Moussa. He remains transfixed with dread. The only word his mind can repeat over and over is the name of Jesus. His brain is too inundated by emotion that he cannot think.

"However." The colonel repeats the word yet again and stops. It is as if he is mentally perseverating or having difficulty communicating what he wants to say next, as if the words are jammed like a piece of raw apple in his windpipe.

Even as the five young people watch, a detectable softness slowly flows back into the officer's round face. He blinks his small eyes three times. Then he clears his throat and finally expands on his single-word utterance.

"However…I discern that you, Moussa, have become like my David, incredible as that is for me to believe." The man whose presence fills the room continues to speak but pauses between every sentence.

"You are a new man purportedly because of Jesus. Just like my son, I see it in your eyes. I see it in your body. I hear it in your voice. Because I see in you, Moussa, what I witnessed in my David years ago—an inexplicable change of being—I cautiously welcome you to my country. Bring shalom wherever you go, and when you leave, pray for the peace of Jerusalem."

Moussa examines the face of the man he would have hated only a month ago and compels words to come out of his mouth. "Thanks to you, sir," he says as he bows his head. "I most assuredly will bring peace to your land during my visit because of Jesus."

The colonel stares at Moussa for a while. Then he grunts, and his eyes move away. He nods at Aly and then looks at Kameel.

"Longtime friend of my son," he says as his face flirts with a smile, "I have only two things to say to you: Welcome again to Israel and—please, let David drive while you're here. I am hesitant to say it, but sadly, you are a true menace behind the wheel."

Kameel laughs and replies, "You know me well, Colonel. I assume you're thinking about the occasion four years ago when I collided with the light rail train."

The burly colonel shakes his round head and replies, "Not at all. I'm recalling your most recent visit to Jerusalem when you foolishly attempted to navigate your car through a narrow archway in the Old City only to get it wedged between the two stone walls. If I remember correctly, it took the police twenty minutes to extract you from the vehicle, and that was only after they were compelled to break the windshield to remove you because you had passed out inside."

"Ah yes, that time," Kameel says slowly, nodding his head with its unruly curls. "I believe I had low blood sugar that day."

"And here I thought all along that you were experiencing delayed effects from the poison of the stonefish," Daniel comments drily, his face sober.

David winks at Aly and asks, "Have you discovered yet that your esteemed professor Kameel is an accident waiting to happen?"

Aly smiles sheepishly and admits, "I've only seen him try to walk through one closed door so far."

The four young people laugh while the colonel coughs into his hand. Moussa, who is finally beginning to relax, permits himself to smile at the others.

David breaks up the lighter moment when he announces, "Hey, you reformed Philistines, it's time for us to make our way up to Jerusalem and get you three checked into your hotel. Transportation is waiting for us out front."

David, Kameel, Daniel, Aly, and Mahmoud—who is now Moussa—all say their goodbyes to Colonel Abramovich. Moussa is the last one to leave. Before he closes the door behind him, he looks over his shoulder and says, "I never imagined I'd see the day when I loved Jesus, and I never ever thought I'd see the day when Jesus would ask me to love an Israeli colonel."

The senior Abramovich considers Moussa for a moment, then grunts and sits back down at his little desk.

CHAPTER 9

Emily and Her Parental Units

Emily navigates her gold '74 Super Beetle with its hand-crank sunroof into her parent's driveway after three days on Marco Island. It is evening. Her parents are home. The dreaded encounter cannot be avoided.

As she walks through the house, she sees them in the back inside the pool enclosure. Her mother is reclining in a lounge chair, reading a book, and her father is busily scribbling on one of his familiar yellow legal pads. For a fleeting moment, she envisions retreating to her bedroom and avoiding them altogether. No conflict. No mess. No fueling the flames of the familiar family conflagration.

When she pauses several steps from the triple pane sliding door that she has walked through twenty thousand times since she was six, something changes her mind, and she continues forward. She hesitates again with her fingers hovering over the handle of the door and inhales deeply. She stands before the sheet of glass long enough to exhale loudly through her mouth, then opens the door and steps outside.

"Hey guys," she says with a bright smile as if she is just returning from a shift at work.

Both parents look up from their preoccupations. Her mother's eyes are blue pools of sadness. Relief floods the face of her father.

"Where have you been?" Joy Parker inquires as she lays aside her book. "You didn't reply to any of our texts or phone calls. The only evidence we had that you were alive were your posts on social media."

Her mother's voice is filled with worry and sadness, but all that Emily hears is accusation. A thick curtain woven of invisible iron mesh immediately unfurls and clangs down between her and her mother.

"Visiting a friend," she replies with a coolness that nearly causes the pool to freeze. It is a tone that has become very familiar to her parents over the last six years.

"You could've taken the time to send us one text, so we didn't have to worry about you day and night," her mother replies.

"I left you a note," Emily parries as her face and neck stiffen like dried cement.

"Were you with Natalie?" her father asks as he pushes his reading glasses up on the top of his head.

Emily hesitates. She is aware that she has been doing a lot of that lately. "Maybe," she says as she folds her arms across her chest. "It's really none of your concern where I was. I'm twenty-four now if you had forgotten. My life is my business, not yours."

"Do you have any idea how sad it is for us to see you go down this path, Emma?" her mother asks as she raises the back of her lounge chair to an upright position. She does not get up from her chair. Joy cannot see her daughter's iron-mesh curtain, of course. Neither is she aware of the other two curtains, one her own and one belonging to the infamous thief who seeks to divorce the mother from her daughter.

"I don't know why you're sad," Emily counters with a dismissive shrug.

"I'm happy. Natalie and I love each other. Who can argue with love? Besides," she says, repeating the familiar mantra that flimsily is all she needs to rationalize her behavior, "how can something that feels so good be wrong?"

Emily's mother opens her mouth to speak but then stops herself. Instead, she looks over at her husband, Dan, effectively passing the baton to her teammate for life.

Dan sets his legal pad down and pushes his chair away from the poolside table. He does not stand up because he does not want to do anything that will feel physically intimidating to his daughter. He knows that his words alone will most likely feel confrontational enough. Besides, he knows how several other men have treated his daughter in threatening ways. He despises the thought of it.

The father clears his throat quietly and looks at his daughter. On the outside, his face is a picture of calm. On the inside, his mind is racing to know what to say and how to say it because it never seems to come out right.

"Emily," he finally says, "just because something feels good doesn't necessarily mean it's good for you. Smoking crack or chewing tobacco may cause me to feel good, but it will likely kill me one day. You simply can't equate pleasure with goodness."

"I'm talking about love, Dad, not drugs!" Emily retorts. "A person, not an addiction!"

"Okay," her father says slowly. "Fair enough. Let's say instead that I get to know a colleague at work and become attracted to her. I feel good when I'm around her, so I decide to have a romantic relationship with her. According to your logic, that relationship can't be wrong because it feels good."

"You're talking about an *affair*, Dad!" Emily exclaims as she adjusts the wide, white headband that flattens her hair severely against her skull. It obscures her beauty almost as much as the hijab Aly used to wear. "I'm not having an affair! I'm loving someone who happens to be another woman. No unfaithfulness is involved."

"You're being unfaithful to your husband," Dan Parker replies as he slowly swirls a spoon in his lemonade glass.

"My husband?" Emily asks with a hint of frustration. "I suppose that's a veiled reference to Jesus."

Her father nods his head and looks up from his glass. "Any time we disobey Jesus, we're betraying our covenant relationship with Him. You know very well, Emily, that Romans 1 addresses this subject when it says that people often exchange God for idols. Idols are anything we choose over God, even other people."

"You know I don't believe the Bible says anything against being gay!" Emily snaps as she protectively folds her arms even more tightly across her chest and stomach.

"How can you say that, Emma?" her mother interjects in a pleading voice. "God's Word is clear that homosexuality is a sin."

"I believe the Old Testament passages about homosexuality no longer apply to us today," Emily argues. "They were relevant only for that particular culture three thousand years ago."

"So, what do you do with the New Testament passages?" her mother asks quietly.

"I believe they're referring to homosexual prostitution," Emily explains, echoing what she has heard from some of her lesbian friends. "Prostitution is wrong. Committed and healthy same-sex relationships are as godly as hetero ones."

Dan sighs and runs his hand over his close-cropped graying hair, being careful not to dislodge his glasses from the top of his head. "Emily, people can engage in amazingly creative gymnastics to make the Bible say whatever they want it to say. Shoot, even Satan quoted Scripture to Jesus when he was tempting God's son in the wilderness."

"What exactly are you saying, Dad?" Emily demands as she compresses her lips so tightly they all but disappear.

"All I'm saying, my Golden Girl, is that no objective, knowledgeable student of the Bible would ever dismiss what it says about homosexual behavior," Dan says as he finishes stirring his lemonade. "The only way to override God's words about same-sex romance is to take scissors and cut the references out of the Bible or manipulate the meaning of the original language, so it says what you want it to say."

Emily stares at her father with green eyes aflame with anger. Eventually, she unfolds her arms and strides over to the far side of the pool and stares—with her back turned against her parents—past the canal and out onto the dusky bay. A deep indigo sky hangs over the darkening world like a velvet curtain. The sound of buzzing and clicking insects attempting to penetrate the patio's screen cocoon and a quiet splash generated by a fishtail are the only sounds heard in the silence of the backyard.

After a long time, when it is obvious that her daughter is not going to break the silence, Joy comments, "Emma, we love you so much! Can't you see that we just don't want you to make choices that will hurt you and destroy your future?"

"Choices!" Emily exclaims as she wheels and strides back toward her parents. "Choices! Don't you see? I'm not making a choice here! I was born with this desire. I'm just being who God made me to be! I didn't choose to be attracted to women, Mom!"

Dan slowly massages the back of his neck and grimaces as he ponders how far to venture out onto thin ice. Finally, he says, "An alcoholic could say the same thing, Emily. She could say, 'I was born this way, so I can't help being an alcoholic. God must have intended me to seek pleasure in alcohol, so it's judgmental of you to tell me to stop being me. I don't need treatment; I just need to be true to the person God made me to be.'"

"That's not fair!" the daughter barks at her father with a coldness that makes her face a stone. "Don't you understand, Dad, I'm talking about loving someone, not an addiction!"

There is a short silence, then Dan Parker looks up at his daughter and says solemnly, "Aren't addictions just distorted affections that we pursue even when they're unhealthy for us? God's Word makes it clear that same-sex attraction is not the love God intends for us. So, it, too, may be a type of distorted love."

"Distorted," Emily repeats the word in a low voice. "You're accusing me of being distorted? That's really low, Dad, even for you." She closes her eyes and lets out a long sigh.

"You know I'm not trying to be low, Golden Girl," her father says as he opens his hands toward her entreatingly. "What I'm trying to say—but not doing a great job of it—is that you, like me, like your mother, like every other human on the planet, is born in a state of rebellion. We want what we want and won't take no for an answer. If anyone does tell us no, we accuse them of being intolerant and judgmental and insist that God's Word is being interpreted incorrectly. We don't want anyone or anything to say no to us—even God Himself. We want to choose whatever we desire."

Emily stares at her father and says, "Didn't you hear what I just said, Dad? I was born gay! God made me this way," she insists as she points at her chest with both index fingers. "I'm not rebelling against God; I'm just living out the path He laid out for me." The anger in her voice is now tempered with a pleading tone.

Dan sighs and massages his forehead slowly. His stomach plummets even deeper into the dark mineshaft that has become so familiar to him over recent years. "I know you believe that, girl," he says. "I know you sincerely believe that. But that's where we part ways—and I hate that we're at odds on that point because it feels like it creates such a huge distance between us. I groan because it feels like we're a million miles apart."

The fifty-four-year-old man pushes aside his full glass of lemonade and leans toward his daughter, elbows on his knees. "Emily, you see same-sex attraction as an identity, as who you are at your core," he begins. "I see it as a behavior—a temptation among many other temptations in this world to practice things that God tells us go against how He made us.

Dan shifts in his chair and says, "And even if someday it can be medically proven that a person is biologically predisposed to homosexual desire—which currently there is no evidence for, loudly though some have insisted—I believe you still have a choice to practice that desire or not.

"That's God's message about all our sinful behaviors as seen in Galatians 5. You can walk in the desires of the flesh, or, with the help of God, you can choose to say no to them and walk in obedience to Jesus. It's always a battle—for all of us. We just have different battles."

Emily releases a long visceral groan. "You're never going to accept this about me, are you, Dad? Mom? It looks like Natalie was right. You're both narrow-minded, homophobic, conservative Christians who can't accept what you don't understand. You simply can't or won't venture out of your familiar little squeaky-clean compound."

"Dead wrong!" Dan Parker counters immediately with an intensity that surprises both his daughter and his wife. "Natalie has no clue who we are! I think it's because we're challenging her sin—and your sin—that she has chosen to shoot the messenger. She—"

"What's that supposed to mean?" Emily snaps with furrowed brows and narrowed eyes.

"It means that if anybody is confronted with truth that challenges their errant choices, nobody wants to admit that the messenger is right," Dan explains. "Most likely, we'll defend ourselves and instead find something wrong with the messenger who is triggering our shame. I think that's what Natalie is doing—accusing us of being judgmental and homophobic to deflect the focus away from her guilt and sin."

"What a convenient explanation," Emily announces slowly and with heavy sarcasm. "Every time someone disagrees with you, they're simply deflecting. They're always wrong, and you're always right."

Emily's father sighs and leans back in his chair. "Yes, that sword can cut both ways, but that's not what I'm saying."

This time, it is Dan's turn to get up and walk over to the far side of the pool. When he reaches the other side next to the canal, he turns to face his daughter and his wife. His fingers are interlaced behind his head.

"This is what it comes down to, Emily," he says slowly, carefully, as if any misspoken word might bring down the whole pool enclosure on top of their heads. "Your mother and I love you and your siblings, and we love each other. But even before we ever loved you kids and each other, we both loved Jesus. Why? Because He loved your mother and I first and saved us years before we ever met each other. He showed us through His word that life has a glorious meaning, an eternal purpose beyond simply what can be seen with physical eyes."

Dan sighs deeply and says, "Emily, you used to believe that, too. You used to believe that there is a God who created us and loves us, that He did not leave us alone in this dark universe, that He sent His son to die for us, and that He left His Word for us to follow—a road map to guide us through this brief lifetime. How can we not follow the map that our loving Father left for us? Since we have this map, we don't have to guess about what is right and healthy, and wise. He clearly revealed the straight path to us in His Word."

Emily rolls her eyes at her father and shakes her head. "Why do you always have to repeat yourself, Dad? You've told me these things a hundred times in the past. And I wish you'd stop throwing subtle jabs at me by using the word 'straight.'"

Emily's father continues as if he had not heard his daughter's protest. "And we love you, our precious daughter, along with your four siblings. We love you so much that we'd give our lives for you. We would die for you just like Jesus died for us."

"Yup, Dad, already know that," the young woman with the partially hidden golden hair replies in staccato syllables.

"If you know that we love you, sweetheart, then why won't you listen to us about what's best for you?" her mother asks, her eyes wet with sorrow.

Emily folds her arms and taps her foot on the patio tile. "Because I'm me and you're you," she replies in a sing-song voice that communicates that she has told her mother the same truth many times in the past. "It's my life, and you need to respect it."

Dan opens his mouth to speak, but Emily raises her palms toward him and says, "I don't want you to trot out your old arguments about the abbreviated life expectancy of a gay man or about higher incidences of domestic violence, STDs, addictions, and cancer. You've driven those opinions home too many times, and I've already explained that those things result from gay people being treated with condemnation and prejudice."

"They're not just opinions," Joy says. "They're truths."

"Whatever," the young woman snaps with exasperation as she shifts her weight to her tapping foot. Her arms are still tightly crossed.

"One last thought, Golden Girl," her father says. He is speaking more rapidly now because he senses that his daughter's patience threshold is rapidly reaching maximum capacity, and he wants to say as much as he can, hoping that if even one word penetrates his daughter's defenses, a victory has been achieved.

"There used to be a time when parents instructed their children not to play in the street because of the danger of getting run over by a truck—and our surrounding culture affirmed that wisdom. Today, if a parent warns his child not to play in the street, the culture no longer affirms the parental warning. Now the culture accuses the parent of being judgmental, hateful, unloving, and even phobic about big trucks if he tells his child to play on the lawn instead of the street."

Dan pauses to assess his daughter's reaction. She simply stares past him impassively, focusing her gaze on a boat with bright running lights navigating the channel behind her father.

"The point I'm making," he explains as he walks back to stand five feet from his daughter, "is that I don't think it's unloving to warn someone not to practice a way of life that may end their life decades prematurely. I don't think it's unwise or judgmental to tell them not to play in a street where they could get run over by a garbage truck. But our culture is so enslaved to the concept of rights and being pro-choice about everything that it will insist that choice is even more important than love or wisdom or—even health and life itself."

Something inside of Dan tells him to stop, but he is on a roll and keeps arguing his point. "'Even if it kills you, choose what you want,' is what the dark side whispers. Choice trumps authority with no apologies. Choice is exalted even above common sense. Heaven forbid that anyone should warn someone that he might die young or that raising children with a father and a mother is far healthier than two parents of the same gender."

Emily continues to stare over her father's shoulder with the look that indicates she has stopped listening, and Dan knows he's said too much. He tilts his head toward the patio floor and sighs. His shoulders slump a bit as he asks quietly, "Can we pray for you, Golden Girl?"

Emily shakes her head decisively. "Nope. I've heard enough. I'm tired of you coming at me. All I want is for you to love me and accept me for who I am. Unfortunately, you have a well-established track record indicating that you're incapable of doing that. You raised me to believe that God's love is unconditional, and then you turn around and love me with so many conditions. To me, that's blatant hypocrisy."

"They're not conditions, Emma," Joy can't resist saying. "Our love for you has never changed, and it will never change. It's just that there's love and truth. Telling you the truth doesn't mean we don't love you."

"I'm done!" the young woman says as she unfolds her arms and strides over to the sliding door. As she opens it, she announces in clipped words thrown over her shoulder, "I'm going out. Don't wait up—I'm not twelve anymore!"

Dan and Joy watch helplessly as their daughter speed walks through the family room and exits the house through the front door, slamming it behind her. The father and mother stand beside the pool for a long time, transfixed by powerlessness and grief.

Eventually, Dan notices that his wife's shoulders are shaking. He gently lifts Joy's face to his with one finger and sees tears flowing down her fair cheeks. He groans softly and pulls her into his arms. He kisses the top of her head and says, "Apparently, we can't argue her into seeing the truth." Then he rests his chin gently on his wife's head and adds, "I've told myself that a hundred times, but it doesn't seem to stop me from trying to do it the next time."

"I'm a bit guilty of that, too," Joy says as she sniffles and wipes away tears from the cheek that is now pressed against her husband's chest. "I think we're convinced that if we say just the right thing, she'll finally hear us, just like she did when she was seven."

There is a long silence. "I suppose we could do what a lot of other parents have done and just accept it as our daughter's orientation or identity—her new normal," Joy comments without conviction.

"We could," her husband says into his wife's hair, "but we can't. Unlike those who view God's Word as mere suggestions or a collection of uneducated guesses, we're convinced that the Bible holds truth from a loving Father God."

"Sometimes, I think it would be so much easier to just give in to the voice of the culture," Joy says with a sigh. "Just believe that it's not that big of a deal and avoid all the conflict. Embrace subjective truth and give up on the absolute truth of God's Word."

"No doubt, it would be easier," Dan agrees as he nods his chin over his wife's hair.

"But then I hear Peter saying that if he had to choose between listening to the world around him or to God, he would listen to God," Joy says.

Dan nods again. "Yes, we who believe in Jesus are an unusual breed. We believe in a God we cannot see; we love those who hate us; and in many ways, we look forward to dying."

Joy chuckles softly and remarks, "One writer even referred to a believer in Jesus as an amphibian, a person called to live in two worlds."

Dan pulls away from his wife and looks at her with a twinkle in his eye. "You do remember that amphibians are cold-blooded creatures."

Joy smiles weakly and nods her head. Then her smile fades, and tears begin to flow again. "Oh, Dan, I don't know what to do about our Emma-girl. I feel like we've lost the precious daughter we raised with so much love and care. I have no idea when or if she'll come back to us. Oh, I'm so, so—" She chokes and stifles a sob.

Dan looks up through the pool screen into the night sky and says softly, "You know what we need to do when we feel so sad and powerless."

Joy nods her head. "Talk to our best friend who can calm the fiercest wind and quiet the wildest waves."

The wife and husband get down on their knees for the umpteenth time in their married lives before the presence of their Savior, who cannot be seen with physical eyes. As they pray, the cool Gulf breeze of late December flows through the screened enclosure, teasing their hair. Simultaneously, another wind gently blows through them, and the overwhelming sadness in their hearts is slowly tempered by a growing sense of unearthly peace.

Toward the end of their conversation with God, Joy prays, "Jesus—Dan and I are so quick to forget that this battle is not primarily intellectual. We forget that we can't debate our daughter into obedience to you. At the deepest level, this is a spiritual battle that only you can win, Jesus. Please help us remember that our fight is not against flesh and blood but against the rulers, against the authorities, against the powers of this dark world, and against the spiritual forces of evil. Lord, we know we cannot fight this war in our human strength.

"So, Holy Spirit, please, please speak deeply into Emma's heart. Open her ears to hear your voice and obey you. We know that it is not by our might or power but by your Spirit alone."

The husband and wife pray on their knees a while longer. The indigo curtain slowly gives way to a darker curtain as the sun drops far beneath the horizon. Eventually, Dan concludes their time with Jesus.

"We don't pray first and foremost that our dear daughter rejects her practice of same-sex attraction," he says earnestly. "No, we ask above all that she might fall in love with you because only then will she surrender her idols and obey you out of a deeper affection. Remove all counterfeit loves and addictions from her heart. Instead, open the eyes of her heart to see the genuine, true love that only comes from you. May she then be inspired to love you in return with all her heart, mind, and strength, Jesus.

"Lastly, show us how to love Emily with your love. If we truly believe that you are her first parent and love her far more than we do, then we can surrender her journey into your loving hands, you who are the good and strong father. Yes, only when I remember that truth will I be able to release her into your care instead of falling into the temptation of controlling her life. We thank you so much for Emily, Jesus. Please help us not to get in the way of your love for her."

The father of Emily Joy pauses and then adds, "Yes, forgive me for always opening my big mouth."

Joy opens her eyes and laughs softly. "Amen to that, Jesus," she says. "Amen to that."

The husband and wife stand up and hold each other beside the pool for a long time. They talk, and they cry, and they laugh.

And then they cry again.

CHAPTER 10

The Inimitable Carmelita Cortez

As the sun is setting, the two young men from the Academy stop for supper at a small Mexican restaurant not far from the high school. They are eating their meal of tamales, tacos, beans, and rice when Armando, who has noticeably drawn into himself since they entered the city limits of La Puente, points toward the front window of the restaurant with his fork.

"In seventh grade," Armando says as he chews a mouthful of refried beans, "my best friend, Adrian, was from the Philippines. His mom worked across the street in that strip mall at a check cashing store. One day, a guy walks in, shoots her in the face, and runs out with all the cash he can carry. A week later, they install a bullet-proof screen—a lifetime too late for Mrs. Ocampo. Two months later, Adrian and his father move away to Sacramento."

Jack groans. The heavy darkness he felt when they stopped at Armando's old house grows even heavier. It weighs on his chest until he feels like he cannot breathe. "The violence around here feels evil," he comments, half to himself, half to his friend.

"You ain't heard nothin' yet," Armando mumbles as he continues to stare across the street. "If a cross was placed at every spot where someone was murdered in this city, you'd see a dozen of them in a two-block radius around us."

Armando falls silent, his fork still pointing across the street. His gaze remains fixed on the strip mall.

"Are you okay, man?" Jack inquires of his friend.

Armando rips his eyes away from the window and looks at Jack. "I'll be fine," he says with a sigh. "Too many memories here."

The man who used to be known as Syko Loco eight years ago stares through Jack as he shifts his thoughts away from Adrian and his mother. A few seconds later, his eyes light up suddenly.

"I do have one good memory from this neighborhood," he comments with a smile. "It was in front of that BP on the corner where I had my first kiss," he says, nodding his head toward the gas station down the street. "Her name was Alicia Hernandez. She had brownish-red hair with eyes as big and brown as...as walnuts."

"Walnuts," Jack repeats, laughing so hard he has to put his hand over his mouth to keep his food from falling out. "Seriously? Alicia had very wrinkly eyes."

"Okay, okay, Juan, I mean acorns," he cries out, correcting his first descriptor. "They were acorns. Isn't that what the poets say when they are speaking of big brown eyes?"

Jack laughs again and begins to tell his friend that poets might use the word "chestnuts" when a human ball of energy suddenly rolls up to their table.

"Is that you, Manny?" a high-pitched voice inquires at a decibel level just short of a scream. "Manny Vasquez?"

Armando looks up at the woman standing beside their table. He does not have to look far since the woman is vertically challenged. His mouth falls open, and his eyes grow large as he says slowly, "Carmelita Cortez?"

The woman, who appears almost as wide as she is tall, squeals loudly, and her whole body from head to toe vibrates with excitement. She stretches out her short arms and leaps to tackle Armando's neck in a tight embrace. The surprised man attempts to speak, but his voice is muffled since his face is buried in the woman's chest.

Eventually, the woman releases her victim as a mousetrap might release a rodent, and Armando is able to speak—and breath. "Is that really you, Carmelita?" he asks incredulously as he rises to his feet. He is a foot taller than the diminutive woman who is beaming in front of him like a bride recessing after her wedding.

"Si, Manny, it is I!" she cries out in a strong accent. The woman's eyes are so large with excitement that Jack thinks they make her look a bit deranged.

Jack pushes his chair back and rises to his feet. Wiping his mouth with his napkin, he asks, "Armando, are you going to introduce me to your friend?"

Armando is unable to respond to his roommate because the short woman is already talking so fast and with such animation that he has no choice but to listen. He glances at Jack with a wry smile. Then he shrugs his shoulders and raises his eyebrows.

"I haven't seen you in years, Manny!" the woman known as Carmelita exclaims as her long, black vertical curls bounce and swing around on the edges of her face in rhythm with the staccato movements of her body. "*Muchos años*! You've grown up to be a man! You're handsome! You're strong! Tell me you're still a man of God, Manny. Please tell me that. I will accept no other answer."

Armando glances quickly at Jack again and nods his head. "Yes, Carmelita," he replies with a larger smile, "I'm still a man of God."

"Gracias a Dios," the round woman cries out as she raises her round face and small but thick hands toward the ceiling. *"Gracias a Dios!* I do still talk to Jesus about you; you should know. I do, Manny! I am not lying. I have been praying for you since I last saw you at the Iglesia del Salvador. How I have worried about you, *mi hijo!*" she says the last two words so fast that they sound like one to Jack.

When the woman, who speaks faster than any person Jack has ever met, pauses to breathe, Armando sees his opportunity. He quickly jumps in and says, "Carmelita, this is mi amigo, Juan. He is also a believer in Jesus. Juan, this is Carmelita, my spiritual mother. She helped me grow in the Lord when I was a baby believer."

In an instant, the woman pivots and directs her radiant attention toward Jack. She throws her arms into the air again and lets out another excited squeal. Then she rushes around the table to where the target of her greeting is standing—a motionless clay pigeon before the blast of a shotgun.

Jack soon finds himself wrapped in the same embrace his roommate was engulfed in moments earlier. The top of the woman's head comes halfway up Jack's chest as she hugs him.

When Carmelita releases Jack, she announces, "A friend of Manny's is a friend of mine! No questions asked. No, not one. *Gracias a Dios!*"

After Jack separates from the woman's embrace, he notices a fragrance emanating from her body that reminds him of lilacs. It is so strong that his eyes begin to water. He stifles a cough with the back of his hand.

Armando invites Carmelita to join them at the table. The ebullient woman responds to the invitation with another squeal of joy.

Once she is seated, she starts talking and does not stop. She explains that she needs to be at her son's house in West Covina by 8:00 that evening to watch her granddaughter, Lucia. No, she doesn't need any food. She would like some water, however—without ice. Yes, she's still at Iglesia Del Salvador. Yes, it has been five years since she last saw Manny at the wedding of Carlos and Juanita in Whittier. As she talks, she fingers one particularly large curl on the right side of her face as if it is the favored one among all of them.

Jack listens with a smile on his face as Carmelita and Armando reminisce about the past with alternating tears, laughter, and sentence-long prayers uttered randomly by the spiritual mother with her hands and face raised in the air. The woman is ecstatic. Under the fluorescent lights, her eyes glisten, and her cheeks glow like small, polished apples ripe with redness.

Jack has never seen a face as elastic as Carmelita's. One moment, her countenance is twisted into a look of agony to such a degree that it appears that she is grimacing in severe physical pain. The next moment, her visage is transformed into the brightest, most joyful expression as if she is beholding Jesus himself. Later, she looks like she is growling and, a minute later, weeping. Jack gazes at Carmelita's quadruple chin and thinks of the tiered waterfall in Armando's backyard where he had eaten breakfast just that morning. It feels like two days ago.

An hour passes, and soon it is 7:45 p.m. The sun set hours ago, and it is dark outside the restaurant.

Jack is growing restless. He attempts to get his roommate's attention with a small cough. Armando glances at him and acknowledges his nonverbal message with a nod of his head. A few minutes later, amazingly, Armando finds a way to interrupt Carmelita's recollection of when she first met her spiritual son shortly after his spiritual rebirth.

"Carmelita," he says in a gentle voice that Jack has never heard before from his roommate. "*Mi amigo,* Juan, and I," he comments, nodding at Jack, "are on a mission tonight, a mission for Jesus."

The round woman with the large, brown eyes—probably very similar to Alicia Hernandez' chestnut eyes—cups her hands in front of her lips and forgets what she was just talking about. "What is it, Manny?" she inquires breathlessly. "What is your mission?" Her face is twisted into a look of deep anguish. Jack finds her expression amazingly appropriate, considering what lies ahead for the two men.

Armando glances at Jack and then levels a serious gaze at Carmelita. "We're going to share the good news of Jesus with Sniper," he confides.

The expressive woman's face freezes as her mind, no doubt, races. She stares at her spiritual son for a long time until a look of awareness transforms her face into a mask of horror—which is of no comfort to Jack. She gasps loudly, and her eyes—if possible—grow even larger beneath her raised, beetled brows. When she speaks, it is in a whisper that sounds conspiratorial to Jack.

"You are going to share Jesus with Miguel Herrera?" she asks.

Armando nods his head slowly as he stares into the woman's eyes.

"He's the man who killed your brother, Raul!" Carmelita announces in such a manner that it sounds like she is informing Armando of something he does not yet know.

Armando nods his head again as he compresses his lips together tightly between his thin mustache and thicker goatee.

"*Vaya usted con Dios!*" Carmelita exclaims in a louder voice as she animatedly makes the sign of the cross over her chest.

"*Si, mi madre,*" Armando replies, "we'll be going with God—or not at all."

A grave look spreads over Carmelita's contortionist face. "Miguel is a very bad man," she announces, "muy mal. The devil himself is his closest friend—his only friend." She continues to stare at Armando and then asks, "Why are you doing this thing?"

Jack's roommate replies, "God has revealed to us through the dream of a godly woman that we must go to Sniper."

"Ah," Carmelita says in a protracted fashion as she nods her head in understanding. "When the Father speaks, you must listen and obey."

Armando and Jack nod their heads in unison.

Carmelita folds her small, chubby hands and leans toward Armando as she glances at both men. "I will pray for both of you before I go," she announces with authority. "Yes, I will pray right now, or my name is not Carmelita Cortez."

The short, stout woman bows her head resolutely, and her black vertical curls bounce beside her cheeks like small Slinkies. Then she beings to pray in such a manner—with passion and confidence, reciting passages from the Bible and talking to Jesus as her best friend—that Jack soon finds himself wishing that Carmelita could be his own personalized prayer warrior.

As she prays, the devout woman bobs her head furiously as if the physical motion will send her words hurtling with increased urgency toward the throne of God. Tears flow down her cheeks like liquid love flowing in quicksilver currents.

When Carmelita is done praying, she briefly consults with Manny about the best way to approach Miguel, a.k.a. Sniper, with the good news. Then, after expressing deep regret about her need to depart, she rises from the table and gives Armando and Jack another enveloping hug shrouded in a fog of lilac perfume. As he embraces Carmelita, Jack feels like he is the tall wizard, Gandalf, giving the diminutive Frodo a hug.

Carmelita promises that she will be praying all night for the two "warriors of God." She points a child's finger at Armando and insists that he call her tonight or tomorrow to let her know what happens with Miguel. Then the portly woman turns and waddles away with short, quick steps. Within seconds of her departure, Jack's throat stops itching, and his eyes stop watering.

Armando's spiritual mother is almost out the door when she suddenly cries out loudly and throws her hands toward the heavens once more, drawing the immediate attention yet again of everyone in the small restaurant. Pivoting quickly like a door on a hinge, she hurries back to the table where Armando and Jack are sitting. Her short legs and large body prevent her from running, but she does her best impersonation. She brings with her the strong lilac fragrance. Jack coughs, and his eyes immediately begin to water again.

Breathless with excitement and exertion, Carmelita grabs the edge of the table with both hands and hangs on tightly as if to life itself. She leans down until her face is on the same level as Armando's and only inches away. Between breaths, she announces gravely, "The Holy Spirit told me to tell you something."

Armando and Jack glance at each other. Then Armando turns to his spiritual mother and asks, "What is it, *mi madre?*"

"If Miguel goes loco, mention his grandmother, Cecilia," the short woman instructs Manny. "I knew her years ago before she passed. She loved Jesus and prayed for Miguel every day. She told me that his father was always drunk and would beat Miguel so badly he couldn't see straight. One time, he even broke his arm. Whenever she could, Cecilia would drive over to the house and pick up Miguel. She would take him to her place where he could be safe. She is with Jesus now, but I know she is praying for her grandson from heaven. I feel that in my heart."

"Gracias, Carmelita, we'll remember that," Armando says as he pats the woman's short, fleshy arm that is dark with hair.

"There is one more thing, Manny," the woman confides gravely, her face glowing with perspiration from her hurried return to the table. "I overheard Cecilia tell my mother not long before she went home to be with Jesus that Miguel only loves two things in this world—herself, Cecilia, and his younger sister, Angela Rose. Miguel has no love for any man in this world, but he would die for his beloved *hermana* in a beat of his heart!"

Carmelita leans closer to her spiritual son as if to impart an even more sacred truth. Her face becomes very serious, and she raises her chin in resolute fashion. Then she begins jabbing her stubby index finger against the tabletop and declares, "Angela Rose was raised mostly by her grandmother. Like Cecilia, she is a believer in Jesus! She has had visions of Miguel bowing down to Jesus!"

Carmelita stares at Armando, her eyes ablaze with conviction. Without words, her face communicates, "So there! Mark my words and do not forget them!"

When Armando nods his head in recognition of Carmelita's revelation, the stout woman withdraws her finger from the table and straightens her short frame so that she stands a few inches taller than her seated spiritual son. Her dark eyes dart toward Jack one last time and then back at Manny.

"As you go into the lion's den tonight," the woman admonishes, leaving the young men with one final message, "remember Shadrach, Meshach, and Abednego! Jesus will protect you from the jaws of death!"

Carmelita stares at Manny for a long time and nods her head slowly to communicate emphasis. Her extra chins decrease and increase as her head goes up and down. Finally, she turns and walks away with her short, waddling steps. This time, she does not return. Neither does the staggering lilac cloud that accompanies her body wherever it goes.

"Wow!" Jack exclaims with a laugh. "Big things sometimes do come in small packages!"

Armando nods his head. "Verdad, you are right," he agrees, smiling. "She's one unique woman. God clearly broke the mold after He created Carmelita Cortez."

Jack hesitates because he doesn't want to say what he's thinking.

Fortunately, Armando says it for him.

"It's a good thing that appearing *normal* is not a prerequisite for being a believer," he says with a wry smile. "Otherwise, Carmelita would most likely never qualify to be in God's family."

"She's unforgettable," Jack comments. "A *oner*. Some people you forget minutes after you meet them," Jack observes, "but Carmelita Cortez will be in my memory 'til the day I die. Guaranteed."

Armando nods absent-mindedly as he squeezes his lower lip between his thumb and index finger. "Her appearance here tonight in this exact spot is certainly not an accident, Juan," he remarks. "God is sending us help. He's telling us that He'll be with us tonight for the Sniper rendezvous."

"Speaking of tonight," Jack says, glancing at his phone, "it's almost 8:15 p.m."

"Yes," Armando replies with a hint of impatience. "Yes, we must go, vato."

CHAPTER 11

Rachel and Drew at Caffeine Cove

The next morning, Rachel parks in front of Caffeine Cove beside a forest green, older model station wagon that looks like a rectangular box on wheels. Sitting in the driver's seat is a man she recognizes as Drew Johnson. The two young people get out of their vehicles and meet on the sidewalk. They stare at each other and smile awkwardly.

Rachel's hands are protected from the cold by cherry-colored mittens, while Drew has his shoved into the back pockets of his jeans. Rachel had forgotten how big the young man is, not just tall but broad. He is all of 6 feet 6 inches in height, she estimates, and thick. He looks dashing, she thinks, wearing a blue flannel shirt and a black T that peeks out at his neck.

Drew gazes at the young woman with the striking shoulder-length auburn hair, slightly upturned nose that fits her face perfectly, and her freckles that remind him of miniature ginger stars. The stars are more heavily concentrated on the sides of her nose and on her cheeks. In her hazel eyes, he observes bubbling energy masked by a veneer of shyness. She is uniquely attractive to him.

"Hey, Rachel," he finally says in his deep bass voice as he shifts his weight from his right foot to his left.

"Hi, Drew!" she says as she drives her mittened hands deeper into the pockets of her snowball-white winter coat. "How was the drive?"

"Good," he says, "yeah, it was good. Roads were dry, and traffic was light."

"I was trying to remember exactly where in upstate New York you said you live," Rachel says.

"Outside of Lake Luzerne," Drew replies. "It's a small town. Part of our property actually borders the Hudson, if you've heard of that river or...or if you happen to know where it is."

Rachel laughs brightly, and Drew is reminded of the beautiful chimes he heard on the phone the previous day. "I've heard of the Hudson, of course," she says, "and I've actually driven over it many times on the Tappan Zee Bridge. It's a cool river," she adds unnecessarily and subsequently kicks herself mentally.

"Yeah, totally cool," Drew says.

They both laugh nervously, and then Rachel asks, "Do you want to go inside?"

"Sure," Drew says as he pulls his hands out of his back pockets and strides toward the door. He opens it effortlessly and says, "After you."

Rachel is impressed by his strength and his thoughtfulness. *Chivalry still lives despite the rumors of its demise, she thinks to herself. Or it still lives despite efforts by some to frame it as antithetical to feminine equality.*

A few minutes later, they settle into two overstuffed chairs with their coffees and blueberry scones situated between them on a small table. Rachel says, "I'll pray that the Holy Spirit will guide our thoughts and words today."

"Okay," Drew replies as he watches Rachel bow her head.

When the prayer is done, Drew asks, "I'm curious why you bow your head when you pray."

Rachel taps her chin with a thoughtful finger and wrinkles her forehead and her starry nose. "Honestly, I don't ever think about that. I just do it from habit, I guess. I suppose it's my way of showing deep respect for God, a way to acknowledge that He's big and I'm so small."

"Almost like saluting," Drew offers.

"Yeah, kind of like that, I suppose," Rachel says. "Except that God most likely doesn't salute us back. He probably doesn't bow his head to us when we bow our heads before him."

"Yeah, I suppose he's much bigger and higher even than some Army general," Drew acknowledges.

As they begin to nibble on their scones and sip their lattes, Rachel looks at the young man sitting across from her with his deep blue eyes and brown wavy hair and asks, "So, Drew, how are you doing today? Yesterday, you didn't sound so good."

Drew's mouth is momentarily hidden by his coffee cup. When he sets it back on the table, he replies, "Better, today. Believe it or not, it was just helpful knowing that I would be seeing you today. Like I said yesterday, I really don't have any fans of my new faith back at home. Even my best friend from high school thinks I've gone off the deep end."

"Yeah, your mother especially sounds like she might struggle with your decision to follow Jesus," Rachel observes.

"No doubt about it," Drew agrees. "As an agnostic, Dad is a bit quieter about it all. Heck, he's quieter about everything. But Mom, she wants me to give it up and never look back. Simply said, she sees spirituality as foolishness."

"Do you think she's basically anti-God, or does she sincerely want to protect you from something she sees as dangerous?" Rachel asks.

"Good question," the big man observes as he scrutinizes Rachel's face. "Actually, it's a great question! I think it could be both. She probably wants to protect me, but I also know she's fundamentally opposed to anything that suggests a divine being exists in the universe."

"So, your faith in Jesus Christ will not be welcomed by your parents," Rachel comments. "What about your brothers or sisters? What do they think?"

"I don't have any of those," Drew answers. "I'm an only child."

Rachel laughs, and Drew responds with, "Yeah, I'm one of those kids."

"You mean spoiled," Rachel says, smiling.

"Maybe," Drew chuckles, "or maybe way more mature because I had to learn how to speak 'adultese' at a young age since I had no siblings to talk to."

"I'll give you the benefit of the doubt and go with the way more mature narrative," Rachel says with a wink.

They both laugh and fall silent. Then Drew asks, "So how exactly do I start this journey?"

Rachel pauses for a moment and then suggests, "Why don't you start by telling me about your life up to the moment you believed in Jesus? That way, I won't feel like I'm talking to you in some vacuum but will have some context to work with."

"Okay," Drew says as he grabs one large knee in his huge hands and leans back in his chair. "Let me think where I should start." He pauses for a long time and then launches in with, "The first thing I would say to you is that my life is meaningless."

Rachel tilts her head to one side, and her auburn hair slides over her right eye. "That's a dark comment, to begin with," she remarks.

"What I mean," Drew explains, "is that I grew up in a family where my father viewed God as unknowable, and my mother believed that God was non-existent. Of course, for my mother, if there is no God, then everything is here by sheer blind chance, even humans."

Rachel nods her head and says, "Okay, that follows—without the existence of God, we're not intelligently designed beings."

"My mother isn't a poster child for evolution," Drew clarifies, "but she does quietly embrace it as scientific fact. Because of her, I grew up believing that there is no God and that humans are simply evolved animals. From that beginning point, I didn't have to be a rocket scientist to deduce that life ultimately has no meaning since we're all here by accident."

"You actually thought about that when you were young—that life has no meaning without God?"

Drew releases his knee and leans forward to reach for his coffee. "When I was a kid, I laid awake many nights thinking about it," he says, nodding his head slowly. "I even had nightmares about it."

"What kind of nightmares?" Rachel inquires.

Drew sips his coffee flavored with pumpkin spice cream and answers, "I had this recurrent dream that I was walking across a vast prairie all by myself. In every direction, I saw flat land covered with knee-high grass. For what it's worth, the grass was brown, dead. There were no mountains, no water, no buildings, no animals, no people, no God. I was terrifyingly alone on that endless prairie.

"Whenever I had those nightmares, I would wake up screaming and run into my parents' room. I had to be close to someone even if they didn't know how to be close to me."

"There are some philosophers who would tell you it's normal to have existential angst in this world," Rachel says. "They would inform you that the authentic man or woman will stand face to face with the emptiness of the universe and go bravely into the dark night of aloneness."

"Whose side are you on?" the young man from New York says with a chuckle.

"I think you know," Rachel replies with a reassuring smile. Then she adds, "It's just so sad to me that you were all alone with that level of fear as a kid."

"Yeah," Drew acknowledges with a nod of his head, "It was mega intense and weird. I mean, what nine-year-old kid worries about being in a universe without God?"

Rachel gazes intensely into Drew's large blue eyes and says, "A nine-year-old boy who's spiritually sensitive, that's who. You sound like you were in touch with something that many adults banish into their unconsciousness. Maybe you didn't have the defenses to shut it all out."

Drew looks at Rachel thoughtfully and says, "I also had repeated nightmares about death. I dreamed that I was buried deep under the ground and being eaten by worms and beetles."

"Ugh!" Rachel exclaims. "Super, ugh! What terrible nightmares! How did you even want to go to sleep at night?"

"I didn't," Drew admits. "I didn't want to go to sleep, but neither did I want to be the last one awake. I hated it when I knew my parents were asleep, but I was still wide awake. I felt like the whole world was sleeping, and I was the only human awake on the whole planet. I felt totally and terribly alone."

"A psychologist would probably diagnose you with separation anxiety," Rachel suggests with raised eyebrows.

Drew looks at the young woman with a look of surprise on his face. "How did you know?"

"Seriously?" Rachel inquires.

Drew nods his head and laughs. "I saw two different shrinks when I was young. Both of them said I had separation anxiety issues. They might have been right—my parents were both highly involved in their work and emotionally unavailable. But I always thought there was more to it than just a deficit in my parents."

"I couldn't agree more!" Rachel says eagerly. "I've always thought that separation anxiety isn't just about the parent-child attachment but about the God-human attachment as well. If we're not rightly attached to the God who made us, we'll experience an underground anxiety that may never dominate our lives but may leak out in other, subtler ways. In fact, I sometimes think all anxiety has its roots in our separation from God. We kind of experience a true-to-life archetype."

"Wow," Drew says as he stares at the redheaded woman across from him. "It sounds like I'm not the only one who thinks about deep stuff."

Rachel smiles wistfully and says, "No, you're not." There is a period of silence before she redirects the conversation. "So, how did you deal with your anxiety?"

"'The rush,'" Drew replies without hesitation.

"The rush," Rachel repeats.

"Yeah," he says. "When my anxiety led to depression and my depression to emptiness, I had to find something to comfort me and to make me feel alive. The rush helped with both of those things."

Drew pauses to take a bite of his blueberry scone and chews in silence as Rachel observes him.

"When I was younger," he eventually says, "I got into skateboarding and then doing tricks on my Haro bike, which wasn't easy since the frame was a bit heavy. Those moments were my earliest experiences with 'the rush.' Later, I graduated to snowmobiles and dirt bikes. Bungee jumping off the Lake Luzerne bridge above the Hudson River was also exhilarating. Sports could also generate the rush, as we talked about at the student commons with Jack."

Drew hesitates and sighs deeply. "Of course, you can probably imagine that I was also attracted to anything I could ingest that would give me the rush, or at least some sort of high. Marijuana, opioids, alcohol, sex—I used all those things to feel fully alive. Even acid a few times, but that stuff scared me—I hallucinated about being alone forever in hell. Ironically, I didn't even believe in hell at the time."

Drew swirls the last of his coffee around in his cup and then stares into the fireplace for a long time. Several times, Rachel is tempted to speak, but before she can ask another question, Drew shares his thoughts.

"Pete and I were doing heroin that last night," he confides quietly.

Without thinking, Rachel reaches out and places her hand on Drew's arm.

The big man looks up, and Rachel finds herself looking into twin well shafts that run deep into Drew's subterranean self. The water at the bottom of the wells is mourning. Neither of them speaks for a long time, but in the silence, they communicate more than any words ever could.

Eventually, Rachel removes her hand. Drew clears his throat which is thick with emotion.

"So, when Pete died," he says in a tight voice, reluctant to speak the words that convey such a harsh reality, "I could only think of two things: kill myself and be with Pete or call Jack. Fortunately, I chose the latter—especially when I remembered what you said about walking to Australia."

The young man inflates his cheeks and then lets out a slow, loud breath. "If you and Jack hadn't talked to us that day on campus, I'm convinced I'd be dead, Rachel. Those worms and beetles would be eating me right now. Pete—" The words that are supposed to follow catch in Drew's throat. His eyes run away from Rachel's face and find refuge on the floor.

"It wasn't an accident that we talked to you that day," Rachel says without hesitation. "Jesus knew you were going to need a rock to stand on in the near future."

Drew nods his head slowly and looks up at the young woman. "So here we sit today to help me develop an alternative to the rush. I've found out that physical pleasures never last and that what comes after the rush leaves me feeling worse than when I started."

The big man sets his empty coffee cup on the table and then announces bitterly, "What a fool I've been! I knew from first-hand experience that the rush wasn't going to last, but I kept going back to it like a dog to its vomit. I was willing to tolerate its bitter consequences just to feel a brief high."

"To be human is to be hungry," Rachel says, thinking how literally true that has been in her own life. "We all need to fill ourselves with something, and there's a lot of somethings out there in the world. But there's only one thing that's meant to fill us on the level of ultimate satisfaction, and that's actually not *something* but *someone*. Only the God who created us can satisfy our deepest longings—the God who your dad says can't be known and the One your mother claims doesn't exist."

"Until very recently, God was never a legitimate contender in my mind," Drew confesses. "In fact, if any of those *rushes* I talked about had given me a reason to live, I probably wouldn't have asked Jesus into my life. Heck, if even one of those things had given me a high that lasted, I would have settled for it. Who needs meaning in life when you can feel good all the time with self-generated pleasure?"

"*Maybe* you would have settled for pleasure," Rachel counters. "I'm convinced, however, that the emptiness you experienced in life was because you didn't have that meaning you referred to. So, even if you had found something that gave you consistent pleasure in this world, I still think you would have been empty and unhappy in the end. You're made for meaning, after all, for a destination, not for random pleasures along the way—not for an infinity circle of empty existence.

"Well," Drew says as he rubs his eyes with large fingers, "I suppose we could say that the point is moot since none of the rushes brought me lasting pleasure. I've always been searching for something more. I just didn't know what it was.

"I probably thought that the right drug or the right girl or the right job or the right movie or binging on the right TV series would make me happy," he comments. "I had even gotten to the point where I was thinking about expanding my opportunities for novel pleasure by experimenting with bisexuality. I reasoned that novelty might promise new pleasure when old pleasures had grown old and unfulfilling. But if I'm honest, I already decided several years ago that none of those things would be the ultimate answer."

Rachel looks down at her feet and then back up at the young man sitting across from her. She hesitates and then says, "I rarely talk about it with anyone—it's one of those...private things, but binging on food or controlling its intake has always been my 'go-to' pleasure, if I can call it that. It's the pseudo-relationship I've turned to since I was a young girl. And like you're saying, Drew, it can offer a fleeting sense of satisfaction. But obsessing about food is just another counterfeit currency in the search for meaning in life."

"Counterfeits never satisfy," Drew admits. "They always have some type of punishing kickback that can be devastating. I think, of course, of Pete and...and the ultimate price he paid."

Rachel nods her head slowly and says, "God wasn't humoring us when He said that we reap what we sow. If we sow pleasure and worldly success, we'll always want more and more, but it'll never be enough. We'll just end up reaping that emptiness you talked about earlier."

"So, it was appealing to me," Drew replies, "when I heard you and Jack speak of something—or someone—who could satisfy my intense hunger and fill my deepest emptiness. Honestly, it was a no-brainer that I asked Him to come into my life considering how low I was and since I saw no other options."

"Have you noticed anything...different since you became a believer in Jesus?" Rachel inquires. She hates to admit to herself that she fears there has been no change, that Drew will report that nothing definitive has happened inside his heart.

"Oh, yeah, there's definitely something going on inside," he says with a smile. "I struggle to put it into words, but I absolutely sense that I'm not alone anymore. There's a...there's a presence, you might call it, inside of me that wasn't there before. And I also see, especially in the last two or three days, that I don't have the same desire to do certain things I used to do in the past."

The large young man hesitates and shakes his head. "It might sound weird, Rachel, and I can't exactly explain it, but I haven't had a drink or smoked anything since I prayed with Jack to receive Jesus. I've been as sober as...as a choir boy. And it's not like I'm trying to be a choir boy. I'm not trying to be good. I just have new desires that seem to have replaced the old ones."

"That's amazing, Drew!" Rachel says with genuine excitement. "The Holy Spirit who now lives inside of you is transforming your affections to be more like His. He's giving you power to do what you could never do on your own when you were living far away from Him. You're a new creation, Drew."

The hulking offensive lineman leans toward Rachel and fixes intense eyes on her. "The things you're telling me right now—they're more than just what I need to hear; they are what I *must* hear," he insists. "Keep going, Rachel."

Rachel nods her head and keeps going. She pulls out her notepad and her Bible and, one by one, walks through the basic pillars of faith in Jesus. She talks about the Triune God: the Father, the Son, and the Holy Spirit. She addresses temptation, sin, and forgiveness. She discusses the importance of spending time in the Love Letter and with other believers.

She covers the topics of how to pray and how to practice the presence of God. She speaks about heaven and hell and the fact that this earth is no longer Drew's ultimate home. She also explains the personality of Satan and how, as a new believer, Drew will draw increasing attention from the enemy. As a result, he will need to know how to protect himself against spiritual attack.

Rachel goes on to read passages from the Bible that speak of God's plan for Drew's life and how he can learn about God's specific will for him. She briefly outlines the attributes of God's character and how Drew will spend the rest of his life only scratching the surface of how huge and amazing God is. Finally, she talks briefly about how to share his new faith with others when the opportunity presents itself. Drew furiously takes notes as Rachel teaches.

Four hours pass, and soon it is midafternoon. Rachel and Drew leave the coffee shop and drive to Rachel's favorite seafood restaurant situated on the bayfront. Drew orders salmon, and Rachel gets her favorite seafood: scallops. Drew insists on paying for the food for the body since Rachel is giving him amazing food for the soul. They spend the next three hours talking further about Jesus and how Drew can walk out his new faith.

After they leave the restaurant, they drive to a hiking trail that follows the shoreline of the bay. They walk and talk for another hour until the sun falls into the ocean and leaves a splash of fiery orange in its wake.

It is completely dark when they return to the coffee shop and stand on the sidewalk where they had first met that morning. It feels to Rachel like she met the young man three days ago instead of eight hours earlier.

"This day has been awesome!" Drew raves in his bass voice. His face is painted with the green, red, and blue hues of Christmas lights that decorate the shops along the quaint street. "I've never experienced a day like this, Rachel! You've given me amazing context for this new life in Jesus and a plan about how to keep growing. How can I ever thank you?"

Rachel blushes, but the familiar red that rises so easily in her cheeks is washed out by the colorful lights.

"I'm so glad I could be here for you," she replies. "I've never had to explain my faith to anyone as much as I did today. Your thoughtful questions really challenged me, Drew."

"Well, good," he says with a deep, resonant laugh. "But I still have one question left."

"Okay, what is it?" Rachel asks.

"Can we talk again?" Drew inquires as he adjusts the backpack on his shoulder. "Can I come back to Connecticut and learn some more about—I mean, *v* you?"

"I would like that," Rachel replies without hesitation. She has thoroughly enjoyed the day with this young man, who is now her brother in the Lord. She pauses for a moment and chews on her lower lip. Then she says, "I'll talk to my parents. Since you said your family doesn't celebrate Christmas, maybe you could come and spend Christmas at my house here in Mystic. Is that too weird to ask?"

"Not at all," Drew says as he reaches out and touches the arm of Rachel's coat. "I'm all over that idea."

"Christmas is only three days away, so we'll have to figure this out straightaway," Rachel says. "I'll talk to my parents when I get home and then text you later tonight to let you know if it works or not."

"Sounds like a plan!" Drew says. He pauses and clears his throat. "Before I go, can I try to pray for us?"

"Wow, of course!" Rachel says. "Go for it, Drew!"

The young man reaches out and takes one of Rachel's cherry-mittened hands in his huge hand. He bows his head and closes his eyes. Then he prays, "Jesus, I thank you for rescuing me from a meaningless life when I wasn't even looking for you. You weren't even a thought in my brain, and yet you came after me and found me. And now you've brought Rachel into my life to teach me how to live as your follower. Help her be patient with me as I share all my questions and doubts with her."

The tall, broad man in the blue flannel shirt pauses and then says, "Jesus, you saved my life through Jack and Rachel. I thank you so much for that."

There is a long silence. "Amen!" Rachel eventually adds with a laugh.

When Drew releases her hand, she reaches one cherry mitten into her bag and extracts a book. "Since Bibles sound like they're rather scarce around your house," she says, "I want you to have mine. I've got four or five others back at my parents' place."

"Seriously?" Drew says, looking very surprised. "Are you sure?"

"I haven't been so sure about anything in a long time," Rachel replies with a smile that adjusts the ginger stars on her cheeks.

Drew takes the Bible from her and places it carefully into his backpack. Then he looks down at Rachel and asks, "Can I give you a hug before I go? If you don't want one, that's ok. Just thought I would ask."

"Sure," Rachel replies with a shrug as her heart skips a beat.

Drew takes the young woman in the white coat into his arms and envelopes her in a hug. For a moment, the outside world ceases to exist for Rachel. She feels an unfamiliar tingle travel up her spine, and she feels like weeping.

After a long embrace, Drew pulls away and, without a word, climbs into his green turtle—as Rachel thinks of the boxy car—and drives away.

As the taillights of the rectangular station wagon fade into the distance, Rachel looks up into the night sky and says, "Well, Lord, I can't wait to see what plans you have up your sleeve. I really like this man, but as you know so well, I'm afraid to like anyone too much. Please guide my steps in this... friendship and help me not to expect too much. I submit myself to your will with Drew. Help me to always trust you that you are the One who gives me every good and perfect gift."

While Rachel is gazing up into the dark vault above, large white stars begin drifting down toward her, floating on the blackness of the night. As the fluffy flakes alight on her hair and face, she smiles and raises her arms into the air.

"Thank you for this day, Father!" she exclaims as she rises on her toes and reaches toward the heavens above. "You know how badly I needed encouragement, to know that I was seen by someone. How amazing it is, Jesus, to be reminded that I'm never alone because you're always with me!"

CHAPTER 12

Stewart in the Blizzard

Stewart awakens to a loud howling that he initially mistakes as the cry of a timber wolf. His watch tells him that it is mid-morning, so why is it so dark in the cabin?

He sits up and gropes around for his glasses on the rough-hewn nightstand. When he locates them, he perches them on his aquiline nose and peers through the gloom at the front wall of the cabin. The Cyclops eye is no longer open. A thick lid of snow has closed it completely. Stewart soon realizes that the howling sound he hears is generated by the wind whipping around the small structure.

He crawls out of his warm cocoon, thinking again of Admiral Byrd at the bottom of the world. Immediately, he is assaulted by the biting cold that invaded the one-room cabin after the protective garrison of warmth abandoned its post hours ago.

Stewart resuscitates the fire by adding pieces of dry bark and blowing on the dying embers that have survived beneath the ashes. When a flame appears, he adds more kindling and eventually several small logs. Before long, fingers of warmth reach out from the stony mouth of the fireplace and reclaim the ground that had been lost to the frigid air. Stewart consumes a quick breakfast and then retreats again to his sleeping bag.

He spends hours in the Field Manual. The last thing he reads about is the account of Elijah squaring off against all the prophets of Baal at Mt. Carmel. *How difficult for the lone prophet of God to be so outnumbered,* Stewart empathizes. *How good that God protected him from all his enemies when he was so alone.* Stewart has not forgotten that feeling alone and outnumbered is a way of life for him.

Drowsy from the warmth of his sleeping bag and the revitalized fire, Stewart lays his Bible on his chest. He stares up into the shadows of the vaulted ceiling and remembers. Eventually, his heavy eyelids close...

He is in high school, a place of anxiety and torture. He is in Algebra class with Mr. Moyer. The third-hour class begins poorly when Stewart rushes into the crowded classroom thirty seconds after the bell has rung. He is late because Billy Reisch—the boy whose father infamously is the town's pipeline for the distribution of marijuana and miscellaneous other drugs—had accosted him in the bathroom.

Stewart's familiar nemesis, who is built like a fire hydrant, had grabbed his glasses and thrown them into a urinal. Then, with a wicked sneer on his pimply face, the bully had said, "You're nothin' but a fag, Olson. My sixth-grade sister could beat you up with one hand tied behind her back."

When Stewart rushes into Algebra class after thoroughly washing his glasses, he is not only late but emotionally shaken. Tragically, as seems to so often happen to those who are condemned to a life of public shame, insult is soon added to injury: Stewart does not realize that he had failed to zip up his pants before leaving the bathroom. Eagle eyes in the classroom that are always scrutinizing him for anything that can be publicly exposed for the purpose of scathing humiliation quickly zero in on his gaffe and call it to the attention of everyone in the room.

The familiar sound of derisive laughter, shaming comments, and the terrible pointing of fingers thunder over him like an avalanche. An equally familiar heat rushes into his cheeks and begins to throb in his ears as he stumbles his way to an unoccupied desk in the back of the room. Invisibility is his only ally in the world of criticism and humiliation. To be seen is dangerous.

Stewart throws himself into the chair and attempts to hide behind his backpack. He zips up his pants as covertly as possible.

Don't be seen, a voice hisses in his head. *Die*, is the next message he hears.

Stewart's tense body is just beginning to relax when Mr. Moyer calls him up to the chalkboard to present his step-by-step solution to a problem only he had gotten right on Wednesday's quiz.

Kind old Mr. Moyer—always attempting to build his student's fragile esteem in the eyes of his peers; foolish old Mr. Moyer unwittingly exposing him to the possibility of more public shame. Good intentions fraught with massive danger. Despite Stewart's near-panic-attack-level of anxiety, a fragile hope of redemption rises within him as he leaves the safety of his fortress in the back of the room and makes his way toward the front lines.

As he walks down the aisle between the desks, he sees the angelic face of Faith Tverberg turn back to look at him from the front row.

Stewart's heart is immediately awash with love. Ah, here is the intelligent and beautiful girl he has entertained a secret affection for since the sixth grade when they completed a science project together. Here is his beloved Juliet, who has inhabited his fantasies for the past four years. How many times has he saved her from the jaws of a lion or the attacks of evil men? Too many to count. Maybe this is the day he will finally confess his concealed love to the woman who has been the single illumination in his darkness.

Stewart is so captivated by Faith's glossy brown hair and pixie nose that he does not see the foot slither like a serpent into the aisle in front of him.

His right foot strikes the premeditated obstacle, and he lurches forward. Unable to right himself, he loses control of his flailing body and falls forward toward a face plant on the unyielding floor. Instinctively, he reaches out for something to break his fall. The only thing his grasping fingers find is something soft and glossy. He hears a loud scream even before he hits the floor.

Stewart opens his eyes and finds himself staring up at the cruel fluorescent lights and Faith Tverberg's face. Her hair, a moment earlier as beautiful as that of a princess, is now in total disarray. Still on his back, Stewart holds up his hand and sees two glossy, brown hair extensions dangling in the air. Against his better judgment, his eyes travel to the angel's face, and he observes that the seraphic countenance has morphed into something much less heavenly.

Wordlessly, the girl's face screams the shame that accompanies total humiliation. Stewart knows the feeling like he knows the back of his hand.

There is something else—it radiates from the windows that open to Faith's beautiful soul. The eyes of his beloved are scalding him with a malevolence he has never witnessed on the fine-featured face. Previously, he would never have imagined that the light of his life was capable of such an annihilating glare. Stewart's extensive fantasy world constructed entirely around Faith Tverberg over a period of four years wobbles for a few seconds, then comes crashing down in a moment. The collapse is epic.

Stewart pushes himself up onto wobbly knees, keeping his gaze fixed on the floor. It is strangely intriguing to him that he has never noticed that the tiles beneath his feet are actually a shade of brown, not the dark green he always thought they were. They are the brown of dead leaves before they rot into compost. A vision passes before his eyes that he is a four-legged animal, not a human being.

Out of the tops of his eyes, he sees the faces of those around him. They are laughing with utter abandon. Incredibly, some of his peers are pointing at him again.

He dares to lift his eyes a few degrees and watches Randy Hickman open his mouth and yell something from between his barbed wire braces. The contortions of his face communicate to Stewart that the message is meant to destroy him. Oddly, he cannot hear what Randy is shouting because there is something wrong with his ears. All the noise in the room is muted as if coming from a great distance.

Worst of all, he feels very small, as if his position on his knees is his proper height in relation to his classmates. Everyone else is so big. They are higher—more than him. He is far less than them. They are human, and he is the animal in his vision.

Eventually, after what feels like an eternity, Stewart raises his eyes with supreme effort. They are heavy, like boulders of lead. He registers Faith's despising visage one last time—just long enough to memorize its contorted features for a lifetime. He knows he will never look into her face again

He labors to his feet like a fighter in the ring trying to shake off a devastating uppercut. He feels unsteady...crooked, somehow. Destroyed by the events of the last five minutes, he stands unmoving, naked in the middle of an ignominious no-man's-land, equally unable to move toward the chalkboard or back to his desk. Nowhere is safe.

He thinks he hears Mr. Moyer's gentle voice saying something to him from a hundred yards away. He cannot discern the words.

He stands unmoving in the middle of the mobbish gauntlet for a long time. Slowly, like ice-cold mercury in his veins, two sensations creep through his crooked body. First, he feels an ocean of rage and hatred surge up against the breakwater of his forehead. He is vaguely aware that he hates everyone in the room. He hates everyone in the school. He hates everyone in the world. But he hates himself even more. He must die since he cannot kill them all as much as he would like to in the moment.

The second thing he senses is a weird disease that has afflicted his face. It feels like the onset of horrible, disfiguring leprosy. Like a macabre horde, it travels through his whole body, invading even his interior self, until he is engulfed by the deadly sickness. He feels monstrous, grotesque. Franken-stein-esque. Worse than that, he feels alien. A seductive voice in his head—it might be the sweet voice of Faith Tverberg, now garbled with rage—convinces him that he does not belong to the human species.

What is the word he learned in ninth grade English class for the talented and gifted students? *Transmogrification*. Yes, he has been transmogrified into a horrific creature, worse than a Halloween hunchback—the reverse story of the Beauty and the Beast. Unhuman. Unloved. Unwanted. Far outside the fellowship of every other normal high school student in the universe.

A strange stiffness possesses his grotesque, accursed body like the dark spell of a witch. He is the Tin Man. He is Pinocchio. He is a wooden soldier. He is a machine.

Without willing it—his brain is not accessible in the disembodied place of the moment—he turns mechanically and staggers away from the soon-to-be legendary site of Stewart Olson's "outing" as an animal. As he nears the door with lurching, uneven steps, the distant laughter, and the castrating humiliation slowly fade from his conscious awareness.

By the time he finds himself in the hallway, the transformation is complete: He is a walking statue. He is beyond feeling, hearing, and hope. He has ceased to exist on the inside. Now he must die on the outside as well. Yes, die...

Stewart is awakened by the howling derision of his classmates that suddenly accosts his ears at full volume. His eyes open slowly. He does not know where he is. At first, he fears that he is lying on the floor in Mr. Moyer's Algebra class back in Two Harbors. A fleeting image of Faith Tverberg's face rushes past his mind's eye.

Mercifully, he comes back from the long hallway of the past. He is alone in the Hiding Place. The howling is the blizzard wind whipping the isolated cabin like an enraged equestrian whipping his steed. Yes, like him, the cabin is a beast to be beaten.

He reclines in the encroaching gloom of the late afternoon for a long time, staring up at the exposed beams of the ceiling. His brain tells him that if he were capable of emotions, he would be weeping at this moment.

Eventually, Stewart unzips his sleeping bag and immediately encounters the cold air that has reclaimed the room. But he does not feel the frigid temperature. After all, he is wooden.

For the first time in a long time, he is the android again, the living-dead robot with the human-like face. In that moment, it strikes Stewart why Admiral Byrd was able to withstand the cold and loneliness of the isolated Antarctic shack.

He, too, was dead.

Stewart gets up and walks as if in a trance to the far side of the fireplace. Getting down on his knees, he focuses on a floorboard—the floorboard. Wooden fingers clutch the end of a beckoning board that is raised a half inch above its peers. The fingers pull hard on it. It yields to the unhuman digits with a screeching cry.

He gazes numbly into the dark cavity beneath the displaced board. Then his hand reaches into the darkness and gropes around for the object of his search. It does not take long for him to locate it. His groping fingers touch the bitterly cold steel. 4140 ordnance steel. The feel of death.

Slowly, as if in slow motion, he extracts the twelve-gauge shotgun from its resting place of seven years. He holds the firearm at arm's length and examines it closely.

He knows the gun well. It is an old acquaintance. He knows the two long, ruthless barrels with their vacuous black eyes, the uncompromising stubby triggers, the cherry-wood stock. It has a name: Deliverance. After the loss of Faith Tverberg in his inner fantasy world, the shotgun became his new comforter and friend. It promised him escape from unrelenting pain—even as recently as last summer.

He gets up from the floor and retreats to the wooden table. He sits down in the small, lonely chair. He holds *Deliverance* in his hands. He runs his fingers over the blue-metal barrels and the smooth wooden stock. As the shroud of darkness begins to descend over the room already darkened by the thick lid over the Cyclop's eye, the man's woodenness fights to maintain mastery over him.

Inside his head, he hears the increasingly loud lyrics of hundreds of old songs—many of them heavy metal tunes he listened to as a teenager while alone in his bedroom. They speak of his irreparable deficiencies and chant about his abandonment by the despicable human race. They sing of his banishment to an island of utter aloneness reserved for misfit humans. The cold and dark inside of him grow until they are more pronounced than the cold and dark outside of him. The wind screams even more loudly, if possible, against the cabin, cruel kin to the screaming voices inside his heart and brain.

He knows the darkness of this moment better than he knows any human on the face of the earth. On more occasions than he wants to remember, he has gazed into the two dark eyes that mock him and demand that he rid humanity of the blemish known as Stewart. Feeling driven to it, he stares into the depths of the two eyes once again, teetering on the edge of a precipice.

At that moment, another voice, totally unsummoned and unexpected, speaks a different message to his heart. It appears within Stewart like a cheerful melody inserted into a cruelly dark song. It is not entirely novel to the ears of his heart but extremely rare. Contrary to the hateful voices shouting the harsh lyrics in his head, this voice is a bright motif mingling with the chaotic cacophony like a sparrow chirping in a hurricane.

The beautiful motif grows louder and louder until it sounds like a wood thrush singing in the forest as the sun rises. Eventually, it begins to eclipse the darker voices that only minutes earlier had threatened to destroy him.

A while longer, and the soothing motif is all that Stewart hears in his head. Soon, it is not merely the consoling notes of a beautiful melody. Now, he hears the lyrics as well. Words from Zephaniah 3:17 roll through him like a gentle stream of water in the desert: "*The LORD your God is in your midst, a mighty one who will save; He will rejoice over you with gladness; He will quiet you by his love; He will exult over you with loud singing.*"

"I have a name," the lonely man mumbles aloud. "I am not a beast. I am not a wooden soldier. I am Stewart."

The lone inhabitant of the cabin unceremoniously releases his grip on Deliverance, and the cold weapon teeters away from him and then falls. It hits the wooden floor with a dull thud. Stewart rises to his feet, energized by the presence of his new Deliverer, who has been relentlessly rewriting, over the last three years, not only his past but also his future.

Something resembling an invisible clay mummy case that has entombed him most of his life fractures then breaks apart. It falls away from his body and crashes onto the floor, burying old *Deliverance* beneath its shards.

Well beyond the seeing of other human eyes but seen by the eyes of the true Deliverer and His angels, the wooden monster who has been reminded again of his identity in Jesus raises one arm tentatively toward the ceiling and prays to feel something, anything: Joy, sadness, peace, grief—even anger.

Minutes passes.

He feels nothing.

In the end, Stewart sighs quietly and sits back down on the solitary wooden chair beside the lone wooden table. Fleetingly, his heart had been delivered from darkness and had glimpsed the light, but he is not yet capable of abiding in that place. The die of the trajectory is cast in a hopeful direction, but the movement forward seems as slow as the waters of the frozen stream outside the cabin.

Stewart eats a light supper that night since he has little interest in food. The ferocious tempest outside begins to die just before sunset. Before the light is totally swallowed by the voracious night, he opens the door of the cabin and looks outside. As he expects, a solid drift of compacted snow stands between him and the outside world like the wall of a keep.

What he did not anticipate is that the white wall rises above the top of the door frame affording no view of the landscape or the sky. When he examines the solitary eye, he finds that it, too, is covered from top to bottom. He is effectively entombed in the cabin. Never in eight years has he ever encountered such a blizzard. But he is not worried. At least not yet. He will simply have to find a way to dig himself out.

Later that night, as he is falling asleep, Stewart imagines he is with Admiral Byrd standing outside the 12x9 shack that is buried in the Antarctic ice and snow. The miles and miles of interminable white prairie surrounding their meteorological station are interrupted only by hidden crevasses crusted over with thin layers of drifted snow. The sun never rises this time of the year in the Antarctic. It is an eternal night.

Recalling Admiral Byrd's experience in the shack, Stewart's only concern as he drifts into full unconsciousness is that the Antarctic winds have blown snow into his chimney. It will only be a matter of time until he is overcome by carbon monoxide poisoning. He might even succumb to the odorless fumes.

A noise in his dream awakens him in the middle of the night. He thinks he hears the growl of a Peugeot tractor with its clanking treads far off on the distant ice fields. He sits up in his narrow bed and scans the dark room. For a moment, he thinks he is Admiral Byrd at the Antarctic weather station. But something is wrong: there is no ice lining the inside walls of his meteorological shack. He knows because he runs his fingers over the log walls.

Since he was a boy, he developed and refined the ability to be someone else since it rarely was advisable or rewarding to be himself. For nearly a year, when he was nine, he was Tarzan of the Apes swinging through the trees of Africa in Edgar Rice Burroughs' books. For a summer, he was Danny Saunders, the young Hasidic Jew with a photographic memory in Chaim Potok's book, *The Chosen*. For a season, he became Pip in *Great Expectations* living with Miss Havisham, hoping to attract the attention of the beautiful Estella, who looked a lot like Faith Tverberg. In his version of the book, the unattainable young woman eventually succumbed to his romantic overtures.

His most exciting escape from being Stewart, however, was when he became Claes, the humble boy-apprentice who evolved into Nicholas de Fleury, the intelligent, wealthy, and famous entrepreneur, banker, and explorer in Dorothy Dunnett's series set in the 15th century. Through Nicholas, Stewart traveled all over the known world, from Bruges to Venice, from Trebizond to Cyprus, from Lisbon to the deserts of Timbuktu, from Egypt to Scotland, from Iceland to Venice.

Stewart-become-Nicholas was a genius who could master any language on the face of the earth within a month's time, woo any woman with his manly physique and passably good looks, win the approbation of any child with his ability to invent mesmerizing toys and make money grow on trees wherever he went. Yes, gold, women, and adventure were all in a day's work for this version of Stewart.

So, it is that Stewart initially finds it difficult to orient himself to place and person in the dark cabin.

When he finally does remember who he is and where he is, he lies back down on his sleeping bag and stares into the impenetrable darkness. Only the faint glow of a few remaining embers provides a ghost of light in the cabin.

He lies there for a long time without moving. The snow-packed tomb is soundless. He is totally alone. But aloneness has never been a nemesis to him. Aloneness has always been synonymous with safety for Stewart, just as his ability to lose himself in the characters of Tarzan, Admiral Byrd, and Nicholas, among others, has been much safer than being Stewart—much more exciting as well.

But something unusual occurs this night, something unprecedented. His aloneness gives birth to a sensation he has never felt before: It feels like what loneliness might feel like if he were capable of longing for another human being.

"What is this, Jesus?" Stewart mumbles into the darkness of the cabin. "What do I feel?"

He pauses and then says haltingly, "I need someone." The word "need" has not crossed his lips since he was, what, four years old? Maybe never. It feels related to his cry for help in the Cave of Dread and his prayer earlier that night in the Hiding Place.

In that moment, wax melts and flows out of the ears of his heart. He hears the voices of people. At first, he hears the voices at a distance, as if from the bottom of an ocean trench. Eventually, one voice stands out from the others, and he can hear what it is saying.

"Stewart, you must come out of your hiding place, and you must come out now!" he hears Miriam, the prophetess, insist. "How can you love others if you must forever protect yourself?" she asks. "The times are dark, and you have been called. Open the door and come out."

Then he hears Jack and Rachel defending him after Armando bullied him. Such a defense is unprecedented in his lifetime. Rachel says, "If anywhere in the universe is going to be safe, it should be here in our group!"

He also hears Jack's excited voice with its encouraging affirmations after he, Stewart, had discovered the journal in the cave.

Stewart is not aware of it, but when he falls back asleep that night, a whisper of a smile is on his face. Only a whisper, but it is a candle flickering in the darkness.

CHAPTER 13

Tel Aviv to Jerusalem

Outside the airport, the party of five climbs into a waiting vehicle that is smaller than a limousine but has seats facing each other in the back. As they pull away from the curb with Daniel at the wheel, Kameel comments to Aly and Moussa, "I usually take a taxi called a sherut from Tel Aviv to Jerusalem. It's always a Mercedes, believe it or not. It costs me about 250 shekels, and the Arab driver typically drives worse than I do. I've seen my life flash before my eyes many times on the road between here and the city of David. It's only a one-hour journey, but it feels like the longest ride of my life," he comments with a laugh. "Today should be safer with Daniel driving."

Daniel glances over his shoulder at the sound of his name and says, "All of you might be relieved to know," he says in his accented voice, "that it is usually much safer to drive in Israel than in the United States. Fewer people die per capita here than back in America."

David looks at Aly and then at Moussa. "Thailand is one of the most dangerous places in the world to drive, yes?" the Israeli asks. "I've tried to understand why this is so. My only uneducated guess is that the Buddhists don't worry if they die on the highway because they believe they will be reincarnated anyway."

Aly laughs and says, "Yes, the roads are dangerous back home. There are too many head-on collisions because people pass all the time when other cars are approaching. The unspoken etiquette is that the oncoming car will steer over onto the shoulder for them. One of our uncles and several cousins were killed on the roads in Thailand over the last ten years. All of them were on motorbikes. Saudi Arabia, where we lived for a few years, isn't much safer for driving."

Daniel does not turn his head away from the road as he warns, "Just be careful, Aliyah, when you mention Saudi Arabia in this country. You will arouse suspicion quickly if the wrong person hears you."

"Of course," Aly says. "Kameel has also admonished us about this. I'll try to be very careful about sensitive topics and dangerous words."

Kameel glances over at Moussa and observes, "You certainly are quiet, my brother. Is anything bothering you?"

Moussa sighs and rubs his eyes. "No. Yes," he replies. He does not lift his head from its comfortable position on the headrest of the car as his eyes travel over to David. "Your father is a frightening man," he observes matter-of-factly.

The young Israeli shakes his head and looks sympathetically at the man with citizenship in three countries, four if one counts his new citizenship in heaven. "My father as a father has always been intimidating," David confides. "My father as Colonel Abramovich, member of Beth Shin, is downright terrifying. Growing up, I remember hearing stories about men having heart attacks and strokes when my father interrogated them hour after hour. I'm not certain the stories are true, but they make good stuff for legends."

Moussa closes his eyes and soon drifts into a shallow sleep. He hears the voices of his sister and his three new brothers murmuring in the background. He listens to the steady hum of the tires on the road and feels the car bounce and roll. He sees his father's disappointed face and then watches as another face slowly superimposes itself over the previous one. It is the face of Jesus. His Savior and friend is smiling. He is also speaking to him. Moussa strains to hear the words. In the end, he makes out only one phrase: "Do not be afraid of what lies before you." There is nothing else.

Moussa awakens when the vehicle comes to a stop. He opens his eyes in the waning light of the late afternoon and looks out the window of the car. They are parked in a driveway in front of a long, multi-storied building constructed of tawny limestone. The double-door entrance to the large structure is directly in front of him, thirty feet away at the end of a broad stone sidewalk.

Rainbowing away from the entryway are a series of running arches. The arches eventually run into bookend sections of the large structure that partially jut out from the rest of the building like huge blocks. Moussa does not recognize the building, of course, but since Kameel had told them earlier where they would be staying, he knows that he is looking at the King David Hotel in the new city sector of Jerusalem.

The motley group of four men and one woman climb out of the car. The luggage of Aly, Mahmoud, and Kameel is quickly retrieved by two bellhops who scurry into the hotel ahead of them. A very deferential valet takes the keys to the car from Daniel, who still carries his Uzi over his shoulder. The five travelers—three from Atlanta and two from nearby Tel Aviv—follow the bellhops through the arched entryway. Golden letters above the double doors read, "KING DAVID HOTEL." Hebrew letters on the right side of the doorway also, presumably, identify the name of the structure.

David pushes his sunglasses back up on the black wave that is his hair as he ushers his guests into the impressive lobby. "Welcome to the King David," he announces, "one of the most beautiful, and certainly most unique, five-star hotels in all the land. Contrary to what many assume, it was not built by Israelis," he explains, "but by the British who occupied the country up until 1948 when the state of Israel came into existence.

"As you can see here in the front desk area, the lobby boasts a theme reminiscent of the architecture of the Second Temple period in the first century AD when King Herod constructed the house of God. If you look closely, you will also notice Assyrian, Hittite, Phoenician, and even several Muslim themes. The exterior looks distinctly European—just as it should since it was designed by a Swiss architect."

David nods his head toward the other end of the room and says, "If you examine the walls of the lobby over there, you'll discover the signatures of more than a half dozen American presidents as well as heads of state from other countries who stayed at the King David over the last eighty-five years. Some Hollywood stars have also left their signatures on the walls. Later, I'll show you the walkway of fame where VIPs like Winston Churchill and Nelson Mandela have signed their names."

David pauses by the front desk and says to the Ahmed siblings, "Feel free to look around while Daniel, Kameel, and I get you checked in."

Moussa and Aly drift through the lobby and into the adjacent lounge area. As they walk, they scan the sights around them with admiring eyes. They gaze at the stone floor with its Persian rugs, the impressive stone pillars that ascend to the twenty-foot-high ceiling with its ornate decorations, and the rich collection of chairs and couches that populate the sitting area.

Through the huge floor-to-ceiling arched windows in the back of the hotel, they see a beautiful garden area replete with tennis courts and a large rectangular pool with bright azure waters. The pool is surrounded by a small village of umbrellas that look like oversized square wafers. In the distance, beyond a broad valley, they glimpse the western wall of the Old City of Jerusalem. The setting sun is painting the limestone blocks a deep shade of amber. A stand of trees prevents Aly and Moussa from seeing more of the ancient wall.

Five minutes later, Kameel and the two Israelis join the Ahmed siblings by the tall windows, where they are still observing the amazing view behind the hotel. David leads the small party out of the lounge area and onto the elevator. Exiting on the fourth floor, they walk down the elegant hallway toward their room. A bellhop follows them, pushing a wheeled cart with their luggage.

"I made reservations several weeks ago, so I had no problem securing an excellent room with a superior view of the Old City," David announces in a voice full of anticipation. "I'm confident you will find it a delightful place to stay while you're in Israel. It's a Duplex room—it has two levels—with two bedrooms, a Jacuzzi, and a walk-in closet."

When the Ahmed siblings enter the room, Aly is immediately impressed by the rich mahogany wood tastefully incorporated into the room and the plush carpet complemented by distinctive accent rugs. What she finds most impressive, however, is the small veranda that affords a spectacular view of the pool below them and the Old City of Jerusalem in the distance.

"It's absolutely beautiful," Aly remarks as she glances at David, her eyes large with excitement. "We will certainly enjoy our stay. Our time here will be unforgettable!"

David smiles warmly at Aly while Daniel—ever the cautious one—checks the closets and the showers for uninvited guests. Kameel is already testing out the king-sized bed upstairs.

"You are close to hell here," David comments offhandedly to Aly.

"What?" the young Saudi-Thai woman asks, raising her eyebrows. "Excuse me?"

"I said you're close to hell here," the young Israeli repeats with a straight face. A moment later, his face breaks into a smile, and he laughs.

"Beyond that stand of trees out there off to your right," David says, pointing out the veranda window, "is a deep valley where people in Jesus' day deposited their garbage. Back then, the valley was always burning, the rabbis say. Many centuries before Jesus, it was the idolatrous site where the Canaanites sacrificed their children to their god, Molech. Jesus and his contemporaries referred to the valley as Gehenna, the place of fire and burning. In other words, 'hell.' So, as I said, you are close to hell here, Aly."

Aly smiles and looks with admiring eyes at the young Israeli man who is full of energy and appears to always have a mischievous twinkle in his eye.

Moussa, meanwhile, is quiet but not due to fatigue. Ever since the holy visitation at the motel almost a month ago, he has been changing. He is becoming much less focused on the outside world of sight and much more focused on the inside spiritual world. He has been memorizing Scripture whenever he is able to do so and talking to Jesus whenever he is not memorizing scripture. Even at this very moment, he is praying for an opportunity to share his faith at the apologetics conference.

He finds the hotel room comfortable, but unlike his sister, he does not value it beyond a place to sleep. Jesus has delivered him from great darkness in radical fashion and forgiven all his heinous sins, so how can he not render complete and radical devotion to his savior? He is, after all, familiar with being radical—just in a different, darker way. Now that he sees life through the eyes of Jesus, he is increasingly being radicalized by love.

By the time David and Daniel escort their three guests down to the King's Garden restaurant, it is dark. Everyone is still dressed in the same clothes they were wearing when they arrived at the hotel except Aly, who has changed into something a bit warmer for the cool evening air. Daniel is still in his military fatigues sans the Uzi which he left in the room. He has decided that he does not need to tote his larger weapon down to supper. In lieu of the Uzi, he is carrying his Glock 17—not exactly standard issue, but his personal favorite handgun.

The restaurant is located on a terrace overlooking the backyard of the hotel that boasts lush grass, spindly palm trees, and a small forest of hardwood trees behind the pool. Aly cannot help but think that she is looking out on a smaller version of the Garden of Eden.

The layout of the night lighting has obviously been carefully planned and wonderfully executed. Celestial illumination pushes back the darkness, bathing everything, including the deep blue pool water as well as the verdant green of the lawn and the trees. The wafer umbrellas that Aly had seen earlier from the balcony outside her room have been collapsed for the night and stand like slender sentinels around the pool.

As the rest of the small party sits down at a table next to the stone wall that runs along the edge of the elevated terrace, Aly remains standing and observes everything around her. The atmosphere of the night feels magical to her. She does not know it at the moment, of course, but she will fondly remember this evening for the rest of her life.

"What a beautiful view of the garden!" Aly exclaims as she walks over to the terrace wall and looks out over the backyard of the hotel. "This is much better than Gehenna," she says, glancing over at David with a knowing smile.

After memorizing the panorama stretching out before her delighted eyes, Aly turns toward the table where the four men are sitting and walks over to her chair. Just before she reaches it, David springs up from his seat and pulls her chair out. After she seats herself with a nod of gratitude to Colonel Abramovich's son, he slides her gently up to the round table.

Once situated, Aly smiles at David and says, "I can't remember the last time someone treated me like a princess."

The young Israeli with the clean-shaven face and the sunglasses still sitting atop his thick, wavy hair looks down at her and replies, "I can't imagine why not. I've met queens at this very same veranda who were less beautiful than you."

Speechless, Aly blushes and glances over at her brother. Moussa smiles and says, "When you heard we were staying at the King David Hotel, my sister, you never imagined that King David himself would be attending to you."

Everyone at the table laughs as David returns to his chair across from Aly.

A moment later, a server dressed in what appears to be priestly garb right out of the Old Testament approaches them and greets them with a bow. Then, after lighting the seven candles of the large golden menorah that dominates the middle of their table, he bows again and departs.

A moment later, from somewhere on the veranda near the arched windows, live music begins to play. Aly hears a rich, haunting melody played by several violins and a cello. The low buzz generated by the voices of sixty other diners mingles with the notes of the instruments and creates what sounds like quiet background percussion.

Daniel clears his throat and says, "Believe it or not, being the son of the esteemed but challenging personality known as Moshe Abramovich has its advantages. David has instant access to opportunities and places the rest of us only dream about, like this hotel."

David folds his arms across his chest and says, "I suppose it is true that I'm finally being rewarded for all those years of surviving the presence of the iron colonel." He pauses, then qualifies his statement slightly. "Just so I don't leave you with a false impression, I do appreciate the colonel even though I would say he is an acquired taste. On most days, I wouldn't choose any father besides him. He just has always been quite...intense."

After the waiter methodically and precisely places menus on the table in front of each diner, David glances at his American guests and comments, "Speaking of the colonel, supper tonight comes at his expense for the three of you. However, I'm afraid Daniel is on his own and must settle for day-old matzo ball soup."

When the young man breaks out into infectious laughter, Daniel reaches over and slaps his friend on the back of the head, nearly dislodging his sunglasses.

"So, this is how you reward me for saving your life many times over the years," Daniel says. "Next time, I will let you die."

David continues to laugh and says, "Such a demanding bodyguard I have. I suppose I will just have to sacrifice and pay for your meal myself." He pauses and adds an afterthought. "Just keep it under four shekels."

"Four shekels!" Daniel exclaims. "I can't buy an apple with that!"

"Exactly," David replies from behind his menu.

Just when Daniel is about to throw a spoon at his friend, Kameel reveals a part of his personality Aly has not seen before. He interjects, "I'll share my supper with you, my dear friend. I have not forgotten how you helped save my life on the beach in Sharm when I was a boy—how you stood there speechless, doing nothing, watching me die. No, I will never forget that, my dear Daniel."

By this time, the three friends whose paths had crossed in Sharm el Sheik are all laughing uproariously. Aly laughs along with them in a more subdued way because she is too busy observing all the men at the table. She has never seen her professor from Atlanta so animated. *The transparency of friendship*, she thinks.

When she steals a glance at David, the young man is already gazing at her with eyes filled with mirth and mischief. Next to David, Moussa is sitting quietly in his chair, staring out toward the lighted western wall of the Old City. As has been increasingly his habit, he appears to be lost in the labyrinths of his heart.

After their meal has been ordered, prepared, served, and consumed, David licks his lips and pushes away from the table. "Thank you, Colonel!" he sighs with pleasure. "That was the best meal I've had in—years! Tender scallops, rich tahini, handmade gnocchi, delicious focaccia, tasty hummus…."

The junior Abramovich pauses and looks at his friends. "Just so you know, I don't dine like this very often, no matter what Daniel might tell you. I think you three should come to Israel more often—I would definitely be eating better."

Everyone smiles, and they toast the generosity of Moshe Abramovich.

The five young people chat amiably for the next half hour—everyone except Moussa, who still appears distracted. Aly attempts to peer over the terrace wall from her seated position but is unable to do so due to her smaller stature. Eventually, she stands up and gazes out over the pool and the lawn for the second time that evening. She has already put her sweater over her shoulders since the night air has dropped to a cool seven degrees Celsius, according to the weather app on her phone.

After several minutes, Aly turns around and leans her lower back against the terrace wall that crawls with vines. She stares at her four escorts until they finally stop talking and focus their attention on the lone woman in their midst.

"Do you realize," Aly begins in her higher-pitched melodic voice, "that we wouldn't be here tonight if it wasn't for the love of Jesus?"

"It is quite amazing," David admits with a nod as he leans back in his chair. Aly notices that his sunglasses are still resting on the top of his head. He looks mildly amused and pleased as his eyes consider her.

The more serious half of the David-Daniel Israeli duo comments, "The odds indeed must be astronomically long for two Jewish boys, one Egyptian boy, and two former Muslims from Saudi Arabia to come together under the same roof with no animosity. Only the love of Yeshua can engineer a gathering of such diverse people!"

Kameel nods his head in agreement. "Jesus came to tear down the dividing wall between the Jews and the Gentiles," he observes. "He came to bring peace where it was impossible for men and women to accomplish it in their own strength."

"Do you know what is amazing to me?" Moussa interjects quietly.

"What's that, brother?" Aly asks curiously, eager to pull her introspective brother into the outside world.

"We are in the land where Jesus made his appearance from heaven," Moussa says. "He most likely walked on the very ground that this hotel rests on and died on a hill not far from where we are sitting."

The believer in Jesus pauses and shakes his head with its thick black mane that is not that different from his Israeli counterparts. "The incarnation of Jesus is still so incredible to me that I cannot stop thinking about it," he says as he leans toward his friends with excitement brightening his face. "God becomes human so He might sympathize with our weaknesses and die for our sins! What a very strange and perfect intervention!"

There is a brief silence during which everyone around the table slowly nods their head. Eventually, David comments, "Speaking of strange and perfect interventions, Mahmoud-become-Moussa, I've never heard anything like your conversion story in all my days. Jesus appearing to a Muslim jihadist who is on a mission to murder his sister—you can't make that stuff up."

There is another silence among the small party as they contemplate the miraculous working of God. Daniel finally breaks the quiet.

"You will need to be careful during the conference," Daniel warns, always the voice of caution. "They know you're here."

Moussa sits up straight in his chair and looks over at Daniel, bemused. "Who is 'they' and how do they know I'm here?" he inquires.

Daniel answers, "'They' are the Muslim apologists coming to the conference from different parts of the world—not to mention every Muslim scholar in Israel and the West Bank—and they know you're here because someone went out of their way to inform them that you were coming. Word out of the mosques in Jerusalem is that everyone wants to meet the Muslim who saw Jesus. Some are curious and wish to question you about your encounter with the prophet. Only a few plan to stone you."

Aly pushes away from the terrace wall and stands up straight. "Who told them that Moussa was coming to the conference?" she asks the Israeli soldier. "Moussa and I didn't tell anybody except a few people we know back at the Academy, and they certainly wouldn't share that information with anybody. Did you tell anyone, Kameel?"

The Egyptian professor adjusts his big glasses and wiggles his broad nose. "No," he replies with a shake of his head, "I wouldn't jeopardize your brother's safety in any way—or yours either, Aliyah. I did tell Dr. McNeely and Dr. Windsor, of course, but I imagine they would keep that information confidential."

David gives Daniel a knowing look and then discloses to the others, "What we know is that the mole—for lack of a more appropriate term—who leaked the information about your intentions to attend the conference is connected to your academy back in America."

"What? A mole at the Academy?" Aly says in disbelief. "Who could that be?"

"We haven't been able to pinpoint a specific person," David answers.

"How is it that you know this information, and why is it important to you and Daniel?" Moussa asks.

"In Israel, information is survival for us in a world filled with enemies," David states. "Our intelligence is second to none in the world, except debatably the United States—on a good day. Maybe. It is essential that we know anything and everything that could impact our country. We heard the scuttlebutt about you from our sleeper agents in the mosques and then followed up with several other sources to discover everything we currently know."

"What area of the government did you say you work in, anyway?" Moussa inquires. "You seem to have access to a lot of information."

David pauses and glances from Kameel to Daniel and then finally back at Moussa. "I haven't said yet, but Kameel knows."

The younger Abramovich looks at the Ahmed siblings and says, "Since I trust everyone at this table—Kameel vouches for you two, Aliyah and Moussa—I will let you know that I work for Mossad, the branch of the Israeli Intelligence Community that concerns itself with foreign information relevant to the safety and integrity of this country. I am tasked with gathering, processing, and analyzing national security data. That's how I know of the sleeper agent back at your academy.

"Obviously, I'm not at the top of the ladder in the organization, but I'm halfway up," David adds. It probably doesn't hurt that I come highly recommended by Colonel Moshe Abramovich," he says with a chuckle.

"Is Moussa's life in danger?" Aly asks, shivering. She buttons up her sweater and sits back down at the table.

David takes the saltshaker, that is a replica of a Torah scroll, into his hands and examines it closely. When he finally looks up, he asks Aly, "Was your life in danger a month ago when your brother arrived in America?"

In that moment, Aly has her answer.

When her large brown eyes turn to consider Moussa, her brother must sense her concern. He says reassuringly, "At this moment, sister, I would not want to be anywhere else in the world. My prayer from the beginning has been for Jesus to take me wherever he wants me to go—as long as he goes with me—even if it means forfeiting my life in the end."

Aly sighs and says, "I know that, Moussa. That's precisely what worries me."

The young woman turns to look out over the garden behind the hotel yet again. This time, Eden's brilliance is tempered by a shadow that has suddenly fallen over the world.

CHAPTER 14

Armando and Jack: Go Time

Ten minutes after leaving the Mexican restaurant in La Puente, the ex-gangster and the young man from Colorado are parked three blocks from Sniper's house in Valinda. The world around them is very dark—possibly for more reasons than one. They have just finished praying one last time and are about to get out of Julio's Maxima when Jack sees Armando bend down and reach under the driver's seat. A moment later, his hand emerges with a small handgun.

"Insurance," Armando states gravely as he glances over at his friend.

"Whoa! Seriously, dude!" Jack exclaims. "You're not bringing that with you, are you?"

"Why not?" Armando replies with challenge in his eyes. "You know I'm licensed to carry."

"We're not here to kill," Jack insists. "We're here to bring life."

"The Walther is just in case things get out of hand," his roommate says coolly. "I will only brandish it as a last resort."

"Don't you remember what we talked about last night?" Jack asks his friend. "We're not here to rely on our own strength but on God's. Remember the verse we prayed: 'Not by might nor by power but by my Spirit, says the Lord.' Besides, we've come tonight as an act of obedience and trust, not self-preservation."

"We're here to meet with Sniper, the boss of Nuestra Familia Valinda," Armando parries. "He and his gang members are cold-blooded killers! Don't be a sheep among the wolves, Juan!"

Jack turns and looks out the passenger window. He shakes his head and bites his lower lip. Then he looks back at Armando and says, "There's one thing I didn't tell you about Jim Elliot."

Armando ejects the eight-round single stack magazine from the gun, briefly inspects it, then drives it back into the handgrip. It clicks into place, steel on steel. He looks over at Jack and raises his eyebrows, inviting his friend to share his thoughts about the missionary to the Auca Indians—if he must.

"I didn't tell you that Jim Elliot and his four friends agreed before they flew into the jungle to find the Auca Indians that if they were attacked, they wouldn't use any guns to protect themselves," Jack says.

"So, they did bring weapons," Armando comments, pressing his point.

"One handgun, I believe," Jack concedes. "But they agreed not to shoot the Indians because if they killed any of them, they reasoned that they would be responsible for sending them into eternity without a saving faith in Jesus."

Armando lays the gun in his lap and turns to look at Jack's face, that is striated with dark shadows. "So, they had a gun in their possession but didn't use it when they were attacked?" he snaps, raising his voice. "They were surrounded by Indians wielding spears, and they just stood there and did nothing to protect themselves?"

By now, the young man is yelling. He is as angry as Jack has ever seen him.

Armando is not done. "Was it Elliot who had the gun?" he yells even louder, "and he just stood there and watched the Indians drive spears through his friends' stomachs and hearts?"

Jack takes a deep breath, fighting to be patient. "As I already said," he explains quietly, "all of them agreed in advance not to harm the Aucas."

"Even if the Indians were attacking them?" Armando screams, hitting the roof of the car with his fist. "Only a coward would watch his brother being murdered!"

A realization dawns in Jack's mind just in time for him to say nothing. Instead of yelling at his friend to shut up and listen, he falls silent, hoping that Armando will experience a eureka moment.

Syko Loco, as he was once known in this neighborhood, is breathing quickly. Jack cannot see most of his friend's face in the meager light of a nearby streetlight, but a narrow band of illumination frames his fiery eyes. They are filled with hate and possibly even murderous intent.

As Jack watches and prays, the wild, enraged eyes slowly soften.

Eventually, Armando turns away from his friend, and his body slouches in the driver's seat. Jack notices that his roommate is shaking, and he feels a sudden surge of compassion flow through him for the young man who had witnessed the slaughter of his half-brother.

There is an extended silence. Armando does not say a word. He sits quietly for a long time, unmoving. Eventually, he reaches down and slides the gun back under his seat. His movements are slow, weighed down with reluctance. Then he stares out the windshield into the darkness that hangs over the neighborhood like a black shroud.

"I hate Jim Elliot," the ex-gangster finally says, breaking the silence. His voice is trembling with emotion. "I hate Stewart Olson...I hate anybody I perceive as weak. I hate all cowards! Most of all...I hate me."

Armando leans back in the driver's seat and closes his eyes. He sighs several times loudly. "If I had been Jim Elliot...I would have shot those Indians," he mumbles bitterly. "I would have shot them all because I could never allow myself to be perceived as a coward who forsakes his friends. I would have killed them all not to save my life or the lives of my friends but to preserve my rep and slaughter those detestable Aucas."

He pauses for a long time and then spits out the words, "I'm such a selfish man, Juan. I wish I could believe that I brought this gun along to protect my brother. But it wasn't altruism that motivated me."

Jack remains silent as he reaches over and rests his hand on his friend's shoulder.

Armando opens his eyes and grips the steering wheel with both hands. He looks sidelong at Jack and says, "I still haven't forgiven myself." Then he turns and stares out through the windshield again into the night.

Jack finally speaks. "You were thirteen years old that night in the alley, bro. You were just a kid. Don't you get that? You weren't even shaving yet, much less driving a car."

His friend continues to stare out into the night, so Jack adds with growing intensity, "You were outnumbered something like twelve to two, right? You were scared to death and bleeding all over the place. You thought you were going to die, Armando! You thought you would never see another day on this planet!"

Armando leans forward and drops his head on top of his hands that are still white knuckling the steering wheel.

Finally, Jack says something that penetrates his friend's stubborn self-condemnation. "Don't you remember that in the Garden of Gethsemane, Jesus and His disciples were outnumbered maybe fifty to twelve? And do you know what the disciples did in the end?"

Armando lifts his head an inch and mumbles, "They ran away."

"That's right," Jack affirms, nodding his head vigorously. They all ran away—every single one of them. We're talking grown men, not thirteen-year-old boys."

Armando sits up straight in his seat but does not look at Jack. He says, "Like cowards, they all abandoned the God of the universe, and yet...Jesus loved them."

"Exactly right, again," Jack says with growing excitement in his voice. "And later, after Jesus rose from the dead, do you remember what He did? He went out of his way to comfort Peter, the same disciple who had denied Him three times during His trial. At least one of those denials was within earshot of Jesus himself."

Jack pauses and then says, "Jesus forgave his disciples for running away from him at the hour of His death. Will you forgive your thirteen-year-old self for running away from Sniper and his gang when your brother was already dead?"

Armando finally looks over at Jack with eyes that radiate awareness. "You're right, Juan," he admits in a voice not much louder than a whisper, "I need to let go of what happened that night. I need to stop listening to the voices that accuse me of being a coward."

"Especially tonight," Jack admonishes his friend. "If you're going to share Jesus with the man who killed your brother, you need to get this figured out right now, or we'll have to abort our mission. Think about it,

Armando! You will never be able to forgive Sniper if you can't even forgive yourself. Maybe if you can have mercy on that thirteen-year-old boy, you can have mercy on the Miguel Herrera boy whose father beat him every day."

Armando looks at Jack and sighs deeply. He replies, "I thought I had forgiven Sniper, but you're right—if I can't even forgive myself, how can I ever forgive Raul's murderer?"

Jack glances out the passenger window and then back at his friend. "Several minutes ago, you said you hated everyone who appears weak. Does that mean you need to forgive others besides Sniper and yourself?"

"Like Jim Elliot and Stewart Olson?" Armando asks without hesitation. "I just met Jim yesterday, in a manner of speaking, so I don't think I need to forgive him for anything. Besides, if I'm in my rational mind, I honestly do admire him for not shooting those Indians. I was just directing my anger at Jim for not protecting his fellow missionaries when I was actually hating myself for not protecting Raul. And maybe for not being able to protect you tonight, Juan—if this whole thing goes south."

There is a long pause before Armando says, "I do need to ask forgiveness from Stewie, though—I'll call him Stewart from now on to show respect. Clearly, I can now see that I'm quick to hate anybody I perceive as weak. It's easier to hate someone else's weakness than it is to hate my own—although I'm pretty good at doing that too."

"I think Stewart would appreciate that," Jack says. "He would find you much safer if you would stop being his prosecuting attorney and instead be the defender of those who are not so much weak as they are broken beneath the crushing weight of this world."

Armando rubs his eyes and then his forehead with the fingers of both hands. “In that spirit,” he says with a deep groan, “I think it would help to think of Sniper not as Sniper but as Miguel Herrera, a creation of God who’s been broken by sin—his own but also his father’s.”

Jack nods his head. “I like that,” he says, “to see Sniper not through the eyes of this world as some gang banger loser but through God’s eyes as a broken child who needs love and compassion instead of more violence and hatred.”

“I agree,” Armando says, “but we can’t forget that he’s a dangerous man, just like those Auca Indians who killed Jim Elliot and his friends.”

“That’s true,” Jack agrees. He pauses and then says, “As an interesting aside, I read somewhere that after the Auca Indians were finally befriended,” Jack says, “they admitted that the only reason they killed the missionaries was that they came without their wives and children, meaning that they were there for war, not peace. The Indians were actually afraid and were just defending themselves against the intruders.”

The two men fall silent. They are in Ecuador, picturing the tragic encounter between the five missionaries and the Aucas that later miraculously led them to receive the gospel.

Eventually, Armando takes a deep breath and lets it out slowly. Then, he prays, “Jesus, I don’t want to see myself through my own eyes, through my earthly father’s eyes, through Satan’s eyes—through any other eyes but yours. If I don’t see myself through your eyes, I’ll see myself as a coward, a *cobarde*. I’m unforgivable, then. I’m shameful. I’m a mistake who will then see others as mistakes.”

Armando rests his head on the steering wheel and prays, “Tonight, at this exact second, I see myself through your eyes—a sinner, but a forgiven sinner loved by you. I’ve always known that in my head, but now...I’m beginning to experience it in my heart. Even if I don't see Sniper—Miguel—in a few minutes, this night has changed the way I see me, others, and you, God. I thank you, Jesus, that every day you are changing me degree by degree into the man you created me to be—into a man after your own heart."

When Armando falls silent, Jack prays, "Holy Spirit, we're all masterpieces created by you but later marred by sin. All of us. Miguel is your masterpiece, too, but ruined by sin. Make us as brave as Jim Elliot and his friends tonight. And, if possible—no, I know it's possible for you—if it's your will, keep us safe. May we be the tip of the spear tonight and not receive the tip of the spear. Amen."

When Jack is done, Armando adds one last request. "Father, prepare Miguel's heart and the hearts of any homies who are with him tonight to receive the light of the gospel of Jesus Christ that resides in these jars of clay."

Armando slaps Jack on the chest, then abruptly gets out of the car and closes the door quietly. He walks around the front of the car to where Jack is just climbing out of his seat. They both lean against the passenger door and stare up into the dark sky where a few stars can be seen, largely muted by the city lights.

Jack asks, "Okay, then, what's the plan, bro'? Do we just walk up to his front door and knock, like we're making a UPS delivery?"

"Sounds good to me, holmes," his friend replies.

"Before we go, I'm going to send a quick group text to our friends from the Academy," Jack says. "We might need all the prayer cover we can get."

It does not take long for him to complete the text since he had created the group on his phone earlier that day. His brief message reads, "Armando and I are going into enemy territory now. Please go with us in the power of the Spirit! Pray that we'll speak the right words and that the hearts of the people God brings across our path tonight will be open to His amazing love."

Jack pockets his phone, and the two Academy students walk away from the car into the dark night.

"Ready or not, it's *go-time,*" Armando announces with a grim smile.

CHAPTER 15

DREW'S GOOD NEWS IS BAD NEWS

Drew arrives at his home outside Lake Luzerne early in the morning on December 22nd, after his time with Rachel. He climbs into bed at 1:00 a.m., then wakes to his phone alarm even before the first blush of frozen scarlet kisses the brittle edge of the winter horizon. Still dressed in sweatpants and a T-shirt, he pulls Rachel's Bible from his backpack. He holds it gently in his hands for a long time, slowly running his hands over the brown leather cover and gazing at the shiny silver edge of the stacked pages. It feels precious to him.

Eventually, he opens the book as someone might open an old treasure map—carefully and with great expectation. It takes him a while, but he locates the book of John and begins to read. The words are all new to him since he has never attended a church in his life. As he reads, he experiences a strange sensation. He can only describe it as a growing appetite. He is eating the words of the book he holds in his hands and becoming hungrier as he eats. It is unlike anything he has ever experienced with other books he has read in the past. He goes on reading for hours.

Over the next several days, Drew interrupts his journey through John and Acts and Romans and the other books of the New Testament only to help with the animals in the barn and the veterinary clinic—and to text Rachel a few times. When he does eat—which is only in the morning when he rises and late at night—he consumes his meal in his bedroom while he sits at his desk devouring every verse and chapter he can from God's word.

He is surprised by the powerful emotions that sweep over him at unexpected times. One night, long after his parents retired to their bedroom, he weeps for several hours, not for sadness but for something that feels like what might be joy. He does not know for sure because he has never felt the emotion before.

Never has he been so focused. Never has he had such a clear picture of the purpose for his life. He entertains the growing thought that he has entered another world that had been completely hidden from him just weeks ago. Now he does not want to leave it for fear that he will never be able to access it again.

It is not a magical world. It is not a science fiction world. No, it is a solid world, more real than anything he has ever experienced. Inside this new world, something is awakening within him that has been asleep for twenty-four years. No, dead for twenty-four years. He slowly becomes certain of the fact that he will never sleep again.

On the second night after his rendezvous with Rachel, Drew has a dream he will never forget.

He opens his eyes and finds himself back on the prairie of despair he visited countless times in his childhood nightmares that stretches out forever in every direction. This time, something is different. He is not alone!

People of all ages are walking with him. They are striding with great purpose toward something that never appeared on the prairie when he was a child: a towering snow-capped mountain rising majestically above the surrounding flatlands. Drew immediately senses that existence is not about a circle of life with no destination, going nowhere forever. No, life is about moving toward something that will go on for an eternity.

Streams of water cascade down the mountain and form a broad, glassy river that flows through the prairie like liquid silver. A jungle of tall grass, thick bushes, and towering trees flourishes along the river. A lone lion stands by the river, watching the people as they travel toward the mountain. Drew instinctively knows that the lion is not a threat to him. He is a guardian. He is the One.

Drew awakens the next morning with a distinct feeling that the despair of his childhood nightmare has forever been supplanted by hope, joy, and presence. He is convinced that he will never be alone again.

On Christmas Eve Day, he walks the ninety feet over crunchy snow from the house to the hodgepodge complex that includes the pole barn, the greenhouse, the veterinary clinic, and his father's studio. Unlike the last time he approached his parents, he is not dreading the encounter. Today, he is brimming with confidence and joy. He has a spring in his step, and he is humming a worship song he cannot get out of his head. Emptiness has been replaced by a long-desired fullness that the rush could never replicate, and he is seeing the world in a totally new way. Talk about a paradigm shift, and not over a period of decades, but weeks—even days.

The young man enters the greenhouse and smiles at the warm, fragrant wave that rushes to meet him like an old friend. At the same time, there is something new about it all, as if he is experiencing everything around him for the first time with heightened senses. He saunters down the center aisle of the amazing structure that is the brainchild of his mother, a woman who has never been afraid to think outside the box—except about God.

He finds his parents in their customary constellation—working within five feet of each other but with their backs turned toward their mate and co-laborer. Drew very intentionally drives a proverbial flag in the sand between him and his parents and greets them with an energetic, "Good morning!" His greeting is far too cheery because both parents turn away from their work to stare at their son. His mother's look is one of disapproval, while his father's countenance conveys curiosity.

His mother is the first to speak, of course, with her typical dampening presentation. Whether she intends it or not, both her tone and her words always carry a subtle edge to them that erode their object like a corrosive chemical agent. They reduce life, discourage emotion, and constrict the expression of self.

"Who put a quarter in you?" she asks as she eyes her son suspiciously. Drew knows she is examining him for physical signs of drug use. He also knows that she can throw no stones at him since both her and his father smoke marijuana daily.

Drew had already decided before he entered the greenhouse that if he was going to sin against his parents' restrictive rules, he was going to sin boldly. "Jesus did," he replies with a smile he cannot suppress. "Jesus put a quarter in me. No, more like a trillion dollars."

His mother is caught off guard for the briefest of moments. Then she comes right back with, "A quarter only buys you one vinyl single on the jukebox, Drew. Soon the tune will end, and the world will go back to the way it was before." Her long, narrow face, framed by dishwater blonde hair that hangs down to the middle of her back, is passionless.

Drew has prepared himself for his parents' pushback, especially that of his more outspoken mother. "I know that's what you believe, Mom. But my belief in Jesus is not a dalliance. I've given my life to Him forever."

Susan Johnson levels one of her notoriously disapproving looks at her only offspring and crosses arms that are covered by a long-sleeved blue denim shirt.

"It doesn't have to be a bad thing, Mom," Drew says, countering her nonverbal critique.

"It was for me and your uncle Bud," she snaps.

"I know that," Drew says, "but that wasn't about Jesus. That was about grandpa's legalistic religion and his obsessive-compulsive mind."

"I sat in that unyielding wooden pew in my parents' provincial church for fifteen years and was forced to swallow Christian propaganda until it made me sick," his mother parries with clipped words.

"Yes," Drew replies patiently, "but that wasn't about the love of God but about grandpa's belief that you had to earn your way to heaven by being good, or even more true, by not being bad."

"The point, Drew," his mother replies sharply, "is that it turned me off to God and the church forever. I'll never submit to that controlling institution ever again."

"Good," Drew replies not disrespectfully. "I don't think you should. But like you've told me ever since I was little, 'Don't throw out the baby with the bath water.' You don't have to throw out Jesus because your father's controlling personality and his narrow, dogmatic church were a severe distortion of God's real message."

"I hate any God who's associated with my father," Susan states. "He doesn't exist for me. In fact, evolution proves that there is no God in this universe at all. It's just us, Drew."

"That's what I used to believe, too, Mom, but it just wasn't working for me," Drew says. "When Pete died, I was confronted with the flimsiness of my life philosophy—if I even had one beyond my mantra to live for the rush."

"You're young, Andrew," his mother explains. "Everyone is looking for something to fill the emptiness when they're young. Over time, you will find more solid things that will give meaning to your life beyond religious myths."

"Like what, Mom?" Drew asks. "Tell me what your purpose in life is."

For the first time, his mother does not have a ready response. She directs an indicting glare at her mute husband and then looks back at Drew.

"Well," she finally says, "for one, my job, and this greenhouse. And you, son," she adds. "You give purpose to my life."

Drew throws caution to the wind and ventures out onto thinner ice than he has ever tested before.

"Okay, Mom, your job and your son bring meaning to your life," he summarizes. "But apparently, those things are not enough to bring you joy. I've never perceived you as genuinely happy. I don't say that to criticize you, just to be honest about what I've seen over the years."

Susan stares at her son, and Drew sees passion flash in her eyes. Abruptly, the woman unfolds her arms and takes off her gloves. As she looks away from him, she mutters, "All that Jesus has done for me is rob me of my respectful son."

"Wait a minute, Mom!" Drew protests. "You don't have to go there. If I have an opinion that disagrees with yours, that doesn't mean I'm not respecting you. I don't think it has to work that way. I'm just telling you my thoughts, Mom, and my thoughts are that your purposes in life don't appear to bring you observable joy."

His mother raises her chin into the air but says nothing. Her silence only serves to further expose her husband's reticence.

"I wasn't going to mention this," Drew says, "but we're there now, so I may as well keep going." He hesitates for a moment, then says, "Both of you, Mom and Dad, have been excellent models for me when it comes to initiative, diligence, and hard work—even creativity and ingenuity. Seriously, you couldn't have done a better job in those areas. I thank you both for all those things you've taught me."

Drew pauses for a moment, then delivers words with an intrepid honesty that has not been witnessed in the Johnson family for a hundred years.

"You guys just don't know how to be emotionally close to anyone, including me."

Susan and Don Johnson glance at each other briefly, then dare to look at their accusing son.

Drew's father eventually clears his throat and finally weighs in on the unprecedentedly candid family discussion. He discloses, "I'm an introvert, and your mother's an introvert with a smidgen of extroversion. We choose to get as close to people as we want to and need to."

Drew nods his head encouragingly, excited that his father has finally shared a vulnerable thought. "I don't disagree with that at all, Dad," he replies. "I'm just saying that neither you nor Mom make a personal commitment to any relationship. You get as close to people as you need to, yes, but that level of closeness doesn't seem to involve any deep level of self-disclosure or connection."

When neither parent responds, Drew continues. "I'm not saying I'm better than you guys. In fact, I know I'm not. I just believe we would be happier as a family if we would work on building relationships instead of simply tolerating them."

Drew sighs and looks up through the transparent roof of the greenhouse at the gray skies above. "I almost think, Dad, that the way you relate to God is the way you relate to people. You claim to be an agnostic, someone who believes there might be a God but insists we can't know him and therefore can't have a personal relationship with him. When it comes to people, you seem to believe the same thing: others exist, but you can't get to know them, so why even try."

Turning to his mother, Drew says, "And you, Mom, you claim that God doesn't exist. In fact, you're angrily opposed to Him existing. That same anger gets in the way of letting people exist for you as well. Whenever I have an opinion you don't agree with, you get angry and don't want my opinion to exist, or maybe even don't want me to exist in that moment.

"Your anger also stiff-arms grandfather whenever he tries to communicate with you. It's like you won't allow him to exist in your personal space. You simply can't tolerate anyone who rocks your world, whether that be a divinity or a human. With your dad, I think your resistance is mostly about not wanting to forgive him."

Drew feels strong emotion rise in his throat. He swallows hard and says, "Atheism and agnosticism have not worked for this family, Mom and Dad. Both these positions seem to be driven by an underground desire to avoid intimacy with anyone—human or divine. And just for the record, I see that tendency toward privacy in me as well. I never commit to anything, or more accurately, to *anyone*," Drew admits.

The young man who has recently become a new creation pauses to give his parents an opportunity to respond. When they stare at him like a pair of deer in the headlights, he keeps going.

"The reason I was so empty was that I didn't commit to any relationships. Either I didn't know how to, or I didn't want to. Now, I have. I've given myself to Jesus because He first gave Himself to me."

His mother recovers her legendary edge and says in rebuttal, "How many times must I remind you that Jesus is a myth? A myth can't give itself to anyone."

"Mom," Drew says as he attempts to hold at bay the rising frustration he feels, "comments like that are anti-intellectual, and they glaringly contradict your frequent claim that you're a rationalist."

"I'm just stating things like I see them," his mother counters.

"And sometimes you might be wrong," Drew tells his mother for the first time in his life. "You've always dismissed what you don't believe without even considering it. You ridicule it instead of allowing a discussion about it.

"When you summarily state that 'Jesus is a myth' or that 'God is a delusion' or that my faith in God is just a 'hangover' that I'll sleep off and 'come to my senses' the next morning, you ridicule what you don't agree with. You don't engage the person, Mom. You just dismiss me along with what you don't believe. You practice absolute dogmatism, the very thing you claim to hate so much in grandpa. So, I'm left feeling like you don't even hear me."

Drew nods his head thoughtfully and adds, "'Dismiss' is the right word. Do you know what it feels like to be dismissed, Mom? I think you do. Your father did it to you, and now you're doing it to me and Dad."

Drew glances at his father and says, "Yes, you dismiss Dad, too. I can only imagine he feels like you don't hear him, either."

Drew's unprecedented verbal release is driven by years of imprisonment in his heart. His spoken words violate every unspoken rule that has held sway in the greenhouse for two decades.

A small miracle is occurring—a son is defying all the unspoken family rules that kill intimacy. Instead, he is daring to give his parents—who wield the power of a god and goddess to the young man—the gift of his candid emotions and thoughts. It is a gift that threatens to undo the 'cold war' that has reigned in the Johnson household for decades, no, for generations. A million dominoes representing an ancient wall of separation are quaking and on the verge of falling in the wake of Drew's honest declarations.

All that remains to be seen is how the mother will respond to this mutinous act of intimacy that represents a gross violation of the family protocol—the old code that for generations has crushed honest communication and forbidden the existence of the true self. Will she receive her son's words as a gift driven by a desire for intimacy, or will she perceive them as a personal attack reminiscent of her father's shaming annihilations?

A silence rumbling with thunderous spiritual power—it is nothing short of a clash between heaven and hell—crushes down on the adult child and his parents. It sucks all the air out of the greenhouse.

Drew finds it difficult to breathe as his mother stares at him with narrowed eyes and a clenched jaw. Even if she had slapped his face and screamed at him, she would not have communicated more loudly that her treasonous son has trespassed over a sacred emotional property line and now will receive the just punishment for his sin.

The only thing Drew's chaotic mind can formulate as his heart pounds against his chest is a single thought, *No wonder I've never spoken these words before. This is mental torture. I now understand why people keep the peace in a family system instead of risking the truth.*

After a terrible silence, during which Drew's father stares down at his waterproof boots, Suzie Johnson's gloves fall to the floor. Then she turns like a steel gate on a post and marches rigidly toward the door of the greenhouse.

Drew is momentarily paralyzed by the rare appearance of his mother's ultimate coping skill that has been so effective in disintegrating her son's resolve in the past. It is the dreaded final defense that only manifests when all others have proved ineffective. It is from hell itself, for it wreaks of separation. It is abandonment.

Initially, the son stands stock-still as he has always done in the past, watching the wretched figure retreat as he feels powerless to do anything. He has wounded his fragile, innocent mother and now must bear the punishment for his terrible crime. What a bad, selfish, destructive son he is. He must be rejected, exiled to the uninhabited outpost of shame until proper penance has been rendered. In fact, he must die.

No! Not today! This time is different. Instead of dying, the son does something he has never done before: he raises his voice at his mother's back.

"You can't just walk away like that, Mom!" he screams. A towering wave of rage surges up within him as he repeats, "You can't just walk out! I'm tired of you turning your back on me when I tell you something you don't want to hear!"

When his mother continues her retreat, Drew breaks out of his paralysis and pivots to face the older male in the greenhouse.

"Dad, aren't you going to stop her?" he cries out. Even as he appeals to his father, he knows his words are falling on deaf ears.

Don Johnson does not respond to his son's entreaty. He continues to examine his boots which must be very interesting to demand such an extended examination. In that moment, Drew understands why his mother has come to despise her husband, for he feels it as well.

In agony and torn, Drew hesitates, but not for long. He abruptly wheels away from his disengaged father. An unbearable panic replaces his anger as he breaks into a run after his retreating mother. Above the sound of pounding blood in his head, he thinks, *What am I doing? I must be crazy!*

He overtakes the retreating tin woman before she reaches the greenhouse door and turns to face her. "Mom," he cries out in a higher-pitched voice, feeling like he is seven years old again, "why are you leaving me?"

The mother, who is a foot shorter than her son, does not even look up. Instead, she sidesteps her son, trying to get past him. Her face is chiseled stone.

"I'm not going to let you leave!" Drew insists, his voice still elevated. He slides over in front of his mother to prevent her end-around run.

The young man takes a deep breath and relaxes the muscles in his neck and shoulders. "Don't you hear me, Mom?" he asks in a calmer voice that is deeper but still pleading. "I want us to talk honestly with each other, but you won't let me speak. You just want me to be convenient for you. You won't love me unless I follow the unspoken rules that protect your heart. Even today, when I challenge you, you turn your back on me. Don't you know I'm left feeling like an awful human being you can't even tolerate?"

After a long silence, Susan Johnson finally looks up at her son and meets his gaze with flashing eyes. "You just told me I'm a terrible mother," she states in a trembling voice. "Why would I stay and listen to further insults from you, of all people, the son I've shed blood, sweat, and tears for?"

"Did I say you were a terrible mother?" Drew asks incredulously.

"That's certainly what I heard!" his mother retorts.

"Well, that's not what I said," Drew insists. "Didn't you just hear me say that I want to know you, Mom, that I want to be closer to you?"

The middle-aged woman stands transfixed in the greenhouse in front of her son. She is no longer in the outside world. She is imprisoned somewhere deep inside herself. Emotion is so strong that it has taken her mind hostage.

She finds thinking ponderous, opposed by some invisible force. She cannot speak any words that invite her son closer because she feels cruelly offended by him. So, she is silent—wordless, once again, like she so often is with her husband. The only difference is that her husband is always wordless with her as well, so they stand in each other's presence with their lips double-stitched shut. So near, yet so infinitely far from each other. They might as well be living on opposite sides of the planet. They never go into the messy, forbidden place known as intimacy. Silence, though violent in its own passive way, feels safer. It is their native tongue.

In the past, her son has always conformed to the unspoken family canon. He has predictably complied with the commandment chiseled into the Johnson family stone tablet that demands that nobody, under threat of exile, is to ever venture into the emotional demilitarized zone.

The commandment's warning is, *Keep out! It insists, Don't talk! It dictates, Don't be vulnerable! It cries out, Don't feel! Don't offend! Don't need anything the other person cannot deliver!* Anger and conflict especially are to be avoided always because they necessarily communicate that its recipient is unlovable, bad, shameful.

Now Susan Johnson's son has defied the ancient commandment and violated the unspoken rule. He has brought anger and conflict—the dangerous things, the shunned things—onto her head. Therefore, he must be shunned, driven into the wilderness like the scapegoat of old.

But something else has occurred that leaves Susan Johnson at a loss: she herself has been angry outwardly. She, too, has disobeyed the high and holy rule. So, she senses some threatening thing hurtling toward her. It feels like doom. She is certain that she will be destroyed by someone else's anger or—could it be true—unbelievably, she will destroy someone with her anger. Whatever is true, she must leave. The only problem is that she cannot move, try as she might.

A shadow of thought wings over the periphery of her brain. She grabs at it with the fingers of her mind, but it eludes her. Tragically, she is left incapable of fathoming that anger and conflict—rather than being supremely dangerous and annihilating—might be the portal to intimacy. They just might expose deeper levels of her heart and so stimulate connection instead of wreaking dangerous and irreparable damage.

Something within the Johnson matriarch feels threatened, even attacked, and so she must protect herself. She feels enraged with her son, and she should be enraged with him. She must move against him somehow, must communicate to him that he is wrong or bad. She must make him sorry for what he has done to her. He must feel the same pain he has inflicted on her.

But what, in fact, has her son done that is so unforgivable?

Susan closes her eyes and shakes her head as if clearing it of a blockage. She vaguely perceives that she wants to "shoot the messenger" even if it is her son, her only offspring. The young man in front of her has fired a salvo at her, aimed at her personhood, accusing her of being bad. At least, that is how she perceives it. He is no longer her flesh and blood. He is the enemy.

Whenever such accusations are leveled at her, she must view the other person as the bad one. She cannot look inside when she feels ashamed because, terrifyingly, she might see that something is "disordered" within her, and she cannot tolerate the crushing moral weight of that. The internal prosecuting attorney would condemn her to death.

Words from the outside world have triggered a rash of thoughts in the inside world, a turbulent mingling of the rational and the irrational. The subsequent emotions that roil within her are a growing hurricane poised to unleash extensive destruction. Hurt and anger, veiled for decades, have the power, when finally released, to maim and kill.

In that moment, Susan Johnson sees at a distance—through the thick fog of her subconscious—the vague outline of four horsemen. The dread equestrians are genocide, fratricide, suicide, and, yes, even...filicide. They ride forth from a heart twisted by long-imprisoned emotions like rage, shame, and rehearsed bitterness. They gallop out like wraiths from hell in primitive response to her son's terrible offense.

The mother shakes her head once more, this time to rid it of the uninvited and terrifying glimpse of evil that resides in her heart. As she attempts to exorcize the darkness within, she hears the outside voice accost her yet again.

"Mom," Drew repeats as calmly as he can, "I'm not trying to criticize you. I'm just saying that we need to be closer as a family. In the past few days, I've felt closer to Jesus than anyone in my whole life, and it's been wonderful. I want that same closeness with you and Dad."

Susan opens her eyes and stares up at the speaker, still not able to translate the foreign language her son is speaking. She cannot shake off the feeling of being under threat. She feels an overwhelming urge to flee from the offending person, even if that person is her only child. He is the enemy. He is dangerous.

No...she is the one who is dangerous.

"Rachel—you know, the girl I met at school—has experienced the same thing," Drew continues, now in a voice increasingly energized by excitement. "She's the girl I went to visit in Connecticut a few days ago. She says that Jesus drew her close to Himself, and now she wants to be closer to her family even though—even though she has been hurt by them a lot over the years."

When his mother remains frozen and mute before him—her whole being clenched like a tightly closed fist—Drew sighs and shakes his head slowly. Then he says in a softer voice, "What I'm trying to say, Mom, is that Jesus isn't a liar or a myth. He's not a religion. He's a loving God—a real living person—who desires closeness with us. When I tasted that closeness, I finally realized what life is about. It's certainly not about 'the rush' for me anymore, but about knowing God and others and being known in return. I want us to be close, too. Does that make any sense to you, Mom?"

Drew knows his mother well enough that he discerns she is torn between fight or flight. But on this occasion, she has encountered an unfamiliar scenario: her son has blocked her usual avenue—flight. She is left with fight as the only option. But Susan does not know how to fight. She can be sarcastic and dismissive, and even silent, but she has never fought with anybody that Drew can remember. Fighting requires engagement, and a certain amount of closeness. It requires the ability to show emotions while modulating them in a socially acceptable way; and the Johnson matriarch does not know how to do any of those things simply because she never has. Neither have her parents, her grandparents, or her great-grandparents.

As Drew stares down at his mother, she looks small to him—smaller than ever before. She appears scared. He knows there will be no more words from her. He interrupted her physical flight, but he cannot prevent her emotional flight. She is present in body but unwilling or unable to be present with emotion or language. He will need to step aside so the small woman can escape. An opportunity that held so much promise for a new level of honesty in the family, tragically, has passed.

Drew is disappointed because he fears that his mother's defenses will be even more impenetrable in the future after this near run-in with intimacy. A deep sadness washes over him, and he is surprised by the tears that form in his eyes.

He takes a deep breath and surrenders. In an instant, he regresses back to his old way of being, the one where he exists without living. He steps out of his mother's way and familiarly sets his jaw. He will not permit himself to cry. He is a Johnson, after all, and Johnsons do not show emotions. They are not vulnerable. They are not seen.

To his surprise, his mother does not leave. She is actually looking at him. She is not blind—she sees the tears in his eyes. As he examines his mother's dispassionate face, Drew thinks he sees her chin quiver. He cannot be certain, of course, but it is enough for him.

Without hesitation, he steps toward his mother and embraces her. He wraps both of his arms around her instead of giving her the customary Johnson single-arm side embrace patented in Sweden three centuries earlier. He holds her for a long time. She does not resist. Neither does she hug him back. He is hugging a granite statue but hugging it, nonetheless. The old eyes of the greenhouse have never witnessed such an intimate moment.

When he finally releases his mother, he briefly informs her that he will be in Connecticut for several days and will return after Christmas. He hesitates, then leans down and kisses the woman on the forehead. Never has he been so close to his mother's face. Then he strides back to where the father statue is standing and gives him a hug as well. For good measure, he kisses him, too.

A moment later, Drew walks out of the green house, through the breezeway, and into the pole barn. He does not even glance into his father's studio as he strides past. He exits the barn and walks the ninety feet to the house to pack for his trip.

He cannot know it, of course, but as he pulls his duffle bag out from under the bed and begins to pack, his mother and father are still standing where he left them in the greenhouse. They are not flesh and blood. They are stone.

Only one person in all the universe can turn hearts of stone to flesh.

CHAPTER 16

Terror on the Beach

Emily jumps into her Super Beetle and backs out of the driveway. She accelerates rapidly down Ibis Street and blows the stop sign at Estero Boulevard. She is feeling something intense twisting around in her stomach and assumes that it is all anger. So, she is driving fast. She is not aware enough to know that there is another emotion mingling with her anger.

She is absolutely done with her father's lectures. Tonight, it was about shooting the messenger. The time before, it was about cognitive dissonance. He had explained in his holier-than-thou fashion that if there is a discrepancy between her behavioral choices and what God's Word says is morally right, she will experience a dissonance within herself, a deep tension between what she wants and what God's Word says.

She will eventually be compelled to resolve the dissonance in one of two ways. Option one is to forsake her behavior and obey God's desires for her. Option two is to choose the sinful behavior and turn her back on her faith or to engage in the exegetical gymnastics necessary to make the Bible say what she wants it to say. Either response will resolve her cognitive dissonance, the former by obedience to God and the latter by 'creative' exegesis that will justify her behaviors or by walking away from Jesus altogether. The argument is familiar to her. Wasn't it Embee who told her the same thing?

As Emily drives north toward the bridge, she slams the palm of her hand against the steering wheel and shakes her head vigorously from side to side. Natalie is right, she thinks to herself—her parents are judgmental people. It is total hypocrisy for them to accept her older brother's wife and then turn around and, in the same breath, disapprove of her partner.

A minute later, she pulls into the parking lot of her favorite liquor store and runs in to purchase the familiar "Russian water." Then she drives five minutes in very light traffic to a spot on the beach just past the pier.

She parks her Super Beetle in the public parking lot, grabs a blanket out of the trunk in front, then walks past the restrooms toward the beach that lies on the other side of a row of small palm trees and a low hedge. She is going to her favorite hangout spot that she has frequented since she was a teenager, the place where she 'serendipitously' met Jaden, her first partner. It was here, five years earlier, that her strong attraction for the attention and touch of a woman was awakened within her.

Emily has totally forgotten the dozens of times she hung out at this very same spot with her parents when she was a child. Her family would attend church Sunday morning, then bring a picnic lunch to the beach. They would build sandcastles, throw a frisbee around, read, nap, talk, and play in the surf until the late afternoon. Then they would stop at a nearby shop for ice cream before making the five-minute drive home—longer during tourist season, of course.

Emily spreads her blanket out on the sand, that is cool now that the December sun has retreated below the horizon. The gulf water rolls silkily over the darkening sand only a hundred feet away. She sits down on her blanket and stares out over the dusky scene before her.

She loves everything about the beach, especially because it is here that she learned how to forget—not just the bad memories but also the good ones that will summon her back to another lifetime and reawaken the dissonance that is so troubling.

The small waves splash brightly onto the beach and then hiss softly over the white powdered-sugar sand. Emily listens to the steady rhythm of the water, feels the gentle breeze kiss her cheeks and sees the dark shapes of pelicans playing follow-the-leader as they skim over the water in search of one last meal before retiring to their rookery for the night.

She sighs deeply as she attempts to purge her mind of every unwanted thought. Eventually, she plugs earbuds into her cell phone. She begins listening to tunes as she sips her liquid comfort.

Emily stares at the vast waters that are shrouded in deepening darkness until her eyes lose focus. She tries not to think about the past or, even more importantly, feel anything from the past. Her goal is to be totally numb—detached from herself. But the detachment is always opposed. Thus, the alcohol.

The previous six years of her life hurtle past her mind's eye like a train, boxcar after boxcar clanking by loudly, painfully, accusingly. Every rumbling and swaying car conjures up nightmares of alcohol binges, drug abuse, forgettable incidents with men, unspeakable things that still haunt her at vulnerable moments, and the depression that followed in their wake like debris from a shipwreck.

How ironic that she initially began drinking because it felt good and calmed her, but now she drinks to not feel bad. The comforter is imbibed partly to reduce the negative emotional and physical residue inflicted by the comforter itself. Ah, the insanity of addiction—a golden serpent that turns around and devours itself.

Emily never glances behind her. The vault that stores her pain, fear, and shame accumulated over recent years remains buried, totally unaddressed, and so it leaks out everywhere in the subterranean world of her life. But neither does she think about the future because then she would have to face the trade-offs she is accruing from the practice of unbridled affections.

She is left to live her life solely between the bookends of the past and future—never learning from yesterday or wisely planning for tomorrow, never owning past mistakes, and seeking the cleansing relief of repentance.

Her practice is to focus on the pleasures of the moment that make her feel good for a time and on the negative emotions she feels toward her parents—and God, and Christians, and intolerant people, and all authority that tries to tell her what to do.

Hating the intolerance of others has proven easier to stomach than focusing on the fruit of her own self-destructive choices. Perceiving a deficit in the character of others is an effective distraction from the consequences of the divorce of her own true self.

As the strong drink begins to perform its familiar function, Emily feels her body relax, and her brain slow down. The giant box cars that were rumbling and careening across her consciousness begin to fade away into the distance. She sighs deeply and closes her eyes.

Uninvited images of Embee, the Academy, and even of Jack appear in her mind like quivering mirages. She battles to silence the pesky words of her silver-haired spelunking guide because they threaten her with truth, and Emily is not dedicated to seeking truth. Rather, she is committed to suppressing it, blindly pursuing what feels good even if it comes at a cost to herself. Great cost.

In the gathering darkness, Emily watches an older woman walking a small dog by the purring surf. She cannot see the woman's face, only the solid form of her body and the trotting dog at her side. The dog...

Of all things Emily's betraying mind could think of at this moment, it dredges up the story that Sunny Livingstone told the Academy students about their two dogs. What were their names—Belle and Summer? Against her will, Emily's mind tells her that she is like Summer, the dog who ran away only to be eaten by a pack of coyotes.

Emily blinks hard and turns her head in disgust to look down the beach toward the pier, a hundred yards away. She attempts to distract herself by focusing on the lights and the downtown area—college student hangout during spring break and tourist central in the summertime. On this December night, it is much quieter. Almost dead, in fact.

She takes another sip of her liquid comfort, and her eyes water. She removes her earbuds and sets them on the blanket beside her. She listens to the gentle waves.

An unwanted parade of thoughts somehow fights its way through the gauntlet of her mind. *I didn't ask to be attracted to women, the first thought says. I didn't notice that I even had that attraction until my sophomore year of college, but I know I was born that way. What else would explain it?*

I've been told by Natalie and Jaden, and many others that my lesbian identity is as defensible as racial identity and that anyone who opposes it is a prejudiced racist and a homophobe. That makes my parents prejudiced people...

My racist parents tell me that my lesbianism is a sin, a behavior I've chosen to practice like another person chooses to practice alcoholism or gambling addiction. The temptation to desire a female is not a sin, Dad says, but to give into the temptation and practice it is sin. But I'm just loving Natalie. How can love ever be wrong?

Emily purses her lips together tightly and sets her jaw. *Who are they to tell me what's love and what isn't? It's not like they get to live my life for me! I get to live my life! It's my choice! What universal standard tells me that I can't do what I want to do?*

The young woman readjusts the severe white headband that crushes her hair. Her hands are rigid with resentment. She digs her feet deeper into the powdery sand and stares out across the waves at a single light bobbing lazily on the distant water.

My parents tell me that the Bible is the universal standard for truth. But how can I agree that the Bible is the source of truth when it tells me that who I love is wrong? After all, God is love.

Emily studied the Bible enough in her undergrad years at a small Christian University in Tennessee to know that it is clearly opposed to the practice of same-sex attraction. Even though she wants to dispute that point—and will always do so in the heat of an argument with her parents—on rare occasions, she admits to herself that the Bible is clear about God's position on homosexuality.

But those occasions are increasingly opposed in her brain by something else that is fighting for dominance.

"Tell me what I'm supposed to do," she mumbles aloud as the simmering anger within her is bellowed into bitter rage. "Yes, tell me what I'm supposed to do, God," she says to the night air that is thick with humidity and salt. "You put me in this hellish bind. You tell me not to be a lesbian, but then you create me with a strong desire to be touched by a woman! What do you expect me to do?"

Emily pauses and then announces aloud in words that are beginning to slur, "You're an unjust, judgmental God, and I hate you! I will never serve a

God who created me with an irresistible desire to disobey your commands and then threatens to send me to hell for it!"

It is then, of course, that words from her childhood crawl up from some deep recess in her suppressed memory: "Let no one say when he is tempted, 'I am being tempted by God,' for God cannot be tempted with evil, and He Himself tempts no one. But each person is tempted when he is lured and enticed by his own desire. Then desire when it has conceived gives birth to sin, and sin when it is fully grown brings forth death" (James1:13–15).

Emily feels hot tears roll down her cheeks that are cool from the December night air. "So, it's all my fault, is that it, God?" she complains bitterly. "This is all about my disordered desire, and you're off the hook?"

She clenches her fists and stares out over the dark waters of the gulf, her vision blurred by two liquids. "You're just going to tell me that I'm a condemned sinner and leave me to my own devices?" she demands with a heavy tongue. "In my humble opinion, Father of the universe, that constitutes neglect and abandonment—even abuse! I can never trust a God who abandons me! I'm going to have to abandon you—"

At that moment, just when a glimmer of awareness concerning who abandoned who slips over the sturdy defenses of Emily's consciousness, rough hands abruptly grab her from behind. In an instant, a heavy body is on top of her. Instinctively, she screams. Immediately, a large hand strikes her on the cheek.

"Shut up!" a voice growls at her. "Shut up, or you're dead!"

Her attacker's cruel, greedy hands quickly travel to places that already pulse with ancient memories of fear, powerlessness, and rage. Terror, like a massive building, collapses onto her body and mind.

She cries out again.

Another vicious blow strikes her cheek, and her head snaps back against the blanket. She struggles to maintain consciousness. Panic threatens to swallow her. She feels herself going away...leaving her body. She melts into the sand beneath her blanket.

Back at the house next to the canal, Dan rolls over in bed and puts his arm around his sleepless wife. "Joy, I feel a need to pray for our Golden Girl," he whispers in the darkness.

"That's always a good idea," his wife agrees. "I'm really worried about Emma tonight. I feel so powerless just sitting here at home when she's out there somewhere, alone and upset. We might as well pray instead of worrying ourselves to death."

A moment later, Dan prays, "Jesus, how often did I plead that you would keep my little girl, Emmie, safe when she was a child?" A sob catches in his throat, and he pauses to swallow hard. His eyes burn with suppressed tears.

"I prayed that you would protect her from illness, from being kidnapped by some random crazy man, from being sexually abused by the babysitter, from friends that would draw her away from you, and even from death in the swimming pool or from a bull shark attack in the gulf or in a car accident. But I forgot to pray that you would protect her from the desires of her own heart."

The man lying in bed with his wife does something he reserves only for his children. He begins to weep. "Oh, God!" he cries out in agony. "Do you know how hard it is to watch your child suffer and feel the helplessness of not being able to protect her?"

Joy turns her body in the bed to face her husband. She gets up on one elbow and rests her hand gently on Dan's cheek. "I know you know the answer to that question," she says in a whisper. "God watched his own son suffer for our sins. There was no greater suffering in this universe in all of history. And certainly, you know that God the father is Emma's first parent. He sees her straying heart all the time and feels the pain of her disobedience even more than we do."

Dan takes his wife's hand in his and wipes away tears with the other. "Okay, God, I'm reminded by this wonderful woman you brought into my life that you know our anguish. I'm so grateful for that because to be alone with this pain would be more than I could endure. I honestly think I would turn to alcohol like my uncles and aunts did. So, please forgive me for the times I've judged them—because I'd be making the same choice they did if it weren't for you. For all I know, I might be making the same choices Emma is making were it not for you living in me."

Dan pauses in the darkness and kisses the back of his wife's hand. "Jesus, my prayer for Emma tonight is a bit different than in the past. I still pray with all my heart that you protect her from death and debilitating illness. But I also pray, as hard as it is to speak the words, that you would allow whatever is needed to get her attention. Even if it is—painful. Even if it takes her way out of her comfort zone. Even if...it is frightening. Open her eyes to see the paths she is on that aren't yours, the ones that belong to the darkness, the ones that I fear will destroy her in the end."

Dan sighs and says, "Is it right for me to even pray such a thing, Jesus? Am I being a bad father for giving you a green light on pain for my own flesh and blood?"

When Dan falls silent, Joy adds, "But Lord, please give her only as much as is needed to open her eyes to see what is true. Nothing more, please.

"Nothing more," she repeats with a groan.

CHAPTER 17

Opening Day in the Holy City

Professor Kameel Majdali, Aly, and Moussa spend their one free day before the conference exploring the Old City of Jerusalem. David leads them through the four quarters of the ancient, walled city in the role of tour guide while Daniel accompanies them as their private security guard.

They visit the Church of the Holy Sepulcher, Gordon's Calvary, the Via Dolorosa, the Mount of Olives, the Wailing Wall, Hezekiah's Tunnel, David's Tomb on Mt. Scopus, and even stop for a few minutes to sip mint tea in the Arab Quarter with Moshe Abramovich's friend, Mahmoud Dajani. Mr. Dajani serves his mint tea in small glasses that contain 25% water and 75% sugar. To his credit, the tea tastes very minty.

The Apologetics and Monotheistic God Studies Conference commences the next day, a Friday, several hours before the beginning of the Sabbath. It convenes at an elegant hotel only five minutes from the King David Hotel. The conference room is moderately large, comfortable, and boasts a beautiful glass half-dome that affords an excellent view of the Old City in the distance. The Jaffa Gate and the Tower of David are prominently on display.

The tables in the room are configured to form twenty-four squares, twelve chairs around each square, three on each side. Aly, Moussa, Kameel, and Daniel sit at a table near the center of the room. Eight other individuals join them at their table—a handful of Muslims, a Christian from Cyprus, and two Hassidic Jews with their long curled sidelocks and impressive phylacteries.

The conference is not large, as conferences go, with a total of fewer than three hundred individuals in attendance. But those who deliver talks during the afternoon and evening of the first day represent the apologetic discipline well on behalf of their respective faiths. Moussa does not recognize the names of any of the speakers but finds their bios impressive. Some are daunting.

The second day of the conference consists primarily of debates between Jews and Christians, Muslims and Jews, Jews and Christians, and even one between Christians and other Christians. The debates between Muslims and Christians generate the most attention from Moussa and Aly, as well as from the rest of the attendees. Professor Kameel Majdali participates in several of them. Living up to his legendary reputation, the first time he ascends the platform in front of the room, he trips on the top step and falls on his face. The crowd gasps and then becomes hushed—except for Daniel, who throws back his head and laughs loudly at the latest gaffe of his childhood friend.

One of the most heated debates of the day concerns the topic of Jesus. Was he—is he—God or simply a prophet? The Muslim apologists, of course, argue that Jesus was merely a man, a prophet like Moses, Abraham, and Muhammad. Muhammad, however, was greater than Jesus, they argue, since he brought the final word from God, arriving with his message centuries after Jesus did.

The Christian apologists, as expected, observe that Muhammed never claimed to be God, unlike Jesus, who made repeated references to His divinity. They point to multiple examples: Jesus claimed to exist before

Abraham was born, He heard and answered prayers, He healed people on His own authority, He said that He was the King of another realm as well as an eternal kingdom, and He commended those who thought He was God.

The Muslim debaters counter with the big gun of their faith, namely, that the Islamic concept of Tawhid advances the absolute indivisible oneness of God. They point to the Shahadah and the Kalima Shahadat, both of which declare the unwavering oneness of Allah. Then they go on to debunk the Christian faith because it absolutely contradicts monotheism when it claims that Yahweh, Jesus, and the Spirit are all divine in nature. They posit that Christianity totally undermines itself when it purports to be a monotheistic religion while simultaneously arguing for a theology of polytheism, namely, that God is a trinity.

Kameel and other believers in Jesus rebut the Muslim apologists with the argument that belief in the divinity of the Father, the Son, and the Holy Spirit is unequivocally monotheistic. They argue that there are three personalities but only one Godhead. In other words, there is only one God who exists eternally in three divine persons. Yes, they admit, the concept of trinitarianism is difficult to understand, but the Trinity, as it has come to be referred to, has been embraced by the church since the time of Christ.

Later in the debate, several Muslim apologists argue that Jesus did not die on the cross, and so He certainly could not have been resurrected from the dead. They concede that Jesus may have been crucified but that He "swooned" on the cross and appeared to His amazed followers three days later after He had recovered from His injuries. Other defenders of Islam allow that Jesus may have died on the cross but that His disciples stole His dead body, hid it, then proclaimed that Jesus had risen from the dead.

The strongest Muslim arguments are reserved for the theory that someone other than Jesus died on the cross.

Kameel explains to the Ahmed siblings that the Muslim representatives at the conference are so adamantly opposed to the idea that Jesus died because that opens the door for the possibility of the resurrection of Christ, which could then easily be forwarded as evidence for His divinity.

Kameel and other scholars on the panel representing the Christian faith bring various arguments against the Muslim claims. To counter the argument that Jesus did not die on the cross, they point out that when the Roman centurion pierced Jesus' heart with a spear, both blood and water flowed from His body, medically indicating that His heart had been lacerated. Obviously, Jesus would not have survived a ruptured heart.

Against the claim that Jesus' disciples had stolen His body and then declared Him risen, the Christian apologists make the convincing point that if the disciples had stolen the body of Jesus and were therefore well aware that Jesus had not risen from the dead, why were they later so prepared to die for their faith?

Subsequent debate from the panel of Christian scholars focuses, first, on the concept of abrogation as it relates to the Islamic Hadith and then, secondly, on the fact that the Quran itself was altered over a period of many years following the death of Muhammad undermining its credibility as an original source. The Muslim representatives counter by dismissing all historical evidence for Christian origins even though dozens of sources—Christian, Jewish, and Graeco Roman—all attest to its historicity.

The final argument against Islam is presented by a Hasidic scholar from New York City. It pertains to Muhammad's frequent admonitions in Islamic holy writ to engage in violence against the infidels. The point is made that the prophet's words contained increasing references to violence toward the end of his life and that such hostility toward unbelievers stands in sharp contrast to the more appealing words of Jesus, who commanded

His followers to love their enemies.

The Muslim scholars attempt to draw attention away from the hundred-plus verses that advocate violence in the Quran and Hadith by countering with the occurrences of violence in the Old Testament. Kameel then drives home the point that Jesus and Muhammad were on opposite ends of the spectrum relative to violence. While Jesus was the God of love and peace, Mohammed was the man of cruelty and war.

When the lengthy debate finally ends, and the conference is about to conclude for the second day, a severe-looking man with a pinched face stands up slowly, pretentiously, at a table in front of the room. He is dressed in a thawb, an ankle-length white robe with long sleeves that imams sometimes wear. His head is wrapped in a white turban. The man looks around the room as if searching for someone. His eyes are piercing and remind Aly of Dr. Hawkstern.

Apparently unable to locate the object of his search, he clears his throat and announces something in a dialect that Moussa recognizes as Palestinian Arabic. He understands most of what the man is saying. His voice is harsh, with a hint of mocking in it.

"Do any of you wish to hear the testimony of Mahmoud Ahmed, the former son of Islam who allegedly had a nightmare about Jesus and afterward shamefully forsook his faith in Allah as the one true God and in Muhammad as his prophet?"

Immediately, a dozen voices cry out from around the room. They also are speaking Palestinian Arabic and are demanding to hear the man who committed *takfir*.

Before long, other voices are heard speaking in different dialects of Arabic. They are loud, insistent, and harsh. Many conference attendees begin scanning the room, no doubt trying to locate the apostate in question. Several participants get to their feet. One man with a thick, black beard waves his fist in the air. The situation in the room continues to escalate.

More men and even a few women are yelling. Still, others rise from their seats, insisting that Mahmoud reveal himself to them. Physical violence seems one impulsive act away. Aly wants to reach out and touch her brother's hand, but she hesitates because several people sitting at their table are looking at them. One man wearing a black and white keffiyeh appears especially interested in Moussa, tilting his head and studying him with narrowed eyes.

Daniel abruptly rises from his chair and barks something in Hebrew into a small radio attached to his lapel. Immediately, several men and women rise from their tables in front of the room. They raise their arms and attempt to calm the storm of voices that is now easily as loud as the wind on the Sea of Galilee during a summer tempest. They are ignored by the agitated crowd.

Just when bedlam appears ready to break out, a dozen Israeli soldiers jog into the conference hall and take up positions around the perimeter of the room. They carry no weapons, at least none that Aly can see, but she suspects that they are armed.

Not long after the soldiers arrive, David Abramovich enters the room. For some reason, Aly relaxes when she sees the intrepid young Mossad agent. She so badly wants to pull her phone out and take a picture of David or capture a video of the unfolding scene around her. In the end, she is wise enough to resist the temptation.

The soldiers are ignored. The crowd continues to escalate in volume. Most of the voices are angry and demanding, while several are crying out for calm and order. A few particularly zealous individuals are jumping up and down while others are sitting in their chairs shaking their heads.

Just when Aly anticipates that tear gas canisters will be fired into the crowd, an older man with a full white beard who is also wearing a thawb climbs up on a chair and stands tottering in the middle of the room. He holds up his hands but does not say a word. Eventually, a few of his religious cronies see him and stop yelling. Others point at the old man until everyone in the room is looking in his direction. Eventually, everyone falls silent. Several sets of hands move in to prop up the unsteady man.

In halting, heavily accented English, the imam announces to the crowd, "Be calm, brothers. If we act like men of peace, this Mahmoud Ahmed will certainly reveal himself to us. Sit down. Be at peace."

One by one, the conference attendees return to their seats until, eventually, everyone is sitting down.

Except one.

The lone individual who remains standing is surprisingly young. He has wavy black hair and a face that appears Asian in its features—except for his forehead and intense eyes. They are distinctly Saudi. He does not have the thick black beard that most conference participants assumed he would have. Rather, he is clean-shaven. He is dressed inconspicuously in khaki pants and a gray pullover. Few of the attendees even remember seeing the young man over the previous two days. Can this be Mahmoud Ahmed, the former faithful servant of Islam and the jihadist who enforced the strictest interpretation of the Quran and the Hadith?

Everyone in the conference hall finds it incredible that the nondescript young man standing in their midst was at one time a man of violence who aroused fear in the hearts of all non-believers, even in the hearts of Muslims who were not devout Sunnis. Standing before them now, he appears to be nothing but a lamb. Where has the lion gone?

While everyone watches, the young man bows his head. He appears to be praying. A murmuring wave rolls through the room.

Eventually, the young man looks up and gazes around at the conference participants. His eyes are as clear as the sky on a sunny day. They are calm. They communicate no anger or fear. Some of those sitting near Mahmoud will later claim that something radiated from his face that could only be the opposite of hate. Yes, his face was full of love.

"I am the one you seek," he begins slowly in a voice that everyone in the room can hear. "I am Mahmoud Ahmed—or at least I used to be. My name now is Moussa." He offers no explanation for the name change.

He pauses for a long time. The room is as silent as a kosher market in New City Jerusalem at the beginning of the Sabbath.

"Let me make one thing absolutely clear from the beginning," Moussa says. "I did not go looking...for Him. Never would I have chosen to pursue Him. Never would I have desired Him—at least not as God. I respected Him as a lesser prophet as I respected Moses and Abraham. But, of course, I never entertained the thought that He was the Creator of the universe."

Moussa has the undivided attention of everyone sitting at the tables, some of it for good and some for ill. Aly, David, Kameel, and Daniel are interceding for their brother as he stands in the center of the room that physically is as quiet as a monastery dedicated to a vow of silence. Despite the ostensible peacefulness, all four Jesus followers know that Moussa stands in the middle of a violent spiritual vortex far more potent than the threat of physical violence in the room. It is one of those rare moments when it feels like a window in the spiritual universe has opened, and God's presence is so real that it is feels tangible. For some, at least.

This time Aly cannot resist. As surreptitiously as possible—which is very surreptitious since she has done it for fifteen years—she takes several pictures of her brother while she is praying. She even captures one brief video of the scene that is unfolding in the room.

"I am—" Moussa begins and then falls silent. "At one time, not long ago, I was like many of you. But I was also not like most of you in another way. Yes, I was a man devoted to Islam, but I was also a man devoted to violence. I collected the verses about violence in the Quran and the Hadith like a child collects seashells on the beach. They were my primary guide. They were my inspiration. Under their direction, I forced people to believe in Allah or gave them the choice of exile or death."

Moussa falls silent for a moment and then nods down toward where Aly is sitting next to him. "I was so zealous that I set out to kill my own sister for takfir."

Another murmuring wave rolls through the room.

"Many of you undoubtedly find it reprehensible that I would turn my back on Islam," Moussa says as he scans the room. "But I tell you the truth when I say that it was never a matter of turning my back on Islam. I never rejected Allah and his prophet. Such rejection by my own sister led me to pursue her all the way from Thailand to America with the intent of killing her. Why would I commit the same apostasy I despised?"

Moussa turns slowly, looking into the eyes of everyone around him. He sees people wearing turbans, keffiyehs, and phylacteries strapped to their foreheads and left arms. His eyes travel over curious faces, angry faces, hungry faces, and even a few smiling faces. He beholds black skin, white skin, olive skin. He even sees one familiar individual from the past—a fellow jihadist from Saudi Arabia. He is briefly shaken when the man mouths the words in Arabic, "You are dead."

Moussa looks away from his former brother and continues. "I did not wake up that morning intent on rejecting the Sublime," he repeats. "That scenario was not even a whisper in the back of my brain. Rather, what occurred was that I was pursued. I was pursued by Him."

The young man clears his throat. "I did not hear Him coming," he says with awe in his voice. "I did not see Him steadily moving toward me. He was a lion in the long grass, quietly approaching, crouching, preparing to pounce. My Islamic faith prevented me from seeing Him. In fact, I was blind to Him."

Moussa looks up at the waning afternoon light that is softly flowing into the room through the glass dome above him. He stands there for a long time, silent as if transfixed by a presence. Aly sees deep passion flood his face and radiate from his eyes. She reaches out and touches his arm.

"I was sleeping," Moussa finally says with wonder in his voice. As he continues to gaze up into the sky, he adds, "It was the middle of the night... He called my name—'Mahmoud'—and I woke up."

Several people in the conference room begin to whisper. One voice in the front of the room grumbles in a low tone, like angry thunder at a distance.

"As a dreamer of dreams and a believer in dreams, I first thought I was having a dream, but I soon realized I was not," Moussa declares as he looks down at the people sitting around him. "Please, hear me on this, my brothers and sisters, so you will never forget. It was not a dream. I was aroused from sleep. I was totally awake. It was the most awake I have been in all my years."

There is a short pause. "He repeated my name four or five times—maybe more," Moussa continues as he glances at the imam with the pinched face who earlier had accused him of dreaming. "I could not believe it," he announces with growing volume. "I did not wish to believe it. I wanted it to be a dream—a nightmare from al-Shaytan! Oh, how desperately I wanted it to be a nightmare from darkness! But—" the young man's voice suddenly grows quiet, and he speaks slowly—"it was not."

More whispers. The voice at the front of the room grumbles again, only more loudly.

"I saw Him," Moussa says matter-of-factly as if he is reporting what he ate for lunch. Then he repeats his words with sudden excitement, "I saw Him! But only briefly because the sight of Him was too much for me. I was struck as with a blow and was filled with fear. I fell to the floor.

"As I laid there, I desperately wanted to run and hide. Oh, yes, I wanted to hide myself from His presence. But at the same time...I wanted to run to Him and wrap my arms around His ankles and embrace Him forever."

Moussa takes a deep breath and admits, "He didn't tell me who He was—but I knew. I knew who He was. I just knew."

The grumbling voice abruptly speaks up and demands, "How did you know it was not Muhammad whom you saw? It must have been God's prophet! You were mistaken!"

Moussa looks toward the sound of the voice. He cannot see the man, but he knows who it is—the familiar voice comes from the man who has traveled to Jerusalem from Saudi Arabia, a man who was his brother in faith only weeks ago. Moussa is silent for a moment. Then he shares a detail about the holy visitation that he had not previously mentioned—even to Aly.

"It was not Muhammad," he announces without hesitation. Moussa pauses, and his face glows with a passion that reminds Aly of Moses in the Red Sea painting back at the fireside room in the citadel.

"The One who appeared to me...had scars...on His hands and on His feet."

Total silence falls over the room as if the listeners are shocked by the young man's revelation.

Moussa does not stop there. He goes on to deliver the clinching statement that most of the conference participants are anticipating by now, whether with joy or great displeasure.

The young man scans the faces of those around him one more time and then makes a triple declaration, "Without doubt, the person who appeared to me was the crucified and risen Son of God, Jesus the Christ."

A third of the conference attendees remain silent, stunned by Moussa's declaration. A third respond with visible animation, talking excitedly among themselves. The remaining apologists begin to denounce the words of the young apostate with loud outcries. Scattered individuals in the conference hall jump to their feet and begin gesticulating with raised fists, their faces contorted by righteous indignation. The room is filled with a resurgence of the earlier intensity.

Before a riot can break out, David Abramovich wades into the maze of tables and raises his hands. "I need order," he insists, first in Hebrew and then in Arabic. He does not yell but speaks in a commanding tone that surprisingly quiets the assembly. Aly marvels at the young Mossad agent who embodies the confidence and strength of Colonel Moshe Abramovich. Like his father, his presence demands attention. Aly's heart feels strangely warm as she stares at the young man. She feels herself blushing.

While David continues to address the restless crowd, Daniel nudges Moussa and Aly and insists that they leave the room immediately. It is not a suggestion. They nod their heads and make their way toward the exit.

That same day, in the evening, David, Daniel, Kameel, Aly, and Moussa make their way through the jumbled streets of the labyrinthine Muslim Quarter of the Old City of Jerusalem. Some of the narrow, claustrophobic-inducing streets are open air, while some are covered with roofed arches that are hundreds of years old. Sometimes they tread on ancient paving stones, occasionally on dirt, and even on asphalt paving.

Fearing what might happen if they are recognized in this part of the city, David provided long robes for them to wear along with keffiyehs to cover their heads. To attract less attention, they divide up and travel through the quarter in two groups instead of as a party of five.

They arrive without incident at a small two-story building that is shoved between several other similar buildings in the middle of a busy marketplace. Offered for sale in the small stalls of the market are goat heads, freshly butchered quarters of cow, fish, vegetables, olive-wood carvings, embroidered tablecloths from Damascus, jewelry, pottery, clothing, delicious-looking baklava and knafeh, and various strong spices the smell of which overruns the marketplace like an invading army.

On their arrival, Mr. Mahmoud Dajani leads them up a stairway to the roof of his store that doubles as his residence. The shopkeeper disappears for several minutes only to return with small glasses of his renowned mint tea served on a silver tray. He brings seven servings of the "diabetes in a glass," as David refers to the sugary concoction. The seventh glass is for his old friend, Colonel Moshe Abramovich.

They sip their tea sitting on cushions around three ancient kerosene heaters that appear to have been repurposed from a local junkyard. Although not cosmetically appealing, the dented and scratched heaters glow invitingly in the darkness, exhaling a warmth that is received gratefully by everyone on this very cool evening in January.

David and Daniel summarize for the colonel what transpired at the conference earlier in the day. David's assessment is that the situation is highly volatile and must be monitored closely. Another option, of course—one that he recommends highly—is to simply cancel the third and final day of the event to avoid any further fueling of potential violence.

The burly colonel's bald ostrich-egg head appears much less bald and egg-like covered as it is by his *keffiyeh*. He would be almost unrecognizable were it not for the impressively pocked face that peers out from the folds of his head covering.

"We always walk the tight rope," the colonel announces in his grave voice that invariably is imbued with a threatening edge, like an unsheathed sword. Moussa takes a deep breath and lets it out slowly. He has not yet learned how to relax around this intimidating man.

"On the one hand," the large-bodied man says, "tourism is our lifeblood. We want the world to visit Israel and spend their dollars and their euros here. Thus, it is unwise for us to overreact to perceived threats and inspire a perception that it is unsafe to visit our country.

"But on the other hand," he says, pausing to sip from the glass that looks like a thimble in his thick fingers, "we must first and foremost protect our country and our people. Security is always first. It is imperative that we keep our citizens safe from both external and internal threats. If tight security frightens some tourists away like so many nervous birds, we cannot lose sleep over the loss of a few chickens. There are so many other things to keep us awake at night."

The six people sitting around the heaters that glow orange are silent. A cacophony of sounds climbs up to their ears from the night marketplace where a variety of merchandise can be purchased—but only after lots of serious haggling. A dog barks in the distance. A church bell from another quarter of the city peels in the twilight. The sound of a jet engine rumbles far away as if from another world and another time.

"Is there anything else, David?" the colonel asks as he shifts his significant weight uncomfortably on his wafer-thin cushion. The inquiry sounds like a growling demand to Moussa.

The junior Abramovich hesitates as he swirls the sugar sediment around in his small glass with his index finger. "Daniel has spoken to several of our sources," he states as he gestures for his friend to speak.

"There is some intelligence, if I may refer to it as such, that suggests potential violence," Daniel reports with a grimace. "The focus of the violence does not seem to be directed toward citizens of Israel. From what I've heard, it's all targeted toward one individual from outside the country."

Everyone sitting in the small circle turns their attention on Moussa, whose face is partially in shadows.

"We must leave, then," Aly says, leaning toward her brother. "We must leave immediately for the peace of Jerusalem." Her small fingers fumble around the edges of her head covering that reminds her of the hijab she wore every day in another lifetime.

Moussa looks at his sister and says, "Listen to yourself, Aly." His voice has a hint of reprimand in it. "Is the woman who is speaking right now the same one who gave her life to Jesus eighteen months ago under threat of death? Is she the one who led me to the foot of the cross where my life was transformed by the Holy Spirit and subsequently forfeited to the King of kings for His service?"

Aly opens her mouth to protest but stops. She is silent.

"Jesus did not die for us and give us new life so we could run away and hide," Moussa declares. "He gave us new life so that we might share the good news just like the Apostle Paul did after his encounter with Jesus on the road to Damascus."

Moussa's voice softens as he says, "Just this morning, I was reading in the New Testament Book of Acts how the apostles were arrested and thrown into jail by the Jewish leaders." He pauses and glances over at the three Israelis in his midst. "Sorry. I don't mean anything personal against the Jewish people. I believe it was primarily the secular Sadducees who put them in jail."

When David smiles and tells him that no offense is taken, Moussa goes on to say, "An angel came during the night and opened the doors of the jail. He woke up Peter and his friends. But did the angel tell them to run to their homes, to hide and be safe? No. He told them to go back to the Temple courts where they had been arrested earlier, to stand, and to tell the people 'The full message of this new life.'

"So, sister, I am under God's authority to do the same," Moussa explains. "I cannot run from Jerusalem. I have to return to the conference and speak to my brothers and sisters just as Peter went back to the Temple and spoke to the people—if the colonel allows the conference to continue, that is." He dares to glance at Moshe Abramovich, whose face, like a full harvest moon, is a muted orange from the reflected light of the kerosene heaters.

The colonel grunts and throws back his head to annihilate the remaining contents of his glass—a bit of tea mingled with the sludgy sugar. Wiping his mouth with the back of his hand, he turns to the shopkeeper and asks, "So what do you think, Mahmoud? What word have you heard in the mosque and on the streets?" The colonel looks over at Moussa, who quickly averts his gaze from the Beth Shin officer.

"Why do you look at me like that?" the infamous interrogator snaps at Moussa. "Do you think I have no friendships with Muslims? I told you I hate and despise all terrorists, not all Muslims. Besides," he says with a wave of his hand, "Mahmoud is a Muslim culturally but not spiritually. It is merely his geopolitical inheritance, so to speak."

The shopkeeper, who is dressed in a threadbare tweed sports coat and a turtleneck that hugs his bulldog neck, rubs his thin mustache with the index finger of his right hand. He rolls his tongue around in his mouth and stares out into the night past the colonel's shoulder. As Aly studies Mahmoud Dajani's scarred and bumpy face, she decides that his skin bears a striking resemblance to his kerosene heaters.

"I have heard things, too," the man eventually confides as his eyes shift to Moussa. "Gossip about this young man's encounter with Jesus is flowing through the streets of the city even as we sit here on our—"

"Mahmoud," David interrupts, "we have a young woman here. Please treat her with respect."

The shopkeeper rolls his small, beady eyes toward David and grunts. Then he runs a small hand over his graying crewcut hair that stands up as straight as a bristle brush and says, "The grapevines in the mosques and on the streets whisper that many people are curious. Some are angry. Only a few seem bent toward...monkey business."

"Monkey business?" Moussa inquires. "What is monkey business?"

"You know," the shopkeeper replies impatiently, "no good. It is what the Americans who come to visit the Holy Land and Al-Quds will say."

"I see," the young man from Thailand replies, indicating that he understands.

The colonel compresses his lips, then twists them this way and that so that they appear elastic. "David? Daniel?" he eventually says, fixing intense eyes on the two young men.

David spreads his hands apart and says, "That's everything I know."

"Nothing more to report, sir," Daniel replies.

The large man groans as he leans forward and stares into the mouth of the kerosene heater. "This is what we will do, then," he announces and proceeds to inform the others of his decision.

CHAPTER 18

Jack and Armando Encounter Sniper

As Armando and Jack walk down the sidewalk, the darkness of the night is interrupted every half block by meager pools of light cast by the staggered streetlights. Moving forward, then, mainly in the dark, they step occasionally—to Jack's consternation—on large snail shells that crunch loudly under their shoes.

"Gross!" Jack remarks time and time again. "What is it with these snails? Shouldn't they be down at the beach?"

Armando laughs quietly, thankful for the distraction. "If it's not Jacaranda sludge or the smog, it's snail slime. LA will get you one way or another, Juan."

Before long, the two men arrive at a dilapidated house that has the numbers they are seeking affixed to the stucco exterior next to the front door. They almost walk past it because the "9" is dangling upside down.

The two spiritual brothers of Jim Elliot hesitate briefly at the sidewalk that leads up to the house. A single naked bulb burns weakly above the front door.

Armando slaps his friend on the back and says in a soft voice, "Thanks for having my back, ese. No matter what happens here, I'll never forget this night. Never."

Jack shrugs and says in a confident voice that contradicts his elevated heart rate, "When you and Violet and Jesus all insist that I obey God's calling, how can I refuse? Outnumbered three to one—what's a guy to do?"

Armando smiles wanly and turns to look at the house. Jack is not certain if it is his imagination or not, but his friend's face looks pale.

As they walk up the broken sidewalk toward the front door of the house that exudes a sinister Amityville aura, Jack prays quietly, "Lord, like King Jehoshaphat said, 'We don't know what to do, but our eyes are on you.'"

When they arrive at the front door, Armando raises his hand to knock. But before his knuckles strike the wooden door, a heavily accented voice growls from the darkness, "Who are you gringos, and why are you trespassin' on Nuestra Familia Valinda turf?"

Armando and Jack turn and look toward the side of the house in the direction of the voice. In the deep darkness, all they see is the outline of a man.

Jack watches his friend swallow hard before Armando replies, "We're here to see Sniper."

The orange glow of a cigarette burning in the dark appears, and there is a short silence. "Sniper's not expectin' nobody friendly," the voice says slowly, flatly, "so you must be trouble. Tell me what clique you roll with, or I'll shoot you in *los juevos*. Knowin' me, I'll blow away your *juevos* even if you tell me."

"We don't roll with any clique," Armando says while Jack reflexively moves his hands in front of his *juevos*. "I'm...familiar with Sniper from years ago and just want to talk with him, real chill like."

There is a long silence as the cigarette glows in the dark again. Eventually, the smoking man steps into the weak circle of light cast by the naked bulb and becomes a five-feet-seven-inches gangster. He is wearing jeans rolled up at the ankles, a white muscle shirt, and a blue bandana on his head. Jack's eyes eventually settle on one feature of the man: the sawed-off shotgun in his right hand. It is pointed toward the ground, almost hidden by the gang-banger's baggy pants.

"You don't dress like a *cholo*," the two-legged watchdog mutters as he flicks his cigarette to the ground and grinds it with the sole of his BK sneaker, "but you sure look like one." The man curses and then asks, "You packin'?"

Armando glances at Jack. He appears relieved. Jack knows why. Then he looks back at the guard who no doubt has been posted in front of the house to look for rival gang drive-bys. "No firearms, no blades," Armando answers.

"You better not be carryin', or I'll make windows in your stomach," the man says very convincingly.

He orders the two young men to turn away from him. Then he roughly frisks them while jamming the double-barreled shotgun into their backs. It is then that Jack's nose tells him that the gangster was smoking something other than a cigarette. He swallows hard and prays to Jesus that the man's finger will be sober on the trigger.

Apparently satisfied by his search, the man steps back and orders the two intruders to turn around. When Jack turns to look at the young man who looks several years younger than him, he notices that his arms are tattooed from wrist to shoulder and that even his neck is fully inked. The tattoos are not professional; they appear to have been stained into his skin by an 'artist' working out of his garage.

"Are you here for *bazukos* or *cremita*?" the man inquires with heavily accented words. "Don't you know the code? No one comes to us. We come to you. You are two stupid *hombres*—soon-to-be-dead *hombres*." The gangster unleashes a torrent of profanity at the two academy students, some of it in Spanish, some in English.

"We're not here for *drogas*," Armando says, shaking his head. "We're only here to talk to Sniper. He knows me. Just take me to him, and you'll find out that he knows me."

The guard raises his chin and looks down his nose at Armando. Then he spits at his feet as he lifts the shotgun to rest on his left forearm. "If this is a war," the man growls between curses, "you two *idiotas* are dead before your bodies hit the ground."

Glaring at the two unexpected arrivals, the gang member swears again and then spits on Jack's shoes. "*Ve*!" he snarls. "Go around the side of the house and through the gate! If you be lyin' to me, Sniper's goin' to use your eyeballs for target practice."

Armando hesitates only briefly before he begins walking toward the side of the house. He is followed a step behind by Jack and five steps behind by the guard dog. Jack dares to glance over his shoulder once. Even in the darkness, he sees the sawed-off shotgun leveled at his back. He prays silently for the tenth time since they arrived at the house.

Jack follows Armando through a gate in a tall wood fence and walks into the backyard behind the house. He feels beads of sweat forming on his forehead and wonders if they are going to die.

Just when a small army of men sitting around a fire comes into view, the guard yells out, "Sniper, a cholo, and a gringo are here to see you. They ain't packin', and they say they don't want no drugs."

The men around the fire scramble to their feet and turn to face the new arrivals. Jack counts them—ten in all. They are dressed similarly to the guard who greeted them in the front yard, except that four of them are not wearing bandanas. Two of them are bald, their shiny heads dully reflecting the orange flames of the fire. The faces of the men are stony and hostile.

Jack is reminded of what he knew from the beginning—he and Armando are not crashing a garden party. He thinks about Jim Elliot and the Aucas. He tries not to think about spears.

One of the bald men, the apparent leader of the group, swaggers up to Armando and Jack. Like the watchdog they met out front, he is not large or tall but wiry and lithe. Jack recognizes him as an athlete even though he probably never participated in organized sports. He has a thick black mustache and equally thick eyebrows.

"A brownie and a fairy," the leader announces to his fellow gang members with a surly laugh. He looks up at Armando because his visitor is several inches taller and growls, "*Que pasa, guey?* You are *loco* to come into my *barrio*! Were you born yesterday?" he asks with incredulity as he jabs a finger into Armando's forehead.

Jack immediately notices two things about the man standing in front of him: He is extremely angry, and he is afraid. Having played football, Jack is familiar with men whose anger vibrates from their bodies. He encountered many such players on the gridiron who played the game with a huge chip on their shoulders. Almost every one of them lined up on the defensive side of the ball.

These players were not just playing the game with high intensity. They were playing it with rage as if every player on the opposing team represented a person they hated—such as an abusive father. They were on the field not to simply tackle the running back or the receiver or the quarterback. Their intent was to harm them, destroy them.

The gang leader reminds Jack of one of those angry football players—except that this man appears angry enough to kill.

Jack also senses a strangely misplaced fear in the man known as Sniper. He is on his home turf, surrounded by his homies, confronting two unarmed men who are not presenting any kind of threat. So why the fear? Of the two emotions—anger and fear—the level of rage in the man obviously concerns Jack the most. He knows that white-hot anger eclipses reason and often leads to impulsive, violent acts such as...murder.

Armando stares at the gang leader for a long time by the light of the fire. Jack thinks he sees a look of recognition on his friend's face. Just when Jack is getting uneasy with the long silence, Armando volunteers, "We're not gang-bangers from another set, Sniper, and we're not here for *drogas*. We're just here to talk."

The gangster, who, like Armando, has a teardrop tattoo below his right eye but, unlike Armando, has four additional ones for a total of five, exclaims, "You're a liar, cholo! How do you know my name if you're not with another set? And you've got the tat on your face—you've killed a man before," he spits out as he gets his finger up in Armando's face again. "Tell the truth now, or I kill both of you where you stand."

Armando quickly replies, "I was in a gang six years ago, but I walked away from the clique after I got shot up. I got the tat because I was planning to kill this one hombre, but I never quite got around to it. He's still alive."

Sniper slaps Armando with the back of his hand and barks, "You still haven't told me how you know my name, Latrino!" The enraged man snarls, and his upper lip curls under his mustache.

Jack's eyes grow wide when he hears Armando reply in a level voice, "You were the man I was going to kill."

The two men are standing sideways to the fire, so only half of their faces are visible while the other half is in shadows. From the half faces, Jack sees that Armando's face is strangely calm while Sniper's face is agitated. Jack begins to pray again.

"Who are you, *gravel belly*?" Sniper demands as he begins pacing back and forth in front of Armando without taking his eyes off his face. He continues his agitated pacing for a long time, reminding Jack of a tiger in a cage.

Eventually, something captures the man's attention, and he stops abruptly. He tilts his bald head to one side and scrutinizes the intruder's face. Then he approaches Armando, his eyes narrow and threatening. He reaches out his hand and runs his finger slowly down Armando's left cheek, and Jack knows he has seen the faint white scar.

"I remember you," the bald man says slowly as the light of recognition floods his surly face. "Years ago, I cut you behind that *groceria* on Brea," he mutters, nodding his head and uttering a string of expletives.

"And we cut your homie good, too—real good. Remember that, Spooky?" he asks, turning to the man on his right who wears a heavy gold chain around his neck. The man's entire face is covered with tattoos and reminds Jack of a heavily graffitied box car. Even the gangster's eyelids are inked. The man called Spooky grunts and nods his small head that bypasses a neck and attaches directly to his chest.

"He wasn't my friend," Armando clarifies in a quiet voice and then pauses. "He was my brother."

Jack holds his breath and studies Sniper closely. His thick black mustache twitches on the left side of his mouth as he stares at the half-brother of the man his gang had brutally murdered. The right side of his face is still obscured by darkness.

Abruptly, the gang leader turns to the guard with the shotgun and barks, "Get an eye on the street, Spyder! This must be a revenge attack!"

Spyder nods his head and melts into the darkness. The other men run after him around the side of the house.

In the flurry of activity, Armando sees an opportunity. He looks at Sniper and says, "We're not here for revenge. The opposite is true. I'm here to forgive you and…and to talk to you about Jesus."

Sniper's mouth drops open as he slowly absorbs Armando's words. But then, recovering quickly, the gangster's hand moves with lightening-speed. Before Armando can react, a knife appears out of nowhere. Sniper presses the blade against the intruder's throat while his free hand grabs the back of his neck. "You die, now, Puente dog!"

"It's true!" Jack interjects abruptly. "If you don't believe him, just ask Carmelita Cortez. We spoke to her earlier tonight. She knows why we're here."

Sniper turns an icy gaze on Jack as he keeps the knife pressed up against Armando's throat. Murder is in his eyes. For a fleeting moment, Jack is sorry he said anything. The gangster sneers and spits out the words, "Carmelita. Who's Carmelita?"

"Carmelita Cortez says her mother knew your grandmother, Cecilia," Jack replies.

Sniper growls a long sentence in Spanish, and Jack is certain he has just been called several derogatory names. "Hiding behind women is not going to save you, dogs!" the man hisses at Jack, twisting his upper lip and mustache into a look of revulsion. "I'm personally going to slit your throats and throw your bodies into the same dumpster we threw that other menso."

Instinctively, Jack cries aloud, "Jesus, we need your help!"

Literally two seconds later, his phone pings notifying him that he has received a text message. Before the gangster can protest, Jack retrieves his phone from his pocket and reads the text, which is from Dr. Windsor: *If you talk to Sniper tonight, tell him I'm praying for his heart. Read Isaiah 1 to him: "Your hands are full of blood...Come, let us reason together, says the Lord. Though your sins are like scarlet, they shall be as white as snow; though they are red as crimson, they shall be like wool."*

Jack looks up at Sniper and says, "It's for you." Then he reads the text and tells the gang member that it was sent to him by a colonel in the army.

While Sniper is digesting the words of the bewildering text message addressed to him by a man he has never met, the sound of upraised voices comes from the front of the house. Sniper's face tenses, and he abruptly removes the knife from Armando's throat.

The body of Jack's roommate immediately slumps, and he sighs with relief.

The gangster sheaths his knife and pulls a handgun from the pocket of his sagging jeans. He quickly runs to the back wall of the house, where he hides in the darkness. Jack and Armando remain standing by the fire.

A moment later, the fence gate bursts open, and a cacophony of voices pours into the backyard. They are all speaking Spanish rapidly and animatedly. Jack cannot understand most of what they are saying, but he does recognize one familiar high-pitched voice that is louder than all the others. The backyard is soon flooded with people and a riotous commotion. Everyone is talking at once.

Suddenly, a high-pitched voice cries out, "Manny! Juan! There you are! I see you!

Gracias Dios! We have been praying for you all the way here, and we will not stop now!"

Out of the darkness, Carmelita Cortez waddles up to the two men with her arms raised toward the sky. She hugs Jack and her "Manny" for the third time that night. Even in the dim light of the fire, Jack sees that the woman's face is radiant. The next thing Jack notices is the overwhelming cloud of lilac fragrance that overruns the backyard like tear gas.

Ignoring the ten gang members who are crowding around her and yelling angrily in Spanish and English, the extraordinary woman scans the dark yard and inquires, "Where is Miguel? Miguel, where are you? Miguel? Come out, Miguel. It is I, Carmelita Cortez. I was a friend of your grandmother, Cecilia."

Even before she is done speaking, Sniper emerges from his hiding place behind the house and walks slowly toward the scene of the small riot. Even though Jack's eyes are beginning to water from Carmelita's strong fragrance, he notices that the gang leader's swagger is not as pronounced as it had been earlier. He looks hesitant and embarrassed.

"Miguel!" the woman cries when she sees the gangster walking toward her. She throws her arms into the air for the second time in the backyard and looks up into the night sky. Then she exclaims, "I see you, Miguel! Gracias Dios!"

For a moment, Jack holds his breath, fearing that the woman will rush up and wrap Sniper in one of her infamous hugs.

The man with the bushy black mustache raises a hand to quiet the loudmouthed woman who is uttering his birth name instead of his gang name.

In the middle of all the chaos, Jack is shocked to see a second woman emerge from the shadows behind Carmelita and glide toward Sniper. She is slim and elegant with long black hair. Her ankle-length white dress stands in shocking contrast to the darkness that is tattooed onto the gang members' bodies.

When the gang leader sees the woman, he stops in his tracks. He looks like he has seen a ghost.

The young woman floats toward Sniper until she is only three feet away from the dumbfounded gang leader whose backyard haven has now been invaded by four unexpected trespassers in the last five minutes. Then she stops and stares at the young man. She clasps her fingers together in front of her waist. She looks nervous.

One of the gang members behind the woman spits out the word, "Frese!" and then curses loudly.

Sniper immediately raises a tattooed arm and stabs his finger at the man who uttered the derogatory comment. "Shut up, Primo, or I'll cut you!" he screams. "You never talk to my *hermana* that way!"

Primo mumbles something unintelligible and lowers his eyes to the ground.

Sniper turns his attention back to the woman in front of him and inquires in a much more subdued voice, "What you doin' here, Angela Rosa? I ain't seen you in years." He does not sound angry, but neither is his voice welcoming.

"Seven, to be exact," Angela Rosa replies. "It has been seven years, Miguel.

You haven't talked to me in seven years!"

Sniper briefly glances over at the fire and then back at his sister. "I been busy," he says with a shrug of his shoulders.

"Too busy to send me one text message?" the woman asks as she lifts her chin slightly. "Too busy to show up at Cecilia's funeral?"

Sniper obviously does not like where this conversation is going. He gestures toward Armando and Jack and asks his sister, "Do you know these *wangstas* from Puente 13?"

Before Angela Rosa can respond, Carmelita interjects, "She doesn't know them, Miguel. But I do. They're *mis amigos.* They would be friends of Cecilia, too, if she was still with us, *Dios la bendiga.*"

"Why are they here but to kill me?" Sniper asks Carmelita with open disgust. "And why are you here, Carmelita—and you, Angela Rosa?" he says in a slightly softer voice. "Why are you all here on my turf? I don't remember invitin' nobody to a picnic."

The hint of softness in the gang leader's voice is not wasted on his sister.

Angela Rosa abruptly breaks into tears. The backyard quickly grows quiet except for the sound of the young woman in white weeping. Even Carmelita is uncharacteristically silent.

Jack and Armando exchange glances. They can hardly see each other because the fire is dying, and the darkness is growing deeper. Armando presses the palms of his hands together to indicate that he is praying. Jack nods his head, and so does Carmelita, who also notices her spiritual son's gesture.

After what feels like minutes to Jack, Sniper snaps something in Spanish at his homies. No one moves. Sniper repeats what he said, only this time it is spoken with a growl. The gang members glance around at each other sullenly, then turn and shuffle toward the gate. Soon, they disappear around the side of the house.

When the men are gone, Angela Rosa tentatively steps toward her brother and leans her head against his white sleeveless wifebeater shirt.

When Sniper stands unmoving with his arms hanging stiffly at his sides, Carmelita interjects, "Aren't you going to hold her, Miguel?"

Sniper gives the round woman a look that communicates something between "shut up" and "if you weren't a woman, I'd kill you where you stand." A moment later, however, he lifts his arms and gingerly wraps them around his sister.

The sight of Sniper with his severe bald head, gang attire, and inked body embracing Angela Rosa with her white dress and long black hair that glistens in the firelight is a study in contrast. Jack thinks of them as a visual oxymoron. Carmelita touches her hand to her mouth and begins to sniff. Armando and Jack relax a bit but are careful not to move.

Eventually, Angela Rosa says something so quietly that Jack strains his ears to hear her words. "Why haven't you tried to contact me, Miguel?" she inquires with a mixture of sadness and petulance. "I thought you were dead. I have nobody else but mama." The young woman does not lift her head to look at her brother but continues to rest it on his chest.

Sniper stares over the top of his sister's head into the growing darkness of the backyard. In a voice that sounds flat, devoid of any compassion, he replies, "I am a bad man, *mi hermana. Muy mal.*"

Sniper does not hold his sister for long. He pushes her away from him, not roughly but not gently either. He glances around at the four interlopers who have introduced great disequilibrium and paranoia into his backyard chill-with-my-homies evening and says, "So is this a revenge attack?"

he asks, looking at Armando and Jack. "Is this an ambush?" he inquires of Angela Rosa and Carmelita.

When nobody volunteers any immediate reply, Armando eventually clears his throat and says, "Everyone is here because of me. And I'm here because...as I said earlier because I need to forgive you and speak to you about Jesus."

"And I am here," Carmelita pipes up in her high-pitched voice as she takes a step toward Sniper, bringing the lilacs with her, "because God opened my eyes to see Armando and his friend tonight at the restaurant. When they told me they were coming to see you, I left and called Angela Rosa. I was afraid you would kill them both. Yes, I was very afraid," she says in her richly accented voice. The woman's pronunciation of "kill" sounds more like "keel" to Jack.

Angela Rosa glances at the older woman and then back at her brother. "When Carmelita called me and told me about Manny and Jack's mission, I told her to pick me up and bring me here," she explains. The younger woman pauses and then adds in a quavering voice, "I decided I should come and see you after all these years even though you've made no effort to see me. Miguel, I didn't even know if you were dead or alive."

Despite the deepening darkness, Jack sees Sniper's eyes flash with emotion.

The man shakes his head from side to side and runs his forefinger and thumb over his bushy mustache, opening his mouth as he does so. Finally, he engages in some obligatory cursing and then cries out in exasperation, "So why are you all here in my barrio? I don't have no time for a family reunion or AA intervention."

Armando, Carmelita, and Angela Rosa all start talking at the same time. As sometimes happens in these situations, they all keep talking, thinking that the others will defer to the person who speaks the loudest and the longest. When none of them defer to the others but keep speaking, Sniper releases a particularly vulgar string of invectives and ends by shouting, "*Callate*!"

Immediately, everyone falls quiet, except for Carmelita, that is. She points one of her stubby fingers at Sniper—the same one Armando and Jack had encountered earlier that evening in the restaurant—and scolds the gang member. "Would you speak that way if Cecilia were here with us?" she asks. "I do not think so," she says, answering her own question as she twists her uniquely expressive face into a look of grave consternation. "When did you become so disrespectful, Miguel?"

To everyone's shock, Sniper answers Carmelita's question without hesitation. "The day *abuelita* Cecilia died," he says bitterly.

Surprised at his unexpected and vulnerable admission, the four visitors glance at each other, uncertain how to respond. Not too surprisingly, Carmelita and her huge black curls lead the way.

"Miguel," she says gently as she shifts her considerable weight from one small foot to the other, "I am confident I speak for everyone when I say that we're all here because we love you. I swear this before the face of God."

"I don't do love," Sniper retorts.

Undaunted, Carmelita counters, "We already know that, Miguel. Tell us something we don't know. That's why we're here."

"Are you deaf, Carmelita?" the gang leader growls. He enunciates the woman's name one long syllable at a time. "I said there's no love in me. There's no love in this whole forsaken barrio," he cries, leaning his thin body toward the rotund woman and throwing his hands in the air for emphasis.

He ends his verbal explosion with a long string of expletives.

Carmelita opens her mouth to respond, but Sniper speaks first. "Cecilia was Miguel's only reason to live," he says, glancing over at Angela Rosa. "When she died, Miguel died. Now only Sniper lives."

Jack is tempted to respond to Sniper's words, but he remains silent. He knows this is not his venue. He has not earned the right to speak. Armando is the one who must speak. He earned that right in a dark alley many years ago.

As if on cue, Armando says, "I was dead once, too. At one time, I was only Syko Loco. But then Armando came back. I was raised from the dead."

Sniper looks at the former gang member and narrows his eyes. "What do you mean, you came back?"

"Love made me alive," Armando replies matter-of-factly.

"Love is only for weak men, women, and children," the gangster scoffs in his heavy accent.

"I used to believe that, too," Armando says. "But then I learned that love is for those who have the courage to admit they need it."

When Sniper does not immediately reply but only stares at the ex-gang member with eyes as hard as steel, Armando goes on to ask, "Can we sit down around the fire and talk with you for a few minutes?"

Sniper glances toward the side of the house where his men had melted into the night only a few minutes earlier and then looks back at the most motley group that has ever gathered in his backyard. He rubs his mustache as he contemplates how to respond. Eventually, he grunts loudly and snaps his head toward the fire with disgust.

When everyone has found a place to sit—whether on an upright log or on the ground—and Sniper has fed the fire with an armful of wood, they look through the growing flames at each other. No one has a plan for what they are going to say.

Angela Rosa clears her throat softly and looks at Sniper but says nothing. When her brother rolls his eyes and shakes his head impatiently, she finally begins sharing about how Cecilia led her to Christ when she was only eight years old, not long before the beloved grandmother died. The story is new to Sniper, and he admits as much. But he appears detached and uninterested as he listens to his sister.

Carmelita speaks after Angela Rosa, continuing with the theme of personal conversion narratives. She explains how she became a "Jesus Freak" as a teenager back in the 1970s at a chapel in Costa Mesa and then relates how she was mentored by two older women in the community of faith who took a personal interest in her growth. She nods her head with the bouncy slinky curls and declares that she would have suicided if God had not called her to Himself that night.

Jack is next to speak. He shares very briefly about his journey to faith in Colorado at a time in life when he was feeling depressed and hopeless about the future.

When Jack is done, all eyes shift to Armando.

The young man does not speak immediately. He takes a stick that is lying in the dirt beside him and begins to poke at the embers. He is quiet for a long time as he stares into the fire.

Finally, without looking up, he announces, "I have three faces tattooed on my body. Not even my friend, Juan," he says, glancing over at his roommate, "knows they exist. One speaks of the past, and two are meant for... this night." Armando pokes at the fire again, and a flurry of sparks explode upward, only to die in the night sky.

Eventually, he sets aside his makeshift poker and gazes through the flames at Sniper. Keeping his eyes fixed on the gang leader, he pulls his left sleeve up to his shoulder, revealing the image of a man's face inked on his upper arm. "Raul," is all he says in a flat voice.

Jack turns and leans forward to look at Armando's arm. In the brightening light of the fire, he sees the expressionless face of a young man tattooed in black ink staring back at him. Beneath the image are the letters *R.I.P.*

No one in the backyard says a word. They all know they are beholding the image of the man Sniper and his gang murdered ten years ago. Jack half expects the gangster to make some sarcastic comment about the slain young man, but the bald man remains silent. He is silent, that is until he abruptly rips off his white T-shirt revealing a tattoo of a woman's face that covers most of his upper chest. The woman is smiling, but a tear rests in the corner of her left eye.

"Cecilia," Sniper announces gravely as he looks at his sister sitting next to him.

Angela Rosa places a hand over her mouth, and her eyes rim with tears. She reaches out and touches her brother's shoulder. Sniper grunts and looks away from his sister. He glares at Armando with a face that says, "You're not the only one who lost someone."

Armando holds the harsh eyes of Cecilia's grandson for a long time, then glances at the other three backyard intruders sitting around the fire. When his eyes finally return to Sniper, he pulls up his other sleeve. Tattooed on his upper right arm is the image of another man. This face is angry, belligerent. Beneath the frowning image are the words, "Sniper. CFY."

The gang leader stares across the fire at Armando's arm. His face is stony and gives away nothing.

Armando swallows hard, and Jack sees his body tense. "Yes, I was coming for you, Sniper," the former Syko Loco says and then pauses. "I was going to kill you or be killed trying."

The backyard is briefly quiet except for the subdued crackling of the fire.

Then Armando explains, "I got the hollow tear drop tattoo in anticipation of killing you. I was going to fill it in as gangsters do after they kill a man. I even had a small hourglass tattooed on my back, indicating the unknown amount of prison time I would do for killing you. I fully expected to be arrested for your murder and sent to prison, maybe for the rest of my life."

Sniper stares at Armando with his dark eyes and licks his lips. "You should've never left the alley alive that night," he comments matter-of-factly.

"So, why didn't you kill me, too?" Armando asks, his voice suddenly tight.

Sniper laughs coldly and replies, "Two reasons. You were nothin' but a paragraph, a punk. You weren't nowhere near bein' a man, and even I don't kill boys. But—"

The gang leader pauses, and his eyes fall away from Armando and seek out the flames that are licking greedily at the immolated logs. "But I was goin' to make an exception that night. When I saw the hate in your eyes, I was convinced I had to kill you. I was goin' to break my own code because I knew you'd be comin' for me."

Sniper's eyes are still fixed on the fire as he says, "But then the second reason happened. Cecilia told me not to." The gangster runs a hand over his mustache and chin and then clarifies further, "I heard her voice in my head telling me not to...not to be like my father."

Everyone stares at Sniper as they absorb the gravity of his admission.

The astounding moment is interrupted by two gang members who emerge through the gate and into the backyard. They walk tentatively toward the five people sitting around the fire as if uncertain that their presence will be welcomed. Their hesitancy is accurate. When Sniper hears his men, he turns around and drives them from the yard with a command snarled in Spanish accompanied by an angry wave of his hand. The men pivot quickly and scurry out of sight.

The gang leader turns back to his visitors and looks at Armando. "What is your third tattoo?" he demands. "Show me the third face."

Armando nods his head and then does what Sniper did earlier—he raises his shirt to expose his chest. "Here it is," he says, as the four others gathered around the fire lean in to examine the face tattooed over his heart. "It's the face of Jesus with the crown of thorns on his head. He's the one who by his death and resurrection brought my dead heart to life." Beneath the image of Jesus are the words, *By grace alone.*

Jack shakes his head, amazed at the three tattoos he has never seen before that silently speak profound stories from his friend's life journey.

Mesmerized, Sniper stares at the image of Jesus until Armando pulls his shirt back down. Then the gangster takes a deep breath and lifts his chin. He looks down his nose at the man formerly known as Syko Loco in another lifetime and comments, "So you don't want to kill me no more."

Armando pauses longer than Jack expects, then shakes his head.

"You don't want to kill me as blood revenge for your brother," he states more than he asks.

Armando again shakes his head.

Sniper stares at the face that still bears the scar he inflicted ten years earlier. In his habitual way, he slowly runs his fingers over his mustache over and over. The shifting light of the fire reveals a face that is impossible to read.

After a long silence, the gangster slowly pulls his handgun from his pocket and points it at the brother of the man he had slain in cold blood.

Armando flinches but says nothing. Jack's heart accelerates in his chest. Angela Rosa gasps, and Carmelita's high-pitched voice exclaims, "Don't do it, Miguel! Don't do it!"

CHAPTER 19

THE CHRISTMAS DANCE

The six-foot-six-inch Drew Johnson arrives in Mystic at noon on December 25th. As soon as he enters the Biandi house on Albatross Road, Dr. Biandi's attention is captured by the young man. Drew's sheer size, athletic build, and impressive sports pedigree earn him immediate admission into Samuel Biandi's inner court of admiration that is reserved for only a select few. Rachel has never set foot in that sacred place. Dr. Biandi's veneration of Drew only grows when the young man mentions the medical training he received during his four years in the Marine Corps.

Rachel is surprised to learn about Drew's military service. She does the math in her head quickly and is not displeased to discover that the young man must be very close to her age.

The pre-dinner family conversation centers around the guest in the Biandi house to such a degree that even the luminary, Celeste, fades into the night sky like some unremarkable star in the vast reaches of the Milky Way. Rachel has never seen the star fall so precipitously. She can discern by the look on her sister's face that she is quietly jealous. Rachel is surprised by another look almost disguised in her sister's eyes as she looks at Drew: desire.

In that deeply hidden place where no human sees her or knows her, Rachel shakes her head and cries, *Jesus, please help me! My desire to be chosen by a man is so obnoxiously strong! I'm so stinking vulnerable to being disappointed for the hundredth time. I don't know if I can handle rejection yet again. Please hold me close and let me rest in your amazing love. Help me let go of the need to control. I put my friendship with Drew into your hands. I desire you above all others, Jesus. I really do.*

As soon as she utters the words, peace settles over her. No, it is more like a calming presence that holds her in the wake of the rumbling cacophony of fear and self-accusation. She takes a deep breath and smiles. Once again, Rachel is reminded that Jesus is the One who proclaims His delight for her and rejoices over her with singing. If her Savior is for her, what does she have to fear?

Eventually, the Biandi family and their guest from upstate New York move from the living room to the elegant dining room with its cherry-wood wainscoting, tray ceiling, and decorative wood molding. The large table is blanketed with a snow-white, fine-laced tablecloth that cradles gleaming china, sparkling crystal glassware, and polished silverware.

Drew's first thought is that he is badly underdressed in his jeans, flannel shirt, and green turtleneck. Rachel knows what he is thinking. When he glances at her, she smiles reassuringly and then mouths the words, "You're fine."

The five diners consume delectable flaky salmon, baked potatoes drenched with a heavenly cream sauce, crunchy roasted Brussels sprouts delightfully seasoned, and finally, a decadent chocolate dessert that would be at home on the menu of any five-star restaurant. Two hours after sitting down, everyone pushes away from the ruins of the feast and scatters to different locations in the large house.

Since the chef doubles as the busser and dishwasher, Susan Biandi and Celeste retreat to the craft room to wrap presents while Mr. Biandi retires to his home office to catch up on work emails.

Drew and Rachel drift away from the table and soon find themselves sitting cross-legged on the bay window cushion in the family room at the back of the house. Outside, the white crepe paper trunks of birch trees glisten in the bright light of the December moon. Inside, soft, jingling Christmas music flows out of speakers located in the ceiling. Rachel feels like she is an imposter in someone else's dream.

"Is this the way it usually goes around your house, or is it just this way tonight because I'm here?" Drew asks as he shifts his legs uncomfortably. Apparently, sitting with legs crossed is not a comfortable position for the big lineman.

Rachel tilts her head to one side, and her vivid auburn hair slides over her cheek. "What do you mean?" she inquires.

"Is it typical for your mom and sister to disappear together to do their thing while your father slips away to his office, leaving you all alone?"

Rachel is surprised by the young man's question. "You're wondering if there's a pattern there," she comments.

Drew nods his head and continues to gaze at her with his large blue eyes.

Rachel touches the spot between her nose and eye where tears customarily travel and looks down at the cushion decorated with black sailboats and anchors. "I feel like I've always been so hyper-sensitive to those things," she comments, nodding her head slowly. "I take them so personally."

"I can see why," Drew says in his deep bass voice that randomly reminds Rachel of her favorite operatic performer.

"You can?" Rachel replies as she looks up, blinking away tears.

Drew nods again and says, "Definitely. At first, I was the obvious focus of attention, but as the night went on, I saw a shift occur. Your mother kept looking at Celeste again and again—it's like she comes alive every time she looks at her. And your dad, he began reciting story after story about your sister, the soccer phenom and the academic star. It's like he worships her."

Rachel looks at Drew with such sad, innocent eyes that the young man wants to take her into his arms and comfort her.

"I didn't think it was obvious to others," she says quietly.

"Well, it is," Drew remarks, nodding his head slowly. He hesitates a moment and then asks carefully, "If you're offended by this question, let me know, but do you think it's because you're the adopted daughter?"

Rachel takes a deep breath and lets it out slowly. "I forgot I told you I'm adopted," she says. "You've got a good memory, Drew. And yeah, I'm sure that has something to do with it," she admits. "Also, Celeste's interests are their interests. They've never really appreciated music and art—my world, you know."

"I love music and art," Drew says with a big smile.

Rachel's laugh rings out as pleasantly as a bright bell, a sound that brings a smile to Drew's face.

"Keep those comments coming," she says, "and you'll get past all the sentries around my heart."

There is a silence in the room that harmonizes with the silence of the birch trees outside dressed in their silver coats.

"Do you want to know something?" Rachel eventually asks. The right side of her face is in shadows.

"Of course. What is it?"

"Are you familiar with the Phantom of the Opera?" Rachel asks.

"I think I saw the movie with my aunt when I was a kid," Drew replies.

"Yes," Rachel comments, "there is a silver screen version of it. Personally, I've always been drawn to Webber's theatrical version of it—live, on stage, I mean. It may sound silly and even weird, but as a girl, I identified with the ghostly phantom in the play. Like him, I always felt misunderstood and so alone. I was angry, too, just like the phantom."

Rachel pauses and sighs. Then she looks out into the night and admits, "In my darkest moments, I wished my sister had never been born."

Drew studies the young woman with compassion in his eyes but does not speak.

"As I grew older, I realized that I felt rejected by two sets of parents," Rachel says. "My birth parents didn't want me, and then the parents who chose me the second time around decided that I wasn't what they wanted, either. It got to the point where I thought there was something inherently wrong with me. I couldn't see it, but everyone around me apparently did."

"I'm surprised," Drew says in his unique way of indicating that he has something to say but then waits for his listener to flush it out like a pheasant in tall grass along the fence line.

"Okay," Rachel says, "about what?"

"I would've guessed Cinderella was your favorite story, not the Phantom of the Opera," Drew replies. "You know, that age-old story of how Cinderella is treated like a second-class citizen by her stepmother and sisters."

Rachel glances out the frosted window at the white winter world and confesses, "You're not wrong about that, Drew. I did identify with

Cinderella, too, when I was younger. Unlike her, though, I was never invited to the royal ball."

As soon as she is done speaking, Rachel feels her face grow hot, and she glances at Drew. She is embarrassed about being too transparent, for letting someone see too deeply into her private self.

The young man sitting across from her on the bay window bench smiles and says, "Somewhere in your past, Rachel, you were invited to the ball. Maybe not by the prince, but by the King himself. God invited you to come and join His party at the most beautiful palace in the universe. I received an invitation too, because of you. Now you and I are sitting together at the same ball. Both of us are here by *special* invitation."

Rachel laughs charmingly, and her eyes sparkle as she looks at Drew. "Has anybody ever told you that for a guy, you're really amazing? Especially for a guy who's a big old football player."

The brawny university student leans back, and his brows turn downward, feigning offense.

"Rachel, you keep forgetting that I'm not just any football player. I'm an offensive lineman," he says, stressing the last two words. "Offensive linemen are intelligent, thoughtful, and articulate. We're different than all those other gridiron jocks."

Rachel puts up her hands and says, "My bad; I didn't know that. I thought all football players were cut from the same pigskin."

"Ha-ha," "Drew replies. "After everything you've been teaching me the last few days," he comments, "I'm glad I can finally return the favor and teach you something, even if it is about big old football players."

"Yeah, it's about time," Rachel quips in return.

A silence settles between them as they gaze awkwardly at each other. When the quiet extends for a long time, Drew abruptly gets to his feet with a bit of a grimace due to his complaining legs that have been crossed far too long. He extends his hand to Rachel and asks, "May I have this dance?"

"This dance?" Rachel inquires in surprise.

Drew smiles playfully at Rachel and says, "Yes, this dance. Since we've both been invited to the King's ball, we should do what people do at a ball, and that's to dance."

At a sudden loss for rational thought, Rachel stammers, "But the music—"

"You don't want to dance to 'Joy to the World'?" Drew asks with incredulity. "Considering the current circumstances of our spiritual lives, I can't imagine a better song for us to dance to."

Rachel gazes up at the extended hand of the prince a moment longer before a broad smile relocates many of the small stars on her cheeks and nose and hides others. She extends her hand to Drew and says, "Come to think of it, I agree with you. 'Joy to the World' is the perfect song at the King's ball. So yes, you may have this dance."

Drew takes Rachel's hand gently in his own, and the woman stands up next to the royal courtier. Then he draws her carefully to himself. Soon they are dancing slowly around the family room.

While the birch trees shiver in the cold moonlight, Rachel is suddenly very warm. She is very aware of two things: the two blue eyes wonderfully looking into her soul and the words with double meaning that sing quietly in the background: "And wonders of his love, and wonders of his love, and wonders, wonders, of his love."

CHAPTER 20

Deliverance

Hysterical, Emily cries out a third time as she vainly attempts to shove the heavy body off her own. She jerks her head away instinctively and grimaces, waiting for the blow that will likely render her unconscious to the evil that will be perpetrated against her body and spirit. Instead, the large hand that reeks of beer and the sickeningly sweet smell of pot covers her mouth and nose, and she cannot breathe. In that moment, through the dark shroud of sheer panic and utter powerlessness, she is convinced that she is going to die.

She is terrified that she will never see another sunrise. She will never get to say goodbye to her sisters and brother. She will never speak with Embee again. She will never be held by Natalie—

Her mind races. The rumbling train cars hurtle at lightening-speed past her dimming eyes, and she thinks a thousand thoughts in the span of ten seconds.

She hears voices in the distance, but she is in such a delirious panic that she does not know if they are real or only a wishful figment manufactured by her oxygen-deprived brain. Maybe...they are angels.

The voices grow louder and louder. It is as if they are getting closer. Then she hears a voice yell, "What's going on?"

The cruel weight on top of her suddenly lifts from her body, and the vice-grip over her mouth relents. The evil that descended so suddenly out of the dark night is gone just as abruptly. Miraculously, Emily finds herself gasping for air. Two people are kneeling beside her in the darkness that is barely illuminated by a streetlight next to the public restrooms. A man's voice asks, "Are you alright?"

Emily instinctively shrinks away from the man who is wearing a white polo shirt and khaki shorts.

"It's okay," a woman's voice says reassuringly. "You're safe now. We were walking down the beach when we heard you scream. We're here to help, honey."

"There was a man—" Emily croaks but then can say no more. She is sobbing. Her body is shaking violently.

The woman kneeling in the sand next to Emily takes one of her hands into both of hers. "Yes, we saw someone running away when we got closer," she says. "But he's gone now, sweetie. He ran toward the street."

"Are you alright?" the man inquires again.

Emily's full body sobs continue with epileptic intensity.

Without looking up from Emily, the woman holding her hand says, "You need to call the police, Jack."

"I'm already on it," the man responds as he turns away to speak with someone on his phone.

Minutes later, Emily's rescuers walk her up to the pavilion next to the parking lot. Emily and the woman sit down on a bench under the soothing radiance of several boardwalk lights. The man named Jack stands in front of them like a bodyguard, his eyes alert for any new threats. Emily's convulsing body begins to calm.

While they wait for the police to arrive, the woman—who now has her arm wrapped around Emily like a mother comforting her child—asks, "Did you know him?"

Emily wipes her eyes with a tissue and then blows her nose. She shakes her head and replies in a quiet, trembling voice, "No...I don't think so. I was just sitting...when he grabbed me. He—" Emily notices that her tongue feels thick and that her lips are not speaking the words according to the wishes of her brain.

"It looks like he hit you hard," the man says as he leans down and examines Emily's face under the glow of the lights. "Did he hurt you...in any other way?"

Emily hesitates and then attempts to take a physical inventory. Initially, she has difficulty connecting with her external self, but eventually, the numbness lifts enough for her to access her body. When her scan is complete, she takes a deep breath and tries to stop shaking. Finally, she shakes her head and mumbles, "No, not really."

The man in the white polo, who appears a decade younger than her father, crouches in front of her and is silent for a while. He glances up at his female companion and then back at the young woman. Eventually, he asks, "What's your name?"

Emily does not look at the man but eventually offers her name.

"Well, Emily, this is Alexa," he says, nodding up at the woman next to her on the bench, "and my name is Jack."

Emily nods her head as she stares down at the concrete sidewalk that is partially covered with powdery white sand. She is trying to fight off a strong wave of nausea that threatens to disgorge the contents of her stomach.

"Do you know what's kind of weird?" the man asks Emily, trying to distract the young woman from her discomfort.

Emily glances at the man from the tops of her eyes as she takes another deep breath and blows it out through her mouth. She shakes her head.

"You yelled my name," Jack says, "when the man was attacking you."

He pauses a moment and then qualifies, "Well, you didn't yell my name since we've never met before. But you did scream the name, 'Jack.' Honestly, that's how you got my attention."

"Actually, you screamed three different times," the maternal woman adds as she offers Emily another tissue from her navy-blue clutch. "Each time, you cried out a different name."

"Yeah, it was the first time you cried out that you said my name," the man named Jack says. "Do you remember that?"

Emily glances into the man's eyes and shakes her head slowly.

"The second time that you screamed for help—" Alexa begins but then pauses, her voice husky with emotion. She hesitates and then takes one of the tissues and dabs her own eyes. "Sorry," she says, "I'm a mother of three daughters." The woman swallows hard and then finishes what she is going to say, "The second time, you cried out for your dad."

Emily looks up as quickly as her throbbing head will allow and stares at the woman. Her eyes are wide with surprise.

Alexa wipes away tears that are rolling down her cheeks and adds, "Actually, you didn't use the word 'Dad,'" she says, correcting herself. "You cried out, 'Daddy!' I think that's so touching. I know our girls would want Jack to be there for them if they were in any kind of danger."

Alexa pauses and smiles compassionately. Then the woman says, "Every girl wants a father to protect her—if she even has a father—a strong and good Daddy who loves her with his life."

Emily feels a new wave of emotion rise in her throat against her will, compounding everything else she has experienced over the last hour. "What...what name did I say the last time I screamed?" she inquires in a voice tight with emotional stress.

Jack glances at his wife and then looks back at Emily. "'Jesus,'" he says quietly. "You cried out the name, 'Jesus!'"

As the sound of a lonely siren pierces the quiet of the night, Emily leans against the mother beside her and begins weeping softly. Again, against her will.

The paramedics arrive in their EMS vehicle with flashing lights but no siren.

They get out quickly and stride up to the bench illuminated by the two pools of light. They ask Emily a few preliminary questions to determine the nature of the assault, then assist her into the back of the ambulance.

In the bright mobile triage room, they examine her for injuries. Beyond some bruising on her arms and a contusion on her left cheek, their only other findings are mild intoxication and an acute stress reaction that leaves her trembling and slightly disoriented. Undoubtedly, she is the survivor of trauma.

One of the paramedics, a woman named Heidi who has short, tightly curled blonde hair, notices a stain on Emily's shorts. She immediately informs Emily that she will need to change into some scrubs that they will provide for her. She explains that the police will want to keep her clothing to check for hair samples, clothing fibers, skin cells, or bodily fluids the assailant may have left behind. Emily initially hesitates but complies in the end.

The squad car arrives minutes after the paramedics. Two officers get out—a male and a female—and walk over to Emily and the EMS personnel. They stand in the doorway of the ambulance and ask Emily what happened. Then they ask her if she wants to file a criminal complaint. Once again, she hesitates. She wants what happened on the beach to be shoved into the same crowded closet along with everything else painful and terrifying that has happened to her over the last five years.

She opens her mouth to voice her refusal, but Heidi interjects first, "Emily, you need to use your voice for you and all other women who have been and will be assaulted in the future. Besides, there could be evidence on your clothing that might help us ID the perp. With your help, he can be apprehended before he tries to rape someone else tomorrow night."

Emily rests her forehead on her open hand and shakes her head. She just wants everything to be over so she can go back to her normal life. Eventually, she glances up at Annie, who is looking at her expectantly.

Emily sighs and then turns to the female detective. "Okay," she says, "I will file a complaint."

Annie smiles at her and then gives her a gentle hug. "You're doing the right thing for all of us," she says into Emily's ear. "I applaud your courage. Other women will be safer because of your courage."

When Emily indicates that she is ready to step out of the emergency vehicle, Annie helps her over to the bench, where she sits down with Alexa again.

The other paramedic, named Nick, hands Emily a business card with several phone numbers on the back. One is for a local crisis line and the other for a sexual abuse trauma group that meets in nearby Coral Cove.

After the paramedics have left, the female police officer—her badge identifies her as Det. Williams—begins questioning Emily. "Can you give us a physical description of your assailant?" she asks. When Emily offers her the little information she has, the detective rapidly types Emily's response into her mobile crime pad.

"What was he wearing?" she asks next. Then, other questions follow. "Did he say anything to you? What do you remember about his voice? Did he have an accent? Did you scratch him or bite him? Okay, your clothes have been placed in a plastic bag. Good. We'll take them with us, and they'll be processed by the lab. Did he have any other identifying features, such as tattoos or piercings? What did he smell like?"

The questions go on for ten minutes. Emily does not have much to offer the detective. She is offended that her questioner several times refers to the perp as "your assailant," as if he somehow belongs to her.

When the questioning finally ends, detective Williams asks a reluctant Emily to blow into a breathalyzer to determine her BAC while the other detective walks down to the beach where the assault occurred. Jack accompanies him to show him the site. It is easy to find since Emily's blanket and personal items are still there. The detective takes dozens of pictures and, with the assistance of a powerful flashlight, examines the scene for evidence.

When they walk back to where Emily and Alexa are sitting, detective Williams returns from the squad car where she had retreated briefly and informs Emily that a serial rapist has been assaulting women up and down the gulf coast from Tampa to Naples in recent weeks. Even though Emily has not been able to give them much of a description beyond the man's thick body size and a few details about the sound of his voice and what he said, the detective comments that he could be the same perp. If they find DNA evidence on Emily's clothing, it could be a major break in the case.

Detective Williams zips up her electronic pad in its black carrying case and hands Emily a card. "If you remember anything else," she says gravely, "and I mean anything, call us at this number. Day or night. A detective will be assigned to your case and will contact you in the next few days. You may be summoned to the station for more questioning depending on the forensic results and any breaking developments in the ongoing investigation."

The other officer, Det. Ramirez, smiles grimly at Emily and remarks, "You're fortunate that Mr. and Mrs. Warren were here tonight to interrupt the assault. Extremely fortunate. It did not go nearly as well for the other women this man has assaulted. He's big, strong, sadistic, and clearly has big-time Mommy issues. That's a bad combination in a perp."

The two detectives dismiss themselves and begin walking back to their cruiser.

Before they are ten feet away, detective Williams stops, pauses, and then turns back to address Emily.

"By the way, young lady," she says with a frown, "Another bad combination came to my attention. Sitting alone on the beach at this time of the night while drinking alcohol to excess is one of the most idiotic things you can do as a woman. Didn't you learn anything in college?"

The detective pauses for a moment, then nods her head knowingly. "Oh, yeah," she says sarcastically, "I know you'll tell me you're not stupid.

After all, you're a college grad. Personally, I don't give a rat's behind how many 4.0 semesters you racked up. Tonight, you got an 'A' in stupid partying habits."

The detective pauses again as she glances at her partner and then back at Emily. "For the record, Ms. Johnson," she says, nodding her head, "we came very close to citing you for public intoxication. Doing what you did tonight on this beach is like parking a Lamborghini in Model City, leaving your keyless remote on the dash, and walking away. A crime will happen."

When detective Williams tilts her head down and stares at Emily from the tops of her eyes, the young woman, who is already shaken by the assault, looks away and says nothing. Her blood boils at being scolded in a manner reminiscent of her parents, except that this correction is three times as harsh.

The Warrens linger with Emily for several minutes after the detectives have left. They help her retrieve her belongings from the beach and secure them in the trunk of her Super Beetle. Alexa holds Emily's hand for a while longer as they stand beside her car. She offers the young woman a ride home and tells her that they can bring her back to her car sometime tomorrow.

Emily thanks the Warrens as she successfully fights back her aggravating tears for the first time since the assault. However, she declines their offer, saying that she is fully capable of driving herself home since she lives only five minutes away.

When Emily unlocks her car door, Alexa says, "If you don't want us to drive you home, feel free to call a friend or your parents for a ride. We don't mind waiting here with you until they arrive."

Once again, Emily declines Warren's offer and insists that she will be fine. To herself, she thinks that it will be a very cold day in Florida before she calls her parents. They will only freak out and get preachy. Besides, they rarely drink alcohol and will be totally disappointed by her decision to drink hard liquor, especially when alone at the beach late at night. No, she will not risk exposing herself to their shaming overreaction to her choices.

"Can we at least pray with you, then?" Jack inquires.

Emily hesitates and then nods her head. She is beginning to wish the couple would leave.

After the Warrens have prayed for the calming of her heart and for her future protection—Alexa has an arm wrapped around Emily's waist the whole time—Jack pulls out his wallet and extracts something. He hands Emily her third business card of the night.

"Since you cried out Jesus' name during the assault," he says, "I'm assuming you have some connection with Him. Well, I'm a pastor at the Gulf Area Community Church in Bonita Springs. Feel free to call Alexa or myself if you ever need anything. Otherwise, just show up at church for service on a Saturday night or Sunday morning if you want to check it out. We would be thrilled to see you again, Emily."

Emily nods her head slowly and takes the card. "Thank you," she says quietly, swallowing more of the tears that make her feel far too vulnerable. She slips the card into the pocket of the blue scrubs along with the other two cards.

"Before we go, I want you to know one last thing, Emily," Alexa says in a confiding voice. "Jack and I were supposed to meet my brother and his wife in Ft. Lucy tonight for supper, but they canceled on us because their son had to be rushed to the hospital. He has complex allergies, and apparently, he ate some peanuts that weren't supposed to be in a birthday cake at a friend's house. When my brother called and canceled on us, we decided to come here for a meal and a late-night stroll on the beach."

The woman pauses and then says, "My point, Emily, is that we shouldn't have been here tonight."

"Some people will undoubtedly dismiss it all as coincidence," Jack interjects. "But as believers in Jesus, there are no coincidences for us, Emily. I believe that God summoned Alexa and I here to this beach tonight for the sole purpose of interrupting the evil intended against you." The man smiles kindly at Emily and then adds, "Jesus is obviously very fond of you."

Emily stares at Pastor Jack Warren in the dim light of the parking lot and is silent. More emotions roil in her chest. Eventually, she thanks the couple one last time and climbs into her car. The Warrens leave only after she has locked her doors and started her car.

Emily takes a deep breath and quickly drives out of the familiar parking lot that has now been forever tainted with terror. When she reaches the downtown area, she pulls over to the curb under a bright streetlight where a handful of people are walking on the sidewalk.

After she checks and then double-checks her doors to make sure they are locked, she sits alone for a long time, listening to the loud Super Beetle engine rattle and jingle. Eventually, she covers her face with her hands.

"If you're a good God," she screams into her hands, "why did you allow this to happen tonight? Why? Am I that evil that I deserve to be punished? Do you want to destroy me like the pastor at that fundamentalist church told me you would? Or are you trying to cast the demon out of me that my friend at college said I have inside of me?"

Emily pauses and leans back on the headrest of the car. Her body is trembling from the trauma of the night and with bitter anger. "If you hate me so much, why did you send the Warrens to save me?" she yells. She pauses again and drops her forehead onto the leather-wrapped steering wheel of the car. "I just don't understand you, God...if I even believe you exist."

After a few minutes, Emily lifts her head and stares out the windshield into the night that is dark and heavy. She vaguely registers that her head is missing its broad white headband, surrendered to the paramedics, along with the rest of her clothes. She picks up her phone and stares at the blank screen for a long time. In the end, she thumbs it several times. Soon, she talks to a voice on the other end.

A few minutes later, after punching the red 'hang up' button, she throws her phone on the passenger seat and puts her car in gear. She accelerates, and the quirky engine accosts the quiet of the night with its jangling racket. She steers south and begins the seventy-five-minute drive to Marco Island for her second attempt at comfort that night. The first round had ended very badly.

Five minutes ago, she was torn. Now she feels, suddenly, all-in. How capricious she can be...

As she rolls past Ibis Street a short time later, Emily glances down the road where her parents are probably sitting beside the pool, worrying about her—and praying for her straying heart. She swallows hard. Then she lifts her chin and turns to stare into the darkness ahead that is lit only by the two inadequate headlights of the Super Beetle.

CHAPTER 21

Tragedy at the King David

The next morning is Sunday. It is warmer than the previous day. A gentle breeze blows in from the east, caressing the city like the hand of a mother softly stroking the cheek of a precious child. The Sabbath ended last night at 6 p.m., so the streets in the New City are busier—not a welcome development for security personnel at the conference. The three members of team Atlanta enter the elevator and descend from the fourth floor of the King David Hotel to the ground floor.

As she walks off the elevator, Aly is torn. She does not know whether to feel embarrassed—like a criminal being escorted to prison—accompanied as she is by Daniel and the two other soldiers who have joined them or to feel excited—a famous rock star protected from rabid fans by her three personal bodyguards. Aly normally would have smiled at the thought. But the Uzis in the soldier's hands punctuate the moment with an undeniable gravity. All levity in her mind evaporates. She takes a deep breath and prays to the Bodyguard above all bodyguards.

While in the elevator, Daniel had explained to Aly, Moussa, and Kameel that many of his military counterparts carried assault rifles, but that he and his men often preferred submachine guns like the Uzi in the event of a close-quarters battle. He told them that the Uzi was almost like a large pistol—easy to carry and quickly manipulated when reaction time is a more important variable than the penetrability of the round. Daniel's explanation was TMI, in Aly's opinion. It only served to heighten her mounting anxiety.

When they exit the front door of the hotel and step out into the fresh morning air, a surprise is waiting for them. Parked in the driveway at the end of the sidewalk is a vehicle that resembles a giant, deformed Jeep. It is equipped with heavy armor and oversized donut tires that look like they can churn through a muddy swamp. Some type of large gun rests on top. The vehicle looks huge and formidable to Aly.

David Abramovich jumps out of the tall vehicle and saunters toward the party of six. Aly notices that the colonel's son is dressed in a suit—typical—with no tie—atypical—and, yes, sunglasses are resting on the top of his head. She smiles to herself and shakes her head slightly. She cannot take her eyes off the young Israeli.

The Mossad agent smiles and sweeps his hand toward the oversized vehicle. He announces, "Welcome to the COMBATGUARD. Just like supper the other night in the garden restaurant, this ride comes compliments of the colonel. We will transport the three of you the amazing distance of 500 meters to the conference venue," he says with an amused smile. "What is the old saying in America? Better safe than sorry? Today my father says we will be safe, not sorry."

Kameel smiles and says, "This will be my best ride since Chaplain Joshua drove me through the Sinai desert in his MFO jeep when I was ten years old!"

Aly stares at the vehicle and declares, "It's physically impossible for me to climb up there. I will need to walk to the conference—unless you have a trampoline so I can jump into the front seat."

Daniel shakes his head with feigned impatience and trots over to the imposing military vehicle. He reaches up and pulls down a small metal ladder located beneath the passenger door. "No trampoline required," he says.

One by one, the Atlanta team, the two soldiers, and David and Daniel climb into the COMBATGUARD. Aly feels like she is in a tank. Moussa smiles sheepishly at David and says, "Never, in all my dreams, did I imagine myself riding in an Israeli military vehicle. Do you see the great irony in this moment?"

"God created irony when He died in the very universe He created," the Mossad agent responds with a grim smile.

Less than a minute later, they disembark the vehicle and are ushered up to the third floor of a modern building where the conference hall is located. As they move forward, the four Israelis scan their surroundings with great vigilance. All of them have a finger on the trigger of their weapon, ready to utilize it if the situation demands.

The final day of the fifth annual International Apologetics and Monotheistic God Studies Conference unfolds more smoothly than the previous day. Lecturers lecture. Panel debaters debate. The keynote speaker delivers her morning address. Lunch is served in the same room, followed by more lecturing and more debating. It is during a lecture by an apologist from Nigeria that Moussa experiences a Moshe Abramovich alert. He sees the colonel enter the room and take a seat at the table nearest the exit. For such a big man, he moves with the ease of a cat.

Toward the end of the afternoon, the director of the conference invites Moussa Ahmed to come to the front of the room and join him under the glass dome. This invitation was expected. Moussa had been contacted the night before and asked if he would be willing to address the conference a second time, on this occasion, for a Q&A time with the director serving as the moderator.

As Moussa walks up to the front of the room, he looks out the paneled windows that provide a 180-degree panoramic view of the Old City. For a glorious moment, he imagines that he is living in first century AD Jerusalem. He is on his way to hear Jesus speak in the Temple courts under the watchful eyes of the Roman legionaries in the Antonia Fortress...

A block of thirty minutes has been set aside for the Q&A time. However, as the list of questions texted to the moderator multiplies, it is soon evident that half an hour will not be a sufficient block of time. The decision is made to extend Moussa's time, cutting into the afternoon break.

The young man who recently had a miraculous encounter with Jesus answers question after question: What did He look like? Have you seen Him again? How might I see Jesus? How do you know He is God? Describe your current relationship with your sister and your family back in Thailand. Do you still pray *salat*? Could the appearance have been a dream within a dream? Do you regret Jesus inserting Himself into your life? Do you hate Muslims now? Is it true that, unlike Allah, Jesus speaks intimate words of comfort and love to His followers?

Halfway through the Q&A, a question is leveled at him from the radical Saudi Arabian imam he had encountered the previous day. Not bothering to text his question, the Muslim leader stands up and asks in front of everyone, "Now that you have committed *takfir*, do you fear that someone will attempt to kill you just as you were going to kill your sister?"

Moussa wisely chooses to ignore the question on the grounds that it is presented outside the established text message format.

Many of the individuals in the audience—Jews, Muslims, and Christians alike—seem intellectually curious but not heart-curious. However, Moussa discerns that several of those who ask questions seem to be genuinely seeking God, just like Aly had done for years before her surrender to Christ. To the seekers and the non-seekers alike, Moussa mentions that he is still amazed that Jesus pursued him even when, unlike his sister, he was doing no seeking at all. Accordingly, how can he not surrender his life to the God who saved Him out of nowhere?

After an hour has passed, the moderator indicates that there is time for one final question from the live audience. Even before the moderator gets the last word out of his mouth, a short, rotund man who looks to be a few years older than Moussa, stands up. His attire identifies him as an imam.

"My name is Abdullah Khan," the man announces as his left eyelid twitches. "I am an imam visiting from Saudi Arabia. My question for you, Moussa, is if your conversion to Jesus has changed only the beliefs in your head, or if it has changed your heart as well." When he is done speaking, the man sits down and considers Moussa with solemn eyes.

"The best question has been saved for last," Moussa declares quietly as he nods his head slowly. The new believer in Jesus closes his eyes and utters a brief prayer before he responds.

"Certainly," Moussa eventually answers. "Most certainly. Yes, my beliefs about Jesus have changed radically—the most notable being that I no longer see him as a mere human prophet but as the second personality of the divine Trinity. But even more critical to me than my beliefs, if such a thing is possible, is my personal experience with Jesus the Christ in my heart."

At this point, Moussa places both hands on his chest and smiles. Everyone in the room sees a radiance brightening his face, and they cannot look away from the young man.

"In my *head*, I know who my Creator is and the purpose of my existence," Moussa explains. "I know where I come from and where I am going. In my heart, Jesus has become my best friend. He is close to me, not distant. He is knowable, not unknowable."

"In my *head*, I know I'm going to heaven. In my *heart*, I hear his voice now and sense His presence closer than a brother. I can't explain it all yet, but what I can say is that I know in my head and feel in my heart that I am deeply loved by Him. Yes, that is my most powerful experience of Jesus: He loves me, and He will always love me. I can do nothing to lose His love because, amazingly, it does not depend on my good works but on His ability to love."

The new believer looks around at his listeners and says, "If you remember only one thing I say today, remember this: what makes faith in Jesus distinct from every other belief system in the world is grace. When you choose to live for Jesus, it's not about your efforts to be a good person. Being good will earn you nothing in His kingdom because you can never be good enough for such a holy God. Faith in Jesus is never about your *doing*. It's about what He has already *done* for you.

"Grace tells us that Jesus paid the penalty for our sin against God—a price we could never repay. Never. Jesus loved us so much that He bore the penalty of our offense against the Holy God. He stepped in when the death penalty was announced against us and gave His life in place of ours. But He didn't stop there.

"Grace tells us that Jesus also gave us His righteousness, His goodness. He took our bad and gave us His good—the amazing exchange. Now we are in Him, and He is in us. When God the Father looks at us, He sees His Son, Jesus.

"Finally, grace tells us that everyone who believes in Jesus is now invited to approach God's throne boldly since Jesus is now our doorway to the Father. Because of His death, we have been adopted into the family of God. We are brothers and sisters of Jesus. We are His friends. We have no doubts. We have no worries about divine rejection. In fact, His own word tells us that we are already seated in the heavenly places because of grace."

Moussa falls silent as he looks around at the men and women who have come from many different nations and who represent radically different faiths. Then he says in a hushed tone, "There's one last thing I want you to know."

The young Jesus follower pauses and looks toward the back of the room where Moshe Abramovich is still seated by himself. "Five weeks ago—" he says slowly, wanting his listeners to absorb his every word, "five weeks ago, I was willing to die for my old God because of my hatred for infidels and even for my brothers I considered inexcusably weak in faith.

"Today, I serve a new God. His name is Jesus. I'm still willing to die for my faith, but now only as I bring the message of His great love to my old brothers, the Muhammadans. I am willing to give my life for Him because he has given His life for me."

After he is done speaking, Moussa stands quietly in the front of the room for a long time. Behind him, the late afternoon sun pastels the tawny Old City wall with muted hues of orange and crimson.

Eventually, Moussa thanks the attendees for asking such gracious questions, then makes his way back to his table. Many attendees at the tables clap for him. A few rise to their feet in approval of his message. Others sit on their hands and say nothing.

Aly beams at her brother when he sits down beside her. She grabs one of his hands in both of hers and exclaims, "What a miracle God has done in you, brother! You were so right in what you told me last night. I must not shrink away from bringing the truth of his loving message to our people. How amazing that you did not shrink away in fear today. I am certain Jesus is pleased that you are such a bold witness of His love and truth."

Moussa leans close to his sister and whispers, "I cannot help but speak of Him."

After a short break, two lecturers deliver anticlimactic addresses about future integrative approaches to faith. Then the conference officially ends with a few parting words from the organizers. Among other things, a Jewish woman announces that next year's conference will be held in Rome.

While many participants depart immediately, some men and women linger in the room, chatting and smiling and joking. Three or four are still animatedly debating with one other. At least a dozen people approach Aly and Moussa and speak graciously to them. Half of them are Muslims.

The last person to approach the Ahmeds after all the others have drifted away is the grumbling imam from Saudi Arabia. After appearing so opposed to Moussa earlier, he proves, in the end, to be secretly hungry to learn more about Jesus. He only parts from the Ahmed siblings after he has obtained Moussa's email address and phone number.

When Moussa looks around the room to locate Colonel Abramovich, he discovers that he has already left. He is disappointed. He had hoped to say goodbye to the Beth Shin agent with whom he now feels a strange bond—and toward whom he feels a strong urge to share more about Jesus.

Aly, Kameel, and Moussa are escorted out of the conference room by a different door than they entered. "We can't be too predictable," David comments as they climb back into the COMBATGUARD and drive the thirty seconds to the King David Hotel.

Once at the hotel, they exit the military vehicle and take the elevator up to their room on the fourth floor. They will shower, pack their bags, eat supper, and then drive to Ben Gurion airport that evening. Their flight to Rome departs at midnight.

Aly is amazed that she has been in Jerusalem for only four days but feels like she is leaving something cherished behind. Or maybe, it is someone cherished she is leaving.

The night air is cold. The Atlanta team is walking out of the King David Hotel toward the driveway where the unique military vehicle is waiting. David is behind the three visitors from America, taking up the rear, while Daniel and the two other soldiers are on point. The bellhop is just behind the three soldiers, pushing the luggage on a cart that clacks down the stone sidewalk like a train on a rickety rail.

The luggage is what saves them, initially.

But so does Aly.

After descending the three steps from the portico that shelters the front entrance of the hotel and taking several steps down the sidewalk, she hears something she had forgotten. Words of warning that Miriam the prophetess spoke to her months earlier on the dock by the Aquarium classroom whisper in her head.

Immediately, Aly stops and raises her arm like an advance scout warning her party of danger. Moussa and David come to a halt behind her. They tilt their heads at her, confused.

Just as Moussa opens his mouth to ask his sister why she has stopped, her eyes rivet on the soldiers in front of her, and she screams, "Daniel, run!"

CHAPTER 22

An Unexpected Visitor

Stewart awakens to an empty feeling in his chest—nothing new about that. But something else stirs within him as well. An ache. It does not feel good. He is alone and now feeling lonely as well. He is very familiar with the passage from the Bible that says, "Weeping may tarry for the night, but joy comes with the morning" (Psalm 30:5). On this morning, however, he feels that weeping comes with the morning, not joy.

The loneliness within him is so strong he does not dare feel it for long. "Imploding" is the word that comes to his mind. He must find a way to medicate or distract, or he will implode.

Miriam's words from the night before speak inside his mind again: "How can you love others if you remain in the cave? Open the door and come out."

His heart is a cave. The cabin is a cave. Both are places of escape that are far removed from the world of people. But the tradeoff that accompanies safety is always the same: throbbing aloneness. When will he finally shun safety and choose intimacy even at the cost of risk and pain?

Despite the loneliness that threatens to drive him into the wilderness of numbness, Stewart feels more energy than he did the previous day. He climbs out of his sleeping bag and revives the fire that is on life-support.

After consuming a breakfast of apple and cinnamon oatmeal and dried apricots, he opens his Bible to Matthew 7:7 and reads, "Ask, and it will be given to you; seek, and you will find; knock, and it will be opened to you. For everyone who asks receives, and the one who seeks finds, and to the one who knocks, it will be opened."

Stewart sets his Bible on the small wooden table and stares at the large horizontal logs that form the back wall of the cabin. They are in shadows because the snow has blinded the Cyclop's eye.

As he meditates on his experiences over the last few days, he resolves something in his mind that is as unfamiliar as his slowly thawing emotions. He folds his hands on his lap and looks up at the ceiling. "God, this surprising loneliness is capturing my attention," he says haltingly. "I think you're telling me that I've never let anyone close to me. Am I scared? Proud? Untrusting? I think the answer is yes, yes, and yes. But how do I change all that?"

Stewart pauses, feeling embarrassed by his unusual transparency with God. He is relieved that no one else is in the cabin. He is being too visible, too vulnerable. Safety has always been the primary need—not physical safety but emotional. *Maslow had it wrong if he believed that physical safety was most essential,* Stewart thinks to himself. *Unless you're in a war zone, maybe, where physical safety is threatened day and night.*

"Okay, God, I'm going on record again," Stewart says aloud. "I did mean it last night when I said I...need someone. I need you. Please hear me, God."

Stewart repeats his simple prayer a few more times to make sure he is heard, then rises abruptly from the solitary chair and grabs the small cooking pot and his mittens.

"It's time to get out of this hiding place," he says with conviction as he turns toward the door, the cooking pot shovel in hand. "Miriam told me to come out of the cave, God, so I'm coming out. Even if it takes all day to dig my way out, I'm getting out of here."

A second later, he cries out in surprise and stumbles backward, landing hard on the wood floor. He had just opened the door only to see a figure standing outside where the snowdrift had previously buried the opening.

Stewart's mouth has dropped open, and he is speechless. He adjusts his glasses and stares in disbelief at the sight in front of him.

"Well, aren't you going to invite me in, Stewart?" the stranger inquires. The deep voice is friendly, even jovial.

Stewart is even more dumbfounded that the unexpected visitor knows his name. He sits transfixed on the floor a while longer, his arms extended out behind him and the palms of his hands resting on the cold planks.

"Who—who are you?" Stewart finally stammers.

"Michael, of course," the visitor says without hesitation. "Some people simply call me The Messenger. So, are you going to invite me in or not? I never enter unless I'm invited. You know, 'ask' and 'knock' and all that."

Stewart gets to his feet slowly, keeping his eyes trained on the man named Michael. When he has regained his feet, he backs up toward the fireplace and says, "Yes, okay. Yes. Come in...Michael."

When the visitor enters the cabin, he straightens up to his full height. It is only then that Stewart realizes the man must have been bending over while he was outside. Stewart looks up at him and is shocked for a third time. His unanticipated guest, dressed in a pewter-gray winter coat with a fur-lined hood, is every bit as tall as the titanic Dr. Hawkstern!

The giant named Michael stomps his massive boots on the floor while he unzips and sheds his coat. Then he takes a step toward Stewart, who quickly moves out of his path.

"Sorry, pardner," the man apologizes in his rumbling voice, "I got to get near that fire of yours and thaw out a bit. I'm not from these parts—not used to the cold. Besides, it took me a while to dig through that drift of yours."

"How—" Stewart begins. "What did you use to dig with?"

The imposing figure turns toward Stewart and holds up two hands the size of frying pans. "These here paws," he replies with a chuckle. He turns back to the fire, rubbing his huge hands together.

Stewart steps to the open door to close it. Before he does, he looks outside and sees the tunnel that Michael had dug. It is easily twelve feet long and six feet high! In that moment, Stewart realizes that the whole cabin must be buried under the massive drift. He shuts the door and turns to stare at the huge man's back.

"How long did it take you to dig the tunnel?" Stewart asks, amazed. "For that matter, how did you even know there was a cabin here?"

Michael pivots and looks down at his smaller host. The visitor is dressed in a flannel shirt that is as large as a small car trunk and a forge-gray pair of waterproof pants. His blonde hair is curly and frames a large face that is ruggedly handsome. Curiously, his face is clean-shaven. His eyes are a brilliant azure, the color of the Minnesota sky on a clear summer day. They twinkle like stars on the darkest of nights. Small wrinkles appear at the corners of his eyes as he smiles at Stewart and replies, "Saw the smoke from your fire. Took me most of the night to dig you out even with my big mitts."

Stewart stares at the mammoth man and shakes his head. "I don't know what I would've done if you hadn't dug me out," he says with gratitude. "It would've taken me three days to dig through that drift, and I would've filled up half the cabin with snow."

"Seventy-nine point nine three six four," the man remarks.

Stewart tilts his head at Michael.

"Seventy-nine point nine three six four is the percentage of your cabin that would've been filled with snow had you attempted to dig yourself out."

Stewart opens his mouth to reply, but Michael speaks first. He says enigmatically, "You must have friends in high places, Stewart."

"And that's another thing," Stewart says as he squeezes the bow of his glasses. "How do you know my name?"

"Ah," the big man says, elongating the word, "now there's a good question. What if I told you I knew your name because you look like a Stewart to me?"

When Stewart says nothing but simply stares back at Michael, the man throws his head back and laughs loudly. "Yes, yes, I know—a poor attempt at humor. The truth is that I know your family back in Two Harbors. I've known them for a long time."

"I thought you said you weren't from the area," Stewart says, narrowing his eyes.

"You're good, Stewart," the giant says with a broad smile that reveals strong white teeth. "You're really good. Always so quick with your brain." He pauses just a second and then adds at a threshold Stewart cannot hear, "A bit slower with your heart, though."

Stewart opens his mouth to ask his visitor to repeat what he said, but Michael speaks first again. "Got some grub here, Stewart? Digging that tunnel left me hungry—mighty hungry."

The bespectacled young man smiles his crooked smile and nods his head. "I've got freeze-dried beef stroganoff and some MREs I snagged at the military surplus store in Duluth."

The visitor rubs his chin with an index finger the size of a large carrot and smiles sheepishly. "If you can spare it, I could eat one of each."

"Not a problem," Stewart says. The ache in his chest is gone. It has been replaced by an unusual sensation that feels exciting and warm.

As Stewart prepares the food, Michael sits on the floor with his tree-trunk legs crossed and his broad back against the fieldstone fireplace. He lets out a long groan that sounds like a black bear and asks, "So, what're you doing up here all alone, Stewart?"

Stewart pauses from tearing open the MRE pouch and looks into Michael's dazzling blue eyes. "I've been coming up here for years now," he remarks evasively.

"Now that's an answer," his lunch guest comments, chuckling, "but it's not the answer. Are you always so careful about what you reveal to others?"

Stewart begins to say no, then hesitates. He tries to look away from Michael but finds that he cannot. He answers candidly, "Yes, I'm always careful about what I say to others. It's not like I do it on purpose, though. It's a reflexive habit."

"What's that—a reflexive habit?" the huge man inquires, his thick, wheat-colored brows raised in curiosity. His head is resting against the fireplace, and he is running his large hands through the curly meadow that is his hair.

Stewart removes the MRE from the heater bag and hands it to his visitor along with a spoon. He begins to answer the man's question when he notices that Michael's eyes are closed, and his lips are moving. Stewart stops talking and stares at the huge man.

A few moments later, Michael opens his eyes and looks up at his host. "Sorry, Stewart. Just giving thanks to my Father for your generosity." He takes a bite of the MRE and sighs loudly as a smile spreads over his face. Then, with his mouth full of food, he asks, "What were you saying?"

Stewart regards his visitor for a while, then retraces the five steps back to his single burner cook stove. He is looking down at the stove when he replies, "People always hurt me, to answer your question."

The man seated next to the fire takes another bite of the MRE and inquires, "Do you have a lot of hurtful people in your life, or do you get hurt easily, Stewart?" There is no malice in his visitor's voice.

Stewart feels something cold stir in his heart, and his mouth clamps shut as if steel cables had been lashed over his lips. He is well aware of what is happening. He is in full retreat. Now Michael will never see his heart but will receive some detached intellectual response.

He surprises himself when he opens his mouth and confesses, "I suppose it's true that it doesn't take a lot to hurt me."

As Michael chews, he asks, "How do you react when you perceive hurt so easily, Stewart?"

"I hide," he remarks hollowly as he stares off toward the back wall of the cabin.

"And how's that working for you?" Michael inquires as he sets aside the already-empty pouch.

"It keeps me safe," Stewart comments as he pours some steaming beef stroganoff out of the small pan and onto a tin plate.

"At what cost?" the visitor asks as he receives the second meal offered to him with a nod of his lionesque head. "I can't help but notice that twelve-gauge on the floor." His eyes glance toward the weapon lying beside the small wooden table.

Stewart feels the familiar fire of humiliation burn in his chest, and his mouth again shuts like the drawbridge of a besieged castle.

"You hate me right now," Michael announces, lifting his eyes from the plate of Stroganoff.

"No, I don't," Stewart says in instant denial.

"Yes, you do," Michael returns without hesitation. "When a man withdraws as deeply, and for as long as you have, eventually you hate yourself and everybody around you. So much for 'you shall love the Lord your God with all your heart and with all your soul and with all your mind and with all your strength'" (Mark 12:30).

Stewart stops pouring food onto his plate and sets the pan down on the table. He walks over to the lion-man and thrusts the plate of food toward him as a hostile gesture. He shocks himself when he snaps, "So what am I supposed to do, Michael? I let people know me, and I get hurt. I hide from others, and I end up hating everybody in the universe. I end up alone if I do, and I end up alone if I don't, so why even try?"

"That explains the shotgun," Michael says, nodding his huge head with its curly mane at the weapon. The guest looks up at his host, and Stewart stares into the azure eyes that are suddenly welling up with sadness.

Before he knows what is happening, Stewart abruptly falls onto trembling knees in front of the giant man whose plate is already almost empty. Something deep inside of him wants to reveal everything in his heart to his unexpected visitor.

"What must I do to be delivered from the prison cell of my heart?" Stewart cries out as his glasses slide down his nose.

Michael shovels the last of the food into his mouth and sets his plate on the floor next to him. "Not bad for freeze-dried," he announces, still chewing. "Almost as good as that four-year-old MRE."

The giant lets out a satisfied sigh and stretches his long arms toward the ceiling. "To answer your question, Stewart, you need to seek, you need to ask, you need to knock—all things that a proud, hidden, protected man cannot do. In short, you must become as needy and transparent as a child."

Stewart leans back on the heels of his feet and says, "That's the last thing I want to do. I already said I get hurt when I let myself need. I always get bullied when I'm vulnerable."

"Only a broken and needy heart is open enough to receive God's love," Michael declares. "Every other heart—even if it appears nice on the outside—is guarded, stubborn, and sufficient on its own."

The huge visitor pauses and then levels a gaze at his host that peers into the darkest dungeon of Stewart's heart. "Absolute self-protection is absolutely dangerous," he states. "It's far more impenetrable than a thousand snowdrifts like the one in front of this cabin."

Stewart stares at the man sitting across from him and ponders his words.

When he does not reply right away, Michael says, "But you know that already, don't you, my friend?"

Stewart stares into the man's eyes and answers slowly, "Yes, I confessed to God just this morning that I'm stubborn and self-sufficient." He pauses and adds, "I also told God that I need Him."

Michael smiles widely, and his eyes are again wreathed with the small wrinkles of warmth and compassion. "Indeed, you did," he says with a nod. "Indeed, you did."

The giant man stretches out his legs in front of him until they are almost touching Stewart. He extracts a carving knife from his pocket along with a block of wood. As he begins to whittle shavings off the piece of wood, he says in the deepest voice Stewart has ever heard—a voice that is consonant with the man's unusual size—"God created you and every other human on this planet to know Him, to love Him, and to experience the peace and joy that comes from being a son or daughter in the Father's house. But there is an opposer who fights to rob you of your intimacy with God and destroy your awareness of being His child."

The titan lifts his chin and gazes at Stewart through narrowed eyes.

Eventually, he says, "The enemy is a kidnaper who steals you from your father's house and then convinces you to stay with him, the thief. He whispers into your ear untruths about your Father, persuading you that He is unloving, unfair, and judgmental. This enemy will even attempt to convince some children that their Father doesn't exist, that they are alone in the universe, and that they should trust Him instead. You might call it a type of spiritual 'Stockholm Syndrome' where the hostages bond with their kidnapper even when treated poorly."

Michael looks up from his whittling and once more penetrates Stewart's heart with his piercing eyes.

"The thief hates everything about love and intimacy and only wants to separate you from your Heavenly Father," he says. "You, Stewart, have been opposed by the accuser since you were a toddler. I believe you already know that. He has been winning the battle for your heart most of your life. He has taught you to hide, to hate, to distrust, to blame, and to believe you are safe only when you're alone. All these lies are diabolically opposed to what your father created you for. Diabolically," he repeats for emphasis.

Stewart hangs his head and stares at the floor. "I thought God came into my heart three years ago," he says, "but I still get hurt so easily and hide so quickly. It's first nature for me. Sometimes I wonder if I'm even a true believer. Maybe I'm nothing but a poser."

Michael shakes his head and points the block of wood at Stewart. "Never believe that accusation, my friend. That's a lie from the pit of hell. Yes, through Adam, you were born in sin, separated from God. But then, by grace, God made you alive through Jesus. Yes, the good news is that you've been born a second time, and now you are God's child. No one, not even the prince of darkness, can take that away from you."

Stewart is quiet as he listens to The Messenger's words. He has heard some of them before, even as recently as the fall semester at the Academy, but today they seem to be taking a foothold in his heart instead of being blown away, like so many tumbleweeds, by the slightest wind of doubt.

"There's one thing that rarely makes it to your heart even though you know it in your head," Michael says as he turns his attention back to the block of wood.

When the giant man falls silent, Stewart asks, "What's that?"

Michael stops carving and looks at the young man whose face is covered with five days of dark stubble. "The mystery that has been hidden for ages and generations but now is made known to all the saints," he answers. He pauses and then declares, "The mystery of Christ in you, Stewart, the hope of glory."

Stewart nods his head but says nothing. Michael stares at him with his vivid blue eyes. "Did you hear me, Stewart?" he asks slowly. "Jesus lives in you."

"I heard you," Stewart replies.

"Did you really hear me?" Michael persists.

"Yes, Jesus lives in me," Stewart says quietly, adjusting the weight on his knees. He is concerned that he has disappointed his oversized visitor.

"Do you know what that means?" the man asks.

Stewart shakes his head and replies, "Apparently not."

Michael looks down and begins carving the piece of wood that now is looking less like a block and more like a wand of some sort. "You're an intelligent man, Stewart. I'm sure you know about the largest star in the universe."

Stewart's face lights up. "Yes, I do. It is so large it would require 2,000 of our suns to match its circumference, and it would take a commercial jet more than a thousand years to fly around it."

"What did I tell you, my friend? You *are* smart," Michael says. He continues to whittle away at the wood as he adds, "The Creator God who designed that gargantuan star lives inside of you, Stewart. Can you imagine that? The God who called into existence such an unfathomably massive star with only a word resides in your heart."

Stewart adjusts his glasses and wrinkles up his nose. "I never thought about it quite that way," he admits.

"Well, think about it, my friend," the visitor says. "Consider what it means to be a vessel made of dust which is indwelt by the God who was never created and will exist forever."

Stewart shakes his head and comments, "I know that, but I don't know that. At least, I don't meditate on that truth."

"Well, start meditating on it instead of on that shotgun of yours," Michael says. "Meditate on Him who loves you so much that He has chosen to be your defender, Stewart. Hear His voice instead of the voice of the thief who wants you to believe that you're nothing but a worthless collocation of atoms in a meaningless universe. Don't think about who you are, but whose you are. You belong to the God who made everything."

Stewart nods his head as his thirsty heart guzzles every word.

Michael concentrates on the piece of wood in his hand once more. The two men go on conversing, with Michael doing most of the talking and Stewart most of the listening. Stewart adds wood to the fire three or four times as the two men lounge on the floor in the lonely cabin that is not so lonely anymore. Michael eats three more MREs along with a plate of Stroganoff. Stewart is too intent on what his visitor is telling him—no, teaching him—to have any interest in food.

Six hours after the unexpected visitor arrived, Michael pushes himself up from the floor and rises to his full height. He stretches and growls loudly—like a black bear again. His presence seems to fill the cabin. "Time for me to move on," his voice rumbles like retreating thunder after a storm.

"You just got here," Stewart protests, getting to his feet. "Besides, it'll be dark soon. You can't leave now."

"You've been kind enough to feed me," the giant remarks. "I've returned the favor by leaving you with an admonition to seek and ask and knock. Only those who seek, ask and knock admit that they need a Savior. Just need, my friend. Need *Him*."

Michael dons his winter coat with the fury hood and zips it up. As he is pulling his mittens on, he confides, "The times are dark, Stewart, and you must come out of your hiding place. Hiding people may be safe in the darkness of their minds, but they are selfishly unavailable to love others. Getting hurt is not the worst thing in the universe, my friend. Sitting alone on the sidelines when people are crying out for love is far worse. You must come out."

Stewart stares up at the man standing before him like a thick oak tree and remarks with a sigh, "I've heard that before."

Michael laughs, and his blue eyes sparkle with an energy that brightens the room. It will linger for hours after he leaves. "When God wants you to consider something seriously, He tells you once," the giant says. "When He wants you to hear something and do it, He tells you twice. When He wants you to hear, remember, and absolutely act in obedience without hesitation, He tells you three times."

Stewart looks at the face framed by the huge, furry hood and reflects aloud, "I've heard that same message three times now—from Miriam, from the gospel of Matthew, and now from you, Michael."

"Well, then, my friend, you know what that means," the big man says as he turns and opens the door.

As the Messenger bends down to exit the inadequate doorway, he looks back at Stewart one last time and says, "Remember, don't lock the door and hide. Instead, open the door of your heart and start knocking on God's door. Be prepared to act when it opens. You are being summoned to the front lines of the battle, Stewart. You have an amazing future serving an amazing God if...if you obey."

Michael smiles one last time at Stewart and says, "Later, son of the King." The young man is tempted to grab his radiant visitor to prevent him from leaving.

The mammoth man—he looks even more unearthly huge in his coat with its mammoth hood—negotiates the long snow tunnel and then straightens up and trudges off into the dusk of the late afternoon. Stewart watches his unexpected visitor through the small aperture of the tunnel until he disappears. Then he shuts the door against the cold and collapses into his chair.

The one-room cabin feels different. It is brighter, alive, pulsating with excitement. Often when people leave a room, they leave emptiness in their wake. Michael leaves it full of hope.

Stewart sits in the lone chair for a while, lost in thought. Then, abruptly, he jumps to his feet and exclaims aloud, "He didn't have snowshoes. I must give him mine!"

Stewart grabs his snowshoes from under the bed and throws open the cabin door. He runs like a madman through the snow tunnel without his coat and out into a sunless world. The copper hues of the vanishing light are surrendering to an invasion of dusky purple. The first star of the evening is a pinpoint of light in the velvety sky.

Stewart looks to the east and then to the west and then across the frozen, snow-covered stream at the trees on the far side of the large meadow. Nothing. He sees only the ghostly white landscape framed by dark trees and the twilight sky.

The unexpected visitor is gone. Vanished.

Stewart turns and trudges reluctantly back to the cabin, his shoulders hunched and his head bent toward the ground. Even though he still senses the lingering presence of hope as he closes the door for a second time, the everlasting loneliness is now waiting for him in the cabin. It grips his throat, and he finds it difficult to breathe.

He walks over to the crackling fire that generates a heat reminiscent of the warmth radiated by Michael's presence. *Such a brief visit. Just enough to whet my appetite and then leave me like everyone else.*

Stewart's downcast eyes fall on the object his visitor had been fashioning from the block of wood. It is lying on the floor where his massive guest had been sitting just moments earlier. Stewart bends over and picks up the handiwork of Michael's hands. It is a carving of a skeleton key.

The kind that unlocks dungeon doors.

CHAPTER 23

Sniper Becomes Miguel

Sniper does not discharge his firearm at the former gangster named Syko Loco. Instead, he lowers the weapon and throws it side-armed as one might throw a Frisbee. It sails above the flames of the fire and lands with a thud at Armando's feet.

"This is your chance, Paragraph," Sniper says in a voice devoid of any passion. "Finally, your chance—after all these years." The gang leader laughs and then smiles in a manner that looks more like a grimace. "Go ahead and kill me. I got nothin' to live for anyway. Send me to hell."

Armando is visibly surprised. Just seconds ago, he thought he was a dead man—for at least the third time in his life. He stares at the handgun lying beside him and then looks up at Sniper. Eventually, he picks up the weapon and turns it over in his hands.

He ejects the magazine, examines it briefly to see how many rounds are in it, and reinserts it as he had done earlier in the car with his Walther. Then he raises the gun to a horizontal position and points it toward Sniper just as the gangster had done to him. The gang leader sits as still as a fixed target at a gun range.

Armando licks his lips and swallows hard. He keeps the weapon on Raul's murderer for a long time.

Jack's heart begins to beat rapidly for a second time even though his head tells him that his friend will never pull the trigger. He thinks he hears his friend mumble, "I hated you and lived for the day when I could kill you."

Finally, Armando shakes his head slowly and laughs softly to himself. He looks over at Jack and announces, "Juan and I made a promise never to kill the people God sends us to save. It's very difficult to tell someone about Jesus if they're dead." Armando lowers the gun and throws it back across the fire. It thuds onto the ground next to Sniper.

The gang leader does not even look down at the weapon. He runs his hand over his head that gleams in the firelight like orange metal. His face relaxes noticeably as he comments, "So you are not here to kill me. You are here to save me. All four of you loco people are here in my barrio to save Sniper," he mutters sarcastically. In Jack's mind, the words "save" and "Sniper" do not belong in the same sentence.

Sniper wraps his arms around his knees and strangely begins rocking back and forth slowly. He stares pensively into the fire as he chews alternately on his lip and then on his knuckle.

Something about the man looks young to Jack. Maybe it is his baggy pants or his smaller, lithe body sitting on the ground. He certainly does not look as threatening as he did only minutes ago. He appears to have shrunk into himself. When he finally does begin speaking, he does not seem to be addressing anyone in his present company except, possibly, his sister.

"I was eighteen," he begins. "I was in her room. She would be dead the next day. But I thought she was goin' to die right there before my eyes. I was afraid. I was so sad I could not breathe. The one person in the world who loved me was leavin' me."

Sniper pauses to take a deep breath and lets it out slowly. "She actually opens her eyes. I could not believe it. I saw her eyes one last time. I lean over her bed, so I am close to her face. She tries to talk, but she is so tired. So tired. Finally, I put my ear next to her lips, and I hear her whisper, 'Miguel, be like Jesus'. Those were her last words to me. 'Be like Jesus.'"

Sniper places his hand on his forehead and shields his eyes from his listeners. "I did not listen. I became the father I hated—the man who killed everythin' about me except my body. I turned the hate I had for him against the world. I hated every man. I killed every man who tried to dominate me," the gangster admits with a shake of his head.

"I'm sorry," he mumbles toward the fire. "I'm sorry, *mi abuela* Cecilia, for not listening." He glances briefly at his sister from beneath his hand. Then his eyes fall to the ground.

The angelic form of Angela Rosa in her white dress stirs, and she speaks so softly that everyone leans toward her to hear what she is saying. "You are sorry, *hermano*. Good. Godly sorrow is the first step when you come to Jesus."

Then, anticipating what Miguel might say in response, she adds, "You don't have to earn His love. All you need to do is come to Him and be sorry for what you've done. Yes, it will cost you your life, but He will cleanse you from all your badness. His love is that forgiving." The woman pauses, then adds, "Above all, His love is safe."

Jack and Armando glance at each other. For the second time that night, they know they are thinking the same thing. As they watch the gang leader and his sister, the two men begin praying that Jesus will penetrate Sniper's anger, hatred, grief, fear, and guilt until he reaches the man's hard heart.

In the moment, Jack remembers the words that Shadrach, Meshach, and Abednego uttered just before the enraged Babylonian King

Nebuchadnezzar threw them into the fiery furnace: "…our God whom we serve is able to deliver us from the burning fiery furnace, and He will deliver us out of your hand, O king. But if not, be it known to you, O king, that we will not serve your gods or worship the golden image that you have set up" (Daniel 3:17–18).

Inspired by the faith of these three young men, Jack prays, *God, you are able to save Sniper, and you will save him. But even if you do not, I will serve only you, Lord Jesus. I trust you with all my heart, and I worship you, the Maker of all things.*

Jack stops praying because he is interrupted by words he will never forget.

Are you ready, son? he hears.

Surprised, Jack turns to look at Armando and sees that his eyes are closed in prayer. Then he looks through the flames in time to see Sniper turn away from his sister to look at him. The gang leader's head pivots so slowly that Jack feels as if the scene before him is in slow motion. When Sniper's eyes finally lock on his face, they are glassy. They appear to be looking right through him.

"You and Syko Loco should be dead," the gang leader announces matter-of-factly. "I was going to kill you myself." He pauses and then says, "There's only one reason you're still alive."

Jack returns Sniper's stare but says nothing. He is not listening to the man of dust. He is listening to the words that are speaking in his heart. *Are you ready, son? I am here with you, and nothing is too hard for me.*

Jack feels an overwhelming presence fill him, and he feels a strong urge to cry out. He is tempted to scramble to his feet and jump over the wooden fence that surrounds the backyard. The words of David in Psalm 18:29

shout in his head: "By my God I can leap over a wall." Never has he felt so energized.

What's going on? he asks himself. *Is this what mania feels like?*

Sniper, who has continued to stare at Jack, raises his tattooed arm and points at him. The man's movements are still in slow motion for Jack. The gang leader narrows his eyes and says with no animosity, "You're still alive, *gringo*, because I've seen you somewhere before."

Armando, Angela Rosa, and Carmelita turn to look at Jack.

"Months ago, I had a dream about two men comin' for me," the gangster intones as if he is drugged. "In the dream, it was your face I saw." Sniper's arm is still raised, and his finger is pointing at Jack. "I did not see the other man's face. Tonight, I know that he was Syko Loco."

Something swells within Jack like a gigantic wave cresting, ready to break. It is not emotion that fills his heart; it is something far more powerful than mere emotion. It rumbles up from the deepest mine shaft of his heart, and he says without hesitation, "Yes, we were fighting through the forest of angry trees. We were coming to save you, Sniper."

The gang leader's face freezes momentarily, his arm still raised in the air. Then his countenance reflects recognition, and his eyes abruptly grow large. He lets out an unintelligible cry and leaps to his feet as if a rattlesnake had slithered up beside him.

"You know the dream!" he cries out not as a question but as a statement of fact.

"Yes, Armando and I both know the dream," Jack answers as the powerful surge within him continues to rumble up from the depths. He can barely contain it now. "In the dream, we are coming to help you, but the trees are your enemies, and they try to stop us from reaching you."

"*Verdad!*" Sniper cries as the animated man bends over at the waist and then lifts his head to stare at Jack and Armando like some deranged contortionist.

The mood around the fire is electric. The gang leader's head is nodding like a bobblehead figurine. Angela Rosa has a hand over her mouth, and she is beginning to weep. Carmelita has a knowing look on her face and is loudly repeating, "Gracias Dios." Her hands, of course, are raised toward the night sky.

"Then the trees become dark warriors—demons," Sniper continues with feverish intensity. "They chain me to a rock, and I know I'm goin' to die!" he exclaims. "I thought you two were the ones comin' to kill me, but now, tonight, I find out you were comin' to save me from the demon warriors!"

Jack and Armando stare at each other. They know they are thinking the same thing. Violet was able to reveal only part of the dream. Now they have heard the rest of it. Whether the trees are demons or gang members from the Familia Nuestra Valinda set, they do not know, but it is enough for them that Sniper knows who they are. What is certain now is that the dream foretells the deliverance of the gang leader through the coming of the two strange men sitting around the fire with him at this very moment.

Sniper falls to his knees and clutches his fists in front of his chest. Jack thinks the man looks insane but insane with what? Fear? Anger? Craziness? Joy?

"You do not know how long I've lived in dread!" the man cries out like a madman as his body writhes in the firelight. "Every night, my sleep has been tortured by the demon trees—grabbin' me, clawin' at me, tearin' my flesh!

"Ever since I had the dream, I posted Spyder in front of the house as a lookout. I warned him to be lookin' for two men who would be comin' for me, one of them a gringo. I told him to kill you immediately if you were carryin' any weapons because that would be a sure sign you were sent by the demons. I would know that you had come to kill me just as the dream predicted."

Armando, Jack, Angela Rosa, and Carmelita glance at each other through the flames of the fire, their initial shock and disbelief now tempered by amazement. Jack again hears the words in his heart, *Are you ready, son?*

Sniper continues to cry out, "Even though you came with no weapons, I was still goin' to kill you. But then Angela Rosa and Carmelita appear out of nowhere! So, I know somethin' isn't right. They were not in my dream."

The gang leader's eyes dart back and forth across the faces of his four guests. Then he scrambles to his feet again and leaps over the fire to where Armando and Jack are sitting. He falls on his knees in front of them and cries out, "You must help me! I fear no man, but the demons terrify me! What must I do to be delivered from the forest of darkness?" His voice is a tortured plea.

Sniper's eyes communicate desperation as he looks from Armando to Jack and then back to Armando again. "My grandmother loved Jesus, and she was the kindest person I ever knew," he cries. "You love Jesus," he says, staring at Armando, his eyes wide, "and you're the most forgiving person I know. And the rest of you here love Jesus," he says, his eyes jumping from Jack to Carmelita and then to Angela Rosa, "and you're the bravest people I know darin' to come to this dark hellhole."

The gangster pauses and then announces with total abandon, "I want to know the God who makes people kind, forgiving, and strong!"

Sniper looks nervously over his shoulder and cries, "And you must protect me from the dark warriors in my dreams. They're more dangerous than any man I've ever met."

Angela Rosa is now weeping more loudly than before. Carmelita leans over to the younger woman and wraps her up in one of her infamous lilac-laced embraces.

Armando, who used to be Syko Loco, says to Sniper, who is about to become Miguel, "You must ask for forgiveness of your sins, then declare with your mouth that Jesus is Lord and believe in your heart that God the Father raised Him from the dead. Then you will be saved."

Still on his knees, Sniper folds his hands and presses them against his chin.

He smiles and says, "Your words are familiar to me. How often did my grandmother speak them to me in another lifetime? But I could not hear them then. I would not hear them. Now I do. I want Jesus to wash away my sins and make me into a new man."

The gang leader pauses and then raises his hands toward the night sky. "*Gracias, Dios*," he cries out loudly as a shiver runs up and down Jack's spine. "Your light has pursued me into the darkness of hell itself."

It is a few minutes after midnight in the barrio of Valinda. Except for the muted thumping of a lonely helicopter rotor and the distant wailing of several sirens, the night is quiet. The fire is burning low, and the air is growing noticeably cool.

Many people in Los Angeles are sleeping. Others are seeking escape from their empty lives by pursuing personal pleasures that provide a fleeting respite only to leave a deeper emptiness. Some are engaged in violent conflicts, whether with words or fists, or weapons. Hundreds are gasping for their final breath on the streets, in their beds, or in the hospital. Others are alone, sad, weeping, and wretchedly seeking ultimate deliverance from the sufferings of life through the pseudo-mercy of self-inflicted death.

Most men and women are conducting their lives oblivious to the existence of the unseen, the spiritual realm where true joy and the purpose of life reside.

Something far different is happening in the backyard where darkness has reigned for so long. Sniper bows his head and talks to the God he cannot see with physical eyes or hear with physical ears. It is the first time he has spoken to Jesus since he was a young teenager in his grandmother's house. It has been far too long.

Jack's head is also bowed, but he watches the gangster—who is only three feet away—from the tops of his eyes and marvels.

Kneeling so close to the man, Jack can see his tattoos very clearly for the first time.

His head is inked with a dozen small skulls. They have knives thrust into them, or jagged holes likely blasted open by gunshots. The eye sockets are not empty, as one would expect with skulls, but are occupied by oversized eyeballs that stare out malevolently at the world. Jack's gaze drifts down to the gang leader's neck. He can make out what appears to be a skeletal hand wrapped around his throat.

Jack shakes his head slowly, and a smile spreads over his face. *No one is beyond the love of God,* he thinks to himself. *No one. Not Mahmoud. Not Sniper. Not Drew. Not me! Everyone who calls on the name of Jesus will be saved!*

Sniper concludes his prayer with the words, "And I believe that you raised Jesus from the dead. Sí, I believe that truth now, just as *mi abuela* did! Now raise me, too, because I been dead for many years."

The gang leader of Familia Nuestra Valinda pauses, laughs, and then declares, "Sniper has died with you, Jesus—he is no more. Now Miguel rises with you to new life! Yes, I am risen with you, Jesus!"

The new creation looks up slowly. When Jack looks at Sniper—no, Miguel—he swears that a mask has been removed from the man's face. His countenance has been completely transformed. It is radiant and not from the flames of the fire.

Jack has seen the look before. He knows what has happened. Miguel is now inhabited by the person of God Himself. Nothing on this planet has the miraculous power to change the heart of a man or woman from stone to flesh, from darkness to light, from despair to joy, from utter emptiness to fulness of joy, except Him.

Jack laughs aloud as he reaches out and plants one hand on Armando's shoulder and the other on Miguel's. He digs into the file cabinet of his limited Spanish vocabulary and announces, "*Hermanos.*"

Miguel flashes a smile that illuminates the darkness—the spiritual darkness. Before the new creation can say anything, his sister nearly tackles him as she throws her arms around her brother's neck and hugs him like a long-lost friend, which he is, of course: long-lost but now found. Angela Rosa is still crying—tears of joy, of course—and has no words.

This time, Miguel hugs his sister tightly. As they rock back and forth, he says in a gentle voice, "*Mi, hermana, mi hermana, mi hermana.*" Jack can't tell if Miguel is laughing or crying. Most likely both.

By this time, Carmelita is on her feet, dancing around the four young people.

Her swaying shadow, cast onto the backyard fence by the dim light of the fire, looks like a snowman with a small head on top and two stubby legs beneath. Like Miguel, she, too, is repeating words, except that hers are lyrics in a song that she sings as she moves: "Satan is a roaring lion seeking someone to devour, but *Dios* is the Maker of the heavens and the earth."

At the sight of the squat woman gyrating and singing in the backyard that formerly had been owned by darkness, Jack and Armando break out into hilarious laughter despite their best efforts not to do so.

Jack looks from Carmelita to Miguel to Angela Rosa and finally, to Armando. Everyone is laughing or crying or singing.

What a peculiar scene, he thinks to himself. *The world would not understand what is happening here tonight. Who says miracles do not occur in this universe? The healing of a cancer-ridden body, sight returned to the blind, hearing restored to the deaf, a dead physical body raised from the dead—none of these miracles are greater than the miracle of Sniper's belief in Jesus on this night. A spiritual transformation has just occurred that is more powerful than an earthquake measuring 11.0 on the Richter Scale! Most amazing of all, this spiritual resurrection will endure forever.*

If someone has eyes to see and ears to hear, God will transform that heart. He will deliver it from the domain of darkness and transfer it to the kingdom of His Son, where only light can dwell.

CHAPTER 24

EMILY AND HER FRIENDS

The next morning, Emily is sitting in a coffee shop around the corner from Natalie's condo. Two friends, Jeannie and Taylor, join them. They converse for a long time about Emily's assault. Taylor shares the account of her near-rape at the hands of her then-boyfriend during her sophomore year of college. Then Jeannie speaks about her nightmare relationship with her divorced stepfather, who isolated both her and her sister from their mother and sexually abused them into their mid-teen years.

Jeannie's comments about her horribly abusive father generate a heated discussion concerning the topic of fathers in general. Natalie comments that her father was physically present but emotionally absent. Taylor reveals that her father was a stumbling, fall-down drunk with unpredictable rage. "And your father," Natalie announces to Emily, "may be the worst of them all—a narrow-minded religious fanatic who doesn't know how to love his daughter if she colors outside his rigid lines. I did enough Sunday School when I was young to know that Jesus hates Pharisees like your father."

A rare, fleeting urge to defend both Jesus and her father awakens inside Emily. If she were honest with her peers, she would tell them that Jesus does not hate her father, and that her father is not a "fanatic." But as usual, she tamps her thoughts down yet again and defers to Natalie, the woman with strong opinions and a penchant for controlling others.

Natalie would be highly displeased if she knew Emily even entertained the thought that she was controlling. Since Emily hates conflict and tension of any kind, she rarely disagrees with the stronger Natalie—at least not outwardly. Keeping the peace is Emily's goal whenever possible. She is rarely aware that her coveted peace comes at the price of her own existence. She is absolutely unaware that a slow annihilation is occurring. A death of God's beautiful creation.

Taylor taps her fingers with energy on the rim of her coffee mug, but the expressionless mask she wears over her face does not change. She comments in her quiet manner, "Yeah, Emily, your father is the worst of the worst. At least my father leaves me alone to choose what I want for my life. He even told me that he hopes Jeannie and I are happy together. Your dad certainly wouldn't say that to you, would he?" Her words are a statement, not a question.

Emily's brilliant green eyes glance nervously at Taylor as she adjusts the broad headband that covers a third of the golden hair on her head. Then she looks down into her coffee and dies a bit more.

"I don't think you're totally sold out," Jeannie accuses as she scrutinizes Emily's averted face. "You still hear your parent's voices in your head, don't you?"

Natalie raises both hands in front of her and treads the minefield known as Jeannie carefully. "Hold on now, guys," she says placatingly. "Emily and I have already been through this whole thing—just last night, in fact. She has agreed to meet with my therapist, who will help her navigate the stages toward complete acceptance of being gay. Emily's on board with us, just not quite at the place of total identification. She'll get there soon. Remember, it was a journey for all of us, too."

Natalie pauses, and an elfin grin spreads over her face. Then she exclaims loudly in an attempt to distract Jeannie, "We're a band of blazing queers who won't let anything or anybody stand against us!"

From the tops of her eyes, Emily notices that Jeannie, her butch friend, is still scanning her face as if looking for cracks. Emily eventually looks up and forces a smile. "You're my tribe," she says with a laugh. "You guys all accept me for who I am, and that's why I'm with you."

A cautious smile appears on Jeannie's face, and she says, "Okay, then. I'm pumped that your allegiance is to us and not to your psycho-Christian parents. The American culture will soon leave all homophobes and haters behind. We're all about love and tolerance now. Everybody has the right to be who they are, and if anybody judges them, they should be silenced."

Emily stares at the woman across the table from her and nods her head. Inside, she is torn—still. But an inexorable shift is occurring that, if left unopposed, will soon tip the balance toward a new identity and extinguish the hope of any return to the old Emily. A hard commitment will soon be required of her heart. A person can only walk a tightrope for so long.

She has a fleeting intrusive thought about her father's comments about dissonance before she brushes it away like an obnoxious deer fly.

Emily is thankful that Natalie has not yet inquired about her plans for February. She is waiting to break the news about her possible return to the Academy for spring semester. If she is going to surrender to the nagging summoning that demands a total conversion to a new self, she wants to turn over every stone before she abandons the old.

CHAPTER 25

Mystic Drawbridge

Drew pushes his plate away and wipes his mouth with his cloth napkin. Looking at Rachel, he comments, "Honestly, I never in a million years thought I'd become a Christian. I don't think I was ever opposed to Jesus. I just didn't see how He was relevant to my life. The culture around me told me that I could make myself happy if I had the latest and best version of a smartphone, drove a cool car, wore rad clothes, toned up my body, had a babe on my arm, and a beer in my hand. I bought into the material. I believed it all. I never gave a thought to my spiritual life. Looking back, I was as lost as a bat with no radar."

"But you were increasingly aware of an emptiness in your life," Rachel states.

Drew nods his head as he looks out at the Mystic River that flows next to the restaurant. Unlike the Hudson River in upstate New York, he has noticed that there is no ice on this river that is so close to the ocean.

"For sure," he replies, "especially after Pete's death. That shook me up like nothing else could."

Drew pulls his eyes away from the dark water of the river and looks back at Rachel. "Do you think Pete's in heaven?"

Rachel sighs and purses her lips. "I don't know," she replies. "I certainly hope so. What I do know is that God is the only Being in the universe who is perfectly just and fair. God loves Pete, and He will be true to Himself."

"From my early reading of the Bible, it doesn't sound like everyone goes to heaven," Drew observes, his face earnest.

Rachel glances out the window at the drawbridge that spans the river only a hundred yards away. "There are many people—all of us, some people would say—who don't want to be in heaven," she muses aloud. "They don't seek after God. In fact, they outright reject Him or, I suppose, passively reject Him. Either way, they make it clear they don't want Him to be their Father. They don't think they need God's help. Even though they're spiritually dead, they refuse to cry out to God for new life."

Drew absently fingers the knife lying on the table in front of him. "I was reading this morning in the gospel of Mark where Jesus said that those who think they're well have no need of a physician. Only those who know they're sick ask for the help of the physician."

He pauses and looks at Rachel with his large blue eyes. "Do you think people know they're sick and refuse to ask for help, or is it that they don't even know they're sick, and so they settle for not being well because they think their current life is as good as it gets?"

"Or they know they're sick, but Satan blinds their eyes to who the physician is," Rachel adds.

"Yeah, that too," Drew agrees.

"I suppose it could be any of those depending on the person," Rachel offers. "It certainly seems obvious that people won't go to the doctor if they don't feel sick—or if they're experiencing symptoms but decide to ignore them, hoping that the pain will go away on its own."

"Do you think God allows us to experience pain, so we'll know we're sick and then turn to Him for help?" Drew inquires.

"Yes, I definitely believe that," Rachel says as she pins a loose strand of auburn hair behind her right ear. "Pain certainly led me to cry out to Jesus."

"Me too," Drew offers. "But only because several weeks earlier you and Jack came and pointed me to Jesus. If you hadn't come to me, I wouldn't be here right now. I'm convinced I would've taken my life."

The large young man drums his fingers on the tablecloth and observes, "I was the guy who was sick for years but denied it. I was the guy who didn't even know where the doctor's office was, so to speak. But if I had known the phone number, I'm 95% sure I would've been too proud to schedule an appointment."

"Maybe a lot of people ignore their pain or try to deal with it on their own because they don't believe there's anything beyond the physical world," Rachel reflects aloud. "Like you, they don't know where the doctor's office is or that there even is a doctor who exists in this universe."

"Exactly," Drew says, nodding his head. "That was me. I thought that getting high or drunk or being with a girl or being successful on the football field or getting wild on the dance floor were what made life worth living. As I've said before, I lived for the rush. But when the rush wasn't rushing, I was empty and restless. My only hope, really, was looking forward to the next rush—almost like a feast and famine thing. Full and happy one moment and empty and starving to death the next."

Rachel takes a swallow of her coffee and says, "God's Word does say that sin brings pleasure, but that it's a fleeting pleasure. I don't mean that everything that brings pleasure is sin, only that sinful things are tempting to pursue because they do bring a temporary high. I think that's what food did—or does—for me."

Rachel feels warmth rise in her cheeks at the revelation of her addiction.

"So even food can be sinful?" Drew asks. "I'm in trouble, then, because I love food—and often lots of it!"

Rachel backpedals a bit. "No, I certainly don't think food is inherently sinful.

God gave us many good things to enjoy, including food. However, my relationship with food became unhealthy, even sinful, because I turned to it for comfort, a sense of control, and even to be perfect. Food became my way to comfort myself instead of trusting others. It isolated me. I've now come to believe that anything that takes me away from God and other people is sin."

Drew slides his knife around on the tablecloth, then looks up at Rachel.

He inquires, "Do you mind me asking how the food thing is going for you?"

Rachel sits back in her chair and clears her throat. "I don't talk about it very often," she admits haltingly. "It's something I usually keep between me and Jesus. It just feels too shameful to talk about—you know, one of those secret things."

"I don't understand how that can be so shameful," Drew says candidly. "I'm just sayin'. I've struggled with far darker things than turning to food for comfort and control."

Rachel nods her head and leans toward her listener. "I can see why you might see it that way. I just feel like I should be able to control my food intake—and sometimes I do—severely. Other times, I just get to this type of release point where my control crumbles, and I—I have to eat...more than

I want to. It feels good in the moment but later—ugh!"

"Sounds a lot like me with drugs and alcohol," Drew interjects, "except that I didn't even want to control them. Just enjoy the 'release' phase. I didn't have a moral code telling me that I was doing something wrong, and I didn't have anything else to turn to, so, c'est la vie! Live for the moment even though later I'd always feel worse. I settled because I thought that was as good as it gets in this world. Then the Great Physician showed up—not an hour too soon."

Rachel glances out the large window at the river and then back at the imposing young man sitting across from her. "I've never told anybody this before, but sometimes I would binge out of anger toward my parents. It was my way of throwing their shallow preoccupation with appearances and performance back into their faces. It was my way of doing the opposite of what they pressured me to do. Yes, their obsession with image was unhealthy, but my passive aggressive defiance was just as unhealthy, if not more so."

Drew nods his head and looks at Rachel with a grim smile. "We all need to be honest about our anger. If we can't do it directly, it will leak out in other ways."

There is a short silence before Rachel's face lights up, and she exclaims, "I can't believe how much you've grown, Drew! And in such a short amount of time. I really want to affirm you for that."

Drew looks back at the woman with his disarming gaze. "I don't know what to say, Rachel. Where do I start? Jesus has changed everything for me. I now know the two bookends to life—where I came from and where I'm going. Plus, I know that there is meaning and purpose behind everything that happens between those two bookends.

"Life is making more sense to me every day," he continues. "And I feel joy. Jesus hasn't burdened me with a bunch of rules or crushing condemnation for my mistakes. Instead, he's brought me into a loving relationship with Him and tells me that I'm forgiven. Rachel, He's honestly become my best friend! How weird is that?"

Some of the stars on Rachel's face readjust as she laughs brightly. "Not weird at all!" she exclaims. "Not to me, at least. Yeah, I'm sure there are a lot of people out there who would say you're crazy. But they don't know what it's like to be loved by Jesus. If they did, they would give up everything for that love. Guaranteed."

"Unless they don't think they need a physician," Drew adds.

"Sad but true," Rachel agrees. "But that was you only a few weeks ago. And that was me at one time, too. I guess our hearts just had to be plowed and seeded and cultivated until we were ready to surrender to His love at just the right time. God is rarely early, but He's never late," she says with a smile.

A brief silence settles over the table as the two young people eye each other with awkward smiles. Eventually, Rachel looks out at the drawbridge and says, "Let's go for a walk! The average temperature this time of year is supposed to be, like, forty degrees, but today it's going to be closer to sixty."

"Great idea!" Drew says. "Let's do it!"

When the two young people get outside, they cross the drawbridge and stroll along the quaint main street. The sun is shining brightly, and the breeze is almost warm. Rivulets of water from the melting snow race toward the nearest gutter. In the distance, a small colonial-style church with chaste white pillars in the front and an ornate clock steeple rises majestically above its surroundings.

"I'm worried about my parents," Drew volunteers as they walk up a gradual ascent toward the church. "Mom doesn't believe God exists, and my dad is totally disinterested—even apathetic. He doesn't care much about anything in life except his art."

"Art," Rachel echoes. "Sounds like a man after my own heart. Does he like to paint or draw?" She pictures in her mind an amateur who dabbles in sketching and watercolors.

"He does some still life painting, but mainly nature stuff, like landscapes and animals," Drew remarks. "No people, though. He has no interest in people. Not even me. As stubborn and independent as my mother is, I've always known she loves me. In her own way. Wish I could say the same about my old man."

Rachel looks up at the man walking beside her. She knows he is taking shorter strides so she can keep up with him. "That's so sad, Drew," she says consolingly. "Fathers have so much power—almost a mystical power—but they often don't know that they wield it. They don't realize how much influence they have even when they do nothing. Your heart must yearn for your dad."

"Believe it or not, I've wondered recently if my father's absence contributed to my willingness to embrace God the Father," Drew observes.

"Do you mean that your dad's absence led you to hunger even more for your Heavenly Father's presence?" Rachel inquires.

Drew nods his head as he unzips his light jacket.

Rachel chews on her lower lip and then comments, "Well, that's a good thing, I guess. I've known men who had bad experiences with their fathers that led them to distrust and even hate God."

Drew stares up the hill at the church steeple and remarks, "I ran into a lot of young men in the Marines who were there because of their fathers. In fact, I'd bet money that seventy-five percent of them signed up because they had father issues. You'd think they would avoid an authority-heavy organization like the Marines if they had such bad experiences with authoritarian fathers. On the other hand, maybe the iron fist of authority was familiar to them."

"Or they were there to reenact the father relationship," Rachel thinks aloud.

"What do you mean?" the young man asks.

"Sometimes when people have unfinished business with parents, they subconsciously seek out other authority figures later in life with whom they can reenact the past and finally resolve it."

Drew shrugs his shoulders and says, "Interesting theory. I think there could be some truth in that. Unfortunately, some of the authority figures in the Marines are as dysfunctional as the unhealthy fathers and only end up exacerbating the unresolved issues. They don't scratch the itch; they inflame it."

Rachel nods her head and is quiet for a while. Then she turns to look at the man who is a foot taller than her and says, "You said you were worried about your parents—you mean whether they'll be in heaven or not?"

"It's pretty obvious, right?" Drew says without sarcasm as he glances into Rachel's eyes. "I'm afraid they'll never admit their need for The Physician. They will choose to reject him, like you said, directly or passively. My mom is the direct rejecter, and my dad is the passive one. Either way, they won't admit their need for Him."

"I hear what you're saying," Rachel says. "It's the other way around for my parents. Dad is the active rejecter, and Mom is the passive one who doesn't hate God, but neither does she need Him."

"So, what do we do, Rachel?" Drew asks as he looks down at her again.

The clock on the church steeple tolls once and then begins to play an instrumental rendition of *It Is Well with My Soul.* Rachel gently bobs her head in rhythm with the music and replies, "Well, first off, we need to pray for them. God is teaching me more and more every day about the importance of praying for others. There's a lot of power in prayer because by praying, we ask God to bring His power into people's lives."

"I've got a lot to learn about prayer," Drew admits. "Actually, I have everything to learn about prayer. I do talk to Jesus a lot, but I have more to learn about formal prayer."

"I don't know about that," Rachel counters. "Prayer is simply talking to God, and it sounds like you're already doing a lot of that. Prayer doesn't need to be formal. In fact, if we're too formal, we become too obsessed with the form of the prayer instead of its content. I like it that you talk to Jesus so freely."

"So, we can pray for our parents," Drew says, making a mental list of what he must do to reach his parents with the good news of Jesus. "What else?"

"We need to love them," Rachel answers. "That one is a no-brainer, I suppose. It's been said that Christians might be the only Bible some people will ever read. We need to show others who Jesus is by the way we love them. Our actions and attitudes may speak more of Jesus' love than even a Bible verse or a sermon they happen to hear."

"What does that love look like?" Drew asks as he shoves his large hands into the pockets of his jeans.

Rachel pauses to think and then replies, "You ask good questions, Drew," she observes. "Have I ever told you that?"

Drew laughs and says, "You know you have."

"Yes, I have, haven't I?" the young woman replies with a smile. "Just checking to see how observant you are."

Rachel pauses and then says, "I think we can show love toward our parents by serving them with the same attitude Jesus had when He was on earth. We can do thoughtful things for them even when they're not expecting it. We can give them random hugs and tell them we love them. Maybe that's more of a female thing; I don't know. I suppose we can love them by not taking what they do and say personally when we feel hurt by them."

Rachel pauses and sighs. "I struggle with that a lot," she admits. "I'm so quick to feel wounded and then pull away and protect myself from further hurt. Someone called that 'stonewalling.' I'm terribly good at stonewalling—or terribly bad."

Drew rests his hand on the young woman's arm and remarks, "Of course, you would be susceptible to feeling rejected, Rachel. I know I would feel rejected easily if I had been abandoned by my biological parents and then neglected by my adoptive parents. That must be so painful for you."

Rachel swallows hard and looks up into the large blue eyes. "How do you do that?" she comments in amazement.

"Do what?" Drew asks.

"Know the right thing to say," Rachel replies. "It's like you're inside my head, Drew. Where did you learn to listen to someone's heart so well?"

The man shrugs his massive shoulders and laughs. "I'm an only child," he says. "Maybe that's it. I grew up too fast."

"Maybe," Rachel comments doubtfully. "But I've known a few only children who are anything but empathic. Either you're naturally vigilant to hearing the hearts of others, or you had some practice with someone in your environment."

"Guilty as charged," Drew responds. "Since my father was so checked out emotionally, I became a second spouse to my mom, helping her with the veterinary clinic and the greenhouse. We weren't emotionally close, but we shared many tasks and interests. I know how to be present for my mother much better than my father does. It's not even close."

When they reach the top of the hill, they find themselves standing in front of the snow-white church with its pillared portico that is taller than it looked half a mile away. The building rises high above them, situated as it is on top of a plateau buttressed by a stone retaining wall. Above the notes of the hymn flowing loudly from the church's clock steeple, they talk for a few more minutes.

Eventually, Drew and Rachel turn and begin the descent back toward the river and the drawbridge. The mid-afternoon sun has warmed the world around them to the point that they both shed their spring jackets.

"So, how will your friends at the university react to your decision to follow Jesus?" Rachel asks.

Drew throws his jacket over his shoulder and hums aloud as he considers her question. "All those guys looked up to me in the past," he finally replies, "so I don't think any of them will blow me off. I'm three or four years older than them because of my stint in the Corps. Being older and having been in the Marines earns me some cred. The Few, The Proud, and all that.

"With that said, I'm sure some of them will think I'm temporarily crazy and will simply tolerate me until I regain my sanity. However," Drew says with a chuckle, "I'm never going back to the way things were before. Not a chance. For the first time in my life, I feel sane. So, they'll be waiting a long time if they think they'll get the old Drew back. Now '*Semper Fi*' means more to me than ever—*always faithful* to my God and Savior."

"Have you spoken with Paul and Theo since Pete died?" Rachel inquires.

Drew nods his head and looks sidelong at Rachel. "The sadness in their eyes is so evident, but they won't talk about Pete," he comments quietly. "They have no idea how to deal with death. They only know how to push it into the back of their brains and distract themselves with whatever they can get their hands on."

Rachel and Drew look at each other for a few moments, and then the offensive lineman says with a smile, "I know what you're thinking, girl."

"You think so," Rachel says coyly. "Okay, you who reads the minds and hearts of women, let's put you to the test. What am I thinking?"

Without hesitation, Drew replies, "You're thinking that God is going to use me to speak the gospel to those guys back on campus since I have such a strong platform. Am I right?"

Rachel stops walking and stares straight ahead. "I'm not going to tell you," she announces with feigned resoluteness. "It's for me to know and you to find out."

"Are you serious?" Drew inquires. "You're not going to use that old line on me, are you?"

Rachel lifts her chin and looks away from her inquisitor. It is clear to Drew that a herd of wild horses is not going to make her divulge the contents of her mind.

"Oh, I get it," Drew says slowly as realization dawns on him. "I must compel you to speak. Well, you should know that I served two tours in Afghanistan and mastered the technique of 'persuasive interviewing.' You do know that's a euphemism for something more...coercive."

Rachel remains silent and pretends to be observing the storefront across the street.

Drew suddenly grabs her arm and turns her to face him. "Speak now, or I will need to commence the ancient Chinese art of water torture."

When Rachel remains silent—although a smile is now playing on her lips—Drew bends down, grabs a handful of snow, and deposits it on the back of her neck.

Shocked out of her silence, Rachel screams loudly and impulsively pushes Drew in the chest with all her might. Unprepared for the strong reprisal, Drew loses his balance and falls back into a low-lying fern.

Rachel lingers long enough to ensure that her interrogator is unhurt, then impulsively breaks into a run down the sidewalk. She runs for a block until she arrives at the middle of the drawbridge and stops. When she turns around, she sees Drew jogging to catch up to her.

"Where in the world are you going?" he says, laughing. "Why did you run away?"

Rachel places a hand over her mouth and cries out in a muffled voice, "I'm so embarrassed, and I'm so sorry! I didn't mean to push you that hard, Drew."

The big man laughs and exclaims, "You just did what no defensive lineman has done in the last three games—you knocked me down!" He shakes his head as he gazes at the woman in front of him. "You're something else, Rachel Biandi," he announces with a broad smile.

Before Rachel can reply, the big man envelopes her in a big hug and says, "You're a keeper, girl. You're a keeper."

Rachel laughs and speaks playfully into his ear, "You were right, Drew. You were right about what I was thinking. From now on, I'm calling you the Rachel Whisperer."

The woman who has been adopted twice now, once by the Biandis and once by God, and the man who has been adopted once—also by God—embrace each other for a long time in the middle of the drawbridge that spans the slowly flowing Mystic River.

Something special is unfolding. Something that is not accidental but orchestrated. Just weeks ago, the man was contemplating suicide. Just days ago, the woman was feeling abandoned by everyone around her who was supposed to love her. But on this day, both Rachel and Drew recognize that their lives are beginning to intertwine in a way they would never have imagined.

Of course, the Conductor of this orchestra is God Himself, the One who says, "All things are possible with me."

CHAPTER 26

Attack at the King David

The explosion comes first. It is deafening and thrusts the four-ton COMBATGUARD several feet into the air. Even before the vehicle crashes down into the fresh hole beneath it, the blast wave slams against the seven people on the sidewalk like a speeding locomotive. It lifts them off their feet and throws them backward as if they are ragdolls.

Aly is most protected from the blast wave since she is directly behind the bellhop at the time of the explosion. Nonetheless, she briefly loses consciousness after she hits the paved sidewalk hard. When she awakes, her head is throbbing, and her ears are ringing loudly. A sharp pain radiates from her chest. She is coughing hard.

Uncertain if she is dreaming or awake, Aly lifts her head to observe her surroundings. The previously placid world has turned into Gehenna, she thinks to herself. In the dark of the night, she sees billowing smoke and flames pouring out from under the military vehicle that is no longer parked level on the driveway. Oddly, it now sits lower and leans away from the hotel at a thirty-degree angle. The air is thick with the sickening stench of chemicals.

Aly coughs hard and turns her head to look for her brother. She winces at the effort. Through the smoke, she sees him sitting on the ground ten feet away from where she is lying. Thank God, she thinks to herself. Then she sees the blood on his face.

She tries to yell at Moussa but cannot even hear her own voice. Bewildered, she shakes her head. Either her lungs are not functioning, or she is deaf. Or both. But she hears other muffled sounds around her—as if she has cotton jammed into her ears—so she must not be deaf. And why does her tongue feel like a piece of wood in her mouth?

While Aly is rubbing her ears, the second wave of the attack appears.

It is not another bomb. Out of the darkness of the night, a hundred feet away, Aly sees four dark figures emerge from the smoke like demons out of hell. When they enter the murky pool of light generated by the floodlights in front of the hotel, she notices that they are running low to the ground carrying rifles up by their shoulders. They are wearing night vision infrared goggles that distort their faces into alien masks. Aly begins reciting the 23rd Psalm and shivers at the prospect of death.

Still coughing, she struggles to a sitting position. Through burning, watery eyes, she sees muzzle flashes stab out of one of the attacker's gun. A split second later, she hears the report. Soon all four guns are firing. Moussa is on his feet. David staggers out from behind the portico in front of the hotel and raises his pistol. Daniel and the other soldiers are nowhere to be seen. Smoke is everywhere. Aly coughs so hard that she finds it hard to breathe.

She watches, as in a dream, as one assailant clutches his throat and falls forward. Another one must have been hit in the leg. He starts limping, falling behind the lead attacker. She sees more muzzle flashes from the lead assailant, who is rapidly approaching the front of the hotel. She watches in horror as her brother is knocked backward by bullets that must have hit him in the chest. He falls heavily on his back.

David is hit, and his body is thrown sideways. Aly sees something dark on his shirt. He leans against one of the columns of the portico in front of the hotel. Oddly, of all things, Aly notices that the young man's sunglasses are not on top of his head. He looks at her and motions for her to stay down. The lead attacker is only thirty feet away now. Aly makes another futile attempt to scream.

Somehow Moussa struggles to his feet, looking very unsteady, and moves in front of David, facing him. Aly watches in horror as she hears more rifle reports. Her brother's body jerks for a second time. He grabs David's shoulders, and they fall heavily into the protection offered by the portico.

She hears the voices first. Then, through the smoke, she sees three figures rush out of the hotel entrance, squat down, and begin firing at the remaining assailants. The attackers fire back with their fully automatic rifles. The noise is deafening. Bullets strike the façade of the hotel and send stone chips zinging through the air like shrapnel. Aly reaches shaking hands up to her head and covers her ears.

The lead attacker runs closer and closer until he is only fifteen feet away. Then, suddenly, he staggers and faces plants into the grass. He does not move. The second attacker, who had started limping earlier, is already on the ground unmoving, as is the assailant who had grabbed his throat. She cannot see the fourth shooter.

Aly looks down at her white sweater for the first time and sees that it is black with some type of residue. Then she notices an unfamiliar red spot slowly mushrooming on the right side of her abdomen. That spot should not be there, she thinks to herself, confused. She touches it, and her fingers come away red. She wretches.

Her head swims, and she lies back down on the sidewalk. She stares up at the night sky and sees the stars winking at her. It looks so peaceful way up there in the heavens where God dwells...So quiet.

She hears voices. She smells rancid smoke. She is coughing again. Someone is weeping. She is the one who is weeping. And talking. She is praying. "Jesus, I thank you that my brother will be with you tonight," she whispers. "Safely home with you. I only ask one thing—take me, too. I don't want to live without my brother."

Then she can speak no more. She thinks the thought in her muddled head that Moussa must have known he was going to die tonight. He died well—while loving his new friend, David. Then her eyes are filled with tears, and the world around her blurs.

Faces float above her. She does not recognize them. Far away, as in a dream, she hears a single lonely siren piercing the quiet of the night. Then she hears many of them. Dozens. They grow louder until they sound like a grieving choir of mothers wailing over the bodies of their dead children.

A voice is heard in Ramah, lamentation and bitter weeping. Rachel is weeping for her children; she refuses to be comforted for her children, because they are no more (Jeremiah 31:15).

"Jesus," Aly hears herself whisper. Then she closes her eyes, and the night is totally silent.

Colonel Moshe Abramovich has not seen a night like this in many years—possibly never. Not like this. He spends it shuttling between the King David Hotel and the Jerusalem Rahavia hospital. Fortunately for him, they are only a kilometer apart.

Seven dead. Four wounded. The worst of it all is that one of them is his son.

His only son.

He attempts to maintain a professional countenance on the outside, but on the inside, the "iron colonel"—as he is often referred to—is unraveling. He is beside himself. Three of his men were murdered on this night from the pit of hell.

He is back at the Jerusalem Rahavia hospital now. It is 4:30 in the morning.

He walks into the room of the small Thai woman from America and stands beside her bed, listening to the beeping sounds coming from the medical devices standing around her like sentinels. No one else is with the young woman. Fortunately, she did not need surgery. He has been told that she lost a lot of blood, but she will recover.

He hesitates, coughs into his shirt sleeve, then carefully takes the woman's small hand in his large hand. He sits down in the chair beside her bed and begins humming a song his grandmother sang to him when he was a boy. As he examines the unconscious woman's face, he once again feels responsible for the attack that never should have happened.

The woman's head is wrapped in a white hijab—gauze—and the light honey-colored skin of her petite face is marred by multiple angry abrasions. One spot on her left cheek has been stitched shut and is covered with clear tape. He pauses to wonder what it would be like to have a daughter, still. He shudders. Then his chest burns with rage, and he stares wildly at the ceiling, fighting back tears.

His feet are sore. His whole body is exhausted. He is having difficulty keeping his eyes open. It is the third time he has been in the Thai woman's room that night.

He is about to leave and walk down the hallway to another room when the woman's eyelids flicker and then open. Her roving, swollen eyes land on her visitor, squinting as she attempts to focus her eyes. The iron colonel stops humming.

Maybe she sustained some type of eye damage from the bomb, the colonel thinks to himself. He leans toward her and nods his head reassuringly.

The young woman attempts to form a word with her lips, but her repeated efforts are unsuccessful.

The veteran Beth Shin officer, who has witnessed everything from a Scud missile landing in his backyard to the aftermath of the coastal massacre of 1978, does his best to comfort the young woman. "Hush," he says, "hush, my child. Close your eyes and rest. You are going to be fine."

When her eyes remain open, he hesitates, debating how much to tell her. In the end, he says, "You were struck by a bullet splinter or a piece of shrapnel. It did not penetrate an organ. If the explosive device placed under the COMBATGUARD had been a fragmentation bomb, you would be dead right now. Fortunately, it was not of that variety. The shrapnel scatter was more limited. The COMBATGUARD is built to absorb the explosive power of sizeable IEDs, so that helped reduce frag spread as well."

The big man groans loudly and shakes his head. He is still distraught that the brazen attack occurred on his watch.

"Your tongue will be sore because you bit it when you were impacted by the blast," he informs the patient. "Also, your throat was bruised by—" he pauses for a moment and then says, "by flying debris."

The colonel absently fingers the large mole on his cheek with his free hand and compresses his large lips. Then he informs Aly, "You lost almost four pints of blood, my daughter, which for your small size, is probably more than half of what is in your body. The bad news is you nearly bled out. The good news is that after all the transfusions, you are now half Israeli," he says, trying to bring some levity into the room. He has never been gifted at humor, so he rarely even attempts it.

Aly opens her mouth to speak again. Her voice is softer than a whisper, and the colonel cannot make out anything she says. However, even the man who has not had a female in his life for years clearly reads the urgency on the woman's face. He knows what she needs to hear.

"Your brother is here, also, in the same hospital," he says, still holding her hand. "He sustained bullet wounds to his leg and hand along with minor shrapnel wounds from the bomb. He also has severe bruising to his chest and back along with two or three broken ribs."

When the young woman with the heart-shaped face and the large, red-rimmed eyes stares at him, he says in his heavily accented voice, "Ah, you do not know, do you? My David gave your brother his vest to wear before they left the hotel. 'Better safe than sorry,' as they say in America. Fortunately, it was not a soft bulletproof vest. It contained hard plates, thick enough to stop even rifle fire. Six rounds struck your brother in the vest, some in front and some in back. None of them penetrated, although they did shatter several plates. If he had been hit by one more round, it would have pierced the compromised armor and killed him."

The weary officer with the round, lunar face watches as tears form and pool in the young woman's eyes. He reaches for a tissue on the nightstand next to the bed and then gently dabs at her eyes. Aly attempts to smile at him but finds that she cannot.

Without warning, a dam fractures deep inside the hardened officer's chest. Quickly, he presses the back of his hand hard against his mouth to contain the powerful emotions that threaten to erupt.

Despite his best efforts at suppression, the iron colonel begins to weep silently. He releases Aly's hand and grips the railing of the bed with both of his. Then he pushes his forehead into the back of his hands. His whole body shakes. When Aly reaches up and touches the man's thick shoulder with her trembling hand, the man's body quakes even more. He weeps for a long time for all the losses that have ripped his heart apart in recent years.

Minutes pass before the thick man stands up abruptly and grabs more tissues. He turns his back to Aly. This time he wipes his own eyes and blows his nose. When he is certain that he has regained his composure, he turns back toward the woman in the bed. His bald head gleams under the fluorescent lights.

Standing beside her bed, he asks, "Do you know why I am weeping? No, you do not, since you did not even know about the vest."

The big man slowly massages his round face with his stout hands. Then he peers through fingers that partially obscure his eyes and says, "I was told that your brother positioned his body in front of my son to protect him from the automatic weapon fire. As I speak, David is one floor below us in the operating room. Even though the surgeons must remove two bullets, they tell me he has a ninety-five percent chance of survival. Your brother's courage and quick thinking spared my son from taking more rounds."

The Israeli officer pauses, takes a deep breath, and lets it out slowly. Then he says, "A man from Saudi Arabia who was a jihadist in another lifetime saved my son's life. What is a Beth Shin officer to do with that?"

Now it is Aly's turn to weep again. The colonel grabs more tissues and wipes her eyes. Then he smiles at the sister of the man who saved his son's life and says sternly, "You must promise me one thing, my daughter. Promise that you will never tell my David that you saw me cry."

The big man takes Aly's hand in his again and says in a grave voice, "I must tell you two more things." He pauses and massages the back of his neck with his free hand. "Kameel was not struck by any bullets," he eventually says. "He sustained minor wounds from glass and metal frags, but he is going to recover quickly—the quickest of all of you. In fact, I'm told he will come up to visit you later this morning."

The Beth Shin officer smiles at Aly, but she sees the sadness in his eyes. Even in her foggy, medicated state, she knows why. She begins to sob.

"Daniel—" the officer begins. He pauses and takes a deep breath. Then he announces, "Daniel was not so fortunate...His body absorbed the full impact of the blast. He and two fellow soldiers were killed instantly."

Moshe Abramovich pauses once more. His face is a mask of grief and rage. "Kameel is grieved," he grunts between clenched teeth. "David also will be deeply grieved. Daniel...was his closest friend since he was a child."

The big man takes another deep breath and says to Aly, "So, we are happy, and so we are sad. Such is life." He coughs and clears his throat loudly before he adds, "The only good news about Daniel, for those of you who believe, is that Kameel says he is in heaven now. He is with his best friend, I am told."

The man with the cratered face shakes his head and stares up at the ceiling for the tenth time that night. "I will never grow accustomed to the pain and the death and the loss in this world," he says, releasing a long, angry groan. "There are days when I wish—secretly, mind you, another promise for you to keep—I wish I knew that there was something beyond this world, someone beyond this world who would make everything right. Maybe a part of me wishes that I knew David's best friend and—David's best friend."

Aly swallows painfully and grimaces. Then she whispers very softly, her words thick and barely intelligible, "Don't stop wishing."

Two weeks later, the Atlanta team flies out of Ben Gurion International Airport for the trip back to America. Physically, all three of them have healed reasonably well and have been told that they should have no lingering effects from their injuries. Despite their positive prognosis and their significant healing up to now, the Ahmed siblings are not looking forward to sitting on the plane for the long flight from Rome to Atlanta.

Moussa has been brooding since the attack because he feels personally responsible for the deaths of the three soldiers and the bellhop. He is convinced that if he had not come to Jerusalem, none of this evil would have happened.

One silver lining in the storm cloud of the tragic attack in Jerusalem, however, is that Moussa has come away from it with a strong aversion for violence in any form. The tragedy at the King David has only convinced him further that Jesus is the God he wishes to serve for a lifetime and beyond. After all, Jesus is the God who is love, the One who teaches peace and love, not war and hate.

The attack has left the new believer with a lifelong "souvenir." He believes that people will find it foolish for him to think such a thing, so he speaks of it to no one. He has decided that the healing, angry scar left by the bullet that pierced his left hand will forever remind him of his Savior, who had both of His hands pierced when he was nailed to the cross.

David is out of the hospital and steadily recovering. He remains deeply saddened by the loss of his best friend. Daniel's death reopens the wound from the loss of his dear mother, Deborah, as well. He will not even allow himself to think of the other person he has lost—the grief is just too overwhelming to feel.

Since he was too weak to attend Daniel's funeral, his father brought the funeral to David in the form of a live video feed from the small church on the Mount of Olives where the service was held. Daniel had offhandedly mentioned to David years ago that he wanted to be buried in the Garden of Gethsemane near the ancient olive trees that some scholars estimated were more than two thousand years old. Daniel had reminded David many times that the gnarled trees were old enough to have witnessed their Creator, Jesus, praying in anguish in the garden before His arrest and subsequent crucifixion so many centuries ago.

David is convinced that if trees were capable of tears, the olive trees certainly would have wept on that fateful night when their Maker was betrayed—and most likely at Daniel's funeral as well.

Aly found herself hesitant to leave Israel. She was befuddled by her reluctance until she realized that she had developed a fondness for Colonel Abramovich's son.

As she ponders her relationship with the colonel's son on the flight from Tel Aviv to Rome, she tells herself that she will never see the Israeli again. If she tells herself that message once on the four-hour flight across the Mediterranean, she tells herself twenty-five times. She reasons that she will never see David again because her fondness for the young man flows merely from proximity and shared suffering. Her affections are nothing more than an infatuation that developed during the many hours they spent visiting each other in their matching wheelchairs during their recovery in the hospital.

On the flight to Miami, Aly and Kameel are pleased to hear that the grumbling imam from Saudi Arabia, Abdullah Khan, who had spoken with them after the conclusion of the apologetics conference in Jerusalem, has remained in contact with Moussa during the two weeks since the attack. The Saudi man had reached out to Moussa repeatedly even while the new believer was in the hospital, peppering him with questions about the young man's new faith.

Most often, the imam asked Moussa to tell him what had changed inside his heart since he had believed in Jesus. He asked the same questions over and over: Did he really feel close to God? Did he know that he was going to heaven when he died or simply hoped that he might? Did he miss anything about Islam? Did one member of the Christian Trinity indeed refer to Himself as a Father who could be approached as a child might approach his daddy? Did he sincerely sense a profound love from Jesus?

It is in the Miami airport, while waiting to board the connecting flight to Atlanta, that Moussa receives a call from Abdullah informing him that he has chosen to believe in Jesus. Moussa immediately shares the amazing news with Kameel and his sister.

Everyone waiting to board the overseas flight stares with amusement, confusion, or disdain as three young people abruptly begin dancing, albeit gingerly, and shouting in the gate area. A few people dismiss the odd behavior as a mini flash mob dance. Several onlookers laugh and join in the celebration with the three believers. Soon, thirty people, who have no clue what is going on, are dancing alongside the Atlanta team. Aly will never forget the spontaneous party as long as she lives.

"What's the latest news from Colonel Abramovich?" Aly asks Kameel, looking at the professor who is sitting between the Ahmed siblings in row 27 on the flight to Atlanta. He spoke with you after your call from Abdullah, right?"

Kameel nods his head as he unfolds his tray in preparation for the soda and snacks soon to be dispensed. "Yes, I did," he comments. "He's still very unsettled about the attack at the King David."

The young Egyptian removes his glasses and begins cleaning the thick lenses with a handkerchief. "The colonel says it doesn't fit the typical M.O. of a terrorist attack."

"What's unusual about it?" Aly asks as she looks around Kameel and eyes her brother, who is sleeping in the window seat with his head resting against a pillow.

"According to Colonel Abramovich, the more accurate question is what's not unusual about it," the professor clarifies as he attempts to straighten a stray curling hair in his thin mustache. "The weapons used by the four attackers were not typical, the explosive materials in the sophisticated car bomb were literally unheard of in an attack on Israeli soil, and the three men who were killed in the ambush were not known terrorists. Also, there is evidence that the assailants planned to survive the attack. Part of that evidence rests on the fact that the fourth shooter fled from the scene of the attack—not the action of a typical terrorist dedicated to suicide in order to receive an automatic ticket to paradise. He is still at large, by the way."

"If they weren't terrorists, then who were they?" Aly asks, thankful that her brother is not awake to hear these details. "We know it certainly wasn't a random attack, and it was too well planned to be the work of an amateur.

Who else would have perpetrated such an evil act and why?"

"Those questions, my dear Aly, are best reserved for Beth Shin," Kameel replies. "Our focus now is to finish the 'J' term course and help you and Moussa decide what your future holds." The Egyptian closes his eyes and leans his head back against his seat.

"I'm so sorry for your loss," Aly repeats for the tenth time in two weeks.

Without opening his eyes, Kameel sighs and says, "Thank you, Aly. Yes, he was my best childhood friend. We shared so many adventures. Certainly, I'll never forget him. The good news is that Christians never say goodbye, only, 'See you later.'"

"I'm so thankful I had the chance to meet him," Aly comments, nodding her head.

"Yes," Kameel mumbles. The Institute professor begins to say something else but slips into unconsciousness before he can finish his thought. The man will sleep through the soda and snacks.

Aly sits for a long time staring at the seatback in front of her. She tries to sleep, but her eyes will not remain closed. She decides that the seven days in the hospital caused her to bank too many hours of sleep despite the frequent interruptions from medical personnel. Besides, the wound in her lower abdomen is beginning to throb. So, she prays.

She prays for everyone back at the Academy, students and professors alike. She offers petitions for her parents and her two younger sisters that they might surrender their lives to Jesus. Her thoughts even drift to Saudi Arabia, and she prays for Abdullah Khan. Lastly, she prays for David Abramovich even though she convinces herself, once more, that she will never see him again.

When she finally falls asleep an hour later, she is back on the terrace behind the King David Hotel. The night is pleasantly cool. The stars are glittering like jewels, and a full moon is climbing high in the black vault above. Kameel is sitting with her at the round table along with her brother, Moussa. Daniel is there as well, complaining to David about the measly four shekels he was given to purchase supper. Everyone is laughing. Daniel playfully punches David in the shoulder.

When Jesus walks up behind Daniel and rests his hands on the young man's shoulders, Aly smiles as if it is an everyday occurrence. Daniel cranes his neck to see who is behind him. When he sees Jesus, he jumps to his feet and turns to face his Savior. The two men smile at each other and embrace. Then Jesus says to Daniel in a gentle voice, "It's time to come home, my friend."

Only Aly hears the words Jesus speaks to the Israeli soldier. As she gazes at Jesus and Daniel, she notices a young woman standing in the background. She is beaming at Daniel.

Daniel's face begins to glow with joy, and he replies without hesitation, "I'm ready, my Lord." He glances over his shoulder at David, who is busy kibbitzing with Kameel and Moussa. Sadness mingles with the joy on his face.

"I won't say goodbye to you, my friends," Daniel says in a voice so quiet that the three other men do not hear him, "because we've always told each other that when we're called home, we'll simply say, 'See you later.'"

Daniel pauses and says to his preoccupied friends, "So, David and Kameel, I'm the first one to say it: 'I'll see you later, brothers. I'll be praying for you until we're united forever.'"

Aly glances away for just a moment to look at David to see if he heard Daniel's words. When she looks back to where Daniel and Jesus were just standing, they have left—along with the mysterious young woman. Aly sheds a single tear, and then, remembering the smile on Daniel's face, she also smiles.

Just then, David turns away from Kameel and notices that his friend is not there. "Where's Daniel?" he asks Aly, concern written on his face.

She hesitates, then says, "He had to leave. But he told me to tell you and Kameel that he will see you guys later."

David nods his head slowly and smiles at her, holding her eyes with his for just a bit longer than usual. Then he turns back and begins talking and laughing with Kameel and Moussa again.

It is at that moment that Aly believes—at least in her dream—that she will see David Abramovich again after all. Her waking self may take more convincing.

"Thank you, Jesus," she whispers. "My times are in your hands."

Then she falls into a deeper sleep still.

CPSIA information can be obtained
at www.ICGtesting.com
Printed in the USA
LVHW032117181022
731001LV00003B/29